PUCKED UP *plans*

BOOK ONE

TAYLOR DELONG

For Vicci,
Your boundless support and friendship mean the world to me. I'm so grateful to know you and appreciate everything you do to help spread the love of my books.
PS I wrote this book before we became friends, but Lennon's middle name is quite fitting.

PUCKED UP PLANS PLAYLIST

One Beer Hardy
There Goes My Life Kenny Chesney
Almost Maybes Jordan Davis
Papa Don't Preach Madonna
A Baby Changes Everything Faith Hill
Made for You Jake Owen
Right Now Van Halen
Brokenhearted Karmin
Accidentally in Love Counting Crows
Can't Help Falling in Love With You Ingrid Michaelson
How Would You Feel Ed Sheeran
Still Falling for You Ellie Goulding
Terrified Katharine McPhee
The Only Way to Love Vanessa Carlton
I Met a Girl William Michael Morgan
Love You Like a Love Song Selena Gomez & The Scene
Butterflies Kasey Musgraves
Unaplogize Carrie Underwood
Daughters John Mayer
('Til) I Kissed You The Everly Brothers

CHAPTER 1
TATE

unning late for preschool pickup, but what else is new? Although today it's not totally my fault. The DMV was busier than I expected. Who knew you needed to make an appointment? Or get there before it opened? Guess that's on me for not doing my homework on Vermont's motor vehicle services.

The worst part is I didn't even get to the front of the line, so I have to go back another day and waste yet another few hours to register my car and get a license in our new state unless I remember to make an appointment ahead of time.

I pull into the spot nearest the door of the preschool. Aubrey waits outside, along with an adult worker who doesn't appear too pissed off. There's another little kid sitting next to Aubrey on the bench. I sigh in relief I'm not the *last* one for pickup. Glancing at the clock reveals I'm only a few minutes past the noon dismissal time, except every minute beyond the stated ending time results in more fees, something I can't worry about now.

Out of the car, I apologize before I reach the woman. She's only a few years older than me, but since Aubrey's new to the school, I haven't met all her teachers. I had hoped to enroll her as soon as we moved, but there was a waitlist. Again, that's on me for not checking things out sooner. Except "move to Vermont" wasn't on my radar until about a week before we arrived.

"I'm so sorry. I got stuck in a line at the DMV." Maybe the truth will get me a little more sympathy than just an apology.

"Not a problem, Mrs. Winchester. It happens to the best of us. It's why we have a fifteen-minute grace period."

I like the sound of the grace period but cringe at the "Mrs." moniker. I'm hardly a Mrs., especially not to Aubrey's father.

Hiding my shudder and not letting my ignorance show, I smile at her. "Thanks. I won't let it happen again." I mentally slap my forehead. It will happen again. Most likely soon. I can't help it. Ever since I was "late" six years ago, I can't seem to get in gear to be on time for anything. At least when it relates to my daughter. Looking to Aubrey, I coo, "Hey, Bree. You ready to go?"

Thankfully, she hasn't figured out my tardiness yet. And since she's not sitting here by herself, she's in good company. Or maybe that's me because I'm not the worst parent at Apple Tree Preschool. At least not today.

Behind us, a truck's engine roars, drawing awareness from all of us waiting on the curb. However, my eyes quickly revert to the other little girl. Clad fully in Aspenridge College attire, complete with a backward hat on her petite head hiding her messy dirty blonde hair, she hops off the bench. Planting her feet, her legs wide, she crosses her arms over her chest with a huff.

"You're late, Keeley. Again." Her small squeaky voice doesn't quite match the shade she's trying to throw at the adult picking her up.

"Tell me something I don't know."

The gravelly voice turns my head. I come face-to-face with a man about my age, give or take a year, with the sharpest blue eyes. A faded scar slices the right eyebrow almost in half. Days' old scruff covers his rounded chin and cheeks. He flashes a smile at the girl and even though it's not directed at me in the slightest, I swear my ovaries weep.

He turns that same wicked smile to the preschool teacher.

"Ms. Hannah, I'm sorry I'm late. Feel free to charge me for your wasted time out here with Lennon."

Hannah's cheeks tinge pink. *I feel ya, girl.*

"Not a bother. She's never a problem."

At the teacher's comment, the man's eyebrows rise in challenge.

I know nothing of this spitfire, but based solely on her attitude and how she carries herself, no way she's completely innocent.

"Did you at least get to the store and get more yogurt?"

My focus is back on the little girl.

Lennon. Unique name.

She's petite for her age, standing a few inches shorter than Aubrey. I suppose she could be in a younger class. I shouldn't assume she's the same age as Aubrey because she's out here with her.

"Yeah, no. Sorry, Squirt. Guess a trip to the grocery store is in our future."

Lennon rolls her eyes. I have to stifle my laughter. How so much sass can live in one tiny human is mind-boggling.

Bean, don't get any ideas, I think as my girl observes the interaction. While she's not a perfect angel all the time, she mostly keeps her attitude in check and is sweet, caring, and a loving five-year-old. And at the moment, my best friend.

"I had to go yesterday with Momma. Now today with you. Who will it be tomorrow?"

He kneels in front of her. "Would it help if I told you I got ice time for tonight?"

In a flash, her attitude disappears, replaced with an elated expression. Just as quickly, she mirrors his image, one eyebrow in the air. "Just for me?"

"Only you."

"At Nordic?"

"Even better." He pauses, heightening her anticipation. I can't help but be invested in finding out what his answer is. Even though I don't have a clue what they are going on about in the slightest. "At Aspenridge."

At the mention of the college, she leaps into the air, throwing herself against his chest. With little effort, he catches her. She loops her arms around his neck and exclaims, "That's the most 'mazing thing ever."

"I thought you might like it. Even if we have to go grocery shopping before we get there, right?"

Her hands cup his cheeks. "Can we get marshmallows? You ate all of them last week and didn't replace them."

This kid is a riot. I'm so entranced in their conversation, I almost miss Aubrey patting my leg. I peer down at her. The face I've loved since the minute they put her on my chest looks up expectantly at me. "Mommy, what are smarshmellows?"

"Only the best thing ever." The guy's voice pulls my attention away from my daughter to him yet again. There's a twinkle in his eyes, a shit-eating grin on his kissable lips.

Down girl. Don't even think about it. Don't even think about him.

Lennon wrinkles her nose, the confusion evident on her adorable features. Addressing my daughter, she wonders, "You've never had marshmallows?" Aubrey shakes her head. Lennon regards the man. "Keeley, we need an extra bag for Aubrey. Think that's doable?"

This time I can't help the chuckle emitting from deep within me. What preschooler talks like this? Certainly not mine.

"I'm sorry," I apologize. "Does she always speak like that?"

He trains his gaze my way, piercing me with a stare. But not in a bad way. And his eyes don't even ogle me. Which is probably for the best.

"Unfortunately. She's definitely wise beyond her five years." He engages in a stare-down with the little girl. With the two of them so close together, I notice the resemblance in the eyes, nose, and cheeks. It's cute they have such a sibling bond. "Can we grab a bag of marshmallows for you? Lennon's treat. It's her turn to buy."

Lennon's little eyes roll again. "Don't be 'diculous. I gotta save my money for new skates. I told you last week." She puts a lot of emphasis on the word *told,* drawing it out beyond the one-syllable word it is.

"Guess they'll be my treat then." Lennon nods fervently in agreement.

Lost in his cobalt eyes, I suddenly remember my manners, shooting down his idea gently. "Oh, no. You don't have to do that. We can grab them the next time we go to the store."

"It's no trouble. Especially since she's never had them before."

Polite as ever, Aubrey pipes in, "Thank you. I can't wait to try them."

I don't think she understands what's involved here. She knows she'll be getting marshmallows, which she'll probably hate. The girl's sweet tooth is nonexistent, the main reason she's never had them.

The man shifts Lennon to his hip, situating her in such a way only a guy with experience can do. Offering his hand, he declares, "Lennon will bring them into school next week. I'll make sure they're in a sealed plastic bag, so they aren't a temptation to open before she gets home."

I'm not sure how to react to this man's kind gesture. Is this a Vermont thing? Should I get used to this weird sort of encounter? The sharing of food with virtual strangers?

"Uh, thank you?" I hate how the phrase comes out as a question, but my confidence has gone missing since I'm still contemplating what's happening. Besides, the way he studies me, his penetrating gaze is a tad unnerving.

"Sure thing. A friend of Lennon's is a friend of mine. And everyone should know what marshmallows taste like." His left eye shoots a wink in my direction. At least he's not judging me for not serving my kid marshmallows before now. When he looks down at Aubrey, I swear her cheeks flush.

Get in line, girl.

Oh my god. I have to get my mind out of the gutter.

His hand is still outstretched, waiting for me to shake it. "Nice to meet you…" He trails off, his hand still in the air.

"Tate," I provide, hoping it's my name he's waiting on. His genuine grin confirms it.

"I'm Lennon," the girl states, "and he's Walsh."

I frown at her introduction. I could have sworn she called him something else. Twice. How did I get that so wrong?

"Aubrey," my girl states shyly.

"I know, silly." Lennon giggles, her comment going over Aubrey's head. I breathe a silent sigh of relief, wanting to keep her from being made fun of, if even only teasing.

"Well, we should probably be on our way. Gotta make a run to the grocery store before rest time."

Lennon shakes her head. "No thanks. I not tired."

"If you want to skate, you know the deal. Rest first, skate later."

"Aw, man. But Dad."

I don't hear the rest of her protest nor what he replies as my ears stick on the "dad".

He's her father? Not the older brother? My head spins with this news.

Why I'm so shocked is a mystery. Maybe because I've yet to meet a dad as young as him. Or because Aubrey's "Dad" wanted nothing to do with her before she was even born. None of his family did. Until the accident.

"Are you okay? Did we lose you there for a moment?" Walsh's apprehensive voice brings me out of my head before my thoughts diverge on a horrible path.

I wave away his concern. "Sorry." I bite back any beliefs about him being the dad. I've been the brunt of too many "you're a little young to the be the mom" judgments to last a lifetime.

Scanning him over, maybe he's not as young as I originally thought. There goes my mind making assumptions again. Good thing he's not in my head. His T-shirt displays the same college name as Lennon. I don't miss the way the words stretch across his broad chest. Nor the way his biceps pop the sleeves.

"Okay then. Nice to meet you, Tate." Without waiting for a response, he bends down to my daughter, his daughter still perched to his side. "Nice to meet you, Aubrey. Be sure to let me know how you like the marshmallows, k?"

My daughter nods shyly at him, then moves to cling onto my leg. I'd like to think her reluctance is because she's shy with new people, especially men, but I'm pretty sure it's just him. He's got some kind of trance over her.

"See you next week," Lennon bids as her father walks away.

I take it as my cue to finally leave the preschool. I don't see Hannah any longer. Hmm. Wonder when she went inside.

"Come on, Bean. Let's go home. Mommy's got some work to finish." I grab her hand in mine, even though my car is only a few steps away.

As I tighten the buckle of the car seat, she gives me a peculiar look. "Where's my dad?"

Shit. She hasn't asked in a few years, but she's at the age now she understands more, yet I'm still unprepared.

A month ago, I would have had a different answer for her.

But now? How do I explain to the five-year-old she'll never get to meet her sperm donor because he's dead?

CHAPTER 2
WALSH

Lennon jabbers away as I buckle her into the car seat. I catch every other word, too focused on the raven beauty parked next to me. Damn. Where the hell did she come from? More importantly, why am I so intrigued? Like I don't have enough issues in my life already? Especially of the female variety.

"I love you, Squirt. I can't wait to skate with you tonight."

Her mouth stops moving as she contemplates my statement. "You said just me." A fire of determination floods her blue eyes, the shade so similar to my own.

I respond with a dramatic hand to my chest. "Yeah, but I figured you'd make an exception for your old man."

She throws her head back in exasperation. "Poppa's old, not you, Keeley."

She gets me every time with that damn Keeley, but I can't let it show. According to her mother, I'm supposed to reprimand her, force her to call me *Dad*. As much as I love hearing "Dad" from her mouth—ever since she first babbled it—some days I feel too young to be a father. And I want to be more of a friend, so I let her continue to call me Keeley. Until she abuses the privilege or stops treating me with the respect a father earns, I'll allow the name.

"So, yes, I can skate with you?" My lips form a pout, and I give her my best puppy dog eyes.

"Silly face. I guess I'll allow it."

I swear I don't know where she comes up with half the shit she says. Her mother, my ex, Megan, blames it all on me, but my mother claims I wasn't half as sassy as Lennon is at her age. Between you and me, I blame Megan.

"Thanks, Squirt."

A kiss to the top of her head, I set off for the driver's side, ready to tackle errands with my best girl.

Hours later, we're at the rink at Aspenridge. It's become like a third home to me in the past three years I've played hockey for the college.

Lennon practically grew up at the ice rink. She took her first steps at "my" rink, and one of her first words was "tick." She was born in the offseason, in September of my junior year of high school, but at less than a month old, Megan or my mom had her on the sidelines once practices started. Bundled up in a stroller or the baby Bjorn, we made it work so I didn't have to give up the most important thing in my life. Now, she ranks highest, but hockey is a close second. I'm grateful every time she lights up about going to the rink. More so when she laces up her skates.

Megan didn't fight me when I had her on skates a little after her first birthday. She loves watching her zoom around the ice almost as much as I do. Whether it's private ice time, open skate, or lessons, Lennon's not picky as long as she's on the ice. Hockey may not be in her future, but she's got ice in her veins, and until Lennon decides she wants to give it up—which will be never if I have any input— we both agreed neither of us is allowed to take it away.

Dressed in her "skate" attire—purple snow pants, a light blue fleece, black snow gloves, and a helmet—she kicks her legs excitedly while I lace up her skates. We started with the Velcro ones, but the girl wasn't having it and demanded lace skates like Daddy. She has tiny feet, so my first pair, which my mother still has, are still too big. We found a pair on a tag sale site, thinking no way she'd want to lace them up every time. As usual, the girl proved us all wrong and never hurries us or begs us to tie them faster.

She wears a sappy grin, happy to be in the rink where I play hockey. Because as much as she loves the rundown Nordic rink, the Aspenridge arena is state-of-the-art and brand-new, even the practice rink currently reserved for us.

"I can't believe I get this whole place to myself," she marvels, eyes fixated as the Zamboni finishes its loop around the ice.

"You agreed I could join you," I remind her.

She sizes me up, her eyes narrowed and nose scrunched, darts her eyes to the rink, then back to me. "You take the visitor half. I'll keep the home team side."

"Big of you." My clipped tone does nothing to dissuade her or change her mind.

The fact she knows the rules of hockey warms my heart. She's become the unofficial team mascot for the Aspenridge Maple Moose men's hockey team, and she never fails to make the guys laugh. It helps assuage some of the guilt of losing parenting time to play college hockey.

Her skates all tightened, she hops down off the bench and hobbles over to wait for the Zamboni to clear the ice. The minute she gets the thumbs up from the driver, she's off, one foot in front of the other, gliding toward the center of the ice.

For five years old, she's got the mechanics down pat. Even when she stumbles and falls, she picks herself up and keeps going. She takes breaks often, her petite legs getting tired from the constant motion around the rink, but she wears a smile on her face the entire time. And she never wants to leave when it's time to come off the ice, an attitude I had to curb quickly. One "If you give me a hard time when it's time to leave, you won't be able to come back," and she learned the lesson. As much as I'm biased, she is the best kid.

I watch her from the bench for a few minutes. Out on the ice by herself, skating around, practicing different stops she's picked up here and there, having fun. Her smile brings an immediate one to my face. I can't help the pride exuding off me at not only her skill level, but her love of skating.

Joining her, I signal her over so we can skate together. She obeys, and we spend the next half hour gliding around the ice. When she gets tired, she's up in my arms or on my shoulders, sounds of glee emanating as she cheers me faster.

"Faster, Keeley. Go faster," she commands, her voice full of pure elation, an emotion she wouldn't be able to fake.

When I'm finally tired, I make a move for the exit.

Kenny Ferguson, Aspenridge's rink manager, sits in the stands, off to the side of our stuff.

"I didn't realize you were the special VIP this evening, Ms. Lennon. Looking great out there."

Lennon's lips curve into a smile. "I know. Did you see my spiral?"

If it's what I think she's talking about, it resembled nothing like a spiral a figure skater might do, but Kenny plays along.

"Best one I've seen all day." Radiating confidence, my girl beams at the compliment. "Walsh, got a second?"

I sit Lennon down on the bench, quickly unlacing her skates. "Squirt, I'm going to talk with Mr. Kenny for a minute or two. Take off your gear. There's water and a snack in the cooler. Be back in a flash."

A nod of her head confirms she got my message. I don't bother with my skates, following Kenny just out of earshot of Lennon.

He motions for me to have a seat on the bleachers, sitting after me.

"I have a proposition for you."

"I'm all ears."

Over the three years I've been at Aspenridge, I've gotten to know Kenny well. He's at every practice and home game, occasionally even traveling with the team to the local away games. As much as I'm loyal to the Nordic rink, I'm building a good rapport with the bigwigs here. You never know when you're going to need something.

"We're hosting a onetime clinic the Saturday after Thanksgiving, and we need volunteers." Before I can even digest the question, he continues. "I've seen you with the young kids, how you are with Lennon. It's only a two-hour commitment and would spruce up any résumé."

My mind churns with adding one more thing to my plate. I'm already overworked between classes, hockey, and my part-time job at Nordic rink, not to mention Lennon. It may only be a "one-day" commitment, but it could also mean less time with her that day.

My attention diverts to her. She's sucking down the squeezie I had the forethought to loosen the top of earlier. Lost in her own little world, the idea of giving up what little time I already have with her weighs heavily on my heart.

"Before you say no, just tell me you'll think about it. It doesn't interfere with Aspenridge games or practice. I already checked." Kenny must sense my hesitation. He sweetens the deal, making it almost impossible to say I won't at least consider it by adding, "Did I mention volunteers get free ice time?"

Blowing out a breath, my gaze back on Kenny, I agree, "I'll think about it. It's about the best I can do."

His mouth breaks out in a smile. "Thank you for even considering it. I know how full your plate is, but you were the first person who came to mind when the opportunity arose." His scrutiny drifts to Lennon. "She entertains herself well on the ice."

"I often wonder what runs through her mind as she skates. I've asked her, but she won't spill her secrets."

His chuckle resounds around the empty arena. "Whatever you're doing, keep doing it. She's going to go places in the rink and in life."

"Thanks. Taking it one day at a time, learning from my mistakes. With no parent handbook to guide me, all I can do is my best."

"The best advice I ever got as a parent. Still trying to follow it with my teenagers." This time, his chuckle is more subdued.

"I try not to think that far. If I don't acknowledge she'll ever be a teenager, she'll stay this little forever, right?"

"If only that were the case. It goes by in the blink of an eye. The days might be long, but the years are short. Cherish them."

As much as I've heard the same advice so many times before, it seems different coming from Kenny. Almost as if he truly means it rather than a platitude.

He stands up, and I follow suit.

"When do you need an answer by?" I ask as we walk back to Lennon, still sitting on the bench.

"Two weeks or so." As we approach, Lennon turns her head and smiles up at us. "Little lady, make sure you come back soon to skate."

At the very insinuation of more time on the ice, her eyes twinkle. "I'm free tomorrow, right, Keeley?" She makes a similar face to the one I gave her earlier, except her puppy dog eyes and pouty lips are more adorable.

"We'll talk about it in the car, Squirt."

"Her enthusiasm is priceless. Make sure you don't squash it." With a pat on Lennon's head, he walks away, his parting words lingering in the air behind him.

Despite her best efforts at holding it back, a yawn breaks free. "Come on. Let's go home for a bath. Thank goodness Mimi already fed you dinner."

I quickly shuck my gear and pack up all our stuff. Shouldering the bag on one arm, she finagles her way into the other.

"Can I sleep with you tonight? I promise not to get out of bed."

"No."

"Just this one night. My pillow misses your bed. And your blanket is so much softer than mine."

The girl's got a million excuses at bedtime about why she can't fall asleep or why she needs to sleep in my bed. She has the same blanket, but the five-year-old in her thinks I'll fall for any and all excuses.

"No."

"But, Dad."

Bringing out the "Dad" means business.

"I said no, Lennon Victoria."

She crosses her arms over her chest and pouts.

Nice try, kid. You may be adorable, but I won't give into your demands.

At least not all the time.

CHAPTER 3
WALSH

walk out of sociology, my head spinning. A few weeks into my fall senior semester, and this elective is kicking my ass. I don't have the time or motivation required to dedicate to doing well. I'm not sure what I was thinking at the end of the semester last year when I agreed to it. Must have been the elation of a Division III Frozen Four championship win, thinking I could tackle anything.

As long as I end up with a C, I'll get credit, keep my grant, and not be put on academic probation. I only like to ride the bench in my jersey.

Perhaps Millie will take pity on me and help in some way.

Because your mother doesn't help enough.

Free babysitting, meals, laundry, a shelter for me and my kid, among other things. Yeah, probably best not to ask her for help. Dad's no help with college, since he barely skated by in high school. And not my kind of skating. Possibly one of my sisters, Juliet or Marina. I'll text them later to see what their availability is.

It's lunchtime on campus at Aspenridge College. Because the weather's mild for September, the quad is packed. Blankets lay among the grass, students soaking up the early autumn sunshine, and at least two organized games of frisbee transpire. Leaves on the trees standing guard are beginning to lose their green.

"Keeley. Where you headed?" my teammate, Ezra Hamilton, calls, jogging over to match my stride.

"Student Center. Gonna grab a snack before taking off for the afternoon."

"I'll join you."

Ezra's a sophomore this year. Another Vermont boy, he grew up on a farm about three towns over. Our high schools were in the same league, so we played against each other years ago, but I didn't know him well before he started playing for Aspenridge. He's a hell of a center, scoring a quarter of our goals last season as a freshman.

"How's Lennon?"

Of the other players, he's the first to ask about her. He's got two kid sisters at home, one about Lennon's age and a younger one. Not the same as having your own kid at our age, but of all my friends, he understands her the best.

"Can't sit still. Sassy. A lovable pain in my butt."

Ezra laughs, and I can't help the smile on my face.

As much as she's all that, she's mine, all thirty-five pounds of her. She was the shock of my life, unplanned in every way, but I wouldn't trade every sacrifice I've made in the last five years. Not if it meant I wouldn't have her. Life as a teen dad isn't for the faint of heart, but I'm fortunate for the support of good people and family in my life. Without my village, I would have drowned. I don't often fathom where my life would be if Megan had made another choice years ago. I also don't allow myself to think of a life devoid of being able to follow my dreams. Fortuity in my life is an understatement. I don't take any of it for granted.

"You get your sisters on skates yet?"

"Nah. Mom won't let them. 'Too violent.'" He shakes his head, a sardonic laugh bubbling out. "I'm lucky they get to come to a game or two."

"Next time they're here, let me know. Lennon would love to entertain them."

My mind drifts to her friend with the hot mom.

Tate.

Straight raven hair. Brown doe eyes. Creamy white skin. The hint of an accent not from these parts enhances her allure. I haven't seen her since I picked Lennon up Friday at preschool, but she hasn't strayed far from my mind. Which is a problem in so many ways.

Hockey.

Lennon.

She's a mom.

Classes.

Lennon.

Since she was born, my priority has been Lennon. I'm fortunate to have a flexible schedule with her, which allows me to pursue a college degree and play the sport I love. Because hockey would be the first to go when and if the schedule gets to be too much. It wouldn't be college, though I could take a year off, get a job and go back.

The first year of college was an adjustment, especially with a toddler. Megan and I were struggling to come up with a schedule that worked for both of us to spend time with Lennon without compromising our goals. Before Lennon, Aspenridge wasn't my first choice of school. With Lennon, it's been a godsend. I get to play hockey, attend class, live at home, and work my schedule around my daughter.

Are there things I sacrifice and have to miss? No doubt. I'm not as tight with some of the other players on the team because I'm only on campus for classes and hockey. I don't live with them, either in the dorms or the hockey house. I'm not going out every night—hell, even weekend nights—seeking a good time. Even when Lennon's with her mother, if I'm not at practice or a game, I'm working a shift at the Nordic rink.

Or catching up on missed work from the week.

Or my dad has me doing something around the house.

Or I'm sleeping.

Ezra holds open the door to the Student Center, and it's chaos. For as many people are outside, there are equal numbers inside.

"The cafeteria or Bites & Bytes?" Ezra wonders.

I check the time on my phone. I have an hour before I have to pick up Lennon from school. My eyes drift to the full line at the door to the cafeteria. "Bites & Bytes."

With the rotating practice schedule, my time on campus each week isn't consistent. I don't eat many meals here. A quick bite for breakfast some days, lunch here and there, is about the extent of my usage of Aspenridge's food services.

Ezra follows my lead to the snack shop. It's a small café serving sandwiches, snacks and grab-and-go items with a self-serve coffee station. Across campus, there's a fully-staffed coffee shop serving fancy drinks. I tend to be a regular Joe guy, so this suits me well. Economical to the wallet and schedule.

"Did you catch the Boston game last night?"

"The beginning. Crashed hard after practice and studying for an exam in medical ethics."

"You missed a good one," Ezra jests with a hanging of his head. "Goalie let in two right in a row. Pulled him in the beginning of the first. It was like he'd never played before."

I chuckle. Even the pros have bad days. It bodes well to remember when I'm playing like crap. I have no lofty notions of playing for the NHL. Some of my teammates do, and I'd give my left nut that one or two will make it there. For me, it's about the love of the game. The thrill of chasing the puck from one side of the rink to the other. The rush as it hits the net. The camaraderie of being part of a team.

Would it be great to play hockey for a living? Beyond question, but it's not in the cards for me. Maybe one day it was. Before Lennon. As much as I want to give her the world, experiencing it with her and finding the things she loves outweighs the effort and skill required to make it as a professional hockey player. The salary would be awesome, but the travel and time away from her would devastate the relationship between us. Something I'm not prepared to do.

A few of the other members of our team join us. We push together two square tables, making the space our own. Baskets of fries, onion rings, and mozzarella sticks are placed in the middle of the table. Give it five minutes before they're wolfed.

"Keeley, the blonde was back last night at the house. Asking about you," Clayton Hibbert prattles with a wink of his eye.

"Which blonde?" He makes a motion with his hands indicating large breasts. Very large breasts. Which is the least bit helpful to narrow it down.

I don't sleep around, especially not with bunnies. A handful of one-night stands tips the scales for the college experience. I'd rather spend my time doing more productive things—hockey, studying, spending time with my kid—than sleeping my way through a gaggle of college co-eds or worse, sleeping with the same girl a teammate has or will bed. Gross. No thanks.

"Bianca. No, Erika. Shantel." He lifts a shoulder. "Not sure."

None of those names sound familiar, but gun to my head, coming up with the names of the girls I messed around with would be impossible. "Where and when was she asking for me?"

"Hockey house. Wanted to know when you'd be back," Gabe Kolligan supplies, wiping mayo off his mouth with his sleeve. Sometimes these guys are worse than Lennon.

"Want me to get her number next time she stops by so you can tap it again?"

"If Keeley doesn't want it, save it for me," Moe Strickland insists.

"Pass." I savor a bite of the Cuban sandwich. Of all the food on campus, it's my favorite. The way they cook the pork does it for me. Mom's tried to replicate it, but though she's a fabulous cook, this one hits differently.

"What time did your *friend* leave this morning?" Tristan Ford wonders, talking to Clayton.

Clayton checks his wrist at the nonexistent watch. "Uh, probably still there. Told her to make herself comfortable for round three."

Six sets of eyes whip his way before the chorus of voices rings out.

"You left her in the house alone?"

"You're going back for thirds?"

"Better triple wrap your dick."

"That's what I'm talking about." A high five from Cody McGuire.

"Wrong, dude. So wrong."

Their conversation continues, Clayton defending his actions and trying to make the girl out to be anything but a puck bunny.

I eat my Cuban and fries in silence, half listening to their conversation, half wondering if I'll make it in time for preschool pickup to see Tate.

The thought has me furiously packing up my stuff. "Gotta run and grab Squirt. See you at practice tonight."

At the mention of my daughter, the crude hockey players gush. Whenever she's around, they're mostly on their best behavior. They may not think to ask about her, but when I mention her, even in passing, or she's at a game or practice, they fold like softies.

"Aww. Tell Squirt we miss her."

"Ask her when she's coming to skate. My mohawk turn could use some sharpening."

"Let's not give the five-year-old so much power. She already thinks she can skate circles around you." With a wave of my hand, I'm off.

If I time it right, maybe I'll actually get to speak to Tate.

CHAPTER 4
TATE

'm early to pick up Aubrey today. I made sure I planned my day with plenty of extra time built in to get to the school early. It means playing catch-up on some work after she's in bed, but it's worth it. I don't need the reputation of being "the mom who's always late." In time, it will apply. But I don't need to be labeled our first month here.

My eyes scan the parking lot, pretending I'm not looking for a certain white truck I haven't seen since last week. Maybe he's habitually late as well. Didn't the kid mention something about *again*? That could be my imagination. It fills in the gaps of things I want to believe rather than remember things that actually happened.

In the past week, Aubrey's talked nonstop about her new friend Lennon. She accepted my dismissal of her "dad" question and hasn't brought it back up. I shouldn't be okay with that, not for the sake of her wanting to know about her father, but also how she lets the issue slide. I try not to ignore any of her requests often. However, I'm not ready to deal with the backlash of having to explain the situation with her father, as if she'd even understand. Though it's not fair to her, I'm still dealing with my emotions about all of it. Damon's death, his parents' reaction, our move.

Shaking off the bad thoughts bubbling to the surface, I park off to the back of the lot, not wanting to mingle with the other parents standing on the sidewalk, chatting and gabbing away. I don't fit in with most of Aubrey's friends' parents, who are all older, wiser, and way more experienced parents than me. You hear enough about being "a young parent," it's hard to ignore it sometimes. Add to it I'm a young, single mom, doing this all on my own now…I should prepare for my tar and feathering.

I considered adoption for a hot minute, but even with everything I've had to sacrifice for the last five years, in no way do I regret my decision to become a mother at seventeen.

To my chagrin, the doors of the preschool open before the white truck pulls into the lot. Would it be obvious to wait for him?

Yes. Totes obvious.

I stall walking over to the door. Not to wait for the truck, but for the other parents to clear the space. When Aubrey notices me, her eyes light up. My smile is instantaneous, a similar one she beaming on her heart-shaped pink lips. She's always had a way of melting my heart with just a look. Part of me hopes she stays this innocent. The other part knows she won't. Hell, it's how I ended up a teenage mother. I shudder at her repeating my mistakes because I want a better life for her. Not because *she's* a mistake.

"Mommy! You'll never guess what." Her excited voice tickles my ears, matching the enthusiasm on her face. She's usually not this enthused, so whatever it is must be great. At least in her mind. She flies into my waiting arms. Her hugs will never get old.

"What, Bean?"

She can't contain the huge grin, her secret brimming, needing to be let loose. Leaning in my ear, she whispers, "Smarshmallows are in my backpack."

Oh wow. He followed through. I'll admit I was skeptical he would, considering Aubrey hadn't mentioned them again after Friday. Males rarely remember the little things, and for a stranger, even less. I'm excited because Aubrey's happy. My joy has nothing to do with the man who kept his end of the bargain.

Not even a little.

"Yummy. What a special treat for later."

There's a tap on my leg. Peering down, I find Lennon gaping up at me. Her hair's pulled back in an unkempt ponytail today, the front strands of her dirty blonde hair falling over her forehead.

"I didn't let Keeley forget them." She radiates with pride at her great memory, her crystal blue eyes dancing with delight.

"That was so sweet of you. You'll have to thank your dad for us."

"You can thank him yo'self. He's coming now." She motions over her shoulder, and damn. With a matching smile to his daughter plastered on his lips, my heart skips a beat as he struts over. While maybe not arrogant in the full sense of the word, the way he carries himself is a turn-on. And something I definitely shouldn't be thinking about.

I'm so lost in staring at him—I hope I'm not drooling—I don't realize he's spoken.

Shaking out of my stupor, I stutter, "Wh-what?" The heat in my cheeks certainly gives away how I'm feeling.

"Just wanted to make sure you got the marshmallows. We don't need any extra bags at our house."

"I have it on good authority Aubrey has them in her backpack." To confirm but also needing a breather from the heat of the Adonis' gaze currently aimed my way, I appraise my daughter. The girl appears as entranced as I feel.

Aubrey steps closer to me, shying away from Walsh. "Thank you," she says in a whisper, her introverted nature still polite.

"You're welcome. Be sure to let us know how you like them. Mommy can text me. I left my number on the bag."

What? my brain fires at me, the ability to even begin to comprehend what his comment implies getting lost in translation.

Finding my voice, I stammer, "Um, sure. We will. Thanks."

"Keeley, can we go to the park? I think the fish need some bread." Lennon's little voice breaks the hold her father has over me.

"Did you bring the bread?" he volleys back.

Not missing a beat, she sasses, "Packed it in my bag. You think Mimi will mind I brought the whole loaf?"

His head shakes at her admission. "For you, she'll probably make an exception. Had I done that as a kid, I'd still be paying her back."

"It's cuz she loves me more. She tells me all the time."

"Right kid. Exactly." He reaches down and lifts her with one arm, tossing her over his shoulder. The way his biceps flex does not escape me.

Is it wrong I'm so invested in their conversation, in the way they're so comfortable with each other? Who's Mimi? How is she related to these two? I should probably excuse myself from this, be on our way, and not waste any more time on strangers. My feet don't move, and I cannot make them.

"So, yes?" she wonders.

"What's the outlook for you going to bed with no problems tonight?"

How he keeps his voice neutral is beyond me. I have to turn away so I don't laugh out loud at his negotiating with a five-year-old. I cross all my fingers and toes Aubrey—who seems as equally zealous about this as I am—doesn't pick up on any of these habits, cute as they are for his kid.

Lennon cocks her head from side to side, obviously thinking about what she's going to say. I wait with bated breath. If he didn't want us to hear their conversation, he would have walked away. It's not my place to make the first move and excuse ourselves, right?

"Positive." She punctuates her reply with a nod of her head.

A few beats pass to follow her one-word answer.

The outlook is positive.

I don't think Aubrey knows the definitions of either outlook or positive. Although in this case, I'm not sure it's such a bad thing.

Walsh consults his watch. "One hour. No issues when it's time to go. You go to bed with no complaints." He ticks off each condition on his fingers.

"Deal. And Aubrey can come too." Lennon's attention focuses our way.

Taken aback at her invitation, I'm too stunned to speak.

"Mommy, can we? Please?"

"Yeah, please can she come?" Lennon pleads. She clasps her fists together under her chin, her eagerness not something I can ignore.

With Aubrey looking so keenly at me, I have no choice but to say, "Of course. Sounds like fun."

"Yes." Lennon pumps her fist in the air, her enthusiasm contagious. So much joy wrapped up in a petite package. "It's going to be so fun. Keeley pushes the swing super high."

Aubrey peers up at me, perplexed. "Mommy, who is Keeley?"

"Me," Walsh answers. "Walsh Keeley, to be exact." He extends his hand for a shake as the name swirls through my brain.

Walsh Keeley.

So much about this man intrigues me, but more so, the dynamic of his relationship with his daughter.

"But she calls you Keeley…" I trail off, the comment sounding so much worse out loud than in my head.

"It's a long story. If you're joining us at the park, I'll be glad to share it with you."

He flashes me that gorgeous smile, and I seriously feel my knees go weak. An exaggeration for sure, but damn this man has some weird sorcery over me. Emotions I can't unpack now.

"S-sure." I clear my throat, trying again to not be so tongue-tied. "Great. Which park?" I fit my hand into his, realizing he's still holding his out.

"Edison." My face must show my confusion, so he adds, "It's over on Main Street, behind all the shops." The further details still do nothing for me. He shakes his head. "Follow us. It'll be easier."

"Okay."

He starts for his truck, turning about halfway there. "Which car is yours? So I can assure you're behind me."

Embarrassed, I point to my Honda Civic. His truck isn't new, but it's in better shape than my hand-me-down car in much need of an upgrade. Which won't come soon. Hondas are notorious for lasting hundreds of thousands of miles, and I've been banking on that being true since I bought the car years ago.

Walsh motions over his shoulder. "Mine's the white Chevy truck. You can keep up, right?"

I undoubtedly know he means by following him to the park, but my brain isn't firing on all cylinders. Because yeah. There's no way I can "keep up" with Walsh in any other sense of the phrase.

My nonverbal head bob given, Aubrey and I walk to the edge of the lot.

"You hot, Mommy? You're super fweaty."

Leave it to my mostly oblivious five-year-old to notice how affected I am by the one guy who's talked to me in the last five years. To be honest, he's only talking to me because his kid friended mine. It's not like he's talking to *me*.

"I'm good, Bree."

Maybe *good* is a bit of a stretch, but I'm certainly not going to explain to her what I'm feeling.

I can't even describe it myself.

The drive is less than seven minutes. As we creep closer to the park, something funny builds inside me. I meant what I said about him not being here for me, but try telling that to certain parts of my body currently experiencing a drought. A *long* famine, starved for more than the touch of another human being. Someone other than myself.

And now I'm even "fweatier" than before. Sweat pools on my forehead, something I'll have to wipe away before facing Walsh again. Discreetly, of course.

"Mommy, they have a zip line." Aubrey's animated voice brings my thoughts back to where they should be.

A quick glance in the rearview mirror reveals her gawking out the window, taking in the sight of this new playground.

Ever since she was little, I made it a point to visit a variety of parks, introducing her to various playground equipment. Not that she partakes in any of it. She's content to watch from the sidelines, maybe go in a swing for a brief time, and every once in a while, she'll choose a small slide to go down. I had hoped by going to different ones, her curiosity about the play structures would help get her over her fear. Still waiting for that day.

"That looks super fun. You should try it," I encourage.

"Too little."

I go to argue, to point out the kid currently on the zip line is about her age, but I stop myself. There's only so much boosting I can do. If she wants to do it, she will. In her own time. She's been this way since day one. Or more like nine days past her due date when she finally made her appearance in the world.

"Okay." I peruse the rest of the park. A toddler playground stands off to the side but most likely still too much for her.

This should be interesting.

Parking in the spot next to Walsh, I manage a few deep breaths before making my way out of the car to unbuckle Aubrey. With a genuine and excited big grin on her petite lips, you'd think she was ready to tackle everything at the park.

By the time we're out of the car, Walsh is holding Lennon. While he's not an overly big guy, she seems even smaller in his arms. My heart squeezes at the protective way he carries her. Aubrey won't ever have that.

I don't let my mind go down that path of thinking. It's our reality, and we both have to be okay with it. Hopefully, I love her enough to make up for it.

"Where to first?" Walsh asks, sweeping his arm out toward the playscape.

"Swings!" Lennon cheers.

Instead of heeding her suggestion, he assesses my daughter standing next to me, holding onto my hand like the good girl she is.

"Shall we hit the swings first, Aubrey?" he queries, waiting patiently for her answer.

"Otay," Aubrey finally mutters.

At her approval, he starts off toward the swings.

The park is mostly deserted at this time of day. A few moms stand off to the side chatting among themselves as their kids play nearby.

Off to one side, there's a tall climbing structure, which Aubrey won't foot on. Off to the other, two sets of swings: a set of four for older kids and another set for the younger crowd. The ones more Aubrey's speed. A playscape stands in the middle of the park, offering different methods of climbing apparatuses: stairs, an arc of rungs, a climbing wall, as well as a wall with a rope for the most daring. Three or four slides shoot off in different directions providing a means back to the ground.

Walsh walks around the perimeter of it all, his gaze set ahead of him on the set of "older" swings. Lennon chatters, going on about something I'm not able to make out completely.

Six feet away from the swings, he sets her down, and she barrels her way to the swing, shimmying her little self up, grabbing onto both chains when she's in the middle.

"Ready, Keeley," she calls out, motioning her head for him.

Aubrey observes her new friend intently from her position next to me, making no move to join in on the fun.

Almost as if he can sense her hesitation, Walsh crouches down next to Aubrey. "You want to swing too?"

Aubrey dismisses his question with a head shake.

"She's definitely more inclined to sit on the sidelines than participate," I fill in to assuage his bewilderment. "Give her a little time to warm up to the idea, and she'll maybe want to go in the toddler swings." I follow my comments with a nervous giggle, an action I can't explain. Must be the proximity to this man.

During the brief interaction, Lennon's hopped down off the swing, coming over to join us where we stand.

"Are we swinging or not?" Her question is more inquisitive than impolite. She looks first to the adults, then to Aubrey.

In my head, I beg Lennon not to provoke Aubrey or make her uncomfortable. It's my way of protecting my kid, shielding her from the cruelties of life. And while I won't be able to do it forever—or much longer, in all honesty—the longer I can keep her from the hurt of other kids, the better in my book.

Almost as if she can read Aubrey's reluctance, like her father did mere moments ago, Lennon stares at Aubrey but speaks to her father. "Keeley, I think it's a green swing kinda day, wouldn't you say?"

"I couldn't agree more," he replies, pride exuding off him at his daughter's ability to put the focus on someone other than herself. She may have the body of a five-year-old, but his comment about being wise beyond her years couldn't be more accurate.

Lennon holds out her hand to Aubrey. Without a moment's indecision, Aubrey lets go of mine and tucks her hand in Lennon's. My heart catches at this simple gesture, the childhood innocence of the two of them extending way beyond what it truly is.

The two girls walk from us, hand in hand, to the other set of swings while I'm left standing in awe at the kindness of this stranger, the perceptiveness and cleverness occupying one tiny human.

It's not until Walsh voices, "You coming?" do I discover I'm rooted in place.

"Um, yeah. The green swings."

He ambles ahead of me, and my eyes dart down to his pert ass. Inwardly, I scold myself for noticing.

He's off-limits.

You're not his type.

You can't date anyone at this point in your life.

But damn. Walsh Keeley would be a mighty fine choice.

CHAPTER 5
WALSH

n my humble opinion, my girl's got a heart of gold. I'd like to think I've had a minor part in cultivating it, but she came like this. She certainly doesn't get it from her mother. I may have "loved" her once, but Megan's not what one would call friendly. She's way more cold than warm, although her icy demeanor has thawed since first learning about Lennon. Almost as if a motherly instinct lay dormant inside her.

Ever since she was little, Lennon's had this way about her, this natural ability to read people's emotions. To back off when needed, to let other people have the limelight, as in today's case. I don't know how she senses it, but she's hardly ever wrong. She's got an old soul, surely.

Focusing on Lennon's behavior allows me to ignore the beauty walking a few paces behind me. I keep inserting myself into her life: buying marshmallows for her kid, leaving my number so she can text me how the kid likes them—can you say ulterior motives—and now inviting them to the park. Sure, much of it's for Lennon's sake, something I'm convincing myself to seem a little less obvious. I should not be this wound up about a woman, the mother to one of Lennon's friends, nor someone I met less than a week ago.

By the time I reach the toddler swings, Lennon's already sitting in one, having scrambled into it on her own. She never lets her size hold her back, and when the girl wants something, she's balls to the walls and keep out of her way until she gets it. It will get her far in life, when she uses it for good. Not at bedtime against me, especially when I'm exhausted from the day.

Aubrey stands to the side, her fingers fiddling, her eyes wide, an unreadable expression on her face. The one mirroring her mother's. She's not quite the spitting image of Tate, but they share a similar shape of their faces. Aubrey's hair is chestnut brown to her mom's darker, almost black, locks. Where Aubrey's eyes are more hazel, Tate's are a deeper chocolate brown.

No, Walsh. Do not go there.

Tate goes over to Aubrey, bending down to her level. I ignore the way she folds herself, her butt sticking out, curves fully on display in the crisp linen shorts she wears. "You want to swing yet, sweetie?"

"I'll watch Lennon."

The gleeful expression on her face is in contrast to a girl who's just going to "watch" someone else. But who am I to force her into something she doesn't want to do?

I stand behind where Lennon sits, waiting somewhat patiently. "Let me know when you're ready to swing. I'm happy to push you too."

Lennon twists her torso and studies me with a kindhearted expression, my heart bursting with love for my daughter. A love I never felt until she came into my life, one growing stronger with each passing day. "She'll be ready soon, Keeley. She just needs an extra minute."

"I think you're right," I respond to her thoughtful comment, pulling the swing back, just the way she likes it. Letting go, the swing powers forward, her giggles and delight as joyful as ever.

She's always loved the swings. Now that she's a little older and extinguished her fear of not holding the chains with a death grip, she loves the "older" swings, going as high as she can. She hasn't yet mastered the art of pumping, but it's not for lack of trying. Skating athleticism doesn't translate to swings.

"Wheeeee!" she shrieks, laughing and having a grand old time.

I propel her as high as I can without it being too dangerous—don't need any more of those judgy mothers on my case again. Seriously, the kid's had blades of steel strapped to her feet as a toddler, but the swing's going too high?

After a few minutes, I sneak a peek at Tate and Aubrey. The girl stands at her mother's leg, and the smile she sports is still big. I wave her over, and surprisingly, she doesn't hesitate. She pulls her mother along behind her, who hoists her up into the swing next to Lennon. Taking her position behind Aubrey's swing, Tate smiles kindly my way. I'm not entirely sure what I did to earn such a warm and inviting beam, but I'm grateful for it. There's something mesmerizing about her, a feeling I haven't experienced in a long time.

Dare I say ever?

No. It's been two quick encounters. Focus on the kids, not your neglected cock.

Except I have the faint suspicion it'd be more than just sex with her.

Fortunately, Lennon's voice diverts this runaway train of inappropriate thought.

"All done. How about we feed the ducks now?"

"Sure, Squirt." I allow the swing to come to a stop on its own to give her a last few sways. She brings her legs in to stand up, which invokes the gasp. You know the one—from the mother who's appalled at the young man who's allowing the kid to stand in a swing. *Stand!* Still holding onto the chains. Me in arm's distance.

At first, I think it's Tate, which saddens me. Sure, her kid's less courageous than Lennon, but she doesn't seem like one of "those" moms. But I guess I'm stereotyping her into that category. Just because she's young doesn't mean she can't judge other parents.

"Oh my god, he's right there. As if he'd let her fall," Tate mumbles, confirming the aversion to my lack of helicopter parenting isn't her.

"So it's not just me who can't stand being judged?"

"Gosh, no. I try to have a tough skin and let things roll off my back, but I don't get why people can't mind their own business."

There's clearly a story—or several—inferred by her reply. And she's not referring to just the current situation.

"We'll have to compare notes one day."

"It'll take more than a day," she deadpans. I kinda get stuck on her comment, the nonchalant way she tosses it out there, still being affected by it.

Rather than rush to catch up with the three of them, I linger behind. To ogle Tate's ass. As much as I really shouldn't. But it's right there. In plain sight. I may have some willpower, but at the end of the day, I'm a guy. One who hasn't been laid in a while. When presented with an opportunity, I'm not ashamed to notice.

I only look away when pressure ignites at my zipper.

Down boy. She's not here to play with you.

Oh, but if she was…

Snapping out of thoughts only leading to problems, I fall into step with them, my stride being double or triple theirs. Especially Lennon's.

The loaf of bread dangles from her fist, swaying side to side. She wasn't kidding when she said she brought the entire loaf. Minus the one piece she nibbled on during the drive. I shouldn't let her waste an entire loaf of edible bread on fowl, but she'll have to face the consequences of Millie Keeley, not me.

Lennon leads the brigade to the pond. We come here enough, she has a favorite spot. Once in place, she struggles to open the bag, though the determination set on her face is quite endearing. Frustrated, she hands it to me with a huff. "Keeley, open this."

"Manners, Lennon."

"Please."

I should correct her use of "Keeley," especially in front of strangers. Perhaps this is the thing Tate will judge me for.

The bread clip off, I hand it back to her. "Remember to share." She shoots me a stank visage, one I've seen all too often with her mother. On my five-year-old, it's not as repulsive. With the parts of my disposition Lennon inherited, hopefully it will stay that way.

She offers two pieces to Aubrey before taking two for herself, then she demonstrates how to rip the bread into pieces, which is best for the ducks. I can't stifle my laughter.

"I'm sorry," I apologize to Tate. "She can be a bit bossy and a little overbearing sometimes. Feel free to reprimand her if she's too much." My eyes cast to hers, our gazes locking. The midday sun reflects in her brown orbs, the color bolder.

"No need to worry. She's adorable. Aubrey's always been more of a follower and tends not to stand her ground much, and she seems quite enamored with Lennon." A tinge of pink heats her cheeks. Immediately I wonder why. "So, Keeley?"

Oh, right. I owe her an explanation.

Before I begin, I sit on the grass, knowing we'll be here a while. Because Aubrey seems to be amenable to whatever Lennon chooses. For as much of my personality she inherited, it's my greatest fear she'll grow up to be a "mean girl" like her mother can be. I'm constantly trying to counteract it, vigilant to step in before things escalate. I won't be able to control that forever, but if she learns from a young age how to treat people, it will carry over as she grows up.

Hopefully.

Tate follows my lead, although she doesn't sit as close as I would like.

"For as long as I can remember, I've gone by Keeley. To everyone but my parents and most of my teachers. Lennon's first word was 'Dad' and not because she was babbling the 'd' sound. If there was any way for her to understand what she was doing, she totally did it to piss off her mother." Saying it aloud always makes me chuckle at the absurdity of my thinking. But I'll swear she did it on purpose until my dying breath. Without a glance in Tate's direction, I shake the comment away. "Maybe she was two when she first called me Keeley, repeating it after hearing someone else. Maybe I reacted too over the top to it. I can't remember anymore, but ever since then, she's done it. Now it's beyond the point of her doing it to get a rise out of me. It's almost second nature. And while I'm her dad first, as long as she doesn't abuse the privilege, I'll let it slide."

I glimpse Tate's way for her reaction to the story. Quiet throughout my explanation, her expression bears no air of judgment. And the way her lips turn up into a half smile is charming.

"From a stranger's perspective, you two seem to have quite the relationship."

"Thanks. Just doing the best I can for her, which isn't always easy."

"Ain't that the truth."

She fuses her lips, almost as if she wants to say more. And I wish she would. I want to know so much more about her. Exactly how old she is. What her story is. Her likes and dislikes. What turns her on.

Uh, no. Perhaps not that. I want to know, but I certainly can't ask. Not in this friendly way we are sorta getting to know each other. At least as parents to our daughters who are forming a friendship.

I haven't said anything in a while, and I'm most likely gawking at her. Thank goodness Aubrey runs over.

"Mommy, gotta go potty." Her face scrunches, and she bounces from foot to foot.

"Okay, Bean." Hopping up off the ground, her eyes scan the vicinity. "You'll have to hold it. I'm not sure there's a bathroom here."

"It's most likely closed for the season," I inform her regretfully.

"I gotta go bad. Real bad." Poor kid seems on the verge of tears, one leg crossed over the other.

"I gotta get her home. Thanks for the invite. We'll have to set up another playdate for the girls."

Tate doesn't even wait for my response, just scoops Aubrey up in her arms and makes a beeline for the parking lot.

Wonder how far they live from here and if she'll make it home. I shudder at the thought of having to clean the damn car seat. Although urine is by far easier than poop or vomit...

"Can we stay? I didn't finish feeding all the bread to the duckies." Lennon holds up the rest of the bag. Gratefully, it's almost gone.

"Of course, Squirt." I dig a piece of bread out for myself and mosey closer to the water. "What are you making us for dinner?"

Without missing a beat, my five-year-old replies, "I didn't get the memo from Mimi, but whatever it is, you're going to eat it and like it."

A deep rumble tears out of my chest. She parrots words she's heard too many times to count. And her delivery is spot-on.

I tuck her into my legs. "That's my girl."

"Always, Keeley. Always."

Sassy and sweet. A perfect combination.

CHAPTER 6
TATE

My mood shouldn't depend on whether I see Walsh each day, but apparently, it does. Or maybe my period's due soon. Ever since getting pregnant with Aubrey, it's been inconsistent. Showing up when it wants, whether it's been twenty days or forty-five. I should contemplate birth control, but working single mom to a five-year-old equates to barely having the time to pee on my own, let alone get to appointments. It's on my list. Just way down at the bottom.

Because other people have picked Lennon up from preschool, it's been like a week without seeing him. Yes, I've counted. No, I'm not ashamed. I should be, but well, I'm not.

Here's the thing—I have his number. But I haven't used it yet. I can't tell him she liked the marshmallows because I'd be lying. And I don't want to start a friendship out on a lie.

A friendship? Let's not get ahead of yourself there, Tate.

She spit the thing out before she even bit it. I should be happy she's got a tiny sweet tooth. In this case, it meant I ate the entire bag because I didn't want it to go to waste. He went out of his way to get them for us. The least I can do is eat and enjoy them, even if my kid doesn't.

So, yeah. And "thanks for the marshmallows" seems like a cop-out. Especially days after the fact.

I think what's really got my panties in a twist is the ex. Lennon's mother. She's drop-dead gorgeous. Even though she walks like she's got a stick up her ass—and I've yet to see her smile—she's still so pretty. And her makeup game is on point. I gave up trying for the smokey eye look. I'm lucky if I swipe the lids with a single color.

She seems such the opposite of Walsh. Guess they proved the whole "opposites attract" thing true.

Right. That's why she's the ex.

Still. He was with her at some point, enough to get her pregnant.

This internal debate I'm having in my head has to stop. It will be easy enough once I get Walsh out of my head.

Easier said than done, of course.

Friday after Aubrey's long day at school, I stupidly choose to stand and wait outside. Off to the side of the door and the other parents, I don't miss the stolen glares or the hushed whispers. Maybe this time it's because I'm new, not because I'm younger than them. And I am much younger. Especially the one whose youngest of five is in Aubrey's class. She just turned forty.

Am I judging her for having five kids? Absolutely not, but that's about three too many for my liking.

The door to the school opens, and kids come pouring out. I notice Lennon first, Aubrey trailing behind her. She talks nonstop about Lennon and a little boy, Isaiah. Whenever I ask her to point him out to me, she gets shy, her face blushing beet red. She's got it bad for him.

Lennon stops in front of her mother. Crossing her arms across her chest, her little foot stomps twice. "Momma, where's Keeley? He's supposed to pick me up today. You said so this morning."

"Your *father* got caught up at school." Huge emphasis on the father. For whose sake, I can't ascertain. "I didn't need another late fee," she adds, further boggling my mind. Sure, the kid isn't a typical five-year-old, but there are still boundaries to set.

"He gets a pass this time," Lennon mumbles. "School is impor-tant. But I still get to go to Mimi's now, right?" Her attitude seems to change drastically. For a moment, at least.

"He's going to pick you up at the restaurant."

The biggest scowl I've ever seen appears on Lennon's face. If she were my kid, I wouldn't think it cute in the slightest, but seeing as she's not, it's stinking adorable.

"I don't wanna."

"We all have to do things we don't want to do." She enunciates each word to correct her use of "wanna."

Rather than get caught up in their drama, I nuzzle Aubrey in my arms. "How was school?"

Her grin reaches her ears. She leans in close to me, bursting with a secret she wants to divulge. Whisper-yelling, she announces, "We had donuts!"

Donuts. The only "sweet treat" my kid will eat. I can't even stand the sight of them anymore after bingeing them during my pregnancy. It's the only explanation I have for why she's so obsessed with them. Although her favorite is old-fashioned plain. Ironically, those were a last resort when I ate them.

"Your favorite," I enthuse while trying to hide my distaste.

Her expression sours for a moment. "I had to brush off the 'prinkles and frosting. But Isaiah ate them and gave me his donut. So I got two!" Her story finishes excitedly. I can't tell if it's because she got to eat two donuts or because she shared with Isaiah. Probably a little of both.

Before I can ask her, Lennon's defiant, "No" accosts my ears. My curiosity piqued, my head whips around. She's standing her ground, feet planted firmly on the sidewalk, arms crossed over her chest, a glower set deep.

"Lennon, don't make a scene," her mother hisses at her in a low, growly voice.

"I don't wanna go to the restaurant. I'll just wait here for Keeley to pick me up."

My feet move ahead of my brain. My mouth misses the memo as well because I say, "Lennon, you want to come to our house for a playdate? Then maybe Daddy can pick you up when he's done?"

My belly coils at my boldness. If I were Lennon's mother, I would hate to be put on the spot like I did to her. A stranger undermining my authority? No thanks. Since the words are out of my mouth, I can't haul them back. Nor do I want to. It will finally give me an excuse to not only text Walsh, but also to see him.

"And you are?" Up close, Lennon's mom is even more gorgeous. Flawless skin, almond-shaped eyes, perfect nose. The only "imperfection" I see is light circles below the eyes.

Standing Aubrey on the ground, I reach my hand out. "Tate Winchester. My daughter Aubrey and Lennon are in class together. We all went to the park last week to feed the ducks." *Stop rambling,* my brain advises. In this case, my mouth listens.

Lennon's mother scans her eyes up and down me. My baggy T-shirt and leggings hardly compare to her flowy skirt and button-down blouse, but there aren't any visible holes and the clothes are clean. My standards have lowered in the last few weeks while I try to get my act together and settled here in Vermont.

"I'm supposed to let my kid go home with a stranger?" she finally spits out.

"Tate isn't a stranger, Momma. Call Keeley. Ask him." Her attitude does a complete one-eighty.

Should I be offended I'm letting this five-year-old stand up for me?

Lennon's mom's pouty lips turn into a bigger frown, especially at the use of "Keeley." Walsh's perception is spot-on. I stifle my giggle.

She doesn't address Lennon's wishes for a few tense minutes as she ponders what to do. Honestly, I have no idea which side of the argument she's going to land. An exasperated sigh follows a glance at her watch.

"Fine. Go to their house. I'll have your father pick you up there. What's your address?" Lennon wraps herself around the woman's legs at the news, then quickly grabs Aubrey's hands and starts some little dance and cheer. Aubrey's excitement mirrors Lennon's.

I rattle off our address, earning a sneer. I bet she thinks her shit don't stink either. *Bitch.*

To ease some of the tension—not because she's handing her kid off to a stranger, but because she's edgy—I also give her my phone number.

"Do you need a car seat?"

Oh crap. Didn't think this plan through. I hate removing and installing the car seat. You'd think I'd be a pro at it by now, but I fight with it every time. Every damn time. And I just had to remove the cover because Aubrey didn't make it home in time from the park and peed all over it.

Fun times in the life of a mom. Single or not.

Lennon's mom shakes her head. "No. I don't have time to switch it out. I'll follow you to your place. Which car is yours?"

"The blue Civic." I sheepishly point it out, intimidation taking center stage.

"K. I'm in the white Audi SUV."

Of course you are.

"See you in a bit."

I rush Aubrey to our car, so many theories swirling through my mind about what's happening. At the forefront is what Walsh is going to say when he finds out.

Too late now to chicken out.

Megan—aka Lennon's mom, I learned—dropped her off and ran. Didn't come in to make sure it was safe or anything. I'm more surprised because I would have thought she'd be the kind of person who would want to snoop. Not for her daughter's sake, but out of curiosity.

Clearly, I'm as judgmental as everyone else.

I set the girls up at the small kitchen table with some fruit while I continue to process how I ended up here. I need to text Walsh, let him know I have his kid, give him my address so he knows where to pick her up.

Digging the phone from the bottom of my purse, I see he's beat me to the punch. Weird. Wonder how he got my number.

I waste no time opening up the Messages app.

WALSH

Hey, Meg let me know you have Lennon. I didn't get the entire story, but I owe you one. For Lennon's sake. Thank you.

Feverishly, my fingers type out a reply.

I'm not sure what overcame me, but you're welcome. Happy to have her. Anytime.

I hit send before I word-vomit every single thought floating through my brain. My stomach ripples when the three dots appear.

Leaving here in five. What's your address?

No rush. Woodland Condos. Building A #5

Cool. See you soon

We'll be here

As soon as the conversation ends, butterflies flutter inside me. The notion of seeing him again starts a chain reaction in my mind.

I should change my clothes.

I should redo my hair.

I should tidy up the mess.

I should put on some makeup.

That one's inspired by how gorgeous his ex is. And I really shouldn't care. I'm not trying to win any contest, let alone his consideration as anything more than his daughter's friend's mother. However, try telling my ego.

By the time I've done anything, there's a knock on the door. As my father always taught me, I peer through the peephole, Walsh's handsome smile greeting my eye.

Damn. How did he get here so fast?

My pulse revs up to a Daytona racing speed, stealing my breath and any sort of semblance of composure. When the door isn't answered fast enough, he knocks again.

Frantically, my eyes scan the small living room. Toys litter the carpet in two corners, and a basket of clean clothes sits off to another side. It's too late to do anything about any of it now.

Deep breath in. Slowly release.

With slightly twitchy fingers, I pull the door open, my smile instant when Walsh flashes his. A full, thousand-watt grin sure to dampen my panties.

"Hey." If the smile didn't do it, the one-word greeting surely does.

"Hi."

He holds some kind of container in one hand, opening the storm door with the other, making no move to enter until I invite him in.

Point one to him for being a true gentleman.

"You got here quick."

"We don't live far from here." His eyes peruse the living room, his gaze back on mine quickly. Not like there's much to see. "Cute place."

"Ah, it's home for now."

"Oh, right. You're new to town. Where did you move from?"

"Cedarvale, Kansas. Still learning the nuances of Vermont. So different from where we lived."

"Happy to show you around town. Just say the word."

I want to agree to his offer. More like, "Hell yes. Let's go right now," but I keep my inner unruliness contained.

"That would be greatly appreciated."

An awkward silence enters the room. My thoughts run haywire for what to say, how to get him talking. He doesn't seem upset about having to pick Lennon up, nor that she's here.

Walsh breaks the quiet. "Here. This is for you. As a thank you for taking Lennon." He shoves the container at me.

"Uh, thanks. You didn't have to do anything special. It's nothing. Plus, Aubrey loves having another kid to talk to."

Or she would, had they had time to do anything but eat a snack.

"It's from my mother." He scratches his head, appearing to be thinking hard. "There was something about simmering."

"What is it?" The question barrels out of my mouth without thought.

"Her famous chili. And if Aubrey eats it, please don't rub it in. Lennon hates the stuff, yet Mom consistently makes it, as if she's going to miraculously change her mind one day and like it."

I chew over how to respond. Do I tell him the truth, which would mean telling him about the marshmallows? Or do I just let it go and simply thank him for his mother's kind gesture?

Two excited five-year-olds bound into the room, interrupting us before I can say anything.

Lennon skips to Walsh. "Keeley, you're here. Momma dropped me off to play with Aubrey. But we didn't get to play. Can we stay a little longer? Please?"

He bends down to her level. "It's not up to us whether we stay. Remember, we talked about the hosts having to invite us to stay longer?"

Her hand slaps her forehead gently. "I keep forgetting." She turns to Aubrey and me, then back at her dad. "How do I get them to invite us?" she whisper-shouts.

Thankfully, Aubrey takes the hint. "Mommy, can Lennon stay longer, please? I didn't even get to show her my room." She doesn't quite have the same presence as Lennon, but her request works just the same.

"Sure thing, kiddo. And Walsh brought us special chili for dinner."

"Ew," Lennon mutters, coupled with a face of disgust.

However, my kid's eyes light up. "Like Nana used to make?"

"We'll have to taste it later. For now, go play."

She fist pumps her approval, grabs Lennon's hand, and scrambles down the hall to her room.

Walsh stands there, his gaze traveling back and forth between where the girls disappeared and me.

"Her room's completely kidproofed if that's what the concern's for."

"No. I trust you." A huge weight lifts off my shoulders. "Was she just passionate about chili?" An underlying tone of jealousy hides in his comment.

My shoulders raise in a shrug. "She loves chili. It's one of her favorite foods. And I don't make it as well as my mother, yet she still eats it."

"What kind of voodoo did you use to get her to eat it? 'Cause I'm going to need some for Lennon."

My chuckle echoes around the small room, eliciting another grin from Walsh. Not a replica from earlier, but handsome just the same.

"She's always been a hearty eater. Sometimes she's less picky than me."

Recognition illuminates his face. "Wait. You never texted how she liked the marshmallows. Did she love them? I still can't believe she's never had them before." As if he realizes what he just implied, he quickly amends, "No judgment."

I wave it off. "It's weird, I get it." I deliberate for a few seconds, but I can't lie to him. Not to his face. "Honestly, she hated it. She barely had it in her mouth before she spit it out."

His eyebrows shoot upward. "How is that possible?"

"I'm sorry. You bought them for her and everything, but…"

He cuts me off. "I'm not worried about one bag of marshmallows. I'm stuck on the fact she didn't like it."

Realizing we're still standing in the entryway, I suggest, "Have a seat. Can I get you something to drink? Water, apple or orange juice, milk? Coffee or tea?"

"Water would be great, thanks." He toes out of his shoes, flashes me a smile, and settles on the couch.

Meanwhile, the butterflies return in full force as I head to the kitchen. It's separated from the living room by a wall. I'm thankful he can't see me.

It's not like this is anything other than two parents chatting while their kids play in the other room, but it seems different. More…I don't know how to describe it. It certainly has to do with the fact he's a guy. And he's kinda my age, though I never pinpointed exactly how old he is, so maybe I'm off. But he's a young dad. Maybe that's where our similarities end. Although, I'd never willingly choose to hang out with his ex, and she's definitely around my age. Age isn't the only thing we have in common.

He's easy to talk to. In the few brief conversations we've had, I've let my guard down. Even though I hardly know anything about him besides a few tidbits I've gleaned over the two exchanges we've had, he's different from anyone else I've been friends with. Different from the two guys I've dated.

As if "dated" in middle school counts.

Or, as if "dating" and Walsh belong in the same sentence.

Two bottles of water in my hand, I inhale deeply and exhale slowly, attempting to calm the nerves trying to creep in. Normally, I'm not this skittish around members of the opposite sex. I'll blame it on being out of practice the past few years. Hard to have a dating life with a little one on top of juggling everything else on my plate.

I have to let this idea of dating go. It won't happen. Not with Walsh, not with anyone. No time, no babysitters, no desire.

The last one is a lie. It gets lonely sometimes, but the first two reasons put a huge damper on any kind of "life" I want to have, dating or otherwise. Especially here in Vermont where I only know my aunt and the few people I've met at Aubrey's preschool. Aunt Marsha's been nothing but kind to us—offering us a place to stay and helping get it set up while we get settled, securing Aubrey a spot at the preschool, inviting us to Sunday dinners, which I've yet to take her up on. I don't want to take advantage of her kindness, which includes pawning my kid off on a virtual stranger.

Back in the living room, Walsh is checking something on his phone but puts it down immediately when I appear. One bottle goes to him before I sit on the other end of the sofa.

It's not a huge sofa, and both my libido and heart take notice. Damn, he smells nice. Fresh, like soap. Woodsy.

"So, what brought you and Aubrey to Vermont?" he questions, taking a swig of his water.

"Go right for the jugular, why don't you?"

Walsh shows no shame, and a simple shrug of his shoulders is his only action.

Forced to answer him, I say, "The short version is I needed a change. I didn't expect to move so far away from home—my parents, the help they offered with Aubrey—but I felt trapped there. My father's sister lives here in Vermont and offered me the place to stay rent-free until I got my bearings. I couldn't pass it up. Plus, I have fond memories of New England summers from a few visits when I was a little older than Aubrey." Now it's my turn to shrug. He doesn't need to know the real reason I moved away from home. Not wanting the focus on me, I ask, "Have you always lived in Havenwood?"

He doesn't seem to mind the conversation turned to him. "I was born here. Moved a few times within the town, but Havenwood has always been home. It's convenient for classes, too."

His comment catches me off guard. "You're a student?"

I never planned to attend college right out of high school, even before Aubrey came into the picture. However, I always figured I'd go at some point. I'd like to think I'll keep the promise to myself one day, way, way in the future.

"Yeah, a senior at Aspenridge. The degree's a bonus for playing on the hockey team." A chuckle rips out from deep within him, finding his own words hysterically funny. I smile, but it's half-hearted.

My eyes assess his athletic build, scrutinizing the way his body is so fit. "What position do you play?" An internal hand slap because I'm certain of one position in hockey: goalie.

"Left wing. Offense," he adds when my face contorts to confusion. "Front line, on the left side." As if that makes it less confusing.

So I change the subject to something I'm a bit more familiar with. "What's your major?"

"Athletic Training. I love the sport, but I have no grand notions of playing much beyond college. My ideal job would be to work as a trainer for the hockey team at Aspenridge. A pipe dream at best."

His tone reeks of defeat. And I have to know why.

"Why?"

Relaxing back onto the sofa, he expels a deep sigh. A motion of his hand in the air waves away my question. "Story for another day."

A sure way I'll get to spend more time with him.

Most likely at a playdate.

For our children.

Not as anything else.

The girls' reemergence in the room disrupts our conversation.

"Dad," Lennon starts, "Aubrey has two American Girl dolls. Two!" She holds up her fingers in case he missed the way she stressed the number. "I don't even have one. What's up with that?" I choke back a laugh how she phrases her question. And I don't miss how she called him "Dad."

"Have you ever asked for an American Girl doll?" he lobs at her.

She tilts her head to the left, contemplating her answer. "Hmm. No, I guess not. I'm asking now. Can I get an American Girl doll? Please? Pretty please?" Her eyes bat, her almost cherub face too cute and nearly impossible to say no to. I have to bite my tongue not to agree to give her one.

"Put it on your list."

Her fist shoots in the air, happiness emanating from her enough to light up our small living room.

When she can't contain her excitement any longer, she races back down the hall, Aubrey on her heels.

"I wouldn't have pegged her for a doll kind of girl." The observation tumbles unabashedly from my lips. Heat creeps into my cheeks at my insinuation.

Walsh chuckles at my comment, which helps ease some of my embarrassment. "I'm pretty sure she's not. Though she seems a little young for American Girl. Aren't they, like, ridiculously expensive?"

"For sure. Aubrey's are hand-me-downs. They were mine. I don't think she understands the concept yet, but one day she will. Especially when she's got dolls no one else has because they're already retired."

Walsh's eyes scan my face. Unsure of what he seeks, I tense under his scrutiny. The cobalt color deepens the longer he stares. When he finds what he's searching for—or realizes his stare is making me uncomfortable—he drags his eyes away.

An uneasy silence ascends the room, and I wonder how my comments about dolls seemed to have gotten us so off track. I can't help but wonder what's running through Walsh's head, but much as I want to know what he's thinking, I'm equally glad he can't read what's overtaking my brain.

After what seems like forever, he finally glances back my way. He goes to speak, but the girls return, my daughter leading the way this time.

"Mom, Lennon and me are hungry. Can we have a 'nack?"

"You had one not too long ago. But if Walsh and Lennon can stay for a little while, I can heat food for an early dinner," I suggest.

Lennon, standing beside Aubrey, voices, "You got anything besides chili?"

"Lennon Victoria," Walsh chides from his position on the couch, his voice full of mortification. "Where the heck are your manners?"

She feigns thinking about the question as if she's going to give him an answer. Instead, her little shoulders raise in a shrug.

"Pretty sure I've got some chicken nuggets in the freezer I can cook for you."

My girl faces her friend. "Mickey Mouse ones. Yum. So good." To prove her point, she rubs her hand over her tummy.

"Tate, no. You do not have to serve her dinner. It's probably time we head home. I happen to like Mimi's chili."

My eyes meet Walsh's. Somehow the awkwardness from earlier has subsided. Also, I don't want him to leave yet.

"If it's because your mother's expecting you at her house, then we'll do it another night, but if it's for any other reason..."

Lennon interjects, "We live at Mimi's house. She not 'pecting us."

Walsh's palm slaps his forehead. "I swear, child. I don't know what to do with you sometimes."

I probably shouldn't encourage this kind of behavior from his kid, but I can't help it. And as I mentioned, I want him to stay.

"Chicken nuggets for Lennon, chili for Aubrey and me. Walsh, what will it be?"

Three sets of watchful eyes settle on Walsh, patiently awaiting his answer. Some of us more than others.

An internal debate wars in his head, and my breath stills as we wait for his decision.

Throwing his hands in the air, he declares, "What the heck? If you're sure you don't mind, we'll stay."

I don't have a chance to confirm when the shrieks of two little girls ring out in the small space.

Can't say I'm not celebrating the same way on the inside.

CHAPTER 7
WALSH

'm not sure what makes me agree to stay, why I can't just say no to Lennon, pick her up, and carry her out to the car.

Other than I have no intention of going home right now.

"What can I do to help?" I ask Tate as she shoos the girls back to Aubrey's room while she prepares dinner.

"Keep me company in the kitchen."

"I can do that."

I follow her to the back of the small condo. There's not much to the place. I'm guessing it has two bedrooms, and I can't imagine they're big if the size of the living room—and now the kitchen—is any indication. I noticed a few boxes against one wall in the living room, but the kitchen seems all unpacked.

"When did you move in?"

She motions for me to have a seat at a black card table situated against the wall with three folding chairs around it. The sink's full of dishes, but what there is of the small counter space is clear.

"About a month ago." She sets to work on our dinner, pulling a bag of nuggets from the freezer. "How many will Lennon eat?" I'm too busy focused on her ass, I miss the meaning of her question. Thankfully, she holds the bag up for me, cluing me in.

Trying for nonchalance, I answer with a lilted, "Three?"

A bob of her head, she declares, "I'll make a few extras just in case. Aubrey might enjoy a few with her chili."

"I still can't believe she eats chili. My mother's going to want to meet you."

The words slip out of my mouth unintended. *My mother's going to want to meet you?* Um, what? Why would I even say that? What does it even mean? Why would she want to meet Tate? Beyond the obvious. She's beautiful, is raising an adorable and polite daughter…

I derail this line of thinking at the sight of Tate's cheeks flushing red. Because I just suggested she meet my mother. I'd blame the fact I was tired from practice today, but Coach let us go early, so it was a short one. Not sure what's gotten into me.

Tate. Tate's what's gotten into me.

Tate still staring at me, I cough to cover up my asinine statement, changing the subject. "How did you find out about Apple Tree Preschool?" There, a safe topic.

She ponders her response for a few seconds, to shake away the memory of what I said. "My aunt suggested it. She knows the owner who pulled some strings to find a spot for Aubrey. She's only been there two full weeks, but she already loves it. I thought the transition was going to be tougher for her, but she seems adjusted and wakes up every morning eager to attend." The trance broken, she continues working—nuggets on a tray for the toaster, chili heating in a pot on the stove.

It's not a gourmet meal, but she's comfortable in the kitchen, juggling the numerous foods, pouring milk into sippy cups, plating carrots and grapes. On autopilot, she moves around the small space. Megan can barely boil water, and while she's competent enough to cook frozen foods, she would have checked and rechecked the bag for directions several times.

Again, I force my thoughts away from drifting down a path they shouldn't go.

"It's an excellent school. This is Lennon's second year. She already told me she plans to stay there for kindergarten too."

Tate swivels around. "Is that an option? I didn't realize they offered a kindergarten class."

I chuckle. "No. Pre-k5 is the highest they go. I hate to break her heart so early in the year this is her last year. Better to enjoy the bliss for as long as possible."

"Gotcha. I'm glad there's a cutoff date of September first. Aubrey wasn't ready for kindergarten this year."

"Same for Lennon. Not about being ready, but her birthday's in September."

"Aubrey too. The fifteenth."

"Huh. Lennon's is the eighteenth."

Weird.

Tate seems to read into that connection as well, looking as if she wants to say more but instead gets back to work. Soon after, she calls down the hall, "Dinner's in five minutes. Bean, set the timer." My confused expression must give me away as Tate continues. "She knows she needs to wash up before meals. She likes routine, so she sets a timer on her Echo once I give her the warning."

Damn. I don't know whether to be impressed with how obedient Aubrey seems or to be thankful Lennon's not that rigid. The whole "five more minutes" seems to go in one ear and out the other with Lennon most of the time. It's not all her fault when the adults don't stick to the rule.

Almost exactly four minutes later, the water turns on down the hall, Aubrey's voice coaxing Lennon to make sure she washes her hands too. I listen for the complaints from my daughter, but surprisingly, they don't come. What I hear are their footsteps thundering down the hall, the two appearing in the kitchen a few seconds later.

"Washed up, Mommy." Aubrey takes a seat in the chair facing the wall and points to a chair for Lennon. Without a word, Lennon slips into the seat Aubrey suggests, waiting patiently for the next direction.

"Len, you feeling okay?" I don't mean for the comment to sound so alarming or to imply she's sick, but who is this kid, and what has she done with my daughter?

"My tummy's just hungry." She eyes the plate of food Tate puts in front of her, noticeably lacking any kind of sauce. "You got ranch?" She peers up at Tate inquisitively.

"And she's fine," I mutter to myself, holding in my laughter. It's a rude way to ask for something as a guest. However, Tate doesn't seem fazed by it, yet it's Aubrey who hops out of the chair to cater to my daughter's demands. "Manners, Lennon," I insert, mindful of the lack of my own.

"Can I please get some ranch?" she amends, only slightly better. I add it to my mental list of things to work on with her.

Aubrey hands her a bottle, a different kind than she's accustomed to. And I predict what's coming even before her face scrunches in disgust.

Jumping in before she says anything ruder, I grab it from Lennon's hands. "Squirt, it won't hurt you to taste it. Here's a little." I pour a minuscule amount on her plate, dip one piece of a nugget into it, and hand it over. Lennon eyes it wearily, almost as if she's never seen a nugget covered in ranch dressing before. After what seems like an hour, she puts the damn thing in her mouth. Out of habit, my hand cups under her chin, prepared for her to spit out the offending food. Which never comes. She chews—way more than she needs to for the tiny bite—and swallows, offering a thumbs up in my direction.

"More than acceptable," she states, motioning for more ranch.

Forgetting we have an audience, Tate's stifled laughter catches me off guard. My eyes search hers out. Her hand hides her smile, her eyes alight with amusement.

Something in Tate's eyes immediately relaxes me, staving off the embarrassment I should feel at Lennon's behavior.

"You slay me, kid," I sputter instead, pouring more ranch on her plate. Looking at Aubrey, she devours the chili, in the way a five-year-old can do. "Lennon, take notes. No complaints about the dinner, and she's enjoying it. Want a taste?"

She has the decency to look over at her friend, who swallows a bite and smiles at my daughter. Lennon's expression sours further, complete with an "Ew" before going back to her frozen chicken nuggets.

"Can't say I didn't try."

To add insult to injury, Aubrey keeps her spoon in her bowl, her head cocking up to me. "It's so yummy, Mr. Walsh. Just like Nana's." Without waiting for a response, she goes back to eating.

Stunned into silence at her compliments, I don't realize Tate puts another bowl of chili in front of the empty chair. "Sit. Enjoy your mother's food."

I obey her directions, the thought of her having to stand while she eats not even a blip on my radar. Lennon's manners have rubbed off on me.

Lennon's eaten one full nugget as Aubrey chimes in, "More please, Mommy," handing an empty bowl over to Tate.

I eye my daughter, who's analyzing the exchange. "Seriously, Len. Watch and learn. Your etiquette could use some enhancement."

"Those are big words, Keeley. Was that even English?"

My hand smacks my forehead to the tune of Tate's laughter. "Just eat your nuggets, Squirt. We'll circle back to this conversation at a later time." My eyes meeting Tate's above Aubrey's head, I mouth, "I'm sorry."

She waves away my apology. Aloud, she states, "I'm loving this dinner entertainment."

I wince at her comment, reading into it too much. However, her mouth continues to grin widely at me, and I can't help but smile back, embracing the awkwardness.

"The first one's free, but if you want more, you'll have to pay up."

It's not until Tate's expression changes do I grasp what I've said. I'm not even sure how to decipher the countenance on her face, nor which part of my comment elicited it. I don't know what it is about this woman that has me twisted up inside, bringing out a side of me I try to keep hidden until people get to know the real me. With her, I can't help it. If I'm being truthful, there's a part of me who wants her to see my true self. As long as it doesn't push her away. If that's the case, he won't be allowed to come out and play for a long while.

Instead of saying something else as utterly ridiculous, I finally clue into the fact she's standing up and eating her dinner. And my butt's firmly planted in the only available chair.

Rushing out of it, almost knocking the chair down, I stand. "Tate, sit."

Her head shakes before the two words are out of my mouth. "No, I'm fine. You're our guests. And I didn't have to cook dinner and still had a delicious meal. Finish yours." She points at my half-eaten bowl, leaving no room to argue.

As much as I shouldn't give in so easily, I fall back into the chair. Thank goodness my mother isn't here to witness this debacle of behavior, both by her son and her granddaughter. She'd surely have some words for us.

We eat the rest of dinner in silence, except for Lennon's usual "food noises." I hardly notice them anymore, but Megan hates the way she hums whenever she eats, no matter the food.

By the end, Aubrey consumed two toddler-sized bowls of chili, some carrots, and two nuggets. Lennon's barely eaten the three she started with. Tate offers them both a wipe for their hands and face and excuses them back to Aubrey's room to play for a little while longer. The wide grin on Aubrey's angelic face matches Lennon's squeal of delight.

Slumping in my chair—I've seriously given up at this point—Tate slides into the seat Lennon vacated.

"Please tell your mother the chili was delicious." The smile she presents reaches her eyes. Everything about this woman is so genuine.

"I will. She'll be happy to hear it. I may omit the fact Aubrey ate two bowls. Purely selfish reasons on my part." Here I go again, admitting truths to this woman I'd normally keep inside.

"If Lennon doesn't out it first." A twinkle in her left eye stirs something inside my pants. I almost don't recognize the feeling of lust starting behind my zipper.

Tamping down those thoughts, I say, "Accurate." She's got my daughter pegged.

Tate surveys the kitchen. "I should clean up this mess." There's a wistfulness in her tone, propelling me into immediate action.

"Let me." I make quick work of clearing the table, setting the dishes on the counter. My eyes search around for a sponge, finally spotting one on the side of the faucet. There's a dishwasher next to the sink, which I open, stopped because it's full of dishes. "Clean or dirty?" I turn to Tate, perusing me with wide eyes, disbelief swimming in the brown orbs.

She shakes her head, clearing away the trance she's in. "I'm sorry. What was the question?"

"Are the dishes in the dishwasher clean or dirty?"

"Is there water on the top of the glasses?"

A reasonable question, I pull out the top shelf. "Um, yes?" It's not a definite answer because it seems like there could be, but it's also too hard to tell.

"Oh my god. Tate, do not let him empty your dishwasher."

When I turn around at her voiced directive to herself, she's out of her chair, in the space I occupy, trying to shove me away from where I stand. I've got a good fifty pounds on her, and it's not cocky to admit it's all muscle. Playing a college sport will do that. She makes a respectable effort at trying to heave me out of the way, but I stand steady, not budging an inch.

A stare-down commences, fire fueling her brown eyes to widen.

"Let me do this, Tate. You fed me and my kid dinner. It's the least I can do."

"Dinner you brought and frozen nuggets. Hardly a hardship. This isn't your mess, nor your responsibility to put away *my* dishes." Heavy emphasis on the my. As if I thought they might be mine.

Cognizant of the small space and opened door of the dishwasher, I rest my hands on her shoulders, moving her back to her chair. She puts up a good fight, only relaxing when I don't back down.

"Sit, Tate." My gaze locks with hers, the tone of my voice not allowing an argument.

"Thank you," she all but whispers, but the sentiment it carries speaks volumes.

With a "you're welcome" in her direction, I get back to work.

If only my momma could see me now.

CHAPTER 8
TATE

Walsh's two words play on repeat in my mind.

Sit, Tate.

His growly voice isn't the only thing affecting me as I do what he demands and sit in the chair while he puts away my dishes.

This angle offers a glorious view of his backside, though the baggy sweatpants he wears conceal an accurate assessment of his ass. My imagination has no qualms filling in the details.

He's pushed the sleeves of his Henley up his arms, the ink on his left forearm catching my notice. I can't make out what it is from this view and file it away to ask later.

He takes it upon himself to locate where the cups and mugs go, flexing his arms as he puts each one carefully on the shelf. Upside down, just like the others already there.

A slew of emotions surge through me at watching this man—a stranger—empty my dishwasher. My father emptying ours at home five times in the last year would be a generous number. The contrast between Walsh offering to put away the dishes he didn't use versus my father, who always used more than half of them but grumbled his way through the task, strikes a chord.

Beyond that, it's the fact there's a *man* in my kitchen, making quick work of this simple task. A man who makes me feel things I haven't felt in years. Or ever, if I'm honest. The feelings Walsh elicits in me are foreign, but hell if I don't want to keep experiencing them.

Once the top rack is bare, he moves onto the bottom, quickly finding where to put the plates. The silverware basket in his hand, he opens up drawers one by one, searching for where they go. He's a man on a mission, so I don't point out where they're kept. With only three drawers to choose from, his hunt is quick, and before I can stop him, he's closing the filled drawer.

He doesn't shut the dishwasher, instead filling it back up with the day's dishes piled in the sink. The ones left there earlier because I was too lazy to empty the dishwasher when the cycle ended.

"Walsh, no. Leave them. You've done enough." My voice holds little conviction, but it hardly matters. He turns his head, his glare striking my words down.

"I have to atone for our behavior," he speaks as he resumes his task.

I want to interrogate him, ask what the hell his comment means, but the words get stuck in my throat. Because selfishly, no matter why he's doing it, it's one less chore I'll have to do after Aubrey goes to bed. Which means I can spend more time reading. I'm in a good part of my book. Just when the hero and heroine realize their sexual attraction toward the other.

Heat rises to my cheeks. And it has little to do with the plot of the book. It's all about the man's backside I'm currently ogling.

Walsh hums to himself while he does the dishes. The tune is familiar, but I can't place it. Lennon barrels into the kitchen, ending any possibility to ask what the song is. She has something on her mind, but Walsh cuts it off. "Perfect timing, Squirt. We've got to get home to Mimi." Her mouth opens to refute, but his stern look closes it.

Aubrey and I walk them to the door. Lennon sits down, putting her sneakers on the wrong feet. Walsh mentions it, but she doesn't fix them.

"Pick your battles," I mumble, keeping my voice low so he doesn't hear me.

"The doctor assured us she'd eventually right it on her own. I had given up the fight even before her mother brought it up at her physical. It's more important to wear her skates on the correct feet, which she does." Guess my comment wasn't quiet enough.

Uncertain of a comeback, I smile at him.

"Lennon, please thank Tate for having us and for making you dinner."

"Thank you, Tate. Thanks for having ranch I like for the nuggets."

"Lennon!" Walsh chides in a hushed tone.

She turns to face him, a retort set on her lips. Like moments ago, she stays silent. Facing back toward Aubrey, she hugs her. "See you at school on Monday."

"Yep. I'll be there." I can't help being proud of Aubrey's enthusiasm, brought out by this new friend.

"I'll be in touch about next Thursday," Walsh says with a grin.

Thursday? I'm about to question it when the playdate plan the girls concocted slams into me.

"Right. Thursday. See you then." My voice hitches on the last part of the comment. Thursday is six days from now. Will I really not see him until then? My heart deflates at the thought.

"Unless I see you sooner." With a wink in my direction, he shepherds Lennon out the door, pulling it closed behind him.

"That was so fun, Mommy." Aubrey practically jumps into my arms. "Can I call Nana and let her know about the chili? Please?"

I can't ever deny a call to her grandmother.

"Sure thing, Bean. Then it's time for bath and bed."

Without arguing, she races off to find the iPad.

We FaceTime with my parents once a week at a minimum and every time, she's as excited to see them as the last. There's always a bit of sadness when they say goodbye, but it lessens each day.

It nearly broke me the first time, knowing I had taken her away from the only family she'd ever known. I love my parents and am forever indebted for everything they've done for Aubrey and me, but as much as I tried to keep myself afloat living with them, I felt like I was drowning, every day the boat taking on more and more water, trying to sink itself with me in it. I needed to get out, live on my own, and prove to myself, and them, I knew what was best for my daughter and me.

But Damon died and the threats and custody battle began. The Melansons, Damon's parents, lost their only son, and Aubrey was a piece of him, a piece they felt entitled to. It didn't matter they tried to force me to get rid of the baby or hadn't offered any help—financial or otherwise—the five years of her life, they suddenly wanted to be grandparents.

Personal letters, emails, phone calls, a declaration letter from a lawyer vying for custody, they came after me in all the ways. It was a losing battle for them, but rather than fight, I chose to escape. It wasn't an easy decision, and my parents encouraged me to stay, but I didn't have it in me. Running away was the easier choice, because I could support Aubrey and me on my own. I didn't know if I could endure a custody battle.

And when a past visit to Aunt Marsha's farmhouse came up in my Facebook memories, I concocted a plan, one Aunt Marsha helped put into motion.

Aubrey's adjustment to life with just the two of us, a life without daily access to her grandparents, has had ups and downs. It's not her style to lash out, to be mad at me for moving away, but her comments every once in a while let me know she hasn't totally forgiven me. I'm okay with that.

One day she'll learn why we made the move.

The weekend passes quickly, reminders of our dinner with Walsh not far from my mind. Nor is the upcoming time on Thursday. After a low-key weekend with a few drives to explore our new town, the first part of the week drags.

Work is more tedious, the doctors in my ear droning on and on and on. Since high school, I've worked for a group of doctors doing medical notes transcription. It started part-time, with one doctor, but over the years, it's billowed into a full-time position. And it's completely remote, which is why it wasn't an issue for me to move so far from home.

While I can't see myself doing this work for the rest of my life, I won't deny the setup I have is too cushy to pass up. Even after giving birth to Aubrey, I still put in hours to "protect" my job.

I try to accomplish most of the assignments while Aubrey's in school, which works well on Tuesdays and Fridays since the days are longer. On the shorter days, I put in hours after she's asleep, and a few hours on the weekends too.

Every time I get frustrated with a comment I have to rewind repeatedly to make sure it's accurate, I remind myself if it weren't for this job, I'd be working a lot more hours, not at home, and I'd most likely have to hire a babysitter, eating into the time I have with Aubrey. It usually does the trick to keep me motivated to soldier on past the mumblings of certain doctors. Until I'm ready to give this job up to pursue something else, I can't risk them letting me go. Unless I all but stopped doing my work, it's unlikely to happen, but I won't take it for granted.

Megan picks up Lennon on Monday and Tuesday, and even though it's Walsh on Wednesday, all we get is a quick wave and a "see you tomorrow" as he whisks Lennon away from school.

As much as I try not to let it show, Aubrey picks up on my prickly mood at the insufficient Walsh interactions.

"Mommy, can we make muffins for our playdate tomorrow? I think Lennon will really like blueberry ones." Aubrey's voice carries from the back of the car.

"She would, huh?" I'm not convinced she will, but blueberry muffins are Bree's favorite.

She's silent for a few minutes. "Or chocolate chip. She'll like those."

Stopped at a light, I sneak a peek in the rearview mirror. Her nose is upturned at the mention of chocolate chip, the mere thought an abomination in her mind.

"Think we'll have time for both this afternoon, or do you need a nap?"

Her eyes glow with excitement, meeting mine in the mirror. "I just need a small resty. Maybe while they bake in the oven?"

"Sure thing, Bean."

Her "yay" rings out in the car, above the country music playing low on the radio. Thank goodness Vermont has a few stations. Sirius XM isn't quite in the budget yet.

Aubrey jabbers away as we eat lunch and prepare the muffins. True to her word, when I slide them into the oven, she climbs on the couch with her blanket. Eventually her eyes close, and she drifts into slumber. I use the time to catch up on a few more files, choosing only those I won't have to replay more than twice to understand.

An hour later, muffins cool on the racks, Aubrey's still asleep—I'll give her another thirty minutes—my phone pings with a text.

Pausing the audio in my ear, I check it. Just the sender's name kicks up butterflies in my abdomen.

WALSH

> Tomorrow still good? Please say it is because it's all Lennon's talked about this week. She may be more excited about coming to your house than she is about skating tonight. Which is kinda a big deal. For the sake of my sanity, please don't cancel

A hearty laugh tumbles out of me until I remember to cover my mouth to not wake Aubrey. Even though she's in the other room, the walls are thin, and the space is small.

I'm not sure my flirty banter of pretending to cancel would come across in a text message, so I give him the truth.

> Yes, still good. What do you guys want for lunch?

> I was going to grab sandwiches at the deli by Aspenridge. What do you and Aubrey want? Does she eat sandwiches? They have grilled cheese, peanut butter and jelly, all kinds of deli meats. Actually, let me send you the menu

I keep my giggle low at the way he writes his text as if speaking. And I can hear his voice in my head. His throaty intonation, unique to Walsh.

Thankfully, another message brings me out of my head and reroutes my thoughts.

Link

> No rush. Just before 11 tomorrow so I have time to order and grab it after class

K

I bite my bottom lip into my mouth, my fingers hovering over the keyboard for what I really want to ask. He kinda implied he'd be staying, if that's what he meant by his "so we can crash here again" when we set it up. "We" means the two of them, right? I've been banking on that since last Friday, which is why I'm hesitant now. Because if he tells me he's just dropping her off and bolting, I may feel a lot like Lennon would have had I said no about tomorrow.

> Hope it's okay I'm inviting myself for lunch. But if you prefer it just be the girls, that's fine too

"No." My beliefs so strong on the subject, I speak aloud to the empty room. I compose myself before I all but beg him to do other things besides having lunch.

> Feel free to stay.

> And thanks for lunch. I'll let you know what we want later tonight.

> *happy emoji*

With a renewed sense of determination—from a simple text exchange—I get back to work, pounding out more charts than usual in twenty-five minutes.

In anticipation of our playdate, I clean the condo while Aubrey's at school. The boxes yet to be unpacked get relocated to the closet for the time being. I sweep, vacuum, and mop the floors. All the rooms get a dusting and the bathroom receives a thorough bleaching. It's the most I've done since right after we moved in, and probably the most I'll do for another few weeks.

I attempt to work for an hour but am distracted the entire time. A few charts get finished, but the rest will have to wait until tonight or tomorrow morning. I make a list with an order of priority.

Even before I leave to pick Aubrey up, nerves flutter inside me. It's another unfamiliar feeling in the sense it's been so long. I shouldn't be having these types of feelings for Walsh, the father of Aubrey's friend. Try telling that to my neglected libido.

Arriving at the preschool way earlier than needed, I struggle to stay focused on the pages of the book I'm reading. Which isn't such a tremendous problem since the storyline's making me all hot and bothered. Coupled with what's happening in my real life, it's a lethal combination. Instead, I text a friend from home.

> Hey, hey. How's it going? How goes the search for the perfect man?

I don't expect a response immediately. She's got class on Thursdays, but hell if I can remember what her schedule is. When my phone jumps on my thigh, I'm a little surprised.

CARLEY

> "Perfect" and "man" do not belong in the same sentence, girl. At least in my experience. And certainly not here in Bumfuck, Idaho.

Her message makes me giggle.

> I've got ten minutes until preschool pickup. Call me?

The phone rings instantly.

"Is it wrong it still weirds me out when you mention things like 'preschool'?" is her opening greeting.

"Hello to you too. Was going to confess I miss you, but now I'm not so sure."

"You know I love your munchkin, but we're twenty-two, babe. We are way too young to be discussing preschool."

A shudder runs through me. I always interpret her words to be biting, even if that's not her intention. Probably because she's always commenting about me being a teenage mom. And if I didn't love her the way I do, I wouldn't stay in touch. But she's the only person in the world other than members of my family who'd have my back in any situation. And as much as there's a lot of resentment toward me being a mom this young, she was the first one to defend my choice to others who gave me trouble. As long as I've known her, Carley continues to amaze and surprise me, never knowing exactly which way she's going to swing on a subject.

Holding back what I want to say, I turn it to her. "So, how's the scene out in Idaho?"

"It sucks. Even off campus, there are little prospects for a one-night stand. Seriously, I've gone through all the members of the male species in a one-hundred-mile radius. How's Vermont?" she volleys back.

"Beautiful."

"Everything you imagined?"

My eyes discern Walsh's truck pulling into the lot.

"And more." The comment is breathy, my heart rate picking up at the mere sight of his truck. Because it means I'll get to see him soon. And he'll be in my space shortly thereafter.

"Hello? Earth to Tate. Where the hell did you just go?"

Shaking out of a Walsh stupor, I answer her. "Sorry. The dad of Aubrey's friend pulled in."

"See, that I could get on board with. Is he a DILF? He's a DILF, right? And how much older?"

Her inquiry hits me rapid-fire, but for a strange reason, I don't want to divulge details about Walsh, wanting to keep him all to myself. As if she will ever meet him or something. As if he'll ever be anything more than "Lennon's dad."

"I'm not sure of his exact age, but he's definitely a DILF." I cringe as the acronym leaves my mouth, objectifying Walsh in that way. But indeed he is a dad I'd love to fuck.

As if reading my mind, he steps out of his truck and glimpses my way. His eyes hide behind his sunglasses, but I'm betting they're lit up as evidenced by the broad smile plastered on his face. I can't help but return one of my own.

Gosh, I've got it bad for him.

Crap.

I all but utter the word aloud, giving myself away to Carley who's chattering about something or another. Most likely a hot, older guy. Who may be a dad. Which in no way describes Walsh. A dad, yes. Older, no.

He waves me over. The nerves from earlier flurry stronger with his invitation.

I cut my friend off mid-sentence. "Car, I gotta go. Doors are opening. Talk soon. Love you." My finger jabs the red button, effectively ending the call before she can accuse me of giving her the runaround. No doubt I'll have a dozen text messages by the time I get back to my car.

A need to compose myself overcomes me, so I delay a couple of minutes to check myself in the mirror to calm my nerves.

"It's just a playdate for your kids. This is not a date for you. He's just a man. A hot, sexy, college hockey player man, but still. You've got this." Emphasis on the *hot* and *sexy* and *hockey player*.

The broad shoulders.

The powerful legs.

The brawny arms.

My pep talk does little to quiet the pounding of my heart or the slowing of my pulse. When Walsh waves me over a second time, I get out of the car and walk toward him. Trying to wear some bravado on the outside, I make my way to him, hoping he doesn't see through my act.

"Hey. You didn't specify what chips you wanted with your sandwich, so I went with barbecue. But I got salt and vinegar for me so we can trade if that's more your style."

His offhand comment about chips has me stumbling. Right into him. He makes quick work of bracing me so I don't fall, steadying me by my shoulders before removing his hands, making sure I won't fall. His touch ignites fire, the flames felt places with no contact.

"Whoa. You okay?"

Embarrassed, I can't look him in the face, so I stare at his arm. Despite a slight chill in the October air, the sleeves of his button-down are rolled up, his tattoo on full display.

Without realizing what I'm doing, I grab hold of his arm, yanking it so I can inspect it in more detail. Lennon's name in swirly script on top of black, newborn footprints, her date of birth below meets my vision.

"This is so cool. Are those her actual footprints?" At first glance, I assumed they were just a reproduced image, but upon closer examination, there are lines and crevices, intimate details carefully etched on his arms. Inked reminders of the miracle of life, preserving the memory of her tiny feet.

"Yep. I had them transferred from the identification card."

"Wow. I love it." My fingers trace her feet, his skin soft under my touch. He doesn't pull his arm away, and I'm still holding onto it, caressing his skin. I wonder if he senses the jolts of energy on my skin at our connection.

My brain yells at me to remove my fingers from his arm. It takes me a moment to comprehend the message, but then I let go, as if his hand was burning mine.

Which it is. Figuratively.

"Thanks."

The opening of the school doors cuts off any more he's going to say, kids exiting the building with the usual end of the day happiness. Lennon and Aubrey hold hands. Lennon skips to us, tugging Aubrey behind her. My girl does her best to keep up, but coordination isn't her thing. While she stays upright, she's more like a raggedy doll being tugged behind a kid.

"Hiya, Keeley," Lennon exclaims, jumping into his outstretched arms, letting go of Aubrey's hand at the last minute. Bree stumbles slightly, but I'm there to catch her.

"Squirt. How was your day?"

"We made applesauce. With real apples and a press. It did not taste good." She sticks out her tongue to prove her point.

Afraid to upset her friend and disagree with her opinion, Aubrey whispers in my ear, "It was yummy. Not as good as the one you make."

Walsh leans in closer to us. "Do you put sugar in the one you make?" His smug grin confirms he heard what Aubrey said.

Ignoring the way his proximity heats my cheeks, I reply, "Only apples."

Lennon's distaste shows on her adorable face. "Can we talk about it later? I've been waiting weeks to watch *Little Einsteins* with Aubrey."

"It hasn't even been one, you goofball." Walsh fits his fingers under Lennon's armpits, tickling her to the point of laughter.

A child's laugh is a sound I never tire of, even when it's not my kid.

"You want to follow me?" I suggest, needing a reprieve from being this near to Walsh, short as it may be.

"Yep."

Aubrey in my arms, I turn away from him and head to my car.

This will definitely be an interesting afternoon.

CHAPTER 9
WALSH

Lennon's enthusiasm for going to Aubrey's house overrides her exhaustion. Because she's tired. We stayed at the rink for over three hours last night, and she loved every minute, even when she wasn't on the ice. I thought she'd pass out on the way home, but the thrill of her playdate kept her awake. And she woke up super early this morning in anticipation.

Lennon yawns from the back seat. "Len, you tired?"

"Nope. Don't need a nap. Just lunch and TV."

"Yeah, okay girl," I mutter so she can't hear me.

Luckily, Tate's place is nearby the preschool, not giving her a chance to fall asleep. I wouldn't be surprised if she falls asleep while watching the show, and if not then, on the way home. She'll be with my parents since I have practice, so I make a mental note to keep the playdate short if needed.

I park in a Visitor's spot, a few away from Tate's in front of her building. Lennon's already unbuckled by the time I get around to her door.

"Was the engine off?" I ask sternly.

"Of course." She refrains from rolling her eyes.

It's a discussion we've had several times. When she first learned to unbuckle her seat, she liked to do it while we were driving. A jaunt to the police station and a lecture from a police officer drilled the rule into her head. She's pretty good these days, but when she's excited about something, she often forgets.

"Love you, Squirt."

"Duh, Keeley. Tell me something I don't know." This time, her blue eyes roll.

"I got you a surprise from Crisp & Crunch." We don't go there often, so when we do, it's a treat.

She lights up. "It's a brownie, right? You got me a brownie?"

"You'll have to wait and see. After you eat your lunch. And you'll have to share with Aubrey if she wants some. Because that's what we do when we eat meals with friends."

"Tate's so pretty."

Her comment comes out of left field, and I'm stunned into silence at the delivery of it.

Especially as it doesn't relate one iota to what we're talking about.

Regaining my composure and my wits, my eyes travel toward the woman in question. "Yes. Yes, she is." I can't help how my lips quirk up at the mere sight of her. Not since before Meg and I got involved have I felt something akin to this toward a woman.

Shit.

These feelings are not okay to have about Tate. She's a parent of Lennon's friend.

Explain that to my cock.

"Keeley?" Lennon's voice pulls me out of the stupor I find myself in.

"Yep." I don't even know if she asked me something, but I can't let her see me sweat. Metaphorical or not.

With Lennon in my arms, I grab the bag of food from the front seat, and stride over to Tate and Aubrey, following them up the steps.

An erratic heartbeat drums in my chest, the rhythm vibrating through all parts of me. I trudge on, Tate and Aubrey leading the way inside. I toe out of my sneakers and lower Lennon to the floor, instructing her to do the same. Either lost in a trance of her excitement or because she's too tired, she sits there unmoving.

With a chuckle, I slip them off her feet as she yawns again.

"You're not going to last, Squirt." I send up a silent prayer she doesn't get too overtired before we leave. I'm not in the mood for a tantrum, especially in front of Tate and Aubrey.

"Shall we eat first?"

"We made muffins," Aubrey exclaims excitedly in response. She disappears down the hall, water running in the distance shortly thereafter.

"Lennon, why don't you go with Aubrey and wash your hands? You remember where the bathroom is?" Zoned out, she doesn't move nor respond. I snap my fingers in front of her face, bringing her out. "Time to wash your hands."

"I cleaned them after recess. See?" She holds them out, flipping them so I can see both sides.

Not in the mood for a fight, I express to Tate, "You got a wipe we could have?"

"Yeah, sure." She departs the entryway, returning with a few wipes in her hand, Aubrey trailing behind. She hands them to me, then picks up the bag of food. "I'll get lunch sorted."

A quick wipe to Lennon's hands—at least she doesn't protest—I lift her into my arms, carrying her into the kitchen. Depositing her in the same chair she sat in last time, I tip her chin up.

"You eat whatever Tate puts on your plate or no treats. And I don't want to hear any complaints."

"K."

That was too easy. Maybe I should feed her when she's this excited or tired all the time.

Lunch is quiet, the only sounds of chewing and Lennon's hums filling the kitchen. Tate brought in a stool from somewhere but insisted I use the chair. I thought about arguing with her, but seems I'm not in the mood for a battle with anyone today.

Aubrey finishes her grilled cheese in the time it takes Lennon to eat half of hers.

"Done. We can have treats now?" Lennon pushes her plate toward the center of the table.

"Mommy, can I get the muffins?"

"Sure."

Aubrey climbs down and gingerly walks over to a low drawer. From the angle I sit, I can't see what's in it, but she brings out two containers, handing them to Tate before taking a seat at the table again.

This kid has better table manners than me.

"We have blueberry and chocolate chip," Tate explains, offering Lennon a choice of muffin first. Turning her nose up at the blueberry ones, Lennon reaches for a chocolate chip.

Next, Tate puts a blueberry on Aubrey's plate, Aubrey's tongue darting out of her mouth as she views the exchange.

"Walsh? Can I offer you a muffin?"

I grab a blueberry, knowing full well Lennon won't finish hers, and I'll sample the leftovers.

Taking a bite, the muffin isn't as sweet as I expected, yet it's incredibly delicious. I devour half in a few bites, and after swallowing, I compliment Tate. "These are delicious."

Aubrey pipes in. "Thanks. I help Mommy with the batter." When she smiles at me, crumbs fall off her lips.

"You did a great job. Do you bake with Mommy a lot?"

"Oh, yeah. All the time." Her head bobs up and down, her brown curls bouncing with the movement.

Tate repeats the question to Lennon.

"No. Momma doesn't bake. Only Mimi. But I'm too busy to help."

If there's one thing my daughter is, it's honest. And in so many ways, it's going to get her far in life. However, sometimes I wish she was a little less blunt.

Tate lets the conversation drop, ushering them into the living room for the show. I stay behind, finishing the muffin Lennon barely ate three bites of. This one's on the sweeter side, although the dark chocolate chips give it a bitter flavor. Precisely why my kid didn't eat it.

"Show's all set. Lennon looks like she's about to fall asleep." There's more she wants to say—it's written on her face—but she holds back.

"Oh, she will, no doubt. She's exhausted, but she'll put up a good fight. I'd offer to leave now, but that would only make it worse." It's my turn to have more to say, but I'm not sure I want her judgment. Because the real reason I'm not leaving has little to do with the outburst Lennon will have. It's more because I want the alone time with Tate.

She heaves her body into the seat across from me. "Aubrey will probably fall asleep too. Then we'll just have to do this all over again so they can watch the show." A nervous laugh follows her comment, but the delighted expression she wears contradicts it.

"Thanks for having us. I'm sorry she keeps inviting herself over. When she sets her mind on something, it's sometimes hard to change it. At least not without a battle of wills." I keep my tone as apologetic as possible. I'm only sorry Lennon keeps inviting us because it's rude. I'm not sorry about this time with Tate.

"It's no trouble. I'm glad Aubrey has found a good friend. With her being so shy and scared of her own shadow sometimes, I worry about her." Her gaze casts downward to where her fingers pick a few crumbs off the table.

"I can imagine that's hard, not that I have any experience. Lennon's not shy, and if she could, she'd live her life with her two feet off the ground. Mostly on the ice, but anything she can climb is a close second."

Tate lifts her head. "How long has she been skating?"

"Since she could walk?" I offer. "I don't mean it quite the way it sounds, but the girl was born with ice in her veins. She's so tired because she was at the rink for three hours last night."

Tate's eyes widen. "Three hours? I can't imagine doing something physical for that long, let alone with blades of steel strapped to my feet."

"She wasn't on the ice that long. Forty-five minutes maybe, with breaks in between. She has a way of negotiating what she wants, which last night included staying to watch a local team practice. As much as I put my foot down, when it comes to skating and hockey, I have a hard time saying no." I could elaborate more, but I don't want to bore her. Especially since I get the sense she's not into anything having to do with "blades of steel."

"How long have you skated?"

"I think I was three when my parents put me on skates. But I took to it almost as quickly as Lennon, and by the next year, I was already in love with hockey."

Tate smiles. "So she gets it from you?"

"And her mother." When she doesn't outwardly react, I add, "But that was kinda my doing too."

It was definitely my doing. Meg's not into any sports, but when she decided she wanted to date me, hockey was a deal-breaker. She learned to love hockey and skating.

"Oh." And there's the reaction I expected.

Needing a subject change from my ex, I ask, "Have you ever skated?"

"Once. When I was maybe eight. I hated it. The cold, the layers, the pain of falling. It wasn't my cup of tea." She shakes her head at the awful memory, and I let it go, yearning for more. "I'm going to use the bathroom and check on the girls. Be right back." She pushes out of her seat, careful not to let the chair scrape the floor too much.

While she's gone, I clear the table of the garbage and sneak another blueberry muffin out of the container. They aren't dry like some muffins can be, and the blueberry flavor explodes on my tongue. It has some kind of sweetener, but I doubt it's sugar.

I peek my head in the living room. Aubrey's wide awake, completely absorbed in the show. Lennon's fighting sleep. Her tired eyes meet mine, and she mumbles, "Shirt, Daddy."

I strip out of my flannel, folding it under so the buttons won't be in her way. She tucks it under her cheek, and her eyes promptly shut.

Back in the kitchen, I slip back into my seat. I'm tempted to steal another muffin but refrain, needing to keep sugar to a minimum during the season.

Tate reappears a few minutes later. "So my kid is totally invested in the show and yours is completely knocked out." She eyes my bare arms, and only because I'm staring directly at her chest do I notice the hitch in her breath. I should be more remorseful about how much I affect her.

"I'm going to let her sleep for a little while. If that's okay."

"Of course. I'm hoping Aubrey conks out for a bit. I've got some work to catch up on."

The mention of "work" perks my ears. Guess I never gave it much thought if she has a job. But that makes sense. How else would she support herself? Unless she gets a boatload of child support. In which case, good for her.

"What do you do?"

"Medical transcription."

I rub my chin, not understanding. "Interesting."

She promptly calls me out. "You have no idea what that means."

"Not even a clue." My chuckle overpowers her feminine laughter. Hers has a melodic quality, light and high-pitched, the sound gentle to my ears.

"Basically, it's typing doctors' notes into patients' charts."

"Ah, okay." *Nice comeback, Keeley.*

"It pays the bills. And it's highly entertaining. Maybe it's not my forever job, but it's exactly what I need right now. For both me and Aubrey."

"How long have you been doing it? What type of doctors do you work with? What's the best thing you've ever heard?" I fire one question after another, suddenly completely intrigued by the idea.

"I started in high school for my pediatrician, which is a long, crazy story of how it came to be." She waves the thought away with a roll of her eyes, then resumes. "Now, I've got about a dozen doctors. As for the craziest…"

Not letting her finish her sentence, I can't help but blurt, "How did you find a job so quickly after moving here?"

"I didn't. It's the same job I've had for the past six years."

I scratch my head, trying to make sense of her words. "Excuse my ignorance, but how does that even work? No way you can commute to Kansas from Vermont." Totally into this story, I need a snack and some water. "Hold that thought. Can I get some water? And possibly another muffin? Even though I've already had two blueberry and the leftover chocolate chip Lennon didn't eat." When I hear it aloud, it makes me out to be a pig. "Never mind. I don't need another one. They're so good, my brain wants another even though I shouldn't. Too many treats slow down my skating."

Tate laughs at my rambling. Standing up, she grabs a muffin from the container and drops it gently on my plate. "As long as I save three for Aubrey, you can have as many as you'd like. They'll look better on your hips than mine, especially since you'll have them skated off in no time." Mortification fills her face, and she quickly turns away.

I can't help my eyes drifting to her hips. She's got some curves, but nothing to be ashamed about. It's just the right amount to hold onto and spear myself into her from behind…

If I were into that sort of thing.

Which I totally would be with Tate.

Like she'd give me the time of day. She's got enough on her plate without the baggage I bring with me. Lennon's cute and all, and we're a package deal, but we don't come without our problems, most of which the likes of someone like Tate won't want to be involved with. Nor could I blame her.

Lennon's groggy wail interrupts my thoughts. "Daddy!"

I jolt out of my seat before she finishes the second syllable.

She's sitting up on the couch, tears streaming down her cheeks. I make my way across the living room in three strides, panic filling every vein.

"Lennon, what's the matter?" My eyes scan her for the issue making her cry. A parent's worst nightmare is seeing his/her kid hurt, not knowing what's wrong. The fear of not being able to do anything to help your child may be worse.

My panic lessens when I notice the issue, the vise constricting my lungs instantly waning.

Scooping her into my arms, I cradle her head against my chest. Though she's not hurt, she's most likely embarrassed.

"It's okay, Squirt. We'll clean you up. Don't cry." I hope my voice is soothing enough for what she needs.

"Hey. Is she okay? What can I do to help?" Tate's concerned voice greets my ears, and it matches her expression when I glance in her direction.

"She had an accident," I whisper, careful not to let Lennon hear me, nodding my head toward the stain on the couch.

She jumps into action, the experienced mother shining through. "Let me get you some clothes to change her."

I fall to the floor, my back to the couch, Lennon quietly whimpering in my arms. "It's okay, Len. Tate's getting you some clothes to borrow, and you'll be all dry."

She moves her head away from my chest, peering up at me through wet lashes. Even though she's okay, my heart threatens to break into pieces at her tearful expression. Anything to soothe the pain, physical or emotional.

"I peed on the couch and I'm not supposed to. Don't be mad 'cause I didn't mean to." Her voice shakes, drawing deeper emotions from me.

"No one's mad. It was an accident. You were sleeping." It's all I can do to reassure her everything's okay.

Somehow she got it in her head—thanks to Megan's mother—good girls never pee their pants, even when they're sleeping. On the occasional chance it happens, she thinks she's going to be punished.

I could strangle Joanne for ever putting that ludicrous idea in her head.

Tate's back, a new set of clothes in her hands. "Here you go, Lennon. Some of Aubrey's favorite clothes for you." She leaves them next to me, retreating a few steps, giving Lennon space.

"Thank you," I mouth.

I don't coerce Lennon to move. I'm sure it can't feel comfortable to sit in wet undies and pants, but I allow her the time she needs to process what happened and feel better.

After several minutes, she pulls her head away again. "You're not mad?"

I shake my head. "I'm not mad."

Narrowing her eyes, she's not convinced. She looks in Tate's direction. "I'm sorry, Tate. It was an accident." Her bottom lip quivers nervously as she waits for Tate's reaction.

Tate walks over, taking a seat on the floor next to us. "Sweetie, you don't need to apologize. It was an accident." She reaches her finger out to Lennon's face, stopping just shy of touching it, not wanting to cross any boundaries. My heart leaps out to this stranger's concern for my child. "Daddy can help get you changed so you don't have to stay in wet clothes. Then maybe you guys can stay and watch another episode of the show."

Instant relief permeates Lennon's face. Bobbing her head up and down, she confirms, "My eyes needed a little rest, but they're better now." She stands up and wiggles out of her wet clothing.

Along with being brutally honest, my kid's got no sense of modesty. At least she has the decency to leave her shirt on since it's not wet.

"Let me get you some wipes." Tate scurries away. She's not the least bit embarrassed by any of this. Other women might empathize with my situation, but mothers understand. If ever there was a time for a complete understanding of being a parent, it's now.

Returning, she hands me the wipes, and I get to work wiping Lennon down. After, she puts on the dry clothes, good as new.

I glance over at the blemish on the couch. Too concerned with Lennon's emotions to notice, it's bigger than I first realized.

"This is going to be a bitch to clean up..."

I shouldn't have worried.

Tate's there with some sort of spray. She aims it at the couch, spraying the entire affected area before laying a towel over it.

"It'll be good as new in a few hours. It's not the first time, and it won't be the last someone pees on our couch. Right, Bean?"

In all the commotion, I forgot Aubrey was here.

A slight tinge of pink creeps up on Aubrey's cheeks. With a lift of her tiny shoulders, she murmurs, "Accidents happen."

We all share a laugh.

Once Lennon seems okay, Tate turns the show back on for the girls, setting them up next to each other on the dry cushion of the couch. Kissing Lennon's head, she shifts her eyes from the TV.

"I'm better, Dad. I'll be okay." She's got my shirt wrapped around her, the added comfort and warmth helping her to feel better.

Back in the kitchen, I slump in the seat, my adrenaline crashing. Needing an energy boost, I grab the muffin, stuffing it in my mouth, carbs be damned. Tate pushes an unopened bottle of water my way.

"What do you sweeten these with?" I ask after I've washed the muffin down with a big gulp of water.

"Pure maple syrup. I'd love to say it's because I want to be healthy, but it's because Aubrey hates sugar." My brows lift for the second time today. Tate raises her hands in the air. "It's the oddest thing. What kid doesn't like sugar, right? The same one who eats chili, tofu, and kale chips."

"Wow," I admit, at a loss for something more intelligent. "What do you bribe her with to be good if she doesn't eat sweets?"

The pee on the couch didn't bother Tate, but my comment hits a chord. I shouldn't ever be surprised my daughter speaks the way she does.

Pot, meet kettle.

"I'm sorry. That was rude. You don't have to answer."

Her relief is evident, and her shoulders sink from her ears.

Behind her, a clock glows with the time, and we've probably overstayed our welcome. Not to mention the fact my kid peed on her couch.

"We should get going. You've got some work to catch up on."

Tate's expression pains. It delights me I'm not the only one affected, and what I wouldn't give to see how affected she is. To elevate this to another level, force her out of her comfort zone.

"Oh, okay. Sure. I didn't realize it was getting so late."

We stand at the same time, each of us holding the other's stare. Tate breaks contact first, her eyes slipping to something on her shirt.

An awkward silence accompanies us until she tentatively meets my gaze again. "You want to bring some muffins home?"

"Will you judge me more for taking them or not?"

"It's not my place to judge you at all, Walsh."

She speaks in a hushed tone, my name falling from her mouth in a whisper. My eyes fall to her lips. They beckon to me, screaming, "Kiss me!"

If only I could.

I wonder what they'd taste like.

"I wonder the same." Her words startle me, how she knew exactly what I was thinking unless I voiced the words. My eyes fly back to hers before falling to her lips now upturned into a smirk.

She's stupefied me speechless, always a rare situation to find myself in. Especially with a beautiful woman like Tate.

"We probably shouldn't though, you know?"

"Why the hell not?"

Oops. My filter has completely left the building.

But seriously. I want to, she wants to, why shouldn't we do it?

I step closer to her. She retreats a step. I can practically hear the way her heart pounds in her chest, matched only by a rhythm of my own.

"Because we're parents," she offers.

"Pretty sure my parents still kiss. Don't yours?"

"Well, yeah, when you put it like that."

I take another step toward her. In response, she moves back half a step. "What else you got?"

"Because it's been a while."

"All the more reason. See what you've been missing all that while."

"We shouldn't, Keeley…"

That's what breaks me.

Hearing her use my last name twists something inside, unleashing the parts of me kept locked away since I became a father.

Sure, I've slept with a handful of women since, but I wouldn't initiate kissing. I never had an urge to kiss them. Because kissing always got me into trouble. Never the sex. Sex I can handle, keeping the emotions separate. But not kissing.

Kissing got me Megan.

Kissing got me Lennon.

Until now, I wanted nothing else. *No one* else.

Until Tate.

Now, kissing's going to get me Tate.

CHAPTER 10
TATE

Walsh looks like he's about to kiss me.

To devour me.

To *ruin* me.

And I want him to do it.

Keeley.

It was the name that did it. I saw the change the minute it left my mouth. I have never not wanted to take something back so badly.

His blue eyes drop to my lips before meeting my gaze. "Last chance to say no," he drawls, the hunger reflected in the husk of his voice.

Closing my eyes for a moment, the words tumble out uninhibited. "Kiss me."

It's been years since I've uttered those words. Was the last time really Damon?

The fact sobers me up quickly. It's the only excuse for why I'm the one who steps closer to Walsh. Why it's my hand running down his muscular, broad chest, a plate of steel under my touch.

He towers over me by about half a foot. His breaths come quickly, matching the erratic rhythm of my own. Only worries about Aubrey have had the power to deregulate my breathing. Certainly nothing sexual in the past five years has evoked a reaction so strongly.

Before either of us makes a move—him to deliver on his threat, me to make him—there's a thud from the living room.

"No worries, Mommy," Aubrey's high-pitched voice filters in, breaking the hold Walsh has on me.

My feet rooted in place, all I can do is stare at him.

The way his eyes darken as he waits for my move.

His chest heaving below his T-shirt.

His hands balled into fists at his sides. Not in anger, but frustration.

Another thud sounds, completely breaking the moment, forcing me into action. Instead of reacting to the sounds from the other room where our children play, I push to my tiptoes, leaning both hands on Walsh's chest.

"I'm gonna need a raincheck on the kiss." My lips find the corner of his, a preview of what's to come, after we take care of more pressing matters.

He's unsuspecting, a deer in headlights as my lips linger longer than what would be considered chaste but not long enough to be diary-worthy.

"Tate." My name is a warning on his lips. Of what I'm unsure. But he repeats it, more needy the second time. "Tate."

The third loud noise has me running for the living room, Walsh at my heels. The slap to his forehead echoes around the small room, the only other sound Aubrey's gasp.

"Lennon Victoria," Walsh bellows. Funny how her name is also a warning, but in a much different way. The deep baritone causes her to stop moving, frozen in place.

"Hey, Keeley," she pants. "What's up?" Her hands are raised above her head, her feet planted on the floor, spread widely.

For the first time, I don't want to laugh at her response, wondering what she's got up her sleeve.

"What's going on?" His voice is almost back to normal, the threadiness waning.

"Playing. Is it time to go? 'Cause I'm not ready yet. How about, hmmm…five more minutes? Maybe ten." She seeks out my daughter. Aubrey's fascinated by the scene playing out, the hint of a smile toying on her mouth. But as usual, she's on the sidelines, watching and not partaking in whatever Lennon's doing.

"I think we've worn out our welcome. And by we, I mean *you*, Squirt. It's like I can't take you anywhere." His jovial tone contradicts his words.

Lennon looks over at me. "It's up to you, since it's your house."

"Seriously, kid. Keep pushing buttons, why don't you?" A new emotion peppers his tone: humiliation.

I don't dare peep at Walsh for fear I'll crack up. But I suggest, "Why don't we go for a walk outside? The autumn colors are so pretty."

Lennon thinks it over a minute, the wheels turning in her adorable little head. I don't know what's going to come out of her mouth when she finally decides.

"Sure, okay. I think that's a fine idea."

"How are you only five?" Walsh asks rhetorically.

"'Cause I had five birthdays," she sasses back, picking up the pillows from the floor.

"Right. Let's get our shoes on and head out, shall we?"

We walk around the complex twice, the preschoolers slow as molasses but chatting away as if they've known each other all their lives. It's so sweet to see Aubrey coming out of her shell and interacting with another child. As brusque as Lennon can be, she has this wisdom about her to back down with Aubrey, inspiring her to take more leaps, be more daring. At least in the figurative sense. My girl won't be scaling playscapes anytime soon.

Walsh and I trail behind. The heat from our time in the kitchen has simmered, but if given a match, we'd be up in flames in no time, the spark very much alive. I don't want to bring the kiss back up, not when we can't do anything about it, nor finish what he started. But damn, do I want to.

Back at the condo, Walsh insists it's time to leave and with a pointed glower in Lennon's direction, she doesn't argue. She hugs Aubrey goodbye, then follows it up with one for me.

"Thanks for bringing lunch." I start for my bag. "What do I owe you?"

"Not a thing. It's on me. You'll get next time." He flashes a smile.

If it made me a little weak before, it's nothing compared to now. I have to steady myself—discreetly of course—on the wall.

I could argue with him, demand he accept the money, but I choose to focus on the "next time." It may not be soon, but there will be a "next time." I'll pay then.

Walsh gathers their things as Lennon politely intones, "Bye, Tate. Thanks for having us."

"Anytime."

At the door, Lennon lights up with enthusiasm, but soon her expression falters. "I'm at Momma's tomorrow, aren't I?"

"Indeed you are. Maybe next week." Walsh opens the door, their conversation continuing, secrets we aren't privy to.

My awareness draws to his backside again, his ass in the sweat-pants causing all kinds of dirty ideas to emerge, sending messages to other parts of my body. Ones still turned on by the almost kiss.

Maybe it's better we didn't kiss. It's not like there could or would ever be something between us. Other than as a parent of my girl's friend. So lost in my thoughts of Walsh and the prospect of not acting on any feelings I have for him, I don't realize I've missed half of what Aubrey said.

"What?"

"I said, that was so fun. The show was great. Can I watch another episode after dinner and bath?" Despite the way I've ignored her, she sounds the least bit irritated with me. Although it doesn't go completely unnoticed. "How about in your bed?"

The idea she proposes doesn't sound half bad. "Yes, let's do that. What do you want for dinner?"

I take full advantage of Aubrey being in school all day on Friday. I pound out my work, leaving the last hour and a half before dismissal free. Needing a little time to decompress after the long week, I draw a bath, my Kindle oasis accompanying me. Which seems like a great idea until I get to the sexy part of the latest romance novel I'm read-ing. And instead of focusing on the actual words on the screen, my mind drifts to Walsh, the thoughts in no way pure.

It feels like it's been forever—roughly about six years—since I've thought about a man sexually. Which is even laughable to call Damon a *man*. Glorified boychild is more like it. So the opposite of Walsh, who's all man. It hasn't slipped my notice how his biceps pop in his shirts. The wall of steel of his chest. The thick thighs from hours and hours on the ice.

Yeah, who needs a fictional man to fantasize about when I've got a real one?

Walsh is in no way "mine." In any sense of the word. But does a little daydreaming about the way he would look hovering over me hurt anyone?

Nope. Just my Kindle as it splashes into the water, falling from my fingers as notions of Walsh skate across my mind.

Jarring out of this fantasy world, I sit up in the bath, chastising myself for allowing my thoughts to drift to these places. With Walsh, no less. Besides being out of my league, he can have any woman he wants. As evidenced by his ex. He'd never choose me.

I tamp down any ideas there could be more between us—even after the hot almost kiss in my kitchen. And damn, that was hot. Not just because it's been so long. Because of how Walsh vibrated. Ready to devour me.

And so begins the vicious cycle again.

I climb out of the tub, shoving down all notions of Walsh. Thankfully, my phone pings with a text, bringing me back to real life, where Walsh can only have a starring role in my fantasies.

Then again, when I find his name on my lock screen, it has to mean something.

Yeah, a playdate for his kid, you moron.

Despite the truth, my belly flips at the mere sight of his name. Reminding myself I have to keep these feelings reined in tight, a smile creeps on my lips.

> Hey. Lennon's at her mom's for the weekend. Any chance you're free to grab dinner one night?

Huh? is my initial reaction.

Is he asking me out on a date for dinner? Heat settles in my cheeks and other areas covered only by a towel. A date with Walsh. Until reality slams into me, knocking me down.

I tumble onto the bed I'm in front of.

No matter how much I want to go on a date with Walsh, the actuality is I can't.

Aubrey.

Unlike him, I don't get to ship her off to her dad's for the weekend. Something I've never been able to do, even at home. My parents were around for the occasional night here and there, for a little time to myself, but not a date.

Here in Vermont, a night "off" from Aubrey isn't a possibility. Even if there was the slight possibility of my aunt helping and taking Aubrey for one night, I won't leave her with someone she doesn't know.

But you can get to know her, my mind taunts. She wants to get to know us, otherwise she'd stop inviting us for dinner. It's probably time to take her up on the offer.

But not to leave Aubrey by herself with her.

> No

I keep it short, to the point. As much as I want to elaborate and explain, a simple answer is best.

The dots jump on his end almost immediately.

> No because you have plans or no because you don't want to?

> Neither

Again, I can't get into specifics. Not over text.

So when the phone rings, WALSH displayed in big letters on the screen, my heart rate quickens. I can't *not* answer since we've been texting. I can't pretend I'm too busy for a call.

Shaky fingers drag over the screen to answer.

"Hello?" My voice almost stutters, as if I had no idea who was calling. But can you blame me?

"I don't understand."

No hey. No hello. Not even a hi.

"What?" Because I don't know how else to answer.

"You're going to make me work for this?" his voice rasps out on speakerphone in my quiet room.

I'm so confused about what he means. "Work for what?"

"Dinner. A date. With you, Tate."

"A date? With *me*?" My voice pitches on the last word, making me sit upright on my bed. I couldn't have heard him correctly. Sure, I assumed his invite to dinner meant a date, but it's a little unbelievable for him to voice the words.

His hearty chuckle amuses my ears, a refreshing sound I didn't realize I needed to hear.

"You and me, Tate. A date."

"Great use of rhyme." My hand slaps my forehead. Aubrey's been into rhyming words lately, so that's where my mind went. Not to the actual meaning behind the words. "Sorry. That was lame." He can't see my shrug. Which is probably a good thing because I'm still only wearing a towel.

Not beating around the bush, he drawls, "Can we get to the reason for my call?"

"Which is?"

He exhales deeply. I shouldn't take notice, but even the way he *breathes* is sexy.

"Tate, I don't know your last name, do you want to grab dinner with me tonight?"

"Winchester."

Now it's his turn to be confused. "Huh?"

"My last name. For future reference." I don't know why it's important to tell him. My last name or the added comment. Except I'm avoiding the whole "date" thing, trying not to freak out at his intentions.

"Tate Winchester, you, me, dinner tonight. What do you say?"

I hate to turn him down, especially with the way my body responds to his demand to have dinner with him.

"I can't." My words are small, nothing like the way he issued his.

"How about tomorrow night?"

Damn, he's persistent.

"How about no nights?"

I don't mean for it to come out so harshly, but I'm frustrated because it can never happen. As much as I want it to happen.

"Really? So no dates?" I don't like the defeated lilt to his tone. And yet, it makes my heart soar knowing he's disappointed too.

"It's not that I don't want to—"

He interrupts anything else I was going to say. "Then what is it? Because I thought we had something in the kitchen yesterday. Unless that was my imagination."

"Not your imagination," I assert, giving him a glimpse into my truth before I deflate his bubble of expectancy. "But I have Aubrey." My voice remains steady. I won't let being a mother or Aubrey herself sound like a burden, something she isn't.

"Oh, shit. I'm so used to not having Lennon every other weekend, I didn't consider the fact it's just you. My bad."

I try not to read into his words, the nonchalant way he tosses it out there. Not because I'm jealous he gets a break from her, but at the possibility of how many other women he can spend time with on his "off" weekends.

Surely there's no way now he'd still want to pursue me—a woman with a child she can't dump on someone for a night.

Inwardly, I cringe at the mere thought of doing that.

"I'm sorry," I murmur, not knowing what else to say but needing to fill the uncomfortable silence.

I don't know how I expect him to respond. Seeing how this entire conversation has thrown me for a loop, it shouldn't surprise me when he replies, "But you still need to eat."

"Food seems to be essential."

"Okay, cool. I guess I'll see you around. Bye."

A glance at my phone confirms what I know to be true—he hung up. He's no longer on the other end of the line. Now, instead of feeling puzzled, I'm angry.

Who does that? Asks someone out on a date and when she gives a reason she can't go, dismisses the idea altogether?

Walsh Keeley.

And this is precisely the reason I can't date. Him especially.

Tossing the phone on the bed, I hastily stand up. Mostly dry after our conversation, I stomp over to my dresser and grab clothes.

If Lennon's with her mother this weekend, at least I don't have to see the man at pickup. I have no intention of facing him after the way he abruptly ended our call.

My insides flame thinking about how rude he was. It's so unlike him, at least from what I've seen the few times we've hung out.

You don't know him.

Isn't that the truth.

And now, I probably never will.

CHAPTER 11
WALSH

hang up the phone in a rush.

"Okay, cool. I guess I'll see you around. Bye."

What the fuck did I say to her?

That's so not what I wanted. I wanted a date, damn it. I didn't consider the fact she has no one to babysit Aubrey, but it doesn't change the fact I still want a date. With Tate. Preferably without the kiddos, but since that's not a possibility for her, I'll have to get creative.

I only have one early morning class on Fridays, and practice ended hours ago. Since I don't have to pick up Lennon at preschool and have the night off from the rink, I have the rest of the day to figure something out. Which isn't only about food at this point. I have to atone for the asinine behavior I displayed. Very high school of me.

Heading down the stairs, the smell of lasagna hits me first before I step foot in the kitchen at the back of our house. The space is my mother's domain. It's not big by any means—none of the three-bedroom Cape Cod-style house is—but it's home.

I find Mom putzing around, tossing a salad, a pot of water boiling on the stove.

"Smells great." I peck her cheek, wiping away the small traces of flour transferring to my lips.

"Are you home for dinner? Juliet's supposed to pop by with Gregor."

As enticing as that sounds, I have groveling to do. And for once, it's not with my sister.

Juliet, older than me by four years, moved out just a little over a year ago, giving Lennon her own room for the first time at our house. She's always had one at Megan's house, but since we never made it a big deal she cohabited with her dear old dad, neither did she. And even with her own room, she ends up in my bed a lot of nights. A lot of nights too many. However, college classes, hockey practices, and an energetic five-year-old are the epitome of exhaustion. Besides, for four years, I was used to having her in the room with me. It was an adjustment for both of us. Hell, still is for her.

"Maybe. I kinda need to do something. What time are they coming?"

With the back of her hand, Mom brushes a wayward grayish strand of hair off her face. She's accepted the gray, refusing to color her hair. She tries to blame me for going gray early—making her a grandmother at a young age—but that's such a lie. It wouldn't have been her choice for me to become a teen dad, making her a grandmother in her late forties, but she's been supportive from day one. Dad too, in his way.

Before she answers, she hands me a loaf of bread, a knife, and some butter. "Garlic bread while we chat." My ass finds a seat in the chair at the dinette, just like old times. "Probably around six. But you know your sister."

I chuckle. "So more like seven. Got it."

Juliet was a week past her due date and has been late ever since.

As I spread the softened butter on the two halves of the bread, my mind ponders what to do about Tate. Would she open the door if I showed up unannounced? Do I text her and invite myself over? It's worked previously, but in this case, I have to step up my game. Definitely a surprise.

Waiting for Aubrey to go to bed seems like my best bet. However, I don't want her to get the wrong idea.

Or maybe I do.

Apologizing for your misgivings does not result in rewarding your dick.

"Well, that's one way to make sure no one eats the garlic bread."

My mother's deep laugh breaks me out of thoughts of Tate.

"Huh?" I look down to where she points. Garlic powder covers both halves of the loaf. "Oh. Oops. I'll shake some off."

Mom grabs it out of my hands. "It's fine. I'll throw some shredded mozzarella and parmesan on it and no one will be the wiser." She makes cooking seem so easy, so effortless, even though the reality is not. "Want to talk about whatever's on your mind?"

"No." The word isn't even out of my mouth before I launch into my dilemma. Mom listens as I tell her about how I treated Tate on the phone, my ideas for tonight, all while she corrects for my over-abundance of garlic. "What do you think? How should I approach it?"

"Lasagna," she suggests with a shrug. As if the answer's that simple.

"That's a stretch, Ma. I can barely make mac and cheese for Lennon and the directions are on the box."

If I have my way, Lennon and I are never leaving the comfort of my parents' house. I'm not one of those guys needing his independence or caring if I'm living at "Mommy and Daddy's." College food sucks. Millie Keeley's food is out of this world. And she does most of our laundry, and I don't have to pay any bills. Why would I ever want to leave?

Her hand covers mine with a shake of her head. "My dear boy. Where did we go wrong with you?"

"I wish I could tell you."

"That was rhetorical." She steps away from the table, checking the food in the oven. "Is it for the two of you? I've got two cooking in the oven now, but there's plenty if you want half of one."

Is she suggesting I bring lasagna to Tate?

"Thanks for the offer, but I can't march over there with lasagna and force it on her. What about her daughter?"

"She's Lennon's age?" I agree with a nod. "So she's in bed fairly early."

"Earlier than Lennon, if I had to guess. Because you know my kid likes to drag out bedtime for an hour."

"No different from when you were her age." I go to argue with her—I couldn't possibly have been as bad as Lennon—but she shoots me a glare warding off any rebuttal.

Instead, I ask, "Do I just show up with dinner? You heard what I said to her, right? What if she slams the door in my face?"

"She'd earn my respect if she does. Even more so if she first takes the lasagna." She smiles wide, the fine lines around her eyes creasing. "But you won't know unless you try." She gets back to cooking, leaving me to ruminate how to proceed.

"I should bring flowers." I don't mean to speak the words aloud but am glad I do when Ma agrees with a hum. My decision made, I leap out of my chair and head out of the kitchen, but not before I give her another kiss on her cheek. "Thanks, Ma. I'll accept the lasagna. Be back in a jiff."

Since I don't know her favorites, I grab a variety of different ones at the local florist. Based on the brief conversation we had about her loving the fall, I choose vibrant colors, hoping to emulate the autumn hues surrounding us.

With lasagna and flowers in tow, I pull up to Tate's condo at 7:45. I didn't send a text to warn her or to give her the opportunity to shoot me down. Hopefully, she's a surprise kinda girl. At least I come bearing gifts.

My heart's in my throat as I approach, the feeling similar to the first step out on the ice for the first game of the season. Nervous yet excited. Tonight the emphasis is on nervous. She could open the door, take one look at me, and send me away. Hell, she may not even open the door. The thought makes me cringe.

My first mistake was assuming she could go on a date with me. The second and more egregious was when I hung up on her with little to no reason about my behavior. I'm fully prepared to grovel and endure my punishment like a man.

I have to wipe down my sweaty fingers before ringing the doorbell. As soon as it chimes, another mistake hits me—Aubrey's probably asleep and the bell will most likely wake her.

Nice work, asshole. Way to start the groveling off on the right foot.

As I'm about to freak out and give up, the outside light turns on. The sound of the dead bolt unlocking incites a jump in my heart. The door opens, and Tate stands on the other side, a shocked expression marring her features.

My eyes scan her. Her black hair's pulled up into a messy knot on the top of her head. Moving lower, she wears an oversized T-shirt with the logo of some construction company and pajama shorts.

"Hey." Not my best opening.

"What are you doing here?" There's fire in her tone, an unrecognizable hostility I've yet to experience with her.

"I brought dinner."

She crosses her arms over her chest, highlighting the fact she's not wearing a bra. "I already ate."

Both my heart and ego deflate with her announcement.

"Oh. Flowers?" Unclear why I'm not affirmative with the word, I hold them up in front of the door.

Her deep set scowl softens the tiniest bit. It's the crack in her composure I need.

"I'm sorry, Tate. I was unprepared when you turned me down for a date. Because I wanted to have dinner with you, spend some time getting to know you as more than Aubrey's mom. But I totally get why you can't go out. I thought maybe we could have a late dinner together if Aubrey was in bed. Seeing how you've already eaten, I'll just go." I turn around, but my mom's words from earlier echo in my head. "Here. My mom would want you to have this."

After word vomiting, I stand there awkwardly, the lasagna outstretched in my hands, loitering for Tate to make a move. Any move. But she just stands there, arms crossed over her chest, head tilted to the side, most likely plotting how to avoid me at preschool.

I notice a small stool next to the door, so I place the lasagna on it.

With one more look in Tate's direction, I say, "Enjoy. See you around."

I turn slowly, my feet heavy as I shuffle away from the door. Three steps away, I'm still holding the flowers. With a palm to my forehead, I spin around. And come face-to-face with Tate. I didn't even hear the door open.

Unsteady on my feet, I almost knock her down, but she reaches out to keep me upright.

"Is your mom's lasagna as good as her chili?"

Her inquiry bewilders me. So does her contrite look. Because if anyone should feel that way, it's me. Not her. She did nothing wrong.

"Better," I confirm with a smile.

"Aubrey wanted chicken nuggets for dinner."

"Okay?" I'm unsure why she's telling me this. Before we go any further, I thrust the flowers into her hands. "I didn't know which ones were your favorites. I couldn't leave the store without these. The colors were just so..."

She reaches for the outstretched blooms, bringing them to her nose to smell. "Vibrant. Fall. Gorgeous." The last word falls out in a whisper. "The chicken nuggets weren't what I wanted for dinner." She looks up in earnest at me.

Again, I don't know why she mentions this. "What did you want?" I ask without hesitation.

"Lasagna sounds pretty good now. You hungry?"

Finally catching on to what she's going on about, I exclaim heartedly, "Starved."

"Aubrey's sleeping, so we'll have to be quiet in the kitchen. If she wakes up and sees you, she's going to ask for Lennon."

"I have some experience sneaking around." Tate's eyes widen, and as the words filter through my brain, they sound horrible. "Being quiet in the house," I amend. "That's the only sneaking I do."

Tate doesn't respond with words, just actions.

With her empty hand, she interlaces our fingers. Her hand is warm to the touch. With her hand in mine, I'd follow her anywhere.

The lasagna in my other hand, Tate leads us inside, reminding me with a finger to her mouth about keeping quiet. Inside, I remove my shoes as she shuts the door. Through the living room and into the kitchen we go, still hand in hand.

I don't want to admit the things her touch does to me. How with such a simple gesture, I'm more enthralled with her.

Our hands disengage only after she places the flowers on the table and reaches for the lasagna.

"Does it need to be reheated?"

"Mom baked it halfway. It still needs about twenty minutes." I only sound confident about the time because my mother drilled it in my head. "Twenty minutes at three hundred-fifty degrees."

"Cool. Let me get it in the oven. Help yourself to anything to drink in the fridge." She fiddles with some buttons to preheat the oven before peering lovingly at the blossoms again. "What kind are these?"

I knew she was going to ask. Despite as many times as the florist mentioned the different types, my brain refused to remember. Stalling, I point to ones I can identify. "These are sunflowers."

"You don't say," she deadpans. "How about these?" Her fingers point to the red ones.

"Flowers?"

A hand to her mouth stifles her giggle. "It's the thought that counts, and these were very thoughtful, Walsh. Thank you."

"You're welcome," I murmur.

"I just realized I don't even have a vase. Good thing one's included."

Damn vase cost me twenty-five bucks extra. Money well spent.

"Now you'll have one when these die."

"I'll let you know when that day comes. I'll probably be so accustomed to looking at them, I'll need more." Her cheeks redden with her implication.

"Noted."

I don't elaborate but make a mental note to remember to get back to the florist when I think they may be dead. How long do flowers usually last? That's a question for Millie. She'll have the answer.

Tate places the vase in the middle of the kitchen table, gesturing I should sit. "How was your day?"

"Exhausting. Lennon woke me up around five when she crawled into my bed. She ends up there at least once a week, but I wish she would just get into bed and go back to sleep. Usually, she has to make sure we have a brief conversation before she finally gets the hint and dozes back off."

I'm not used to talking about Lennon with any woman I'm interested in. I don't hide the fact I have a daughter, but most girls aren't looking to talk about my kid. They're way more interested in what I can offer them. And hockey. Then there are the puck chasers who pretend to like hockey so they have an in with the players. My experience with these types is limited as I have little free time outside of hockey and being a dad, but a few have wormed their way in.

With Tate, we connect on a deeper level because of our mutual experiences of being parents. *Teen* parents.

Tate nods her head, fully invested in the story I've lost track of with one glance in her direction. What was I rambling on about?

Oh, right. My day.

"And then it just went downhill from there. Class was boring. Practice was invigorating yet draining at the same time. How about yours?"

I can't ignore the slight pink tinge creeping on her cheeks. "Fine."

There's more to it than "fine," but I don't inquire further. For now.

"What time does Aubrey go to sleep?" The question has little to do with what we're talking about, but once it's out there, I'm interested to see it through.

"Seven-ish is the time we start to unwind for the day. Bath and books or neither if she's exhausted. As methodical as she is, bedtime's never been a time when she craves structure. As long as she's asleep by eight, I'm okay with it. Gives me a couple of hours to myself before I hit the hay."

I want to know when that is, but I don't ask.

"What about Lennon?"

I guffaw at the audacity of a bedtime for Lennon. "The girl has never understood the word bedtime or routine, and especially not in conjunction. It's a struggle to get her in bed by 8:30 most nights, the first of many times I tuck her in." My head shakes at what a disaster every night is. "The nights she's with Megan, I often collapse into bed, no matter if it's early or late."

There's a bit of hesitancy in my voice at the mention of Megan. I rationalize it away—I can't change the fact Lennon has a mother who spends as much time with her as I do.

"Aubrey's always been a great sleeper. Once she started sleeping through the night at about a year. The first year was a little hairy. No, a lot hairy."

"One year's nothing. There's no end in sight for Lennon."

Tate's lips purse. It's not until the words leave my mouth do I cringe.

"Is she the same way for her mother?" Her tone is laced with something unexplainable with the reference to Megan.

"God, no. Meg won't put up with that shit, and Lennon knows it."

"So why do you?"

It's a legitimate question, one I've asked myself repeatedly, never having a decent answer.

"The million dollar question."

Luckily, the timer beeps alerting us the lasagna's done. Tate jumps up, removes it from the oven, and after waiting a few minutes for it to cool slightly, plates a piece for each of us.

"Thanks."

"It looks and smells delicious."

She wastes no time digging in, and I rivet my eyes to her. An orgasmic moan accompanies her bite. Coupled with her eyes shutting, it's all I can do not to get hard. But she's making it extremely difficult.

"So good. Compliments to your mother. Anytime she makes too much, Aubrey and I will take the leftovers."

"I'll pass along the message. Again, she'll be envious. Lennon won't even try pasta with red sauce."

All I get is a nod of her head before she digs back into the food.

Dinner chatter consists of a "getting to know you" session. I learn she has an older brother who still lives at home with her parents, she might want to attend college someday, and her absolute favorite food is pizza. The thinner the better. It's another fact I file away for future reference, the wheels already spinning for when we can visit Pizza Forge to introduce her to the best pizza Vermont offers.

I do most of the asking, but she doesn't seem to mind she gets little information from me. If all goes according to the plans in my head, there will be future time for her to get to know me better.

After we eat, I make quick work of cleaning up, rinsing the

dishes before putting them in the dishwasher. She only protests once. And it's not so much of a "you don't have to do that" but more of a "plates face the other way in the dishwasher." To see how much it bothers her, I leave them the way I arranged them, close it up, and encourage her to join me in the living room.

"Do you watch TV out here after Aubrey's sleeping?" We settle on the couch, an entire cushion between us. My eyes can't help assessing for stains from Lennon's accident yesterday, of which there doesn't seem to be any.

"I tend to hole up in my room after she's in bed."

It's not an invitation, Walsh. My cock needs the reprimand more than anything else.

"So as not to wake her?"

"No. Habit, I guess. It's not that I can't or don't watch out here, but it's just something that happened." She stares at the wall, leaving me with only a glimpse of her side profile. I can't help staring, my eyes outlining the delicate lines, the ridge of her small nose, the round curve of her jaw. Even from this angle, she's beautiful.

You've still yet to taste those lips, my brain prods.

How would Tate react if I made a move? The notion of kissing her appeals greatly to every sense of me, but not if it would make her uncomfortable.

"You should," she whispers, reading my innermost thoughts.

Am I that transparent? Or did I voice my opinions aloud? Her head swivels slowly to face me. Her expression gives little conviction to her request. In fact, her worried appearance seems to convey the complete opposite.

"I don't want you to regret it."

"Will you?" she sasses back. My dick twinges.

I tug her over. Cupping her jaw in my hands, I state honestly, "Yep." My one-word answer gets the reaction I was going for—shock—but I don't let her pull away. "Because I won't get to do it whenever I want."

Any retort she may have gets swallowed by my lips. She lets out the tiniest squeak of surprise, followed by total surrender.

Her lips are soft, as I knew they would be. The remnants of tomato sauce linger, transferring to mine. She yields total control of the kiss, allowing me to devour her lips as I please.

As much as I want to misuse the control, I refrain from total domination. I lead our lips in a duel, a dance of sorts, licking, nibbling, sucking. It's only after I can't stop myself any longer do I seek entrance.

Her lips part enough for my tongue to sneak in. And I'm certain I've gone too far.

Not because it's bad. The total opposite.

It's perfection.

Tate's mouth is the perfect combination of sweet heat, a place my tongue would like to call home for a long time.

My hazy thoughts recognize it's not a possibility, so I relish the minutes I have.

Winding my hands in her hair, my tongue strokes the top of hers, and when she lifts it slightly, I do the same to the bottom.

The little moans escaping Tate urge me on, pressuring me to take everything she gives, to keep going, to *never* stop.

Our lips tangle together. It should be awkward, bumbling, a first kiss between foreign mouths. But it's quite the contrary. It's like our mouths were meant to fuse, to come together like long-lost friends, a beckoning of something beyond our control.

My fingers fall from her hair when she stops the kiss, shoving my chest away, her attempt thwarted by the weak strength she applies.

"Need." Gasp. "A." Gasp. "Breather," she expresses, a breath between words.

As disappointed as I am, it gives me time to take stock of my emotions, the high I'm feeling with one connection of our lips. My heart thunders in my chest, adrenaline coursing through me, lighting my insides. It's a high, comparable only to skating in a championship game when everything's on the line.

I slouch back into the couch, tugging her to my side. This time, she comes willingly, with no fight necessary. My fingers reach out to touch her hair, releasing her black locks from the messy bun.

"You're beautiful." My mouth forms the words I've been itching to articulate for a while now.

Her brown eyes roll. "Please. This is beautiful?" She waves her hand over her body. "Highly doubtful." There's a hint of skepticism in her voice.

"Incredibly," I confirm, a nod of my head punctuating the point.

She's not one of those girls who thinks more of her appearance, even though she could be. She really is gorgeous. And from what I've gleaned about her so far from our few interactions, it's not just on the outside. Beautiful inside as well. I'm also sure she doesn't accept compliments well, so I won't push her to the point of arguing.

I'll have to find ways to show her how beautiful she is.

CHAPTER 12
TATE

Walsh kissed me.

Me. Tate Winchester.

This hunky, muscular, extremely attractive man kissed me.

And damn, what a kiss. No one has ever kissed me like that in my twenty-two years of life. Part of me wonders if it was a fluke. Like some cosmic force pulled us together for this one kiss because surely, not all kisses can be like that. Right?

I mean, I wouldn't mind testing it out at a future time.

"You want to watch a movie?" Walsh's suggestion pops my thought bubble of more potential kisses. With Walsh. Kisses that lead to maybe more than just our lips coming together.

Maybe other parts of us come together as well. As in, his dick in my…

Stopping this train of thought, I pant out, "Yes. A movie. Yes. For sure. Let's do that."

Way to sound so affected there, Tate.

Except I'm a hella lot affected by his kiss. By him being here. By the man himself.

I wasn't expecting him at the door when it rang earlier. He flustered me. Even after making dinner, giving Aubrey a long bath, reading three books, and tucking her into bed, I was still pissed at the way he dismissed me on the phone.

Then he showed up. With flowers. A stunning autumn arrangement of various varieties. It's like he knew my weakness without me giving it up. Which seems totally cliché—what girl doesn't love flowers? My dad came home every Friday night with some "for his girls" ever since I can remember. I've been spoiled and molded to think that's what men did. Boy, was that a wake-up call I learned the hard way.

But no. Walsh. Focus on Walsh.

His showing up with the bouquet nearly set my heart aflame right then. His actions instantly earned him forgiveness. A sincere apology and flowers go a long way in my book, and upon his own accord, he did both.

Damn, two more boxes ticked off my checklist. Major ones, too. And he's so great with kids because he's a dad. I might as well serve my heart and vagina up to him on a silver platter.

Again, Walsh's voice breaks into the train wreck my mind conjures up.

"Any preferences on a movie choice?"

"Huh?" His question requires a lot of processing time because I'm too busy hooking up with him in my mind. Heat sears my cheeks. Hopefully, I can recover quickly, making him think I'm embarrassed by not knowing what he said. And because I want to see him naked.

Cue the redder cheeks.

"I'm not picky. I've got Netflix and Prime. Oh, and Disney Plus." As if any movies on there appeal to him.

"Where's your remote?"

Reluctantly, I move away from being tucked into him and a cool rush of air hits me. Or maybe it feels that way since he was so warm and now I'm practically frigid as I walk to the entertainment center to grab the remotes. Back on the couch, I hand them to him before dropping onto the sofa. I debate whether to move next to him or sit on the opposite side. Walsh decides for me when he all but urges me to curl back into him. The smile sprouting on my lips prompts a similar one from him.

He entangles his fingers in my hair. I don't hate it. "Thanks for not turning me away earlier, especially after the stupid things I said on the phone. This is a nice way to spend a Friday evening."

As much as his tone is genuine, I hardly believe he can think this is a good way to spend a Friday night. Not when he's in college. Surely there are parties to go to, beer to drink, girls to defile.

The last thought turns my stomach.

I lean my head so I can see him. "Isn't Friday night a huge party night in college? Especially on nights you don't have Lennon. Why wouldn't you choose those over this?"

"Can't drink much during the season. And Lennon's not the only reason I don't live on campus."

"Why else?"

"The cost, for one. But also, because it's not really my scene. Even when it's not the middle of hockey season, I have little interest in getting plastered or hit on by rando college girls who only want me because I play hockey."

"Would not being a dad change your mind?"

"I've never given it much consideration." He pauses, gathering his thoughts. The fingers of his left hand continue to twirl my hair and the other hand scrolls through movies on Netflix. "Before Lennon, hockey was always my focus. If I had to guess, I'd assume probably not."

"That's honest and realistic." At least it sounds like it is. What the heck do I know about the partying habits of college seniors?

"*Forever My Girl* good?"

"Whatever."

Once it starts, he sets the remote on the table next to him before inching me closer, which warms me up at how intimate he wants us and turns me on. As much as I want to be turned on by him, now isn't the time. But beggars can't be choosers.

Even though it's not too late, I don't mention how it's likely I'll fall asleep. The motion of his twirls and my head resting on his shoulder do little to encourage me to keep my heavy eyes open.

Only when the body next to me moves do I realize I fell asleep on the couch lying on top of Walsh.

"I should probably get going. It's kinda late."

His groggy voice makes me wonder if he wasn't asleep too. Or is his from nonuse in the past however long I've been asleep? A glimpse at my watch reveals it's a little after midnight. Wracking my brain, I have no clue what time we started the movie or how long I lasted before conking out.

"Probably best," I agree, but make no action to move from my comfortable position. "How was the movie?"

"The first ten minutes were pretty good. Can I get back to you about the rest when I finish it?" His entire upper body shakes with his chuckle, my body along for the ride.

Sitting up, I brush the hair off my face, pulling it back up into a messy bun. "Or maybe it was boring enough to put us both to sleep."

"We could go with that. Or," he draws out, his arms stretching above his head, "the fact I was exhausted, and having you cuddled up next to me was too damn comfortable." He continues, a smug grin on his face. "And sleep seemed like the better choice over doing all the things my mind wanted to do."

"More than kissing?" I whisper, afraid to voice the question. But I need the answer.

"So much more, Tate. So. Much. More." He slides his thumb along my jaw, the softest caress evoking so many emotions inside me. At the forefront, lust.

"Sleep was the smarter choice," I concur. A cloud of anguish washes over his face, vanishing only when I add, "But I want all the other things too. Another time, another place?"

The reality is, "other things" won't come to fruition. Not in the near future.

"Rain check for now, but I'm holding you to them. Tasting your lips doesn't suffice."

With his comment, he leans in, his lips slanting over mine. His thumb moves from my jaw, and with his entire hand, he cradles the back of my neck, tilting my head exactly where he wants it.

His lips are drier than earlier, so I drag my tongue over them to moisten them. He mimics my actions, then delves his tongue into my mouth. My lips have a mind of their own, opening up with abandon, welcoming the intrusion.

The top of my tongue becomes a target for him. He wastes no

time licking every inch before moving to the underside, lavishing it with the same affection.

With little coherent thought left in my brain, I focus on how possessive he is. How much control he wields, but not dominantly. Or maybe it's because I'm succumbing to his will so easily. Because Walsh can kiss. I may lack experience in the bedroom, but I've kissed more than my share of guys.

Correction, *boys.* Yet, I don't think that makes a difference in this situation. Or maybe it does because he sure as heck knows what he's doing.

The way his tongue explores every inch of my mouth.

The way he pulls it back, only to suck my bottom lip between his teeth.

The way he drags me on top of his lap without so much as breaking our connection.

I'm not consciously paying attention to what I'm doing and only hope I'm kissing him back. I must be because he hasn't moved away or had any complaints.

Oh!

He wasn't lying about wanting to do more. The evidence presses against the apex of my thighs.

Gaining my wits back, I unenthusiastically rip my mouth away. Because this kiss can't lead to more. Not tonight. Not here.

Hopefully not never.

"We can't," I breathe out restlessly, feeling every ounce of the adrenaline coursing through me. I didn't appreciate how much I missed this, nor the feeling of being connected to a member of the opposite sex. Especially one who wants me as badly as I want him.

"Not tonight." So much eagerness in his tone and expression.

"Not tonight," I confirm.

"But we can. Eventually?"

Laying my forehead against his, I meet his gaze. "It would be a sin if we didn't."

"Didn't peg you as a religious girl."

"Hardly. Premarital sex and teenage mom would have solidified my excommunication with any church had I been a churchgoing girl."

I'm uncertain what words are coming out of my mouth right now. Being this close to Walsh—my pussy adjacent to his dick—jumbles all my thoughts. The comprehensible ones at minimum. The ones about rubbing myself against him run rampant through my brain. On a loop, taunting me to just slide myself back. Then forward. Back…

I jump off his lap, having to catch my breath again.

"Don't take this the wrong way, but you should go. Home. To your house. Where you live. Not here. Where I live. Like now."

Short of tugging him off the couch and shoving his shoes at his chest, I all but throw him out. Because I don't have the willpower to guard against his sexiness any longer.

Hopefully, when I see him next, I'll have calmed down. Given myself a few orgasms to stave him off.

Who am I kidding? I'll be lucky if I don't maul him in the parking lot of the preschool.

Bad idea, Tate. Terrible.

"Please, go." Even to my ears, my plea sounds unconvincing. I try again after clearing my throat. "I don't want you to leave, but I need you to leave. Because I have no trust in myself if you don't."

Walsh stalks over to where I stand. I retreat a step, but his arms land on my shoulders cementing me in place.

"I appreciate your honesty. That's the only reason I'm leaving. Not because I don't want to pursue more. Because you're asking me to leave. And I would never put you in a position of doing something you're uncomfortable with or don't want. Even though I can sense how much you want it."

I give him more truth. "So much."

"Don't take it off the table."

He doesn't elaborate. I know what *it* is, but part of me wants to make sure. But I hold my tongue.

A brief peck to my lips, a squeeze to my shoulders, he moves away. Shoving his feet into his sneakers, the door opens, and he slips out.

The minute the door shuts behind him, a huge breath releases. One I'd been holding in for so long. It carries a weight off my shoulders, confirming that asking him to leave—not acting on my feelings—was the only choice tonight.

Quickly and quietly, I lock up and shut off the remaining lights before creeping to bed.

At least this time when I get myself off to images of Walsh, it's a new day.

X

Saturday and Sunday pass quickly. My aunt invites us to her house for dinner Sunday night, and I finally accept.

It's just her and a few cats. They somehow sense not to come near Aubrey, and leave her alone until she gets comfortable. And by comfortable, I mean her face isn't a mask of fear if one of them comes in the room.

"She doesn't like cats?" Aunt Marsha guesses, one eyebrow quirked up.

"It's more of the unknown for Bree. She's not used to being around them, so she's squeamish about what they might do."

"They won't hurt her."

"We know that, but until she feels completely at ease with them, it won't matter trying to explain it."

She's got her quirks, but who doesn't? And honestly, I'll take her quirks over having a kid with bad behavior any day.

"She reminds me so much of you at her age. She's your spitting image."

I smile at the compliment. "Is it wrong of me to be grateful she doesn't resemble her sperm donor?"

"Not one bit."

Living so far away from Marsha and only visiting a few times, I wasn't close with her. Since moving here, I'm getting to know her better, and I find myself opening up to her. I tell myself it's to "repay" her for her kindness, but deep down, it's much more. She listens attentively without judgment and gives solid advice, both things my mom isn't great at. Much as I love her and how she's always there for me, Mom and I don't have a close-knit relationship, something I hope to improve between me and Aubrey.

Marsha is my father's half-sister, older by about seven years. Never married, no kids, she volunteers a lot at various organizations here in Havenwood and Wilmington, along with her work as a therapist. She runs her practice out of her home, an office in the house's front. She mentioned once it was to cut costs, but she's not hurting for money. If memory serves, her father passed when she was young, leaving behind a wealthy inheritance.

Her house is exactly the same as I pictured it from trips years ago: an old, large farmhouse she inherited along with the money. The floor, made from wide planks of wood, shows its age, probably as old as the house. Over a hundred years, I'd venture to guess. Big windows let in tons of light but also a draft. In the kitchen, yellowing cabinets practically fall off the hinges, in need of a good repair and major upgrade. The stairs leading to the second level creak with every step. Upstairs, there are four bedrooms—the primary bedroom, two large rooms, and a tiny one, the size of a closet.

Marsha didn't grow up here, having lived with my father, their mother, and her new husband, Dad's father, back in Kansas, but after college, she settled and made her life in Vermont. There's such a sense of comfort here, a feeling of *home* without actually having any family. Throughout our visit today, she reemphasized she's our family in Vermont, and whatever we need, we shouldn't hesitate to ask.

I don't know how to ask her about babysitting without sounding like a horrible mother for dumping my kid so I can get it on with Walsh. I would never mention that's what I wanted to do, but guilt can be a bitch.

"Are you all settled into the condo ? Everything else good?"

"Yes. All good. Aubrey loves school, made a new friend and everything, and I'm slowly learning my way around, only getting distracted by the beauty of fall in New England."

And a certain man I can't get out of my head.

"The exact reason I couldn't sell this house and move back to the Midwest." Her whimsical expression compliments her tone.

"Totally understandable. It's so pretty."

"What are your plans for Thanksgiving? Have you made any yet?"

Her out of the blue question startles me. I haven't given it much thought. I plan to trek home for Christmas, but wasn't planning a visit to Kansas for the few days Aubrey has off for Thanksgiving.

"No."

Aunt Marsha's face lights up with exhilaration. "Great. Come here. I've invited some of the families I've met through volunteering, so there will be other kids for Aubrey to play with."

"Only if I can help with the cooking." The stipulation falls out of my mouth unfiltered, but it's the real reason I was avoiding thinking about it. Because it's one of my favorite holidays to cook, but it seemed like too much work to go all out for Aubrey and me. I would have done a smaller version of our usual meal, but this way, I may get what I truly want.

"Only a fool turns down help in the kitchen. Want to come Wednesday and help prep?" Her smile grows wider. "Sleep over. We'll have a girls' night, and then in the morning, we can watch the parade like I used to do with your father when we were kids." She claps her hands together. "Yes. I like this plan more and more. Are you in?"

Her enthusiasm is contagious, and I agree to it all. Taking a brash leap, I blurt, "Would you ever consider babysitting Aubrey? I have time to myself when she's at school during the day, but occasionally, I want to go out alone for an hour at night or on the weekends. If it's too much, forget I even asked." The entire diatribe falls out of my mouth in one breath. I gulp in air when finished.

She pats my hand. "Of course. I was waiting for you to ask. I didn't want it to seem like I was offering because I didn't think you could handle things on your own."

Her comment strikes me as a little odd, but it's coming from a genuine place. "Aubrey needs to get used to other adults too. But the more we come here, the more she'll be comfortable. Even with the cats." We both laugh as Aubrey squeaks as a cat rubs her leg. She doesn't reach out and pet it, but she doesn't run away screaming either. Progress.

"Absolutely. I remember her mother being the same way."

I study Aunt Marsha's face. She resembles my father in eye shape only. The rest of her features are from her father. Her small crow's feet deepen when she smiles, enhancing her charm. Gray roots top her head of otherwise mousy brown hair, which extends just past her shoulders. She doesn't look a day over fifty, even though she's almost sixty.

We sit and chat with Aunt Marsha for an hour more before Aubrey decides she's ready for a bath and bed. I'm certainly not going to argue with the five-year-old.

"Come again soon, Aubrey." Aunt Marsha leans down and squeezes Aubrey's body into her. Over her head, she meets my gaze. "Come next weekend. We'll work on the menu for Thanksgiving. Do you know how to make Nannie's pecan pie?"

Sadly, I shake my head. "Dad wouldn't divulge the recipe."

Her face becomes a visage of distaste. "Oh, I'll give my brother an earful. Maybe we should make two so you can practice."

The mere thought of having the recipe for the pie in my hands has me ecstatic. "Yes. Two pies would be great. I'll need lots and lots of practice."

Letting go of Aubrey, her hands come together in front of her chest. "Great, that's settled then. And there will be plenty of left-overs." She surveys my daughter whose look mirrors Aunt Marsha's from moments ago.

"Aubrey's not a fan."

Aunt Marsha's hand flies to her chest. "Heavens to Betsy, child. Why the heck not?" Her eyes scan between the two of us.

"It's not Nannie's pie. It's any pie. Or rather, all desserts. The girl has no sweet tooth."

"Oh dear. That's dreadful." Her demeanor is pained, as if it's truly the worst news she's ever heard.

"More for us." I give her one last hug before heading home for the night.

After bath and stories, as I tuck Aubrey in, her face gets serious. "Mommy, I like Aunt Marsha. But I'm not so sure about those cats."

"My girl, never change." She flashes me a bright smile, as if she knows exactly what I mean.

And I hope that's the truth.

CHAPTER 13
WALSH

Practices have been brutal this week. With games underway, practices usually ramp up. For some reason, they seem to be worse this year. Of course, I seem to be the only one complaining. And there's one reason for it.

Tate Winchester.

I can't seem to get her off my mind, no matter how else I distract myself. She's always there.

When I'm in class.

When I'm on the ice at practice.

When it's late at night, and I should sleep, but instead, I'm jerking off. More than when I was a teenager. Like, way more.

It doesn't help I've wracked my brain for ways to get her alone. For a date. For more.

For sex specifically.

Right about now, I wish I lived on campus. Even if I had a roommate, I could ask him to leave for an hour. Can't do that at home.

However, the bigger obstacle is how do I even get her alone? She didn't seem too keen on us doing anything while Aubrey was sleeping. Which I'm totally on board with. Mostly. About half convinced I could keep it in my pants if I were to show up at her place again at night.

More like twenty-five percent. Which is a serious problem to have.

"Keeley! Your line's up. Get your head in the game," Coach Pagano's voice booms, bringing me out of my head.

Right.

Hockey practice.

The rink buzzes with anticipation as our team gathers for practice. The crisp sound of skates slicing the ice echoes around the arena, the sound comforting me. Even though they're good, I don't let it drag up memories from years past. My focus needs to be on my teammates.

I hop the boards, taking my place as left wing. Warm-up drills kick off our training, a time to hone our stickhandling, shooting, and agility. Adrenaline surges as the familiar rhythm of puck-on-stick reverberates, bringing my mind back to the present. Passing drills bolster teamwork and a chance to fine-tune puck control. My head in the game, I execute quick and accurate passes and master dekes to outmaneuver opponents.

"Nice one, Keeley," Moe Strickland calls out as I skirt around the defender straight to the goal, anticipating Cody McGuire's moves before he does. Playing with a handful of these guys the last few years eliminates the guesswork. We're always improving our skills and upping the quality of our game, but we're also learning to read other players, to predict what they're thinking as the next move. It's one of my favorite parts of the game: attempting to read minds.

Practice continues in a scrimmage. Battling against opposing blueliners tests my resilience and offensive instincts. Will I be able to foresee where the puck will go? Who can I stop from blocking a shot? Where can I find the perfect position to be open to snag a pass and shoot on the goal? Today's contest is especially grueling as our defense puts up their guard, not backing down from our attempts at scoring.

"Hibbert, get open!" Coach yells across the arena. "Keeley, other side."

I push off, my thighs protesting every movement, working overtime with more skating than usual. When I reach the other side, I stop, searching for who has the puck. From the corner of my eye, I spy Moe bent over, stick raised in the air, pursuing an opportunity.

"Strickland!" I shout, snagging his attention.

With a slight twist of his hips, the stick connects to the puck, gliding it my way from center ice. Meeting the puck before it's captured by a defenseman, I cradle it and power toward the goal. My breath panty, I don't stop until I have a shot.

Hovering the stick in the air, aiming for the top left corner of the goal, I connect with the puck. A five-second countdown in my head before…goal! It hits the back of the net with a whoosh, the red lamp spinning.

The guys on my team pat my back.

"Nice shot, Keeley."

"Way to commit to the goal," Coach commends. My chest puffs with the compliment.

Skating over to the bench, I use the door, my legs too tired to hop over.

While the next line takes over, I chug water from the Gatorade bottle. Tristan Ford and Andre Greeley face off with mumbles of trash talk, like in a real game. Sometimes it's more contentious against your own teammate to gain an edge. To show the coach what you have. A few of the younger players think it's a way to get ahead. I learned early on to keep it to a minimum. As much as displaying your skills is important, showing off gets you benched.

I get distracted by an excited "Keeley." At Lennon's voice, I turn my head. And I'm not the only one who notices her.

"Little Lennon!" Gabe Kolligan calls.

"Squirt!" Cody bellows, his voice loud above the ruckus.

Lennon's hand gestures wildly in the air, as if she's waving to her fans. Which, in her mind, she is. Dad follows her to a seat directly behind our bench, Lennon's backpack slung over his shoulders. He doesn't seem too irritated drawing the short straw for preschool pickup. Must have been a slow day at work.

"Hey, Squirt. How was school?" I remove my helmet, shaking off the sweat.

"Mostly boring." Her shoulders lift in indifference. If she's bored in preschool, I can't imagine what kindergarten will be like. "Poppa picked me up, and we went to the barn. The lady said I should come back and ride the pony." She peers up at Dad over her shoulder, but his sight bounces around the stadium. His cheeks blush red, chagrined to be called out by the kid.

"Maybe in the spring. When the weather's nicer." The whistle blows, signaling the end of practice. "Gotta listen to Coach's instructions. Stay with Poppa."

We gather on center ice, my legs wobbly from the difficult practice. We have a game coming up this weekend against a rival Vermont college. As it draws nearer, the practice intensity will increase. Despite the challenge, I love the rush of adrenaline, the relentless pursuit of perfection, each repetition and stride propelling me forward, both on the ice and toward my goals in life. The trials faced during practices serve as a reminder that pursuing excellence requires unwavering commitment and an insatiable hunger for improvement.

Coach goes over his list of notes before dismissing us. Before I make it back to the bench, my friends surround Lennon, inquiring about her day, what's new in her life, and when they can skate with her. My girl craves their devotion, lapping it up like a dog with water.

I hear her, "I can't stay. Gotta go somewhere with Poppa," disappointment settling deep in her tone.

A collective "aww" rises from the group. As if they want to spend their time entertaining a five-year-old. As much as the guys, except for Ezra, have no genuine interest in kids, Lennon's different. Whenever she's around, they melt like ice cream on a hot day.

"But you'll come back soon, right?" Gabe requests, complete with prayer hands.

"Duh." She finds me among the crowd. "When can I come back and skate with the boys?"

"We'll have to consult your social calendar. You keep filling it up with playdates." As the words barrel out of my mouth, my mind drifts to Tate. But I can't get too off track. "But I bet Momma will bring you to the game this weekend."

She fist pumps and high fives my teammates. I can't tell who's more excited—her or them. Especially Cody. Big and brawny and the "player" of my friend group, he's got a soft spot for my kid. Which is both comforting and worrisome.

"You're our good luck charm," someone claims. Maybe Andre.

"I'll make sure Mimi washes my jersey," she informs. "Gotta show my team spirit. Number sixteen like Keeley."

My eyes roll of their own accord, but I don't fight it. What's the use? Only when she's inappropriate will I curb the things she says. Otherwise, she'll continue to crack others up with what comes out of her mouth.

"Next time, bring Mimi," another teammate comments.

Neither I nor Lennon are fazed by the request.

Mom's been the "team mom" since I started playing hockey, but more so at Aspenridge. She brings treats to games and practices, serves dinners at our house, and is a listening ear for whenever a player misses home and needs "Mom" advice. Heck, she even rode in the ambulance when a prior teammate had no one to go to the hospital with. And I'm the lucky one to call her Mom.

After another round of high fives—Lennon doesn't miss a player —the team and I head to the locker room to change.

Outside the arena, I catch up with Lennon and Dad. "You riding with Poppa or me?"

"Poppa. His car needs a wash, and I'll watch from the window." Her voice pitches higher with her excitement. Dad likes to take her for the cheap entertainment value. If it's busy, she'll sit for a good hour without complaining, the suds covering the different vehicles fascinating her.

"Great. Have fun. What's Mimi making for dinner?"

She plants her feet wide and fists her hands on her hips. "How the heck should I know?"

"Didn't you ask her this morning?"

"Burgers on the grill," my father supplies, joining our conversation.

"Yum," I say, the same time Lennon yammers, "Yuck."

Dad and I laugh, Lennon's gaze volleying between us.

"Be good for Poppa. I'll see you when you get home." I lean down to her, presenting my cheek to her lips. With a smack, she leaves a kiss. "Love you, Squirt."

"Love you, Keeley."

My father chuckles, encouraging her use of the moniker. I can't blame him. I'm no better.

"Thanks, Dad. See you at home."

I climb into my truck as Lennon and Dad head for the van. The automatic door opens, and he lifts her inside, saying something to make her giggle. I can't hear their conversation or her laugh, but I love watching their connection.

He may not have wanted to be a grandfather so young, but he plays the part well. He spoils her in the best ways, and she's smart enough to know it. I wouldn't trade their relationship for anything.

I'm not sure who's more fortunate: me, for parents who embraced my unplanned teenage fatherhood, or her, for adoring and doting grandparents who never complain about helping to raise their kid's kid.

Definitely a toss-up.

CHAPTER 14
WALSH

The following Friday, after a long shower on my protesting muscles from a taxing practice, I dress quickly, needing to be at school to pick up Lennon. Megan said she was all out of sorts this morning, crying at the drop of a hat about anything and nothing at all.

Great.

I'm jazzed about this weekend. Unlike most weekends, we somehow have an open schedule with no game and not much on our agenda. I plan to lie low and enjoy the solitude.

When I get to preschool, I spy Mom's car. I scratch my head, wondering if I'm supposed to be somewhere else if she's here.

Guess I'll find out soon enough.

I park next to her, and she hops out.

"Did I miss the memo? What are you doing here?"

"Lennon asked me to come meet her friend Aubrey. So here I am. Figured I could take her for a treat." I can't be certain, but I swear she winks. Which makes this whole situation more bizarre.

Out of the corner of my eye, I spy Tate pulling in. She parks a few cars down.

A brilliant plan hits me.

"Hey, Ma. Think Aubrey can join you for the treat? Except, the girl doesn't like sweets, so maybe you could bring them to our house for a playdate. Let them play on the swing set since the weather's warm enough. Although Aubrey's not big on that either. Feed them some dinner." I sweeten the deal a little. "Aubrey will eat whatever you're making."

Mom kinda stares at me, unblinking. Possibly because I'm practically foaming at the mouth for her to agree.

Finally, her head bobs up and down. "If it's okay with Aubrey's mom, I don't have an issue with it. Think she'll agree?"

"When Lennon suggests it? Of course."

She raises a brow. "This should be good. Wish I had popcorn."

The doors to the school open, kids rushing out every which way. It's crazy how even at this age, the kids are excited for the weekend. As if their lives are so hard.

Please, kids. Just wait.

Lennon picks up the pace when she spots me, enthusiasm saturating her face. It's the same reaction I get every Friday when I haven't seen her since Wednesday morning. Sometimes Tuesday night if I have an early practice or study group. Which was the case this week.

I squat down, my arms open in anticipation of her flinging herself at me. "Missed you, Squirt. How was your day?" I cuddle her close, ignoring her squeals of protest of "too tight," soaking her up as long as she'll allow it.

"It was a boring day. 'Cept for recess. So fun."

"At least your day wasn't entirely boring. Glad to know my money's being well spent."

Mom comes over. Lennon squirms down out of my arms and rushes over to her.

"Mimi, you came. Let's find Aubrey so you can meet her." She grabs Mom's hand in hers and yanks her toward Tate and Aubrey, calling out so they don't leave before she can get to them. I trail behind, my mind already conjuring up what Tate and I can do with a couple of free hours this afternoon and early evening.

"Aubrey, this is Mimi. Mimi, this is my friend Aubrey. Say hello."

I roll my eyes at the way she orders my mother around. In all fairness, it's how her mother introduces her to most people. It should come as no surprise Lennon picked it up. How many bad habits has she picked up from me?

Not answering that.

Mom plays along. "Hello, Aubrey. It's nice to finally meet you. I've heard so many great things about you from Lennon. I'm Mimi."

Aubrey stands behind Tate, her head peeking out from the side of her legs.

"Bree, say hello to Lennon's grandma." Aubrey gives a tiny wave.

As the scene plays out, the bubbles of hope and excitement inside me wane. I truly don't think Tate will have a problem with Aubrey coming to our house, but I didn't consider Aubrey not wanting to go with a stranger to an unfamiliar place without her mother.

Hmm. A monkey wrench in my plan.

"Mimi, can Aubrey come to our house for a playdate today? I'll be extra good at bedtime. Please?"

I love when my kid can read my mind. It's definitely a gift we share. Ma gives me a look, a cross between "how the hell did you get her to do that" and "why am I not surprised?"

"I think Daddy has some errands to run, but if it's okay with Aubrey's mom, we'd love to have her come play with us."

Holding my breath, I glance at Tate, remembering she hasn't yet met my mother.

"Tate, this is my mother, Millie. Ma, Tate, Aubrey's mom." *And the woman I want to fuck while you watch our kids,* I elaborate nonverbally.

Jeez. My mind is on a one-way track to hell.

Maybe it won't be so bad if Tate's with me for the ride.

"Nice to meet you, Mrs. Keeley."

Ma frowns. "Millie, please. Mrs. Keeley is my mother-in-law."

Tate's face tints pink, becoming more endearing. "Oh, um, okay."

Lennon reminds us why we're still standing in the parking lot. "Tate, can Aubrey come play at my house? You and Mimi can have a chat. Like you did with Keeley at your house."

"Or," I interject expectedly, "you could help me with my errands."

Tate's demeanor turns questioning as she ponders my suggestion. She doesn't understand "errands" is code for sex. With her. At her empty condo.

Instead of answering either of us, she squats down to Aubrey's level. "Do you want to play at Lennon's house?"

Not able to stop myself, I disclose, "Mimi's making meatloaf for dinner," hoping it's enough of an enticement to convince her to go.

It piques her interest and after a short while—of which I hold my breath—her head nods up and down.

"Otay."

Internally, I fist pump. Half the battle was getting her there. Now, I need to get Tate to agree to my "errands."

"Do you want Mommy to come with you?"

Aubrey muses for a beat but gives nothing away. It's not until her, "I go meself, " does my heart skip a beat. Getting closer.

Tate's face registers shock, and I swear she exclaims, "Wow." She quickly schools her expression and smiles. "Sounds good. You're going to have so much fun."

"Yay!" Lennon yells, making Aubrey jump at how loud she is.

Do not ruin this for me, kid. Don't be a cockblocker, I chastise mentally.

"Do you want me to follow you to your house? I don't have an extra car seat."

"Walsh can put his seat in my car. It'll only take a few minutes."

"Oh, okay." There's a trace of reluctance in Tate's voice, but I can't make out why.

"Unless you're more comfortable driving her yourself."

Please say no.

Please say no.

Please say no.

"I go with Lennon," Aubrey states, settling the debate.

In five minutes, I secure my seat in Mom's van. To be on the safe side, I persuade Aubrey into the permanent one.

Tate gives Mom her phone number with explicit directions to call her with any issues. Mom assures her she'll be fine. I assume Tate's only hesitation is because Aubrey doesn't know my mother well, not that she doesn't trust her.

"Of course. Do what you need to do for a few hours. We'll have a great time playing, and I'll feed her dinner. Pick her up at seven?"

Tate worries her bottom lip into her mouth.

"She'll be fine," I whisper from her side. "Mom will call if there are any problems."

My words help to lessen her anxiety. "Thank you, Mrs—Millie. I appreciate it." To Aubrey, she says, "Be a good girl for Lennon's grandma. Use your manners and listening ears."

"I pomise, Mommy. I be good." She does something with her hand. If she were my kid, it would be a dismissal, but that doesn't seem like something Aubrey would do.

Taking Tate's hand, I lead her away from the car and step up on the sidewalk so Mom can pull out. Scanning the surrounding area, I lean in close to Tate's ear. "What do you suppose we do for a few hours without our kids?"

"I thought you had errands to run."

"Only those involving driving to your house and getting you naked."

She sucks in a breath, the hair on the back of her neck standing on edge at my insinuation and proximity.

"What do you know? Those exact errands were on my agenda today too. The whole 'getting' naked part was going to be later, before my shower, but I can alter the timeline."

Damn, her sass is downright sexy.

"One car or two?" My question comes out raspy, her direct effect on me.

"Whichever option gets us to my house faster."

"I knew I liked you for a reason. Come on." I waste no time dragging her to my truck. "Make sure your car's locked. We'll come back for it later tonight."

Once in the front seat, she fiddles with her key fob before the lights on her car blink on and off.

"I somehow feel you had a hand in this. It seems too convenient for your mom to have been at pickup today and for Lennon to have devised the plan herself."

"You've met my daughter, no?" Stopped at a light, I chance a look over at her. Sitting pretty in the passenger seat in jeans and a sweater, a smirk adorns the lips I can't wait to kiss. "I swear I had nothing to do with my mom being here nor Lennon asking." Because I'm nothing but truthful with Tate, I add, "But I did clear it with my mom first because I was working on a way to get Lennon to ask, but Scout's honor, she did it on her own."

Her dubious expression doubts me, but since she's agreed to my plan, I'm not concerned.

"I hope Aubrey's okay. School's the only place she goes without me. And we had a rough first week with the transition."

I reach for her hand, linking it in mine. "Mom will call if she's the least bit sad. I think she'll be okay. Lennon will make sure of it."

"She seems to read Aubrey well."

"It's eerie how she can read people sometimes."

Before long, I'm pulling into the lot of her complex. "You can park in my spot. 275," she directs. Before I even have the truck in park, her door swings open.

I relish watching as she hurries up the stairs and fiddles with the door, struggling to get it unlocked. She's adorable when she's flustered, and I can't wait to see how far I can coax her and how receptive she'll be during sex.

"Are you coming?" Her voice pops the bubble of my erotic thoughts, but it also gets me moving.

"Eager, much?" I question, stepping inside the door she holds open for me.

"Will you think less of me if I say yes?"

Instead of answering with words, I first grab her hand and bring it to my groin where I'm already hard. "Absolutely not. How fast can you get undressed?"

"Lock the door and lose your shoes," she requests over her shoulder, taking off for her bedroom.

Her demands followed, I head down the hall she disappeared, finding her bedroom, the only door on the left. She shimmies her jeans down her legs as I enter. For a moment, my eyes get lost on her. This gorgeous beauty I get to make mine for the afternoon.

And if all goes well, for more than today.

Completely naked, she climbs up on the bed. As I undress, a moment of sheer panic coats her face at what we're about to do. The blanket folded at the foot of her mattress soon covers her.

I go to protest, but it dies on my lips. Like her daughter, I need her to be comfortable with this. As much as she wants this, something's stopping her. Once I figure out what it is and we move past it, we'll have plenty of time to get to the main event.

Reluctantly leaving my boxers on, I join her on the queen bed, snuggling her in my arms. She situates her head on my chest, staying as covered as she can by the blanket.

"You want to talk about it?" I ask hesitantly, treading lightly, unsure how to proceed.

"It's nothing." Apprehension defies her words. Her lips purse, her thumbs twiddle, and her sight fixes on something across the room.

"Did you change your mind?" Like earlier, I hold my breath, hoping beyond all that's good in the world she hasn't.

"Not entirely."

"Did I move too fast?"

"Yes and no."

"Should I slow down?" As selfish as I try not to be, ending the day without burying myself inside Tate may make me weep actual tears. I'm too close to the goal.

"I haven't been with a guy since I got pregnant."

Her honesty slays me. I can't quite read her reservations. Is she worried it will happen again? Or is it more of letting me know how long it's been?

"Does that worry you?"

"Not completely, it's just, it's been a while."

She goes to say more, but I cut her off. "It had been a while since you were kissed too. Remember how great that was."

Her head slants to gaze up at me. "The best. You're a great kisser, Walsh."

Despite having nothing to do with it, my cock rejoices at the compliment. "I could say the same about you. Fireworks, Tate. We brought the fireworks with the kiss."

"Which one?"

"Both. I can honestly admit they were both explosive-worthy." Taking a risk, I arrange our bodies so she's straddling me, knocking the blanket away. My hands to her waist to steady her, before my eyes betray me and preview her breasts, I stare solidly into her eyes. "This can be too. Give me a chance?" My eyes drift downward to her breasts, and before I perceive what I'm doing, my hands cup each one. Smaller than a handful, there's not much to them, but they suit Tate perfectly.

Two fingers roll the nipples, pulling each to erect, helped by the chill in the air. Tate's breath hitches in her chest, the action the only clue I need to soldier on.

The pink buds are soft under my skin. Applying the lightest pressure, I gently tug, watching Tate's reaction. She rewards me by biting her bottom lip into her mouth, an almost inaudible moan slipping from her lips.

"Do you trust me?" I hope she knows the true depth of my question.

Ever so slowly, her head bobs up and down.

"Say the words, Tate."

"I trust you, Keeley."

My cock jumps, straining to be released. "Fuck." I shut my eyes, the sound of my last name on her pretty lips hitting me way too hard for my liking. Except, I like it way too much.

Her breasts still in my palms, she lets her head fall back, offering her neck for the taking. I lean in, blowing slowly on the exposed area.

Don't maul her neck, Keeley, my brain reminds me. *Don't leave a mark.*

With restraint I didn't realize I had, my lips meet her skin. Softly. Lightly. Tenderly. My tongue peeks out to lick a trail up one side, down the other. My teeth nibble playfully, careful not to mar her perfect skin.

"I want you." Tate whispers the words so quietly, I almost miss them.

"You have me. Tell me what you want."

I hand her the reins for where this goes. However fast or slow she wants it, I'm along for the ride.

And what a ride it's going to be.

"I don't have any condoms."

Everything around me comes to a screeching halt. Her words hang in the air as my actions stop.

Condoms?

Oh, shit. When arranging this afternoon, I didn't consider the damn condoms. No, my brain was too busy listening to my cock's one direction—get inside a naked Tate. Why would *he* be worried about covering up?

"Right. Condoms." My voice is strangled as my brain tries to overcome the fact I'm not prepared for this. I have Tate exactly where I want her—naked, in a bed, primed and ready for sex. And because of my unpreparedness, I have to stop.

My cock shrivels up and weeps.

"Doesn't every college guy carry at least one in his wallet like a rite of passage? That's what I was led to believe."

She's not wrong. But I'm highly certain I didn't replace the one I used when I had sex the last time.

She regards me with a pensive yet rueful expression, her chocolate eyes searing into me.

"I, uh, usually, but not today. I fucked this up royally. My one chance. You're naked and a willing participant, and I've got no condoms. I'm losing major points in your book, aren't I?"

"Honestly, no. Because you're man enough to admit your mistake and not pressure me into doing it anyway. That takes guts. And willpower."

"But we may never get this chance again." My tone is just short of whining.

"Never seems a little harsh, doesn't it? Maybe it won't be soon, but if you think we'll *never* get an hour or two to ourselves, I'm going to be incredibly frustrated for a long time. *Sexually* frustrated, if you catch my drift."

Strong emphasis on the *sexually*. The girl who, less than fifteen minutes ago, would barely let me see her naked, voices the comment. And my dick takes notice, stiffening to nearly painful.

"So, we'll get this chance again?"

She lies sideways next to me, her hand drawing lines on my chest, tangling in the short hair there. "Unless Aubrey has a horrible time at your house today, she'll probably want to go back. If your mom will have her again, of course." I'm about to reply, but she continues. "Oh, my aunt said she'd also babysit her. We have a standing invitation to Sunday night dinners, and we'll be going there for Thanksgiving. For a sleepover. After, I'm sure Aubrey will be comfortable enough for me to leave her with Aunt Marsha for an afternoon or something."

I like the sound of her plans, the wheels already spinning, wondering if we can schedule something now or if that seems too eager since Thanksgiving is still at least three weeks away.

Nonchalantly, I say, "That's cool. I'll make it work whenever's good for you."

She sits up, quirking her brows at me. "What if you have a game? Practice? Something else on your agenda?"

"So maybe we'll pick a date convenient for us both. Better?"

Her smile brightens up the room. "Much."

As much as I'm enjoying the closeness, when I thought up this brilliant—but not so well thought-out—plan, it wasn't to cuddle. It was for sex. At the minimum, sexual things.

My mind prompts there are plenty of things we can do not involving condoms yet still resulting in orgasms.

I slide out of Tate's hold. Kneeling at the foot of the bed, I yank her legs. A startled gasp echoes around the room as Tate reacts to the not-so-smooth motion. It's because I'm rushing. I don't want to waste a single moment before I taste her.

"Spread your legs wider." She obeys instantly, her thighs parting enough to fit my head in between without it being squeezed. I shimmy her body a little more, lifting her legs at the knees to rest on my shoulders.

My tongue licks my lips in anticipation of how sweet she'll taste. I can't wait for the noises she makes and how she looks when she orgasms. Although it may be a little hard to see her face when I'm ravishing her pussy. Next time.

Opening her thighs marginally wider, I trail my fingers up the sides. They quake at the slightest touch.

This is going to be so fun to watch her come undone.

With no further hesitation, my tongue traces up her slit, her "Oh shit" resonating around the room. It's not loud by any means, but it pierces the silence.

"Do it again."

I do. This time, two quick licks rather than one long.

Her hips buck off the bed. I like how she's so receptive to my touch. No matter what part of me caresses her, she reacts.

I suck her clit into my mouth, swirling the nub around before letting go. She rewards me with a long, drawn-out moan from deep in her throat.

Music to my ears.

I raise my head so I can observe her. "More, Tate?"

Her head doesn't even leave the bed. "You can't stop now. I'm close, but not there yet. Not even close enough."

My only response is to swipe again, massaging the inside of her canal. Her flavor on my tongue turns me on more. I don't want to blow before she's done. Heck, I'm not a teenager—I don't want to shoot in my shorts. I should have been more prepared to ache. I should have been prepared with condoms. That would have been smart. Not only for me, but for both of us. Because experiencing sex with Tate is high on my priority list.

I flatten my tongue against her clit. It tips the scales, forcing her over the cliff. While she thrashes on the bed, I lap up the mess dripping out, not leaving a single drop behind.

"Fuck. Fuckity. Fuck. So good. Too good. How?"

Her incoherent words elicit a chuckle. Rubbing my hand across my jaw, I clean up the evidence of her.

Tate lies boneless on the bed, her chest moving up and down in an erratic pattern. She's a beautiful sight. Sated with her orgasm, coming down from the high.

And the image is too much.

Should I be ashamed to admit I lose the battle with myself?

As I stroke my dick, I groan, more out of relief than embarrassment. That's going to be a bitch to clean up.

"Wow," Tate breathes. "I didn't, um, I didn't know it could be so good."

I grunt my agreement.

After sex cuddles aren't my thing. But damn if I don't lie down next to her, pulling her on top of me. It's way too much effort to clean us up, pull clothes on, let alone actually leave.

Tate settles her head on my chest, the pounding of my heart vibrating against her ear.

"I don't know whether I should feel bad you've yet to experience something so great or be grateful I was the one to make you experience it." She interlaces our hands together, the contrast of her small palm against my larger one catching my eye.

"I can't wait for actual sex. It's going to be the trifecta."

"I'm sorry it can't be now. I feel—"

Her finger covers my lips as she picks up her head. "Don't apologize again. What we just did is way more than I thought I'd get to do today. It'll happen when the time is right."

"Whenever it is, it'll be before never."

She relaxes back against me. I can't remember the last time I felt this at ease with a woman without having sex. Was there even a "last time"?

Megan, my mind provokes.

Which is most likely true. We experienced a lot during our four years together, Lennon being the best thing to come from our failed relationship. Meg taught me a lot about myself, a lot about love, and also, what I don't want with a long-term committed partner.

"How much longer do we have before we're due at your house? I feel like I need a shower."

"There was mention about seven," I admit, pulling the detail from the sex fog in my head.

"Alexa, what time is it?"

"Good afternoon. It's 4:36 p.m."

"When is dinnertime?"

"Most nights, around six. Should we shoot to be there for then? Enough time to shower without rushing, right?"

She's quiet for a long while. Or what seems long. I wonder if she's fallen asleep. I wouldn't blame her. All blissed out on an orgasm, no kid to care for. A quick rest is a clever use of our time.

"Tate, you awake?"

"Want me to return the favor?"

I have an inkling of what she's referring to, but I need her to voice the words.

"The favor?"

"A blow job." Her voice shakes on the word blow, making her seem uncomfortable. I never want her to feel that way, nor like she owes me anything.

"We do, but you are under no obligation. I'm not a tit-for-tat kinda guy."

She sits up quickly, wrapping the blanket around her shoulders. "It probably wouldn't be any good anyway."

I find that hard to believe. I've been the recipient of her kisses. "Your mouth on my dick? Nothing not to like."

Straight-faced and no-nonsense, she declares, "You'd be my first."

Both the words and the delivery of her comment floor me.

CHAPTER 15
TATE

push the words out of my mouth. Walsh's cobalt eyes enlarge, complete shock washing over his face.

"You've never given a blow job?"

Not able to answer with words, I shake my head.

I didn't think I'd be telling him this our first time together. Except there's something about his dick almost begging for me to suck.

His mouth opens several times, but no words come out. The adrenaline I felt soon after coming on his tongue has long since vanished, replaced by a feeling of dread at my admission. He's probably mad he went down on me when he won't get the same treatment. Maybe he's rethinking inviting himself over.

My shoulders raise to my ears. "See, wouldn't be any good for you. Forget I mentioned it. At least you got off, right?"

"That's what you think?" He sits up straight, his narrowed eyes meeting mine. "I got off because I couldn't hold myself back watching you come. Because that was fucking sexy as hell, Tate. *You* did that." His tone softens as he continues to speak, and my mind swirls with the possibility of how wrong I may be. "Even if you gave me the worst head of my life, I'd still blow. Receiving it from you. Please don't think anything else."

There's something about the way he words the explanation, the way he makes me feel so special, so respected, helping ease all insecurities. Without him realizing what he's doing.

I make a snap decision, reaching my hands toward his dick. He impels them away before I can make contact.

"No. Not like this."

And the bubble of optimism deflates, all the air hissing out in one big whoosh.

"Right," I grit out. Not in anger so much as frustration.

"Once more. Confirm for me you've never given a blow job to any other guy?"

His question irritates me more. Twice I told him, and he needs further confirmation? Is he trying to humiliate me?

"Never. Not once in my life have my lips sucked a guy off. Or even attempted the act."

The left corner of his lip quirks up into a grin. A contented grin. "Awesome. I'm honored to be your first."

Um, what?

Honored?

Did I hear him correctly?

It's my turn for resolute verification. "Can you repeat that?"

"Your first ever blow job. That'll be me. Next time we're together." Assurance accompanies his words, a sense of he can't wait for it to happen.

"What if I suck at it?" I flinch as the words leave my mouth. "No pun intended."

"Then you suck. And we'll try another time. It's not the end of the world to go without blow jobs for a few weeks. Trust me." He smiles again, a little bigger.

Although he didn't pose it as a question, I answer it anyway. "I do trust you. I already can't wait for next time. We're going to need a lot more than a couple of hours."

This man brings out my bold side, the one who's laid dormant since the day in the school bathroom when she walked out pregnant. I'm digging her. Hopefully, with a few more years' experience —as well as being a mom—she's learned to be more cautious.

"Like a sleepover?" he suggests happily.

The shock value of his words hits like a blow to the head.

A sleepover? With Walsh? How would that work?

His fingers on my chin draw my focus back to him. "It will all work itself out. Don't fuss over the semantics or the logistics of how it will get done. We'll get there. I'm happy to wait."

"What if *I'm* not?" My subconscious mind conjures up the idea. As much as I want this with him, I have some patience.

Maybe.

My knees touch his thighs. He flashes the most ridiculous yet adorable smirk. "Oh, but you will have patience. That's all there is to it." He reaches his arms out to pull me into him, I assume, but instead, he shifts me out of his way and crawls out of my bed. He strides purposefully for the door, his posterior on full display. If I thought it looked good in clothes, I was sorely mistaken.

Hot damn.

The muscles of his powerful thighs flex with each step, his tight ass outlined in his boxer briefs. Like solid globes of muscle. As if he does one hundred squats a day.

Stopping at the doorway, one arm on the jamb, he half turns to me. "Good thing you need to shower. You need to wipe up the pool of drool on your chin."

Dazedly, I swipe my fingers over my face, coming up dry. Realizing he's caught me, his left eye winks as a playful laugh fills my bedroom.

"So, I'll shower first?"

"S-sure," I stammer, my tongue feeling too big for my mouth.

Only when he's completely out of sight do I drop back onto the bed, the breath I didn't realize I was holding expelling loudly.

He called me out on my staring, yet I can't stop the smile spreading across my face.

The fact he somehow got us alone. Even though we didn't have sex—neither one of us taking a chance without protection—it still tops the list of best sexual interactions I've ever had. Jeez, what's going to happen when we have sex?

"It's going to be incredible," I whisper to the empty room.

Without the result of what happened last time—my body can't help but shiver—I don't know if I'll be able to handle the act itself.

While Walsh is in the shower, I imagine it, but as soon as the water stops, I shut down the inappropriateness. One, we don't have time for anything else. Two, I don't want to overthink it too much, make it out to be something amazing in my head that fizzles in reality. Not in a million years do I think that might happen, but still.

Hop off the sex-thoughts train, Tate.

Walsh reappears in the doorway in my towel. Small drops of water fall from his short strands of hair cascading down his naked, broad chest. My eyes can't help but gawk at him. At the sheer muscles in his pecs, a hockey stick tattoo inked on the right one. At his well-defined, six-pack abs, the delineated divots begging to be licked. The trim waist, the cut V lines disappearing into the towel. Who knew those existed outside of fictional book boyfriends?

His voice slices into my perusal. "It's all yours. Hope you don't mind I used your shampoo and soap."

My mouth, dry as the Sahara, forbids me from speaking. My head nods—I think.

Slowly, I get off the bed, my mind on anything but the task at hand. He blocks the exit, and I'm compelled to stop in front of him. The scent of my soap mixed with a hint of something else floods my nostrils.

Walsh, my mind provides. The "something else" is Walsh.

"Tate?"

"Hmm?"

"Are you okay?"

His question tears me out of my salacious thoughts.

"Define okay."

His thumb tips my chin up, forcing my focus on him. The shower made him even sexier.

"We don't have much time," I start, "but all I'm going to think about while I shower is picturing you naked in the same space. It's going to be so hard."

At the second unintentional pun of the evening, my eyes betray me and glance down. It's subtle, but the slightest bulge tents the towel. A heady feeling washes over me, forcing my eyes to close and my arm to reach out and steady myself on Walsh's chest.

I require five deep breaths to calm myself, to refrain from making a move, any move, toward Walsh.

"Tate, I said I could wait, but if you could make it a little easier for me, my willpower would appreciate it. I'm trying to be a gentleman right now, so if you could help me out and go shower, I promise it will be entirely worth it. No matter how long the wait is."

I want to say so many things, question everything he's said. Instead, I obey his request.

Besides, it's not like I don't need the space from him.

Not accounting for how much his being in my personal space would truly affect me, I take the world's quickest shower. He's not in my room when I return, and I breathe a sigh of relief at being able to dress without him observing. The idea of him seeing me naked again, watching me get into my clothes, is a turn-on, but since we can't act on any other feelings tonight, it's best this way. However, it doesn't stop me from debating for a solid five minutes on what to wear. In the end, I decide on skinny jeans and a long sweater.

Walsh relaxes on my couch, scrolling through his phone. He wears the same clothes he came in—black sweats and an Aspenridge hockey hoodie—but his hair's still damp. He's run his fingers through it, and the result causes my heart to skip a beat.

Does this man never not exude sex?

He glances up from his phone while I stand and gape at him. In all fairness, his eyes ogle my body, one scan up and down, a devious simper sprouting on his lips.

"Mom texted. The girls are having tons of fun. She said they'll probably eat around 6:30 and you're welcome to join us. She wanted to make sure I specifically extended her invite to you, as if me telling you to eat dinner with us wasn't enough."

Too lost in the sight of him, I'm not exactly sure I comprehend the words coming out of his mouth. Somehow my brain gets the memo and my mouth speaks. "I'd like that, thanks."

He pushes off the couch, using all of his six feet to stand up straight. A man on a mission, he eliminates the gap between us in five strides.

"I want to kiss you right now, one last proper kiss before we have to be parents again."

"Do it," I challenge, the butterflies in my abdomen fluttering wildly at the mere thought of our lips touching.

"It's going to be so unsatisfying."

The butterflies' wings halt mid-flap, any excitement I felt in the past few minutes draining out.

He shakes his head. "Oh my god. That's so wrong. I just meant..."

Sucking in a breath, I wait for him to speak. I thought we had moved past the awkwardness and were on the same page. But now, it's *going to be so unsatisfying* to kiss me? Why did he bother even mentioning it?

"I want to kiss you."

"You're confusing me," I mutter with a big exhale, the words rushing out like a geyser.

He inches closer. "I want more than just a kiss goodbye."

My brows knit together. "This isn't goodbye. We're having dinner at your parents'."

"And then what? When can I see you again?"

My mouth opens, but no words emerge. As previously discussed, I have no idea. But I'm cluing into what he means about the kiss.

"I want you to kiss me too, but maybe it's better if it's just quick."

His breaking point reached, he mumbles, "Fuck that."

I'm in the air before I can process what's happening as his lips cover mine. My legs wrap around his waist as I slacken into him and the kiss.

Every coherent thought escapes me, solely absorbed in Walsh. The way his mouth greedily devours mine. How his tongue thrusts into my mouth without permission. How our teeth nearly clash because the intensity of the kiss is so molten.

It continues in this manner for a few minutes. With each sweep of his tongue against some part of me, I loosen deeper and deeper. My arms behind his neck, I'm barely holding on. Thank goodness his hands cup my ass, not allowing me to fall.

When I can't stand it any longer, I move my mouth away, filling my lungs with huge amounts of fresh air. While we recover from the kiss, Walsh doesn't let me go, squeezing me tighter, taking away my option to untangle myself.

A few more minutes pass, our collective heavy panting the only sound in the room. My chin finds rest on his shoulder, and he somehow lays his forehead on mine.

"That was…" I begin, the words to finish the sentence evading me.

"As far as kisses go," Walsh inserts, "perfection."

Though he can't see it, I smile. That sums it up extremely well.

I slide down his front, the fact he's hard not eluding my notice. We don't have time to remedy it.

My brain tries to find the words to thank him for today. "Thank you for orchestrating time alone for you to get me off" hardly seems appropriate, yet "thank you" doesn't do it justice either. In the end, I say nothing. Not until I've had a chance to work through exactly what I want to say.

Wordlessly, we both head to the door, putting our feet into shoes, ready for this afternoon to be over. And though it's the beginning of this between us, I can't help but feel a little sad and unfulfilled.

Walsh must sense how I'm feeling or experiencing similar things. At the truck, he pulls me into his arms.

"Not to sound too cliché, but there's something here to explore. You feel it too?"

"Yeah."

With a final embrace, he releases me. "And now I have to pretend in front of our daughters I haven't seen you naked. Or that I can't wait until I get to see you again. This should be fun."

I can't help the snort at his expense. "Hope it won't be too *hard* for you."

A guttural groan tears out of him. He mumbles something under his breath on his side of the truck. I only make out my name.

An unfamiliar emotion takes root. The satisfaction of the power I wield over him makes me giddy.

Walsh refuses to pick up my car on the way to his house. Outwardly, I pretend to fester, but inwardly I do cartwheels of joy getting to spend extra time with him later this evening.

He pulls up in front of his house, a medium Cape on a tree-lined street. Immediately, a sense of comfort washes over me with a glance at the outside. The paint peels in a few areas, but I like how it's not perfect. It reminds me of home, not in style, but emanating a similar vibe to our rustic ranch.

I grew up in a blue-collar, working town. Almost everyone who lives in Cedarvale is roughly in the same tax bracket, a few outliers at either end are the only exception. My family is smack in the middle—we have enough without being extravagant or wanting for more. Our house is the same size as the rest of our neighbors, topping the scale at just under two thousand square feet. Mom uses the space the open floor plan provides well.

When Aubrey was born, neither of my parents batted an eye at losing out on the guest bedroom. Not like it was utilized often. In five years, they did more than accommodate our living space. Maybe one day, we'll be able to go home, but for now, I'm living in the present.

"This is where you grew up?" I ask, taking in other features—the black door to match the black shutters, the patches of grass on both sides of the house, the two stairs up to the door.

"We moved here when I was in middle school." His tone implies there's more to the story, but I don't press for an explanation. He's already highly emotional. No need to poke the bear.

"It's cozy." After the words leave my mouth, I realize how that must sound. Except he's been to my place—the rental I don't pay for —so who am I to judge? Which I wasn't doing by any means.

When he lets my comment go, I release the breath. "It was a hard change, but it's home for now. At least until I graduate and find a job and get my own place." Melancholy undertones layer his remarks. Again, I don't push it. Not really my place, but I hope one day, it will be my place to learn more.

I climb out the passenger door. Stopping in front of the hood of the truck, I wait for Walsh. He joins me, but in fear of being caught in a compromising position, I don't step too close.

"Before we go inside, I wanted to say another thanks. As much as it's going to be difficult to pretend we didn't do what we did, especially in front of your parents, I wouldn't change anything about our afternoon."

He arches a brow in disbelief. "Even though we didn't have sex?"

"Even still. You made me feel so cherished. I don't think I've ever felt that way." Honesty flows out of me around this man like lava from an active volcano.

"It pains me to hear you admit that. However, I'm not sorry I'm the one who gets to show you how you deserve to be treated. Not just in the bedroom."

"Me too. I'm not sorry it's you."

His arms open wide, inviting me to fall into him. And I allow myself a quick hug, breathing in every ounce of his essence, forcing myself away when I begin to feel too comfortable.

He motions me ahead of him, his hand resting on my back as we make our way to the front door. Once inside, he calls out, "Honey, we're home."

Footsteps echo from above us, and soon Lennon appears on the stairs, Aubrey lagging.

"Keeley. Finally. Aubrey and me are starving. What the heck took you so long?" Her actions defy the sass she extends Walsh's way—she jumps into his arms from the bottom step. He doesn't miss a beat in catching her.

"Boring grown-up stuff. Be thankful you didn't come."

Aubrey's exuberant grin and sparkling eyes greet me as she bubbles with excitement. "Mommy, you're here! Do we have to leave yet? Because we didn't have dinner and Mimi made super special biscuits I want to eat."

Lifting her off the ground, I cuddle her into my chest, breathing in her scent. Besides school, this is the only time she's been away from me since we moved. As enjoyable as our afternoon was, I missed her. But seeing her this excited tamps down the mom guilt. We were each having our own fun.

"Hey, Bree. Did you have fun?"

"Yep. So fun. So can we stay? Please?" Her wide eyes plead with me to agree.

"How can I turn down super special biscuits? They're your favorite."

"Yay!" She covers my face in kisses, prompting giggles from both of us.

"Squirt, you excited about Mimi's super special biscuits?" Walsh asks.

I turn my head just in time to catch Lennon's reaction.

"The ones she makes once a week? Oh yeah. Can't wait."

Five. Years. Old. And the girl has mastered the art of sarcasm. I'm not sure if I should laugh or cringe.

She wiggles herself out of Walsh's arms, Aubrey doing the same. They scurry off toward the back of the house.

"How did she learn sarcasm?"

"That would be my tutelage. Megan hates it."

Remembering what he's mentioned before, I smirk. "So let me guess. You encourage it more."

"Bingo." He boinks my nose. "I know it's wrong, and it's inevitable before it bites me in the ass, but damn, it's hysterical."

"I should disagree with you, but you're not wrong. Quite impressive."

He bows, complete with one arm at his waist, the other behind his back. "Why thank you. For only seventy-five dollars an hour, I could tutor Aubrey. Probably only take a few hours before she fully grasps the concept." He pauses a moment in concentration. "Scratch that. First, I'll teach your daughter sarcasm, then I'll teach you how to give a mind-numbing blow job. Two for one deal."

Only joking, his words don't sink in fully right away.

"Just the blow job lessons are necessary. I have a feeling Aubrey won't completely understand sarcasm until she's a teenager. If then."

Despite the fact I have no idea where I'm going, I leave him standing in the front hallway, traipsing to where the girls ran off.

Dinner with the Keeley family is interesting. There's a fun dynamic between Walsh and his mom. He obviously gets most of his personality from her. Gary, his dad, says little but gives off a calm, happy vibe. He thanks his wife several times throughout the meal, complimenting her. I'd say he's going overboard, but it's damn delicious. And I thought my mom was a superb cook.

My two favorite parts of the meal are how Millie gushes over how well Aubrey eats, almost making Lennon feel guilty for eating noodles and the super special biscuits. Not once does she take the bait. The other is sneaking peeks at Walsh. I try to be stealthy, but I doubt I am.

He catches my eyes a few times. The smile he returns nearly ignites a fire within me.

Wouldn't that be an interesting headline for the news tomorrow: "Man invites new girlfriend over for dinner; girlfriend goes up in flames, burning down the house."

Wow, Tate. Overactive imagination?

After Walsh and his dad clean up, Aubrey and I finally say our goodbyes.

Millie starts, addressing Aubrey first. "Aubrey, I hope you had a good time today and you'll come back and visit soon. You're always welcome at our house."

Without prompting, Aubrey replies, "Thank you. I'll come back." My daughter initiates a hug with Millie.

My heart squeezes with her declaration and action. Her being comfortable in a place other than home isn't easy for her. The fact it's Walsh's family certainly has its benefits.

And no, they aren't all sexual benefits.

Next, it's my turn. "Tate, it's been my pleasure having Aubrey and you at our home. Please don't be a stranger." With her embrace, a feeling of immediate comfort washes over me. As she releases me, she whispers not so quietly, "If you have any tips to get kids to try new foods, send them my way."

I can't help the laugh tumbling out. "It's nothing I did. She has an extremely varied palate."

"I heard that, Mom," Walsh exclaims with a pout.

"You were supposed to, boy."

"Thank you for having Aubrey for the afternoon and extending the invite to dinner. We always appreciate your leftovers." When the sentence leaves my mouth, I cringe at how it must sound—begging for food. I'm about to clarify, but Millie saves me.

"I'll remember for the future." She silences for a minute, giving Walsh some side-eye. "Be sure to inform me when you need more than leftovers. I raised a good boy, but he's not perfect."

Should I feel more affronted she's hinting at knowing something is going on between Walsh and me? Because all I feel is relaxed and invigorated.

"I wouldn't expect him to be. So far, I like what I've seen."

Apparently, my honesty policy extends to his family members as well.

"Tate and Aubrey have to be going now. I need to drop them to their car, so I'll be back in a bit. Be useful and give Lennon her bath, would ya?"

I wait with wide eyes for her to call him out on his issued demand. No doubt she perceived his teasing tone, but still. She is his mother.

Instead of reprimanding him, she returns, "At least she smells better when I do it."

Pretty sure my chin drops to the floor. I'm also certain I want to be around to witness more of this dynamic.

Walsh directs us to his mother's car since his seat is still in there. Without hesitation, he leads Aubrey over to the side of the car with the permanent seat. Shock doesn't describe the emotions surging through me. Not because of his actions, but Aubrey's. She doesn't bat an eyelash when he lifts her and clasps her buckle, making sure it's fastened securely.

Shit.

As if I need more excuses to fall for this guy. Now he's got my daughter wrapped around his finger too.

When he climbs behind the wheel, he glimpses at me. His face changes into confusion. "What's wrong? Did I overstep? Oh, she can probably buckle herself. Lennon can too, but I always make sure it's tight and…"

My hand to his, I cut off his apology. "You don't have to be perfect. Just don't hurt us."

I so badly want to kiss him, but Aubrey's watching. And while she might not know what it means exactly, I won't put her in a place to question it.

His eyes travel to the rearview mirror. With a smile and his eyes locked on my daughter's, he promises, "I have no intentions."

Please let that be the case.

CHAPTER 16
TATE

t's almost two weeks until I see Walsh again for a significant amount of time.

The first week, their house came down with some nasty bug. He sent a dozen "I'm dying" texts in three days. I dropped off some chicken soup and a few other groceries on their front porch. When he opened the door to retrieve the items, he legit looked like he could be dying. I felt a little guilty for thinking he was making it up. Thank goodness I never mentioned it to him. It was easier to justify in my mind.

Aubrey and I stayed healthy despite being at their house, which I'm grateful for.

He was busy with hockey the next week so Megan or Millie picked up Lennon from school.

To occupy my time, I put in way more hours at work than normal. I started and abandoned five different books, none of them keeping my attention beyond chapter two. I deep cleaned the condo. Twice. We spent a lot of time at Aunt Marsha's house, planning the menu for Thanksgiving, Googling recipes, making grocery lists for her to shop, and just catching up. I left Aubrey for an hour each time to ease her into getting used to another adult. Just like at Walsh's, Aubrey enjoyed her visit.

Aubrey's invited to a Friendsgiving tomorrow at her friend Callen's house. According to her, he's not really her friend. The entire class is invited, as well as their families. Must be nice to have a house big enough to host so many people.

I'm not dreading it only because Walsh will be there. His game this weekend is on Sunday. He keeps hinting I should come see him play. Since it's an away game, it was an easy excuse to say no.

While I want to see him in action playing the sport he loves—what's not to like about sexiness and athleticism all wrapped up in a hunky body—I know nothing about hockey beyond they wear skates, play in a frigid ice rink, and shoot pucks around to score goals.

Oh, and they fight like toddlers.

Yeah, not high on my priority list.

I've spent today going through a difficult amount of dictation. One was an hours-long surgery. The dictation didn't last that long, but the doctor muffled every third word. It was a lot of rewind, replay, repeat. And I'm still not sure I got it all.

Walsh texts around lunchtime.

Want to hang out tonight?

He's not asking me on a date. He learned that lesson. But I'm unsure what "hang out" implies.

By hang out, you mean...

Lennon and I bring dinner to you and Aubrey. Kids can play freeing up the adults to do whatever their minds can conjure up.

If only that were true...

I've got an entire list of ideas of what I'd like to do with him when we get to be alone together. Which isn't panning out to anytime soon, unfortunately.

We could Netflix and chill. The total PG version

I'll take time with you any way I can get it

My heart jumps at his compliment. Because he's completely genuine with his words.

> You're the sweetest

My phone pings with another text, but it's Aunt Marsha.

> Hey! If the sleepover goes well on Wednesday night, think Aubrey'd want to stay by herself Friday or Saturday night?

It's wrong for me to say yes even if she won't be, right?
Yeah, I thought so.
But what if she was? Then it wouldn't be wrong, right?
An entire night to myself. Whatever would I do with all the time?
For pure shits and giggles, I inquire about Walsh's availability.

> Hypothetically speaking, you free either Friday or Saturday night after Thanksgiving?

> Lennon comes back Saturday afternoon. I've got some team thing on Friday night

> Does this team thing last all night?

> No

I go back to the thread with Aunt Marsha.

> Can we pencil in Friday and play it by ear? Worst-case scenario, I sleep at your house after going out for the night

> Great. Putting it on my calendar now. Is she a hot cocoa fan?

> Negative

> Does the girl eat popcorn at least?

> She'll tolerate it on special occasions

> She makes it hard to spoil her with treats

> She'll be happy as a pig in mud if you make her a plate of fruit

I can do that!

I was so busy texting with her, I missed a few from Walsh.

What are you thinking?

How hypothetical is this situation?

Tate. Don't leave me hanging

Sorry. I'll explain later. Are you coming right from pickup?

Want me to grab Aubrey so you don't have to come out in this crappy rain?

His sweet gesture has me conflicted. My head rationalizes I'm not comfortable with him driving my baby home from school. My heart screams with delight at his sweet gesture.

When I don't respond after a few minutes—because I'm hemming and hawing and overthinking my decision—my phone rings with his name displayed.

"Hello?"

"Hey. I'm sorry. I overstepped again. I thought it would save you a trip since we're coming to your house anyway."

"It's really sweet, Walsh. I just…it's not you, it's me." I don't quite have the words to elaborate where my mind's at. Because I think she'll be fine going with him, and it makes total sense. But I can't help this tightening in the pit of my stomach.

Besides my parents—and now Aunt Marsha—I've never relied on anyone else to help with Aubrey. There's a sense of control I have to let go of to agree to his offer. And I don't know if I'm there yet.

However, not having to put on shoes and trek out in the pouring rain does sound rather appealing…

"You know what? Yes. Pick her up. Tell me what I have to do for the school. I can't imagine you can show up and bring her with you even though they know you."

"Are you sure? I don't want you to regret your decision later."

"Yes, Walsh. I'm sure and appreciate you checking. I trust you." My tone is more reassuring, more confident in my decision.

The knot in my stomach remains, but it has little to do with Walsh.

"Awesome. Call the office and let them know I'll be picking her up. I'll text you when we're on the way." I can practically hear the smile in his voice. "What do you want for dinner? Or should we order later and have it delivered?"

"We were going to make pizzas, but we can do that tomorrow night instead. Does the place next to the grocery store deliver or do pickup? Their menu is extensive, but we've yet to try it."

"Homegrown Bistro? I believe so. Once I get there, we can double-check."

"Cool. See you soon."

Drive safe lingers on the tip of my tongue, but I hold it in. I don't want him to interpret the message the wrong way.

"Tate?" he asks, a little less pep in his voice.

"Yeah?"

"It's going to kill me not to kiss you tonight. If it seems like I don't want to, that's not the case."

Though he can't see, I smile at his words.

"Same goes for me."

"Good. See you later. Bye."

He hangs up without waiting for a response.

Walsh's "on our way" text comes as I'm working on a batch of pretzels. I'm so lost in my head combining ingredients, I jump at the sound of the doorbell.

Rushing to the front door, I throw it back, met with a beautiful sight: my daughter holding a gorgeous bouquet of red and purple flowers. Her smile stretches across her entire face. When she realizes the door is open, it grows bigger. As if that's possible.

My heart stutters in my chest, kick-started only when I hear her voice. "Mommy, Mr. Walsh pick me up from school. And Lennon gets to stay for a playdate."

Her enthusiasm spikes my own. It elevates when my gaze locks on Walsh, who stands off to the side behind my daughter. Lennon sits in his arms, her smile not as big as Aubrey's.

Dragging my eyes from Walsh's blues, I peer down at my daughter and find my voice. "What a great surprise for the afternoon." I open the storm door, motioning them all inside. The rain appears to have let up for the moment, so they aren't soaking wet. "Come in. Let's get shoes off and have a snack."

Aubrey's eyes go wide. "Pretzels?"

"They'll be ready soon."

She hands me the blooms as she scurries past through the door, sitting down on the floor to remove her shoes. Walsh and Lennon enter, and he somehow removes her shoes before setting her down. Is there anything this man can't do?

"Thanks for letting us come over. I'm super excited to play with the American Girl dolls again." Lennon squints, her eyes gleaming with delight. Two tiny buns are pinned on each side of her head.

"It's literally all she's talked about since I picked them up," Walsh reports.

"Aubrey will be excited to play with them too." I motion to the flowers in my hand. "Did you pick these out?"

"Nah. That's all Keeley." Her little nose scrunches. "They smell funny."

"Saves me from having to ever buy you any, Squirt."

My gaze travels from dad to daughter. "Don't let him get away with that, Lennon. Your dad's one of the good guys, and one day, you'll want flowers from your dad. *Especially* from your dad."

She observes me like I've said something funny—not comical—but something she doesn't quite understand. With a shrug of her petite shoulders, she asks, "I go play now?"

"Sure thing."

"Wash your hands first," Walsh prompts after her as she disappears toward Aubrey's room.

Alone with Walsh, I stick my nose in the flowers. "These smell incredible. Thank you."

It's the third bouquet I've gotten from him. The week he was sick, he had them delivered right as the others died.

"You're welcome." Cognizant to not rattle the blossoms in my hand, he pulls me into him. "You smell incredible."

"I hadn't planned on showering until later tonight but managed a bath with the extra time you saved me not having to do pickup." I debate about how honest I want to be with him. Deciding to go for it, I add, "Took under five minutes to get myself off knowing you were coming over."

A groan unleashes from deep within him. Shutting his eyes, he hangs his head back. "And now I'm hard. I didn't need to picture that, Tate. Not when I can't kiss you properly."

My good mood spoils. He's completely right. We can't risk the girls seeing us being intimate. It will send the wrong message. Especially because this is all still so new.

And he could decide at any moment you aren't what he wants.

The timer sounds from the kitchen.

"I made sourdough pretzels." I hand him the flowers. "Replace the old ones with these, will ya?"

"Sure."

He follows me to the kitchen, his presence so large in my small space.

"How was your day?" Walsh disposes of the wilted stems in the trash can and arranges the new ones in the vase. He takes several tries to get it exactly the way he wants. "Remind me to take out the trash before we leave."

He never leaves without doing some kind of chore. Never asked, but always appreciated.

"Thanks," I return with a smile. "Saves me a trip to the dumpster this weekend." I open the oven door, checking on the pretzels. They need one more minute, so I shut the door and set the timer. I'll get too lost in Walsh and forget about what's in the oven. "Work was frustratingly annoying. All kinds of mumbled jargon I couldn't make out and too many unfamiliar words to spell. I'll have to catch up on more stuff tomorrow after the party. How about you?"

I lean up against the counter. Walsh sits at the table, positively edible in his Aspenridge hoodie and sweats. He must have run a brush through his hair today because it's not as disheveled as usual.

"That sucks. I spent the entire day in the library, attempting to write a paper for my sociology class and failed miserably. I have no ideas about how to help our community better themselves in terms of socioeconomic groups."

I chuckle, not understanding. "Yeah, I'll stick with nephrology." His expression turns inquisitive. "All things related to the kidneys and renal systems."

"Shit, it's hot when you talk medical terms." His eyebrows waggle. Hotness overload.

Heat creeps up my neck when the timer beeps again. I exaggerate my ass wiggle as I bend over to remove the pretzels.

"Stop tempting me, Tate. A guy's only got so much self-control." His throaty voice emboldens me further.

"I know a lot of medical terms. A lot." To demonstrate, I list the ones sounding the sexiest. Or that's my intention in my head. "Toxicology. Rheumatoid. Corpora cavernosa."

The last word not even out of my mouth, he hops up, caging me against the stove. His chest rises and falls, his heavy breathing hot on my neck. He presses his semi-hard dick into my stomach.

"When can we start those blow job lessons? 'Cause that dirty mouth of yours needs to be thoroughly punished."

Shit. I didn't anticipate his dirty words.

His closeness, coupled with his erection, lights all the nerve endings ablaze. An inferno raises my internal temperature to boiling. My breath quickens as anticipation prances through me.

"Mommy, are the pretzels ready yet?"

At the sound of Aubrey's voice, Walsh backs up. I immediately feel the loss of him. As much as we can't get caught, having him pressed up against me stirred something deep within, a promise of more. A want for more. No, a *need* for more.

"To be continued." My racing heart slowly calms down.

The girls come dashing into the room.

"Hands washed?" They both nod enthusiastically. "Have a seat at the table." Lennon follows my direction while Aubrey throws her arms around my legs.

"This is such a great day, Mommy. Thank you, thank you."

I sometimes wonder why she chose me to be her mother because she always makes me feel like I'm doing everything right. Even when I lose my shit and have no clue what I'm doing, she has this way of making everything seem better. Before she knew how to talk and could understand what she was doing, on the toughest days, she'd smile up at me, and I knew all would be okay. She was sent to me for a reason. Every day, I send up a prayer of gratitude for making the right decision to become a teenage mom. Aubrey makes every sacrifice worth it.

She isn't stingy with her love and affection to those people she truly cares for, but today, her sentiments rattle me, rendering me speechless as I place the plate of pretzels in front of her and Lennon.

My emotions are out of whack because of Walsh. As much as I want to have sex with him, I can't imagine the toll it will have on my mental health.

"Earth to Tate." Walsh's voice draws me out of my thoughts.

"Hmm?"

"Where'd you go?"

"To a place I shouldn't."

I definitely shouldn't be thinking about sex in front of my daughter and her friend. Especially when it's her friend's father I'm imagining doling out the orgasms.

Who the hell am I and what have I done with Tate Winchester?

"Mommy, may I please have a glass of milk?"

"Yeah, me too," Lennon chimes in.

"Squirt, did you hear how politely Aubrey asked for milk? Want to try again?" Walsh chides.

Lennon shoots her father a side-eye but faces me. "Tate, can I please have some milk too?"

"Sure. Good manners."

Walsh jumps in and grabs two cups from the cabinet. Filling them about halfway with milk, he hands one to Aubrey first, then Lennon. It's Lennon who thanks him first, followed by Aubrey's appreciation.

I hand Walsh a plate with a pretzel. He studies it carefully before taking a bite. The minute it hits his mouth, he lets out a groan not appropriate for little ears. I can't stop the giggle tickling my insides, begging to be set free.

"Oh, that's good. You made these from scratch?"

"Yep. The recipe is labor-intensive so we don't make them often, but when Aubrey mentioned we hadn't made them in a while, I figured it was time. Lucky for you to choose today to come over."

He swallows the bite in his mouth, my eyes drawn to his neck, fixated on the way it moves with the action.

Jeez, Tate. What's next?

He doesn't miss the fact I'm checking him out, and I don't mind the smirk appearing on his lips. Not one bit. My internal body temperature rises. I'm going to have to learn to keep my body in check when I'm around him and the kids.

"We'll be in my room," Aubrey advises as she delivers her plate to the counter by the sink. Lennon barely touched her pretzel but doesn't hesitate to follow Aubrey from the room.

"Lennon," Walsh reprimands, causing her to turn around, hands planted firmly on her hips. "Are you going to finish your pretzel?"

A slight pink tinges her cheeks. "Not hungry." Without further explanation or waiting for further reprimand, she spins and heads off to play.

"She didn't like it?" I guess.

"The girl has no taste. But, more for me." He shovels it into his mouth. I force my attention away from him, busying myself on not staring.

"What should we do with our free time?"

So many answers—all of which are inappropriate with the kids down the hall—flood my mind. "We could start a movie now. Give us something to keep our concentration off other things."

"Probably for the best," he states with a sigh.

I want to tell him about Friday, but if Wednesday night doesn't go well, it won't be a possibility. No need to get his hopes up—or mine—to be dashed.

After everything with Damon, I swore I'd never let another man have this kind of hold over me. Yet here I am, the first guy since him, and it's like I've learned nothing.

But Walsh isn't Damon, and I have more experience now.

I also have Aubrey to consider, which is probably the most important reason to slow this down.

But I have needs as a woman too. And damn it, a girl needs sex every once in a while. Or in my case, at least once after six years.

However, with Walsh, it feels way more than sex.

Friendship.

Companionship.

Someone to take care of me.

I'll just keep my heart and feelings out of it, have a little fun, be rewarded with orgasms. No harm in that, right?

"Have you given more thought to going out on a date?"

Walsh's words throw smoke on the whole "casual" idea.

I focus on him. He's curled up on the other end of the sofa, still totally hot and so relaxed and comfortable at my house. Which isn't conducive to my plan either. Because I want him here. Not just so our kids can have a playdate, but so I can have some fun.

My brain wars with itself over what I want. Truth is, I'm unsure of exactly what I want versus what I'll allow myself to have. What I deserve. A showdown of Tate the mom vs. Tate the woman.

Wonder which one will win.

I finally find the words to answer him. "Every day. It crosses my mind every day."

"And?" His expectant expression begs for a positive outcome.

"I'm working out the details for it to happen."

The blue striations in his eyes lighten with pleasure. "That's the best news I've heard all day."

"You sound like Lennon." I giggle.

"Where do you think she gets it from?"

"How much notice will you need?"

"As long as I don't have hockey, about ten minutes to make sure I'm clean and decently dressed." He holds out his hand. "Give me your phone. I'll put my hockey schedule in so you'll know when I'm busy."

I can't tear my eyes away from him. One, for his happiness, a wide smile the size of Texas beaming at me. Two, for the mere enthusiasm oozing from him for getting to take me on a date. Me. Tate Winchester. And three, for the way he demands things of me, and I surrender.

The phone gets passed his way. I never use the Calendar app for anything, so he has free rein over my entire schedule.

While Walsh does his thing, I half concentrate on the movie, an action film he chose, something I wouldn't pick on my own, the other half drifting to ideas of dating him. Followed by thoughts of sleeping with him. I allow nothing beyond that. I have to protect my heart. Besides, as much as I talk a big game about wanting to have sex, I'm still kinda fearful of doing it.

It seems like I should be ready after all these years, but there's something I can't shake: the fear of getting pregnant again.

I love being a mom to Aubrey, but I can't do it again. Not by myself. Not with someone I barely know. Though what I know about him, I like and enjoy, there's still so much to learn about Walsh Keeley.

We spend the next forty-five minutes watching the movie, fighting any urges of pursuing more. Anytime he's tried to make a move, get closer, lean in for a quick peck, I shove him away. One of us has to be the strong one here. If it utilizes every damn last ounce of my willpower, I'll do it.

The girls wander out, asking for a show. They cuddle on the couch together under a blanket, happily engaged in the action on the screen.

"It's not fair they get to be so close," Walsh hisses in my ear.

I tug him into the kitchen and give him a job.

"Peel these potatoes. Please," I add sweetly.

"This is a lot of potatoes for you and Aubrey."

"Making mashed for the lunch tomorrow. What are you bringing?"

Alarm bells go off above his head. "We're supposed to bring something? I thought all we had to do was show up and eat." His shocked expression is quite adorable, eliciting a flip of my heart.

"Oh. I offered."

"I'll give you some money for them. They can be from both of us." He pulls his wallet from his pocket, but my hand on his stops the action.

"Just peel. I'll make sure you get credit."

He seems to accept that and sets to work.

Walsh takes an absurd amount of time to peel one potato. Seriously. Like fifteen minutes. I've cleaned up everything from the pretzels, started the water boiling, and wrote our dinner order all while he's peeled one potato.

"Good thing you're a good cleaner. You suck at prep work."

"Actually, it's quite genius. Got you to fall for it, didn't I?"

Because yes. I took the peeler from his hand and started peeling the potatoes.

My fingers halt their movements as I study the smug expression covering his handsome features. "You played me?" I sound way less confident than I intend. An unexplained feeling sprouts in my stomach, a knot of dread at how easily I fell for his act. I can't help doubting if everything with him is an act.

"No. I would never. I truly suck. Mom keeps trying to give me small jobs, but I'm so out of my element, it takes forever, and I never do them right." Honesty infuses his tone, matching the truth on his face. His hand covers my hand holding the peeler in the air. "I'm sorry, Tate. It was a joke. I hope you believe me."

The thing is, I do believe him. He's been nothing but honest with me. "I do. But for your antics, you're on double cleaning duty."

He blows out a breath of relief. "Deal. I deserve whatever that is."

I finish peeling the potatoes in silence. While one would think it might be awkward, it's kind of reassuring to not have to fill the space with idle chatter. There are still so many things I want to know about him, but the quiet is nice.

Walsh orders our dinner, but since the restaurant doesn't deliver, he runs out and grabs the food. While he's gone, the girls clean up the mess they made of the doll accessories. In her sweet little voice, I overhear Aubrey telling Lennon, "No, those go in this bin" and "We have to put away everything." Lennon doesn't seem to complain, and I'm glad my girl's not afraid to stand up for what needs to be done.

Once Walsh returns with dinner, we eat together in the kitchen, our conversation focused on our favorite Thanksgiving foods. As I process the scene, my heart pings. It often does when I ponder what Aubrey's missing out on without a father figure. I don't allow the niggle in the back of my brain to suggest Walsh could be him. What a ludicrous idea.

I sometimes picture the future, and the man sitting at the table with us possesses many similar qualities with my potential partner.

After dinner, Walsh gives Lennon a ten-minute warning until they have to leave. He cleans up the mess from dinner and the pot from the potatoes.

"Thanks for dinner. One of these days I'm going to make a trip there. The food was amazing."

"We'll go together. One night without the kids. Whenever that may be."

Instead of permitting myself to be goaded into yet another discussion about when we can go out, I state, "I'd enjoy that."

He removes the towel from the oven handle—the ones I clarified were for drying hands—and peeks down the hallway. "Two minutes." Without warning, he stalks over, which is like four steps. "I'll take even one minute." His lips crash to mine, the action so startling, a tiny gasp of surprise trips out of my mouth.

Mindful of his "one minute" timeframe, I quickly collect myself and lean into the kiss, my lips parting for his tongue almost immediately. His tongue does a quick sweep of my mouth before he pulls away too soon.

"Shortest minute of my life. You were just getting started," I complain. It was barely enough time to even taste the burger he enjoyed for dinner.

"I'll make it up to you next time." His tone implies, "whenever that is." But I ignore it. We'll get there.

Moving out of his space, I state, "You definitely will."

When their time is up, Lennon begs for more. When Walsh denies her request, she goes to complain but stops with his "don't ask again" look. Why does he have to be so damn sexy even when he's reprimanding his daughter?

"We'll see you tomorrow at the party. Don't forget my mashed potatoes." Lennon in his arms, his left eye winks.

As much as I was anticipating hanging out with him at the party, it doesn't bode well I can't get enough of him.

CHAPTER 17
WALSH

Tate and I are the only two adults here at Friendsgiving under the age of thirty. I tried mingling with the other parents, participating in their conversations, but I have nothing in common with any of them. And no one wants to hear about the essay I'm procrastinating writing about the history of sports.

Tate seems to be just as much out of her element. With the connection we share, it's hard to hide the fact I want to touch her. To hold her hand. To kiss the fuck out of her. So I've mostly ignored her. She's holding her own with a few of the moms because my eyes never stray far from her for too long. I may not be in her physical presence, but I'm keeping tabs on her.

The kids are having a grand ole time. The parents set up games and snacks in the finished basement, but most of the kids are enjoying the two bounce houses set up. In the house. There's even a high school girl making sure the kids don't overcrowd them. I lost Lennon the minute we arrived. The last I checked, she was behaving.

We downsized our house when Dad lost his job, and I thought our former house was massive. What it must be like to have this kind of money, to have the biggest house on the block, to have *two* bounce houses in your basement.

For the potluck meal, everyone was supposed to bring something. Either I missed the memo on the invite or I was supposed to know. Don't ask me how. Tate, gotta love her, showed up with mashed potatoes and homemade cookies, which she handed over to me when we arrived at the same time. Stunned by her actions, I barely said thank you. One more thing I'll have to "make up for" when I get her alone.

At this rate, it's going to be never. The odds are not in our favor for even going out on a date. I'd totally offer Mom to babysit Aubrey, but I've already overstepped a lot, so I'm trying to wait this one out.

The twenty kids sit at a long table set up in the dining room. After we plated food for them, we were instructed to disperse, so the adults scatter throughout the first floor of the house, sitting or standing anywhere they choose. I end up next to Tate on the couch in the living room.

Being so close to her and having to behave proves to be difficult. It's not so much I'd throw her down and kiss her in front of all these people, but we can't even pretend to know each other beyond being parents of our kids. Truthfully, I don't give a shit what other parents would think. Neither of us is married, not that it's any of their business. But I get the sense Tate feels differently. Or maybe it's because of the kids.

Hmm. I guess I should ask her one of these days. Perhaps on the date we can't ever seem to schedule.

After sitting in silence, hearing bits and pieces of other people's conversation, I can't take it any longer. "These mashed potatoes are delicious. I should give people my recipe." My eyes catch her lips as they quirk up into a gorgeous smile.

Tate scoops some on her spoon, holding it out in front of me. "This right here is from the *one* potato you peeled." Shoveling it in her mouth, her eyes shut, and I swear she moans, the sound putting my dick on full alert. "Yum. So good."

"Don't make those noises, Tate," I whisper-hiss. "It's unbecoming of a lady. Especially with other people around."

"You must be confusing me with some other lady," she retorts sassily, a smirk on her lips I'd love to kiss off.

Damn. Why does she have to be so incredibly alluring?

Will I ever get enough of her?

The gathering lasts another forty-five minutes after food is served. Tate's cookies are delicious, and I'm not ashamed to admit I grab a few to go. They've got cranberries, white chocolate, and some kind of nuts. Perfect for this time of year.

Lennon sticks to chocolate chip cookies, and poor Aubrey examines the dessert table and practically gags as she walks away. Her mood doesn't change, nor does she throw any type of tantrum about not having dessert. My heart pinches at her uniqueness.

"Keeley, what's on our agenda this evening?" Lennon asks as we depart the party, having said our goodbyes and gratitude to the hosts. I lost track of Tate and Aubrey when I took Lennon to pee. Kinda bummed we didn't get to say goodbye.

"I was thinking, if you aren't too tired, we might go to the rink for a little while."

I barely finish the idea before she squeals.

"I'm not tired. Nope. Not me. I can skate." She shakes her head to punctuate her point.

"Great. Nordic rink?"

"If it's the only one available, it will do." I swear she lets out an exasperated sigh along with her comment. And most likely, it's not my imagination. The girl isn't afraid to preach her opinions.

"Beggars can't be choosers. You want to skate, it's Nordic."

Her eyes go wide at the prospect of not getting to skate. "I want to skate."

"We have to grab our gear. I have it on good authority Mimi's making pizza bagels for dinner."

Her arms shoot into the air, pumping up and down. "Score. Those are like my favorite."

"Gee, I didn't know."

Lennon throws her body into mine. "Yes, you did, Keeley. I tell you all the time."

Scooping her into my arms, I carry her the rest of the way to our truck down the road. Her car parked behind my truck, Tate's buckling Aubrey into her seat.

"Hey, there you are. Wanted to say goodbye and thanks again for the potatoes. Oh, and the cookies were delicious. Got any leftovers at home?"

I mean the words as a playful joke, but my delivery needs some work because it comes out more like I'm expecting her to have them. And to be for me.

"Trying out a new recipe for Thanksgiving. I assume it's a keeper?"

"Yes. For sure. They'll be a hit. I wish we could have them at our meal." My words get away from me yet again. I need to learn how to better control myself around Tate.

"I'll make you a batch if you're prepared to clean my kitchen when I'm done."

The word "Deal" flees my mouth without conscious thought. I'm uncertain what I've agreed to. I only paid attention to the "I'll make you a batch." After that, my brain shut down listening.

Tate smiles at me, and I determine I've said the right thing. "How's tomorrow?" She doesn't allow me the chance to answer before her shoulders slump. "Oh wait. You have a game. You'll probably be tired after being out all day."

Oh right.

Hockey.

"Can we play it by ear?"

She nods, her demeanor akin to being crushed. Before speaking again, she shakes herself out of the funk. "Either way, I'll bake you a batch. Aubrey and I are running to the grocery store tomorrow so we'll grab the ingredients. Need anything?"

Lennon butts into the conversation. "Can you get us a bag of those Mickey Mouse chicken nuggets? Keeley doesn't know where to find them, but I told him you'd know where they were."

Who knew she was invested in our conversation? Another reason for Tate and me to conceal our relationship from the kids.

Tate seems unfazed by my kid's request, addressing Lennon with a broader smile. "Sure thing. I'll add them to my list. One bag good?"

"Better get two. So we don't run out of them too quickly."

"Lennon!" I scold, my voice harsher than usual. One would think I've never discussed manners with this child.

"It's fine, Walsh. I asked," Tate consoles. "Besides, you're always bringing food for us. It's the least I can do." She doesn't seem at all putout, but when I reach into my pocket for my wallet, her hand on my arm stops me. The usual jolt of electricity shouldn't surprise me, yet it does. I'm on higher alert. Or more like worked up after having to control my urges of being in such proximity to her the past two days and not being able to act on them. "It's on me. Please. I insist."

"Thank you, Tate." Lennon gets the words of appreciation out before it even crosses my mind to thank her.

"You're most welcome, Lennon. Daddy can grab them when he comes to pick up the cookies."

She closes the door to the car and makes a move for the driver's door.

"Wait a minute. Please," I include for good measure. She grants my request with a nod of her head.

Digging the keys out of my pocket, I jog to my truck, unlocking the doors as I go. "Get in and get buckled. I'll be right back," I instruct Lennon. Without waiting for an answer, I slam her door and jog back to Tate's car. Knowing little eyes are watching, I don't lean in for a kiss or even make a move to pull her into me.

"I'm not sure what I did to deserve all this, Tate." I want to insert more, but a street full of cars doesn't seem like the right place to wax poetic about her kindness.

"Please. It's two bags of chicken nuggets and ingredients for a batch of cookies."

"It's more. But I can't get into it now, but one day soon I will. When I take you on a date." Lowering my voice, I continue, "And then bury myself inside you." Her cheeks immediately flush red. Not a tinge of pink. Full-on beet red. I fish my wallet out of my back pocket. Grabbing a twenty-dollar bill, I shove it in her hands. "Grab some condoms while you're there. I'll text you a picture of the ones I like."

Even more flustered now, I turn around and leave her standing there. Thinking better of my demand, I call out, "Unless that's weird and uncomfortable in front of Aubrey. If so, use the money to buy yourself a treat, and I'll pick them up the next time I'm shopping." I'm careful not to use the word *condom* as I shout to her.

I say nothing else. With a smirk, I get into the truck. Before I drive away, I send her a text.

> Close your jaw. And for real. Buy yourself
> something with the cash. I'll get the condoms

My eyes stay glued to her, watching her actions from the rearview mirror. She pulls her phone from her pocket, reads the text, and looks up. She mouths, "Soon," then immediately climbs into her car.

Starting up the engine, I mumble, "Soon isn't *soon* enough."

Lennon bursts through the door at home. "Mimi, going skating. You got the pizza bagels ready yet?"

Mom's on the couch, reading a book. Abandoning it, her attention lands on us. "I planned dinner for later since you had a big lunch. You can eat after you skate."

"Hmm. Good plan. I'm not hungry right now." She disappears from the room, no doubt going to get her stuff ready.

I slump down in the chair next to the couch.

"How was it?"

"Fine." The stress from the week catches up with me, and exhaustion tries to claim me.

"Did you talk to the other parents?"

"Tate. Maybe a few more. I don't really have anything in common with them. You should see the house of the family who hosted. They have money to burn."

I don't mean to sound judgmental or envious, but my tone conveys exactly that. Luckily, Mom focuses on the first part of the sentence.

"How's Tate doing? She has somewhere to spend the holiday? Didn't you tell me she's new to town?"

No one can accuse Millie Keeley of not paying attention.

"Yes and yes. Her aunt lives here, so she's going there." Kinda wishing I didn't tell Lennon we could go skating tonight. I'd rather shower and have a movie night. Especially since I have a game tomorrow.

"Okay good. Because they'd be welcome here."

"Thanks. I appreciate it, and she would too."

"What time will you be home tonight?"

"I got the ice until seven. She'll want every minute, so as soon as we get off and changed, we'll be home."

"She is her father's daughter. One day you'll believe me."

She's been telling me that for years, pretty much since Lennon could talk and demanded skates. Possibly even before with something other than skating.

"Keeley, I'm ready." Lennon's voice in my ear startles me. It's not so much loud but near.

My closed eyes open, and I sit up in the chair. I glare pointedly at my mother. "If I ever tried to call you or Dad by your first or last name, I wouldn't be here to tell this tale."

She smirks in return. "Boy, that's all on you. Maybe you shouldn't tolerate that kind of behavior."

I can't even argue with her because she's right.

"Let me grab my stuff."

Lennon's bag is packed and ready to go. I try to make it easy for her. As soon as we get home, she empties it. Once the stuff is washed, the bag gets packed again, ready for next time.

"Give Mimi kisses and tell me all about the party while Daddy gets ready." Warmth spreads through me as Lennon hops up on the couch next to Ma. Lennon's lucky to have such a giving, loving, and kind grandmother, someone who will make sure her father doesn't screw her up too much.

As soon as we enter the rink, my mood automatically changes, the stress of the week melting away. It's why I always push through whatever I'm feeling and don't give up the time on the ice. The rink's always been a sense of peace for me, a haven. Even during grueling practices and games, there's no better feeling than gliding across the ice. In the rundown rink of my childhood, it's like coming home. I've left much of my blood, sweat, and tears on the ice, and I don't foresee that changing anytime soon.

The unique smell of ice invigorates every one of my senses. The crisp, cool air carries a slightly musty aroma stemming from the accumulated moisture and dampness. I could do without the weak odor of sweat and body heat as the scent of exertion mixes with the frozen air, but it comes with the territory.

It takes five minutes to get Lennon's skates on before she's ready to go. I don't put mine on right away, admiring how she enjoys it all, moving from one end of the rink to the other. With the ice all to herself, she relishes the space.

I snap some pictures and videos as she passes me, a huge smile on her face, laughing at whatever is going on in her head.

I could lace up my skates in my sleep, but I take my time, letting Lennon appreciate her calm. As much as I'm going to miss hockey after I'm done playing, I won't hang up my skates as long as she loves it. Hell, even if she gives it up, I'll find a way to be involved with the sport.

Like the clinic next weekend. Kenny sought me out specifically, and I was happy to volunteer.

As if the universe is trying to tell me something, my phone rings, KENNY displayed on the screen.

My eyes on Lennon, I answer the phone. "Hey, Kenny."

"Walsh. Got a minute?"

Lennon's in her glory, occupied and enchanted by the ice. "Yep." Hopefully, he misses the hesitation in my tone.

"Unfortunately, we had to rearrange a few things at the rink next weekend, including the timing of the clinic. We have to push it to four. Does that still work?"

The earlier timing was perfect since Lennon would still be with Megan, but now I'll have to see who's available to babysit. I hate always asking Mom and Dad, assuming they're free and want to keep her.

"That should work. I just have to make sure I have a sitter for Lennon, but it shouldn't be too much of a problem," I confirm, not wanting to let him down or not be able to attend.

"My oldest is home from college for the holiday and would love to hang with her."

Possible crisis averted.

I'm fortunate Lennon's so easygoing that she gets along with anyone, even new people. And it's not like I wouldn't be there if any issues arise. The incentive to sit in the stands at the university rink would probably be enough of an enticement to keep her entertained.

"Sounds good. We'll come around 3:30 Saturday. She'll be excited."

"My daughter too. See you then. Bye."

The phone disconnects in my ear as Lennon comes off the ice for a break. She chugs water from her thermos before appraising me. "You got snacks? All those laps are making me hungry."

"I thought it was your turn to pack the snacks." She narrows her eyes at me, eerily resembling her mother. From a five-year-old, it's not as daunting as from my ex.

"I didn't. Because I'm not the adult."

"Could've fooled me," I mutter, digging into my bag for an apple squeezie. Her entire body vibrates at the sight of it. "Will this do?" I ask, in case her actions don't convey her genuine excitement.

"Oh yes. I was really hoping for this."

I smile, wondering if that's remotely true or not. Either way, it satisfies her, giving her just enough energy to power through the rest of our session on the ice.

Abandoning my phone, I join my daughter on the slippery surface, wondering how I ever got so fortunate for a kid who loved skating almost more than I do.

CHAPTER 18
TATE

My dreams revolve around Walsh.

Being alone with him.

Cuddling him.

Undressing him.

I wake up in a cold sweat as we're about to finally do the deed. I heave all foreboding thoughts aside. It's only a dream. It means nothing.

Aubrey helps me make pancakes for breakfast before we hit the grocery store. Aunt Marsha's shopping for everything we need for the meal on Thursday, but I want to make another batch of cranberry cookies. Now it's two batches. I smile at how Walsh easily convinced me to make a batch for him.

Like he knew I was thinking about him, a text message comes through on my phone.

Wanna know something I don't tell many people?

I feel so special. Of course

I lead Aubrey to the frozen aisle to grab the chicken nuggets for Lennon. She earns a smirk for the way she insisted I get two bags. He's so going to have his hands full when she's a teenager.

I hope I'm around to witness it, a voice whispers in the back of my head. It's years away, but even if nothing transpires between Walsh and me, I hope Lennon and Aubrey stay friends.

I hate bus rides to away games

"That's your secret?" I blurt in the middle of the grocery aisle after reading his message. Aubrey peers funnily at me. Stopped in front of the nuggets, I motion for her to grab two bags of the Mickey nuggets. Instead, she grabs three.

"I think we need more, otay?" she muses optimistically.

Fairly certain we have an entire bag in our freezer, but I won't deny her request. "Sure thing." I scan our basket, checking to make sure we have everything on our list. In my hand, my phone startles me.

WALSH.

There's about a two-second debate about whether to answer the call. For no other reason than because I'm in the middle of the grocery store. The urge to hear his voice wins out.

He doesn't let me get in a hello before he starts right in. "I hate the front of the bus, but if I move farther back, I risk vomiting. It started in high school and has only gotten worse the past few years." There's a reason he's telling me this, which he'll reveal when he's ready. "Want to know why I'm telling you this now?"

"I wondered."

"It's a new game I thought we could play. You in?"

I don't answer right away. A game he wants to play? I'm not much for games. I'm leery of how playing any game with a guy could go wrong.

So very wrong.

At least that's been my experience. But so far, what Walsh has shown me, I like very much.

Not beating around the bush any longer, I give him my truth. "I want to say yes, but I'm in the middle of the frozen foods aisle and not exactly sure what I'm agreeing to."

"You answered my call at the grocery store?"

"Um, yeah. Should I not have?" Unsure of where he's going with this, I'm committed to seeing this to the end, rooted to the floor.

Thankfully, the store isn't too busy. Which seems crazy for the middle of the Sunday afternoon before Thanksgiving.

I can hear the smile in his voice when he speaks again. "I feel special, Tate."

He makes me feel special too.

"How much longer will you be at the store?"

"Shopping's done. Just need to check out."

"I'm going to be sitting here, my cheek pressed to the window, breathing through my nose so I don't toss my cookies for another solid hour. Call me back once you're home to continue this conversation."

"Right." My word's not convincing. Not because I don't want to learn the rules of his new game, but because…actually, I'm not sure why. I try again. "Sounds good. Expect my call in the next thirty minutes." I don't wait for a response, the shopping cart in motion as I hang up the phone. "Come on, Bean. Let's check out and get home."

"Who was that?" Her question comes out of left field. She's usually not so involved in my phone calls. Although, I guess I don't have many phone calls in front of her, my parents and Aunt Marsha being the exceptions.

"Walsh."

At the checkout, she loads the items I hand her on the belt, an unusual expression on her face. I'm about to ask her what's bothering her, but she beats me to the punch.

"I want a dad like Walsh."

It's all she says. Her expression remains the same, and once she issues her six terror-inducing words, she seizes whatever I'm holding and places it on the belt. As if she just told me she was hungry. Not that *she wants a dad like Walsh.*

The air in my lungs stales, making it almost impossible to take another breath. The world around me fades away, my eyes blurring even on Aubrey.

It wasn't enough for her to announce she wants a dad. I could have dealt with that a little better. No. She had to put a quantifier on it.

I want a dad *like Walsh.*

At least she didn't say I want Walsh to *be* my dad.

"Mommy?"

Her timid voice snaps me out of my trance, out of the hole I've fallen into, one of my digging.

I want to ignore what she said, but that's not how we operate, so I give her the next best thing. "Maybe one day."

Okay, not the *next best thing* in the slightest. My words back to her are only slightly above when your parents tell you "We'll see."

I force myself to continue checking out. The items are few, and it's not long before they're bagged and back in the cart. I go through the motions of paying, thanking the cashier only because she spoke to me first.

Walking to the car, Aubrey's words play on repeat.

Is it possible she knows how I feel about Walsh? In a perfect world, I'd love to give her a dad like him. I stop myself from allowing the next thought to penetrate—to give her *him*.

It's the craziest notion, one I can't allow myself to give any type of headspace. Not for me. And especially not for Aubrey.

On autopilot, I load the groceries into the trunk, tighten Aubrey's buckle, and latch my seat belt. Before starting the car, I fill my lungs with a deep breath, blowing it out slowly.

Her questions are only going to continue the older she gets. I'm only going to be able to keep putting her off for so long. Especially now since we've been hanging out with Lennon and Walsh more. Does she see what she's missing out on? Does this stem from there?

"I love you, Mommy."

The timing of her declaration stirs up something inside me, almost as if she needs me to know that no matter what happens, she'll be okay with just her and me.

And yeah, I'm twisting her words to assuage my guilt.

Back at home, I carry in and unload the groceries before calling Walsh back. I set Aubrey up with a snack and a show and hide out in my bedroom to return his call. It rings twice before his voice delights my ear.

"Hey, you."

"Hey. How's it going? Surviving the ride?"

"Managing okay. I think we'll be there soon, thank goodness." There's agony in his voice, like he's on edge. My heart spirals hearing it, wishing I could make it better for him, get him to his destination faster.

Instead, I run interference. "So tell me more about this game you've invented."

"So each of us has to tell the other something about ourselves hardly anyone else knows."

"How do many people not know about your bus thing?" I'm ignorant about organized sports, but they're a team. They must be somewhat tight. And it's close quarters on the bus, right?

"It's not something I advertise, especially this year with being captain. They think I like the front of the bus. And I've never actually thrown up on the bus. I came close once but made it to the bushes as soon as the doors opened. I chalked it up to nerves of a championship game."

I don't care he's talking about vomit. I love the sound of his voice. The deep timbre prattling in my ear has my stomach doing flips.

"Your turn. What secret are you going to reveal to me?"

I think for a minute. Even though it was going to be my turn, I don't have an answer prepared. "I'm not sure I have one as juicy as having to sit in the front of the bus." I laugh at my expense, stalling for more time.

"Truthfully, I just wanted to hear your voice, Tate."

Aww. This guy.

"Now I'm the one who feels special."

"You are," Walsh compliments.

He can't see the way my cheeks flush pink nor the way my stomach tumbles again, making me want more than just his voice in my ear.

"I'm not devastated Aubrey's father died," I divulge.

A gasp echoes on the other end of the phone. He follows it with, "Shit, Tate. We need to discuss this more, but our bus pulled into the parking lot."

"And you didn't puke."

"Nope." He lowers his voice. "Thanks for being the distraction I needed."

"You're welcome. Any time. It was good to hear your voice." Jeez, one would think I hadn't seen him in weeks or months. "Good luck with your game. See what you can do about getting the puck into the net." My light-hearted attempt at a hockey joke falls a little flat.

"That's always my goal. See what I did there?" His hearty chuckle causes tremors of emotion.

"Yeah, got it. Clever." As much as he has to go, I don't want to hang up. "What are the odds you'll be stopping by for cookies tonight?"

"Probably in your favor. Lennon's with her mom for the night. I could come over after Aubrey goes to bed." Expectation clings to his comment.

I don't want to turn him down, but I don't trust myself. However, I'm the one who initiated this, so I can't rescind my invitation.

"Okay." My heart soars as I speak. I'll have to be on my best behavior, not maul him the minute he walks in, even though that will be the only thing I want to do.

"The thought of seeing you tonight will help me power through the bus ride home."

The seams of my heart explode at both his words and getting to see him tonight. Friday and Saturday didn't fulfill my Walsh quota.

"Awesome. Have a great game. Text me when you have an estimated time."

"Thanks, Tate. I will. See you later. Bye."

Like the gentleman he is, he waits for my goodbye before ending the call.

"Bye, Walsh. Skate well." I end the call, not waiting for any response to my well wishes. Because if I hear his voice again, I won't have the willpower to let him go. Even though he can't stay on the phone.

Slipping my phone in my pocket, I join Aubrey on the couch.

She squints up at me. "We make cookies soon?" The girl won't even touch the end product—or any taste tests during the process—but she's all about measuring and adding ingredients.

"Just waiting on you."

Her eyes flick back to the TV for a brief minute before she voices, "I'll watch later." She scrambles to get the remote and powers down the TV. "Let's go."

As much as I enjoy cooking and baking, when she's with me underfoot, it's a bonus, an extra pleasure from the sometimes mundane chore. And though she's only five, she has a good sense of how things work in the kitchen, which ingredients are what, and where we keep them, so she's quite the help.

Aubrey and I spend several hours measuring, mixing, and baking cookies, making enough to serve at our meal, a batch and a half for Walsh, with a few extras for tonight, and about three batches to freeze for Christmas gifts for teachers at the school. When I find a recipe I like, I go overboard. But it's one less thing I'll have to worry about next month.

The kitchen looks like a tornado swept in and destroyed it, but instead of sand and dirt, it brought a flurry of flour and sugar. I've left most of the mess for later when Walsh comes to help. I suspect if we do it together, it won't feel so much like a chore.

After hanging up our aprons, Aubrey takes a bath, not curious the timing before dinner. I advised Aunt Marsha not to cook for us tonight since we'd be there Wednesday and Thursday, so dinner is soup I heat from earlier in the week, using paper everything since I can't fathom adding any more dishes to the sink and counters. I spend little time in the kitchen because seeing the mess makes me a little antsy. After my shower, we spend extra cuddle time on the couch with books.

The doorbell rings around seven p.m. as I'm finishing braiding Aubrey's hair.

"Who's that, Mommy?" Aubrey wonders.

The flutter low in my belly predicts who I think it is.

Moving off the couch, I check the peephole before I answer. Excited doesn't do my emotions justice. He's a little earlier than he implied—with no text message as to his eta—but it doesn't stop me from tearing the door open.

Walsh stands there, his cobalt eyes shimmering under the outdoor light, flakes of our first snow stuck to his hair. Instead of gray, a navy Aspenridge hoodie covers his torso, hiding away his muscles. My mind fills in for what my eyes can't see, conjuring up the hidden, burly biceps. Until my eyes home in on a white bandage tinted with blood on his forehead.

"Walsh. What happened to your forehead?" I hold open the storm door, inviting him in. His fingers clasp a bouquet of wildflowers. Handing them over, he shrugs off his coat and unties the laces of his boots, taking them off one by one.

He dismisses my concern with a wave. "A minor battle wound from a tiff on the ice. Doesn't need stitches or anything, thank goodness. It would have set my timing back even more."

I can't assess his "battle wound" for myself, so I believe him at his word.

"I wasn't expecting you so early. I thought you'd let me know when you were on your way." The words leave my mouth, and I'm embarrassed by how they sound—judgmental and borderline rude. He appears crestfallen, and it does funny things to my heart. I'm about to apologize, but he speaks first.

"Did my text not go through? I sent it from the bus, so maybe it didn't."

My phone's been sitting in the kitchen since I used it to pull up the recipe. Hmm. Must be on silent or I was into the books we were reading and didn't hear it.

"Sorry. Aubrey and I were busy, and I didn't think to check it."

We stand in my entryway, and Walsh's demeanor changes slightly, as if he's embarrassed. "She's probably still awake, and I'd apologize for it, but I kinda needed to see you sooner. And I tried to stay at my house until I said I would come over, so maybe it's a good thing you didn't get my message, but I couldn't stand waiting there any longer. Not when I could at least start on your kitchen mess while you do the bedtime routine."

His ramblings filter in my foggy brain like slime oozing out—slowly. I don't fully comprehend what he's talking about before he steals a peek in the living room. Satisfied with what he sees or doesn't, he pecks my cheek. His action is so jarring, I can't make sense of it. And when he leaves me standing there, completely awestruck and floundering, I fall.

I fall *hard*.

The warning bells clang in my head, but my heart doesn't listen.

No, it gallops after Walsh, needing to be closer to the guy who's currently enchanting it.

This is not good.

This is *not* good.

I can't get involved with a guy right now. A guy who seems to check all the boxes of someone I want to be with. I may not know everything about Walsh Keeley, but there's only about one thing I can find fault with: he doesn't load the dishwasher correctly. I'm sure he's got other quirks and habits I won't adore, but fuck if he isn't the sweetest man I've ever had the pleasure of knowing.

My feet fixed in place, I stare after him for way too long. Breaking out of the Walsh trance I'm under, I temporarily shake off these feelings. Because under no circumstances can I march into the kitchen and act on any of them. Not at this moment. Not even tonight.

I won't be able to last much longer before combusting with lust and desire for this man. It's a lethal combination, the memory of buzzing with hunger for another man always in the back of my head. With Damon, it was different—I was an inexperienced teenager who thought she was in love. Now, I'm still mostly inexperienced, but with the obstacles I've overcome in my life, the need to tread lightly still exists. With so much at stake for me and Aubrey, I can't make a similar mistake based solely on my sexual wants and needs.

Except, with Walsh, it's already been more than sexual, and we haven't had sex yet. Which doesn't permit me to be so casual with my heart and urges.

I follow the sounds of running water to the kitchen, not even a glance at the couch where Aubrey waits for me. The shock of her sitting at the table in the kitchen knocks me for a loop.

For a moment, all I can do is stare. Walsh faces away from us, his arms elbow-deep in the sink. From her position, Aubrey's eyes intently watch his every move. If "stars in her eyes" were more physical and less figurative, her eyes would shoot out of her head. She's got it almost as bad as her mother.

Shit. Which makes this whole scenario even worse.

Tamping down the spell I'm under, I call her name quietly. "Bree, you ready for bed?" I don't address Walsh currently standing in our kitchen, cleaning up *our* mess. If she has questions about why he's here, I'll do my best to answer, hoping I can simply ignore them by changing the subject.

She tears her vision away from Walsh, her googly eyes focused on me. "Otay, Mommy." Slowly, she hops down off her chair, stopping in the middle of the kitchen, her mind clarifying what's happening. Instead of walking to me, she ambles three steps toward Walsh, tugging on his pant leg to garner his attention. My breath ceases with her actions, wondering what she plans to do.

Walsh tips his head to my daughter, his grin big and sweet. "What's up, Aubrey?"

"Is Lennon sleeping?"

His hearty laugh echoes around the small kitchen. "Hardly. But she's getting ready for bed soon with her mom."

Aubrey contemplates his words, soaking up what he tells her, trying to make sense of it. I so want to interrupt, to explain in terms she can understand, to ease her mind. Or maybe that's guilt talking, always trying to protect her from the consequences of choices I've made for the two of us.

"Can you bring her next time you come over?" Her words start timid, as if she's not sure what she wants to say. "She's really fun. Even if it's bedtime. Maybe she can sleep here too." Her smile grows at the idea. I wasn't aware sleepovers were on her radar. Must be because I mentioned today about sleeping at Aunt Marsha's on Wednesday. "Good night, Walsh." Slowly and tentatively, she wraps her arms around his legs, the action so out of character, it leaves me utterly speechless.

His arms wet and soapy, he kinda pats her back with his elbow. "Night, Aubrey. Sweet dreams." His inquisitive gaze finds mine over her head. So many uncertainties swirl among the varying shades of blue in his eyes.

All I can do is gape back, not having a clue how to interpret this scene displayed before me.

If I could, I'd join their embrace, begging for him to make this an everyday occurrence. But I can't. For so many reasons, most of which I've forgotten at the moment.

When Aubrey lets go, she faces me, and a lump clogs my throat. All the sacrifices I've made for us, for *her*—the sleepless nights, the move to Vermont for a new life, dragging her away from the only people she's ever loved and known—gather into a knot of emotion threatening to crack the precipice of the ground I stand on.

Not only have I gone and fallen hard for Walsh, but Aubrey has too. And she doesn't see him as just Lennon's father.

What have I done?

CHAPTER 19
WALSH

Tate's face pales as if a ghost appeared in her line of vision. I deliberate if she's going to be sick, not truly understanding why else her color would be sheet white. Although, she'd probably be green if that were the case.

"I have to, um, put Aubrey to bed," she stammers unconfidently.

"I'll be here." I motion my head to the sink full of dishes.

Tate grabs Aubrey's hand and tugs her out of the room. It's a gentle tug, but something has spooked her.

My mind reels through the last ten minutes while I continue to tackle the dishes. Grateful I came a little early, it's going to take a while to clean up the mess from her baking. However, I'm not the least bit annoyed at the state of her kitchen. If the smile continuously creeping on my face is any sign, I'm happy about it. Because it gives me time with Tate. And I get yummy cookies out of the deal. Win-win.

If I could figure out why she's acting so odd.

Is it because I came earlier than expected?

Is it because her kid hugged me?

Is it something else I did I'm not even contemplating, in which case, will have no way to attempt to fix?

I'm at a loss here and out of my element. It was like the time I showed up at the florist asking for flowers when I didn't know what kind she likes. I fumbled my way through, winning her over with the beautiful fall bouquet the florist suggested. Today's wildflowers were an impulse buy. It might be a problem, but I saw the way her face lit up when she noticed them in my hands. Every time I bring them, she glows. It's all I can do to keep her vase filled with living ones.

Speaking of, I rinse and dry my hands, putting a temporary hold on cleaning to search out where she left today's bunch. I find them on a table in the living room. The hall to the bedrooms tempts me. What I wouldn't give to sneak down and eavesdrop on their bedtime routine. I'll pretend it's for pointers, but it's seeing Tate in her element as a mom.

She's so damn sexy as a woman, but I'd be lying if she didn't land squarely in MILF territory. Though, it's less of a "love to fuck" scenario and more of a "give me everything" one.

Whoa, what?

I have to reassess my thinking here.

I want to have sex with her, and when that happens, it will be so much more than fucking. Currently, it's more of an "if." As much as it might be soon—damn, I hope so—it still seems like there's a possibility of it never happening. Even though there are currently two condoms in my wallet, I don't have any notions of it happening anytime in the immediate future. But when I can figure out a plan to make it happen, I'm prepared. Unlike last time.

Flowers in hand, I go back to the kitchen. Removing the almost dead ones from the vase, I rinse it out and put the new bouquet in, arranging it like I have an advanced degree in flower-making. Is that a real thing? I'd never pursue something so foolish—I'd fail the first course. I file it away to ask the florist of Whispering Petals— Jenny—at my next visit. Even with my few visits, she knows my secrets, and I'm comfortable enough in our friendship to ask how to become a florist. As if it's a secret or something.

Jeez, Walsh. Tate has you all off your game today. And not just the romance one.

Though I scored a clutch goal in today's game, I played sloppy. Our entire team did. Missed shots, extra penalties for our side, incomplete passes. We won, but it wasn't a fun victory—we were the "better" team. The bus ride home was quiet and somber, but it offered me the chance to rest with no one riding my ass about it.

I don't know how much time passes before Tate reappears in the kitchen, but it's way less than it requires to put Lennon to bed.

"Hey. That was quick. How long before she comes out the first time?"

Over my shoulder, I find Tate sitting at the table, her fingers twiddling the strings of her hoodie. It's oversized and paired with black leggings. When my mind wanders to what's underneath, I turn back around, ignoring the tenting in my sweatpants.

"The first time?" Tate finally speaks, her uncertain voice more concerning than her question.

Again I abandon the mess, rinse and dry my hands, and drop into the seat across from her. She visibly retreats from the nearness.

Hmm.

"The first time she comes out of bed."

As if understanding dawns on her, her confused expression fades. "Oh, she won't."

"Ever?"

She shakes her head and thinks for a minute. "No. Once she's in bed, she stays there."

Her words cause me to fall back against my chair. A brief conversation we had about bedtime routines filters through my mind, but to see it in action makes me awestruck.

"I am super jealous right now. Teeming with envy." Which is kind of an understatement, evidenced by the way I beg, "How? Can you teach me all your tricks?"

A shy smile invades her lips. "It's not something I did. Besides, I vaguely remember you mentioning something about Lennon not doing it to her mother." Her brows meet her hairline. The small creases forming do nothing to lessen the attraction I feel toward her. It heightens it.

"I fully admit it's me. That's why I need your help."

As much as I'm kidding—kinda—the way she reacts, it was the wrong thing.

"I can't," she voices in a hushed tone.

"Harsh, but I get it. I'm on my own for a bad habit I created. This is just one reason Millie likes you. You don't enable me."

For the second time, her face goes ashen. Conversely, not only do

I not like it, but it must be something I'm doing to make her feel this way. Wish I knew what it was.

My hand reaches for hers, but she pulls it away before I can make contact. Abruptly, she stands up, a shudder passing through her. Swiping a container from the counter, a bag of cookies on top, she slides it across the table.

"I think you should go."

That's all she says. *I think you should go.*

Her arms cross over her chest, hugging tightly. Like if she lets go, she'd do something she'd regret.

"Go? I didn't finish the dishes. Wasn't that the deal?" That's not the reason I want to stay. Not at all. But it's the only one reasonable enough to change her mind.

"You can have the cookies. I'll finish the mess."

The chair I occupy nearly falls to the floor as I stand up quickly.

"Talk to me, Tate. What happened? What did I do? How can I make this better?"

I've learned there's not always something to be done to make things "better," especially when I'm the one causing the hurt or pain. I'm lost at what I've done or how to fix it.

"We can't."

"We can't what?" I ask. Her shoulders slump, her head tilts, her gaze trains on something on the table. My thumb hooks under her chin, tipping it up. Tears pool in the corners of her eyes, stirring up a shitstorm inside me. The turmoil on her face kicks me into protective mode.

I don't want to be the one to put this look on her face.

I don't want to be the one to cause her stress.

I don't want to be the one to make her any sort of unhappy.

As calmly as I can, I repeat my question. "We can't what?"

"Get involved."

"Involved with what?" My voice sounds naïve, but I truly have no clue what she's going on about.

"Be together."

Oh.

Oh.

"Why, Tate? Because I know you feel this…this connection, this pull. I may not be in tune with all my emotions, but there's more here than merely a friendship because our kids are friends. It's not one-sided."

Right? Did I make this out to be more than it was? Did I receive mixed signals? Wasn't it her that said something about feeling special today? How did I screw this up?

"That's the problem."

I swear, I'll never understand the female mind. But fuck if I'm giving up now. Fuck if I'm giving *her* up. Not when we haven't had a chance to fully explore what's between us. Because there is something here, goddamn it. And if I have to prove it to her, I will. No matter how long it takes, nor how long I have to wait to get her into bed.

The thought makes me cringe. While I pride myself on trying not to be selfish, never getting to experience sex with Tate doesn't fly in my book. Not with the way she has me all tangled up inside. How with just the thought of her, my emotions can't be measured. Yeah, no. Not happening. At least without some sort of conversation.

"Can we talk?" Her head shakes in response. I plow on, not giving up. "Please. I get it's scary, but please don't slam the door on whatever this is without a conversation," I implore. "If you still feel the same way, I promise I'll leave and won't pursue anything beyond a friendship for our kids."

"Oh, crap." Another mixed message from her. The words themselves aren't significant, but the way the sentiment comes across is. Like she didn't consider the fact Aubrey and Lennon are friends. We'd still be in her life.

Using this small unforeseen opening, I slip her hand into mine, leading her to the couch. It pains me to put distance between us, to be separated by a cushion, but it's what she needs.

"Talk, Tate." She doesn't visibly react to my gentle demand. I chalk it up as a good sign.

Sucking in some air, her eyes flutter closed, opening only as she roughly exhales.

"This wasn't supposed to happen."

I wait for her to elaborate, but she doesn't. I could be off base with her implication, but I supply, "I didn't expect it either." If there's one thing I am, it's truthful. She deserves every ounce of honesty I can give her, even if it makes me more vulnerable.

Her lack of surprise doesn't shock me. At least we're on the same page. Hopefully, that will continue.

"I have to think of Aubrey." Again, no further explanation. This time, though, I nod, encouraging her to continue. "I can't let her get too attached."

She stumbles on the word "her." And while she has to consider Aubrey, *Tate's* the one who can't get too attached, I guess based on her tone of voice.

"I don't have a crystal ball to consult where this ends up. Hell, if I did, I'd at least know when we could have sex." I wince at the way my comment will be perceived. I didn't mean to bring it up during this conversation. I can't push her into anything she's not comfortable with.

The faintest smile cracks through the otherwise solemn façade. "It's probably for the best we never took the relationship that far. At least now I won't want what I can't have."

"That makes no sort of sense. Won't you be wondering what it would have been like? Regretting the fact you never took me for a ride?" I physically slap myself for being so crude. For phrasing things so impolitely. As my fingers touch the bandage, I groan at the excruciating pain.

"A 'minor battle wound,' my ass." Her tone affects me the most. Coupled with her use of ass, a fire ignites within me, one I don't want snuffed out.

"You're the only person in my life who truly gets me on such a deep level. That has to mean something."

Her eyes scan my face, lingering longest on the bandage. Even in the dim light of the room, specks of brown twinkle in her eyes. An unspoken agreement of silence shrouds us. It's only uncomfortable because the outcome is unknown.

She finally breaks the silence. "It's not one-sided. And I am scared. Terrified, actually."

Her truths propel me into action. I inch closer. "Matters of the heart always are. With no guarantees."

While I have no proof that's what this is—maybe it's purely physical and the rest will fizzle out—I get the sense to put it all on the line.

"What if it's a risk I can't afford?"

Another inch. "What if not taking the risk costs you more?"

The beat of her heart matches the rhythm of mine. There's a lot at stake here, probably more than either of us realize. And if she decides the risk isn't worth it, I'll keep my promise. I won't pursue Tate the woman. But it will be nearly impossible to avoid Tate the mom.

I hold my breath until she speaks again. "I'm so conflicted. My heart's already gone, and my head needs to convince it it's wrong. We can't do this. We shouldn't do this."

"But what if we should?" I taunt. One more inch.

Even gentlemen are only human.

"Can we go slow?"

Despite what I speak aloud, "We're already moving at a snail's pace," my heart gets tripped up. Because if she has to ask about our pace, it implies we're moving forward. That I can work with.

"Slowish," she amends.

"As long as we don't backpedal and move onward in what we do, I'll agree to slowish." A palpable sigh of relief washes away her angst. Not wanting to press matters but needing some sort of tangible plan, I inquire, "For the love of Pete, can we please find a time to go out on a date? Plan for other things too?"

She swats my chest, not having to reach far since I'm sitting so close.

"Not slowish, Walsh. That's warp speed. Zero to sixty in two point five seconds."

"Um, what?" I shake my head. "I don't think that analogy works. Is that possible? Zero to sixty what in two point five seconds?"

Instead of addressing my concern—which isn't so much of a concern, per se—she speaks one word. One word causing my dick to grow semi-hard.

"Friday." I probe the validity of what she's offering with a raise of my brows. She approves with a nod.

"Friday it is," I confirm. Until reality swoops in. The fundraiser. "No, not Friday. I have a thing Friday with the team."

"Ah, true. And Saturday night you have Lennon." Her hopes deflate, her body sagging with the weight of her disappointment. Can't say I blame her.

"Come with me Friday. It's a fundraiser and lots of people will be there." The words are out of my mouth faster than a shot from a cannon. Then another thought occurs, souring my good mood. "But you probably don't have much time, and a fundraiser with my hockey buddies isn't much of a date. Nor is it sex." Disappointment seeps into every crevice. Why is this so freaking difficult?

"I hope sex lives up to this pedestal you've put it on. It's like the only thing on your mind." Opening my eyes that closed when I fell back against the cushion, Tate's beautiful face greets my sight. She continues speaking, not letting me respond to her comments or her close presence. "What if I told you I had all night? Barring any issues with Aubrey sleeping at my aunt's by herself."

Stupidly, I pull her onto my lap. Her surprise at my actions lasts briefly before she nestles herself comfortably, her legs straddling mine. My dick thickens, her position a total tease. Well, and the fact she said we had all night.

All. Fucking. Night.

"Please tell me you're not joking."

"Aunt Marsha offered. Unless Aubrey gives us a hard time, I'm yours for the taking."

I'm yours.

That has a nice ring to it. A damn nice ring.

"What can I do to assure Aubrey won't give you a hard time? I'll do anything. Pay her money. Buy her vegetables. Have Ma make her a month's worth of chili. Anything. Name it."

Tate's giggle further incites my cock. Then she tilts her head to the side, her features softening.

"I probably shouldn't, but I love how you suggested vegetables. How you know her tastes. It's like you're giving my heart more ammunition against my head."

"I aim to please."

She leans in, waiting for something. A kiss, most likely. So I incline my head, meeting her halfway. "Friday," she rasps. "Everything has to wait until Friday." Not only does she move her head away, she hops off my lap, putting over six feet of distance between us.

"You're killing me, Smalls." A low groan accompanies my words.

"Slowish," she reminds. It taunts me more.

I jump up off the couch. "I should go." It's the last thing I want to do, but if I don't, I don't trust what I might do. If I tip her to the brink, she's likely to pull back everything we've agreed to. I can wait a few more days to have her to myself rather than lose any of this.

"You didn't finish cleaning up the kitchen." Her straitlaced tone halts my actions.

"You said you'd do it."

"That was before you talked me into taking this leap with you. Now, get back in there and clean up. You got your batch of cookies, with some extras for you. You should hold up your end of the bargain." She jabs her hand behind her.

Like a scolded puppy, I make my way to the kitchen, followed by Tate. Just great. Now she'll probably critique how I load the dishwasher and clean up. Not in the mood for that, I load it the way she likes.

When she doesn't sit down, I inquire about her intentions. "What are you doing?"

"Helping. This mess isn't from your one batch of cookies. You want some tea or coffee?"

The timing of her question rattles me. Because it's late and consuming caffeine probably isn't the best idea. But that doesn't stop me. "Co-coffee, please. And a cookie. Or three," I mumble under my breath.

She wastes little time making a pot of coffee. For a solid three minutes, I'm mesmerized by how she moves around the small space. Sure, it's just coffee, but she's so comfortable with what she's doing. She eyeballs the amount of grinds and water. The few times I've attempted to make coffee, I had to measure it meticulously. And then remeasure.

"Keeley, this kitchen won't clean itself."

"Fuck. You know what using that nickname does to me."

"Why do you think I do it?"

I can't let it get to me. Not in any way. It would surely be my undoing.

Death by use of nickname.

Not until after Friday.

We clean for about twenty minutes, side by side, working together as a team. It's stupid, mundane, and domesticated, but there's something comforting about doing it with Tate. It doesn't feel like a chore, just two people getting familiar with each other while making sure the mess gets cleaned up.

When the coffee's ready, she pours two mugs. "I've got almond or regular milk, sugar, and coconut creamer. How can I doctor yours up?"

"You can't. I prefer it black."

Her nose scrunches in disgust. "Ew. Gross. Remind me never to drink from your cup." Her words surprise even her but shift something inside me. If we're fortunate enough to get to that stage of a relationship, I'll be happy to forgo my tastes for hers.

Maybe.

On second thought, I'll reassess in the future.

She adds a splash of coconut creamer to her mug, then stirs it.

The oddest sensation sprouts inside me: a small part wanting to taste hers. But we're not there yet. Instead, I blow on mine and sip it before reaching for my bag of cookies.

Her hand on mine stops me. A spark ignites at the connection. Or rather, the inferno burns stronger.

"Save those for tomorrow. I've got extras." Sliding out of her seat, she grabs a container from the counter and hands it to me. The entire thing.

"Aren't you afraid I may eat all your extras?"

From her spot across the table, her eyes blink. Like she doesn't comprehend what I'm asking.

"You eating all my extra cookies hardly scares me. It's what would happen if I couldn't share my extras with you that does."

A lightning bolt hits. I now totally understand where she was coming from earlier. Because yeah. That scenario scares the shit out of me. And maybe we tread lightly from here on out. And go slowish.

Not wanting to admit my thoughts aloud, I nibble the cookie. Just as good as the other day. Or maybe even a tad better.

"Mmm," I moan around the cranberry taste exploding on my tongue. "Delicious, Tate. Fucking delicious."

"Thanks. Bree and I made some for the teachers for Christmas gifts."

"How many cookies did you make today?"

"Like seven batches, maybe?" It's a question, but her nonchalance implies how *easy* it was.

"And how many cookies per batch?"

"Two dozen."

Mentally I calculate how many cookies. Impressed is one way to show my appreciation. "One hundred sixty-eight cookies in a day? Damn, girl."

"Give or take. I may have eaten a few along the way. Along with some of the dough."

I want that. Eating the dough out of the bowl. Cookies right out of the oven. I don't even care I've done it my entire life with my mother. I want this with Tate. And I have no qualms in letting her know.

"Next time, can I help?"

So "help" is a loose term. Luckily, she rebukes my bullshit.

"You can help Aubrey gather the ingredients. Help her find stuff she can't read. How's that for *helping*?"

I should be more annoyed at how she makes fun of me, but I can't stop the guffaw emanating from my mouth. I point at her. "Shut. Up. I loaded the dishwasher like a pro tonight."

"I'll give you that. But you still wiped your hands on the decorative towel. Can you work on that?"

"If you insist." I did it on purpose. She's so transparent about things done the way she likes.

"Your assistance is duly noted and appreciated."

"Does Aubrey really help you cook and bake?"

Her face lights up. "She does. She's much more helpful when we cook because she'll eat the end product, but she loves being in the kitchen almost as much as I do. How about Lennon?"

"Lennon barely tolerates *eating* food, let alone preparing it. As for desserts, she has little patience for being exact. It's not in her DNA." I gulp more coffee, using it to stall for what I need to ask. "How did Aubrey's father die?"

It's been on my mind since she dropped the bomb earlier, but now's the first chance I've had to inquire.

"Drug overdose." There's no emotion behind the words. "It's the reason we moved."

Over coffee and cookies, she regales me with the story of how he wasn't interested in being a dad, how his family tried to make her get rid of the baby, how she never got a dime in child support. And when he suddenly passed away, his parents decided they wanted a relationship with Aubrey, the only piece of their son they had left.

By the time she's done, she's blown my mind.

At the audacity of his family.

At how much stronger she is than I recognized.

At the relief she feels getting it off her chest.

My eyes drift to the clock behind her. "Shit. Is it almost midnight?"

Tate twists to see the time. "Wow. Guess it is."

Cue the awkwardness of the goodbye. Because I want to kiss her, but I expect she won't let me.

"Friday's only in five days," she mutters. Then she peers at me. "What time is the fundraiser? So I can figure out a plan with Aunt Marsha." Her cheeks flame crimson. With a waggle of her brows, she asks, "What time does it end?"

"It starts at seven, but we don't have to be there then. I think it ends at eleven."

"I'd love for you to say we don't have to stay until the end." Cue an intake of breath as she waits expectantly for my answer.

Which I make her wait for. I interlace her fingers, her skin smooth against the rough edges of mine. "Depending on when we get there will dictate when we can leave. I think the auction's over at nine-thirty, so not before then. I'll need at least an hour to schmooze with the guests."

"What kind of food does the restaurant serve?"

She's testing my memory of the restaurant's menu. "Pub food. Burgers, sandwiches, salads, fries."

"I'm sure Aunt Marsha will feed Aubrey dinner if I ask. I wish you could come over before so we had extra time."

"Why can't I?"

Her forehead creases adorably. "It will be very difficult to get me to attend the event if you ply me with sex before."

A vision of Tate sucking my dick flashes in my eyes. "Duly

noted," I huff out, the words scratching my throat. "Let me know what you decide, and I'll pick you up then."

She nods once. "You should go," she whispers.

"I'm going," I murmur back. Neither of us makes any moves to follow through.

"Thanks for the flowers, Walsh. I neglected that when you arrived. The purple is too pretty."

That's pretty much what Jenny mentioned. Damn, she knows her shit.

"You're welcome."

Our gazes hold a few more beats, then I make my move to leave but not before she remembers Lennon's chicken nuggets.

In front of the door, she bites the inside of her cheek, no doubt a tactic so she doesn't kiss me. I'll oblige her tonight, but on Friday, all bets are off. Before and after the fundraiser. She just doesn't know it yet.

"Will I see you at preschool tomorrow or Tuesday?"

"No. She's with Meg until Tuesday night."

"Oh. More transitions this week than usual?"

"The holidays always fuck with the schedule. Lennon is usually unfazed by it as long as she knows what's coming, where she's going, and for how long. Although Mom said she gave Megan some pushback today. But she was tired. Or pissed at me because I told her she couldn't come to the game." Tate yawns. "But we can talk more on Friday. Or during the week on the phone." I can't leave without at least a peck on her cheek. A little bubble of disappointment pops when she doesn't take it any further, but I can't blame her.

She calls my name as I reach for the door. "Thanks for tonight. For not letting my fear get to me. I can't promise what happens next, but I'm here for it."

"Good enough for me. Night, Tate."

"Be safe in the snow. Text me when you get home." A shudder ripples through her as her eyes watch the falling flakes.

As I make my way to my car in the chilly November air, I can't help but smile. She doesn't comprehend she made it very clear what comes next for us.

I'm yours.

I can't wait to make it official on Friday.

CHAPTER 20
TATE

After starting after we got home from our errands yesterday, it looks like it snowed all night, our first big Vermont storm. People weren't kidding when they said Vermont gets a lot of snow. And I thought we got a lot in Kansas!

I burst into tears when we come outside to the car lacking any snow.

"Mommy, who did this?" Aubrey wonders as she recognizes our car being the only one free of snow.

"Let's find out." I usher her into the car and start it up before dialing Walsh. He answers on the third ring.

"Hey, beautiful."

"When did you clean off my car?" I ask, barely able to get the words out over the lump of elation and gratitude in my throat.

"My dad and I came on his daily coffee run. I needed you to be safe."

The organ in my chest grows three sizes. I'm falling fast and hard for him, but I'm too shy to admit my feelings aloud. Or at least in front of Aubrey.

"Thank you. It was really sweet of you, Walsh."

"You're welcome."

After dropping Aubrey to school—driving at a snail's pace on the light snow-covered roads—I cram half a week's worth of work into the day.

I do the same on Tuesday. Thank goodness it's still a full day of school for Aubrey. I put in extra hours after she goes to bed, but it's worth it to have the rest of the week off.

Around three on Wednesday, with all our stuff packed, we head to Aunt Marsha's.

Aubrey's asked no less than a dozen questions about our sleepover tonight, all of which have made me leery of her agreeing to Friday night. I won't give up hope until she tells me, under no circumstances, is she going to sleep at Aunt Marsha's without me. A simple "no" won't do it.

I may be just a tad bit too excited for Friday. At the prospect of having some time to myself, but also at having the time with Walsh.

Time for a "date."

Time to be adults.

Time to be naked.

The mere thought of seeing him naked again makes me wet.

It also brings an endless cycle of infuriating nerves.

As much as I want to have sex with him, the thought of having sex—with anyone—terrifies me. Scars of my last time are ripped wide open, blood profusely oozing from them. Picturing Walsh helps scab them over until thoughts drift to the actual deed.

Wash. Rinse. Repeat.

Thankfully, I have Aunt Marsha tonight to help keep everything at bay. And tomorrow too.

"Mommy, are you sure the cats won't come into my room tonight?" This is her latest worry. She's asked it at least five times today. Hearing the answer repeated multiple times helps lessens the worry.

"Aunt Marsha and I will make sure they don't."

The cats are growing on her, as long as she goes to them. If one tries to get near her without her "permission," she begins to panic. Neither Aunt Marsha nor I make a big deal out of it, which would only make it worse. There's only the very slim possibility one of the cats would hurt her. It's this thought helping mitigate any guilt over going out with Walsh on Friday.

Aunt Marsha and I spend the afternoon and evening getting the meals and sides prepped for tomorrow. The best part is making Nannie's pecan pies. Two, just as Aunt Marsha promised.

I snap a picture of the old, handwritten recipe—Nannie's shaky penmanship barely legible on the yellowed paper—even though it will be hard to read, and I've mostly committed it to memory.

"Aunt Marsha, why haven't you typed this up or at least written it on another piece of paper?" I ask while the pies bake.

"The recipe's up here, child." She taps her head. "I only brought this out so you could see for yourself what we needed and verify I wasn't making any of the ingredients up."

She's referring to the cinnamon, the secret ingredient you'd never know was part of the recipe. I doubted it at first, but quickly dismissed it. Dad makes the pie every year on Thanksgiving, and not once have I ever tasted the cinnamon. But other than this one pie, Dad's a terrible cook. There's no way he would have doctored the recipe, especially adding an ingredient the recipe doesn't call for.

"Thank you for this, Aunt Marsha. And I don't just mean the recipe, although I can't wait to gloat to Dad tomorrow."

"I'm thrilled you agreed to my crazy invite. Making you come here a day early, prepping and cooking your own Thanksgiving meal, coaxing you into sleeping over so I'm not alone on Thanksgiving morning. It wasn't all for selfless reasons."

"I don't care about the reasons. I'm happy to be a part of all of it." And as I say the words, they are, without a doubt, completely true.

"So, you ready to tell me about the boy yet?"

My jaw falls to the floor with her insinuation. "Wh-what?" I stammer, heat filling my cheeks.

"Tate, you're a beautiful young woman. I'd be amazed if you didn't have a boy chasing after you."

"He's hardly chasing after me." I roll my eyes at the ridiculousness of it. Except with more thought, it's true. Walsh is "chasing" me. And pretty soon, I'm going to let him catch me.

Aubrey's already in bed, sans any cats, nor any way for them to get into the room where she's sleeping. She requested books with Aunt Marsha, further lessening my guilt for Friday. It's hard not to love Aunt Marsha, and I'm so glad for this experience of getting to know her as well as we are.

"His name's Walsh."

She stops with a hand in the air. "Wait. As in Walsh, Lennon's father?"

"Um, yeah. One and the same. But how do you know?"

"Aubrey sings his praises. How he buys her things, goes to the park, comes over, and brings dinner. I didn't realize he had an ulterior motive. I figured he was some nice dad."

"He's that too. And Aubrey's mesmerized by him, one of the main reasons I'm terrified of pursuing a relationship. It's already way more than casual between us, and I don't want to screw it up. If something happened between us, I'd still have to deal with him. As enchanted as Aubrey is with him, Lennon's a great friend to her. I can't let her lose that."

My throat catches as I speak so openly to Aunt Marsha, who listens attentively. I've never been one to communicate my secrets with my mother. At least regarding boys. But there's a certain freedom in sharing these details with Aunt Marsha. Maybe because she's not my mom. Or maybe because she's so different from my mom, so much more accepting to talk about these things.

"So don't screw it up."

I laugh out loud at her advice. As if it's that simple.

"It's like I'm looking for ways to sabotage it."

"I believe that to be true for you."

"But things happen. You trust people, and they let you down. They let your kid down. The one other person in the world who's supposed to love her unconditionally, who couldn't be bothered to meet her."

A tear hits the table, the small dot soon joined by two others.

"Oh, sweetie. Don't cry over that bastard. He doesn't deserve your tears." Aunt Marsha wraps me up in her embrace, and the weight of the world releases from my shoulders.

Only one time before have I ever shed tears over Damon—the day he told me any kid would be better off without him in his/her life. I didn't see it right away, but he did Aubrey a solid by not sticking around. Before he died, I saw news of him stealing cars and being arrested for soliciting a prostitute, all to support his drug habit. Ironic. His parents had money to burn. And though we're both better off without him—and his parents—it doesn't mean I don't feel bad she's growing up without a father. Nor should I jump into bed with the first guy who's made me feel like a *girl* since Damon.

A part of me believes Damon loved me the only way he could, meaning the words he said when he whispered "I love you" in my ear. But there's also a lot of truth in the fact he wasn't capable of loving anyone, including himself.

It's unfair to compare Walsh to Damon. They aren't in the same league. But seeing as he's my only experience regarding sex and relationships, how can I not?

I allow myself to empty my well of tears for Damon one last time. In Aunt Marsha's arms, I cry for myself at sixteen, whose choices led her to become pregnant. And I cry for Aubrey, who through no fault of her own, got the shit end of the stick in the daddy department.

Last, I cry as a final mourning of his death. He chose a life of destruction, but deep down, I held onto a glimmer of hope he'd turn it around. If not for himself, for Aubrey. Wishful thinking on my part for my beautiful daughter.

When the tears have dried, Aunt Marsha cups my face. "He's not Damon. It's okay to be scared. I'd be more concerned if you had no qualms about this. I'm not telling you to let your guard down too far, but on Friday night, enjoy yourself. Enjoy that man who makes you smile. Even if he's not the one, you'll figure out a way to make it work for Aubrey's sake. She's your sun, you're her moon."

When I ask her to clarify her statement, all she says is, "One day you'll understand it better than I can explain it now." She hugs me again with her declaration of love.

We clean up the rest of the mess and head for bed. I get little sleep, and visions of Walsh invade the rest I get.

Like him, I don't have a crystal ball, but what I have is faith in him being who he's shown me. Even if I can't put all my trust in him yet, I have way more trust in myself than ever before. And my gut says to trust him.

Thanksgiving morning, we all huddle on the couch together after devouring a breakfast of baked French toast. Aubrey's enthralled with the parade. She's at the age to sit and watch it, only bored when the announcers come on to chat.

Aunt Marsha and I share in the meal's cooking. Thanksgiving's always been one of my favorite holidays, but I had come to terms with it being just Aubrey and me this year, as lonely and sucky as that would be. My parents don't like to fly and didn't want to make the drive.

It's been such a great day of working side by side in the kitchen with Aunt Marsha, not having to forgo the tradition. I've let her know how happy I am multiple times. It seems the feeling's mutual.

Her friends arrive around two p.m. Introductions are made, and while they all seem nice, the kids are a lot to handle. All older than Aubrey, the minute she tries to engage them—which is huge for her—they run off, leaving her wondering what she did wrong.

After we eat dinner and dessert, they all leave, and the usual post-Thanksgiving calm settles over the house. Both Aunt Marsha and I are too tired to do much of the cleaning, but I packed up the leftovers so they won't go to waste. We've got enough food for the rest of the weekend.

Around six, my phone rings. Aunt Marsha's closest to it, so she answers it.

"Happy Thanksgiving, Raymond. How's Kansas?"

Aubrey appears in the room, and seeing my dad's face on the screen, runs immediately over to say hello.

"Happy Thanksgiving, Gramps!" she coos excitedly into the phone.

They talk for a few minutes, Aubrey telling them all about the parade. They've still got food on their table, but it's an hour later there.

"Hey, Tate. Happy Thanksgiving."

"Happy Thanksgiving, Mom. How was your day?"

"Quiet, without you and Bree. But that's most days."

Ah, laying the mom guilt on thick today. I won't ever mention that to her. She'd probably stop speaking to me. If she had her way, there would have been a compromise made with the Melansons so we could have stayed in Kansas.

"At least you have Robbie and Reyna."

There's a definite change in her demeanor at the mention of my brother and his girlfriend. "They're expecting. Did you hear?"

"Saw it on Facebook. Exciting."

The news was a bit shocking, more so because I had to read it on social media rather than my brother sending a text. I shouldn't have expected more. When I told him I was pregnant, his exact words were, "Guess you couldn't learn to keep your legs shut, huh?"

Despite the strain in our relationship, he's a pretty good uncle to Aubrey. At least once she could talk and was out of diapers. I can't wait to see how it plays out with his kid.

Mom's prattling on about something, but I've tuned her out. And when the notification of WALSH comes across my screen, I rush her off the phone.

"Glad you had a nice day. I've got another call. Tell Dad goodbye for me. I love you both."

Swiping to Walsh's call without a response, I put it up to my ear, answering with a smile on my face.

"Hey."

"Tate, it's Millie Keeley."

My elation fades quickly. "Oh, hi, Mrs. Keeley."

"Millie dear. Or Mimi. Your choice," she politely reminds me. My disappointment lessens. I've only met her a handful of times, but she's an exceptional woman. Even beyond raising Walsh to be the man he is. "Walsh is itching to talk to you, but I had to compliment your cookies. They are simply mouthwatering divine. My husband and son are currently fighting over the last one." She laughs as if it's the funniest thing.

"Thank you. Your praise means a lot since I've tasted some of the deliciousness coming out of your kitchen."

"It's well warranted. Okay, here's Walsh. Hope you had a nice Thanksgiving."

"Thanks. We did. Hope you as well."

There's some shuffling of something over the line, but soon Walsh's "hey" accosts my ear.

"Let your father have the last cookie. I have more for you tomorrow."

"No way. He ate like half a dozen. Is crack one ingredient? It might sound like I'm joking, but I'm dead serious. They're so fucking delicious and highly addictive."

My smile widens. "Thanks. I'm glad the new recipe was a hit with everyone."

"What are you doing now?"

His abrupt change of subject has me shifting gears. "Working up the energy to clean the kitchen. I ate too much stuffing and like three pieces of my great-grandmother's pecan pie."

"Yeah, I always overeat on Thanksgiving, more so this year... wait, did you say pecan pie?"

"Yep."

"That's my favorite pie. Did you know that about me?" I love how serious his tone is. How youthful and eager his voice sounds about something simple as pie. I fall further under his charm.

"I didn't. But now I do."

"What are the odds there will be pie at your house tomorrow when I get there?"

"I'll see what I can do. Any other requests?"

"Hmm, what other foods were served?"

I rattle off a list of our leftovers. I can't imagine they're different from his meal, but he's adamant about saving some stuffing and mashed potatoes for him.

"What time did you decide you want me to pick you up?"

I knew this was coming, but a bout of nerves hit me square in the gut. I already worked out the plan with Aunt Marsha. She'll pick Aubrey up around three and bring her to some fair or something—I stopped listening as soon as she mentioned three o'clock.

I hinted to Walsh the other day about him coming over before the fundraiser, but now having to admit it's an option, I'm being shy.

He reads into my silence. "I'm going to rephrase my question. Don't get mad."

I'm set at ease by this, feeling let off the hook even if it is my hook I'm on. "Why would I get mad?"

"What time is Aubrey leaving?"

"Three."

"I'll be over shortly thereafter. I'll be skipping lunch, so if you could have the food hot and ready for when I get there, that would be most appreciated."

The words don't compute in my head, hearing nothing after "shortly thereafter." The rest of his comment is lost on me. Until it finally sinks in.

"Did you just tell me to have your food hot and ready for you? Are those the words that came out of your mouth, Walsh Keeley?"

I hope he's joking. While I probably would have made sure it was had he asked nicely, I don't appreciate the fact he's instructing me what to do. It leaves a bitter taste in my mouth, and my pulse quickens.

"Down girl. It was only a joke. But one I'm filing away because hearing you all hot and bothered? Damn. Tomorrow is going to be so damn fun."

As much as I hate playing "games," he deserves this one. "No pie for you."

"No. Don't take away my pie. I swear it was a joke, and I won't say it ever again. But please, don't take away my pie."

"It could suck for all you know."

"Did you make it?"

"Yes."

"Then it won't. Plus, you said you had three pieces. If it sucked, you wouldn't have eaten that many."

I'm amazed at his recall of detail. "Not much gets by you, huh?"

"Not with you, Tate."

It's the way he utters it, the emphasis on my name. It opens up a passion I've kept buried for the last six years.

"If I don't go now, I won't want to hang up. I'll see you shortly after three tomorrow. If you text me a more specific time, your food will be warmed up and waiting for you."

"Tate, I was kidding."

"I know. But I want to do it for you." More than he'll ever appreciate.

"I have other plans when I get there. You can warm it after. Night. See you tomorrow."

No chance to get another word in, the phone disconnects in my ear.

"Well, that was rude," I say aloud to the empty room. "I can't believe he just hung up on me."

Still simmering, I head for the kitchen, prepared to relieve my aggression on the pile of dirty dishes in the farmhouse sink. When I get there, the sink is not only devoid of all dishes, but it's gleaming back at me. And I get even more pissed off.

Aunt Marsha and Aubrey cuddle on the couch, the TV tuned to one of Aubrey's favorite shows.

"Uh oh. Who pissed in your Cheerios?"

The cliché makes me laugh, and my frown slips away.

"When did you clean the kitchen? I need to alleviate some aggression, but the dishes are all done."

"While you and Aubrey were on the phone. I'm sorry?" She looks just the opposite.

I throw myself down on the couch. I rarely get this worked up. At least in front of Aubrey.

"The floor still needs to be swept if that will have a similar effect." She hides the smirk beginning to form behind her hand.

"Are they all difficult?"

"Who are they, dear?"

"Men."

"In their way, they are. You'll learn to ignore most of the small stuff, especially if he's good at the big stuff." She earns a laugh when she makes an "O" with her thumb and pointer and pushes a finger through.

"I'll let you know tomorrow. More like Saturday since I'll kinda be occupied most of tomorrow."

"You get it, girl."

Aubrey chooses that moment to clue into our conversation. "What's Mommy going to get?"

"When you're older, I'll tell you. And by older, I mean over eighteen."

Just because I had sex at sixteen doesn't mean I want her to follow in my footsteps. I wouldn't trade my decision regarding her, but hopefully, she can learn from my mistakes.

A cat struts in front of the TV, catching Aubrey's attention. "Here comes Scooter again. Why can't she just leave me alone?"

Aunt Marsha and I crack up with laughter.

"Never change, my girl. Never change."

CHAPTER 21
WALSH

Never have I wanted a day to go by faster than today. The countdown to three p.m. began the second Tate told me what time Aubrey would be leaving. Jitters—freaking jitters—have me on edge. I'm pretty sure when we played in last year's championship game, I wasn't this nervy.

My bag's been packed, checked, and double-checked, since early this morning. I made an appointment at the florist for 2:45. I had to hold my tongue when Jenny asked me what was the occasion. Pretty sure "fucking" would have landed me on her crazy list. Instead, I mentioned something about a first date, and she ran with it.

Tate sends a text in the early afternoon.

> In all the discussions about tonight, you never once mentioned what the fundraiser is for nor how I should dress

> It's at the Orchard View Tavern so more casual than formal, but dressy casual. Half the proceeds will be donated to the sports program at a neighboring high school

> What are you wearing?

I evaluate my ragged T-shirt and jeans but get the sense she wants to know more about what I'm wearing tonight not now.

Khaki pants, a button-down shirt, dress shoes

Thanks. See you later

I'll need to shower at your house. Maybe today's the day we can do it together *tongue out emoji*

Okay

Hmm. Kinda thought I'd get more of a reaction, but oh well.

I pull into the lot of Whispering Petals at 2:45, hopping out of the car as soon as it's parked. The bell above the door jingles as I walk in, the floral scents overloading my senses. I never thought I'd be the guy who marveled at the sight of a bouquet sitting on the counter, but here I am.

Thank you, Tate Winchester.

"Hey there, Walsh," Jenny greets with a smile. "What do you think?" She points to the bouquet sitting pretty in a square glass vase. I went big this time. It's a special occasion.

My eyes scan the different types—the white ones similar to the color of fresh snow, the pink roses standing tall, and the light pink ones adding a muted pop of color. A bunch of green sprigs fill in the gaps.

"Beautiful, Jenny. She's going to love them."

Jenny's hands clap together and she goes all florist, pointing and naming them. Trying my best to remember hydrangeas, Gerbera daisies, Tiger lilies, Bells of Ireland, orchids, and the other words, proves to be difficult. Thank goodness for the roses. Those I recognize and can name.

"How did the wildflowers go over?" she asks, ringing me out.

"She loved them. She seems to love all of them." I rest my elbows on the counter. "How do I get her to divulge her favorites? Just ask her?"

Every time I come into the shop, I let Jenny suggest what's best. They all blend together for me after staring for so long, and I'm more drawn to the colors than the shape or type of flower.

"That would be the most direct way." She laughs at my expense.

"Ask her. I can do that." I have little confidence in doing it correctly. And while it seems like such a simple task, there's a high possibility I'll screw it up.

"Enjoy your first date. Where are you taking her?"

"To a hockey fundraiser at Orchard View Tavern." Jenny's expression falters before she catches herself. "It wouldn't be my first choice, but it's the first day we could make work, and I had already committed to attending with the team. I'm already screwing this up, aren't I?" My head droops down.

"All I know about this girl is what you've told me. But if she agreed to attend it with you, then you're already batting over five hundred."

I pick my head up and stare at her. "I play hockey, not baseball."

She shrugs. "I don't know any hockey analogies appropriate in this scenario."

I wrack my brain, coming up empty. "I see what you mean." My alarm blares from my pocket. I silence it quickly. "Oh, shit. Gotta run." Grabbing the vase with two hands, I tell Jenny, "Thank you. See you next week?"

"She's a lucky one. Keep reminding yourself. Have fun tonight."

The door propped open with one foot, I turn back to her with a little shimmy in place. "Planning on it." I can't be certain, but I think she rolls her eyes at me. Do I care? Nope. I'm on my way to my night with Tate. Not much can bring me down.

It's a short ten-minute drive to Tate's condo. Pulling into a Visitor's spot, I notice an older woman holding onto an excited Aubrey's hand. As much as I want to spend every minute with Tate, it would be a little awkward to meet her aunt like this—with my duffel bag slung over my shoulder practically shouting, "I'm here to defile your niece." I wait with very little patience until the car backs out. The taillights a distant memory, I'm out of my car and up the stairs in a flash.

The doorbell rings, my body humming with adrenaline. At this rate, I hope I don't blow early. How much would that suck? I finally get to have sex with Tate, and I can't hold it together.

I try some calming breaths while I wait for the door to open, but once Tate stands on the opposite side, all rational thinking goes out the window.

My eyes rake up and down her body, cataloging every inch of her. The way she's got her hair pulled tightly on her head, twisted into some kind of topknot. Her face practically glowing. The neck of the oversized T-shirt slid down her arm, revealing one bare shoulder. The leggings. Her bare feet, toes painted a bright pink.

"Wow." I thought I knew what I was getting into, but seeing her, knowing what tonight is, it's overwhelming.

"You're here," she breathes, a sigh of relief loud enough to wake the dead tearing from her lips. Lips I haven't kissed properly in weeks.

Letting the bag drop to the floor, I carefully set the flowers on the side table. Without me having to ask, she jumps into me, her arms wrapping around my neck, her legs around my waist, my arms holding under her ass.

"You should kiss me," I rasp, my voice scratchy from a parched throat.

She brings her mouth closer to mine, her tongue darting out before our lips meet. There's a brief hesitation when they're an inch apart. Not able to stand it any longer, I erase the gap, swallowing her gasp of surprise when they touch.

Fireworks explode with the first touch. My lips on hers feel like they're home. It's been a long time away, but with the contact, everything rights itself.

Tate tries to control the kiss, but my tongue pushes hers back. With her, I crave the domination, the need to power the kiss. It's all I can do to concentrate on the way her lips feel against mine. Feel how soft her tongue is as they tangle. Taste the sweet sugar.

"You ate pie without me?" I speak against her lips, pausing my assault.

"It was one bite. A tease. For you."

I rear my head back, the loss immediately felt everywhere, most notably not from my lips kissing her, but my cock. He's getting hard and angry, waiting for his turn.

"Don't tease me. It's not nice."

The corner of her mouth quirks up, the slowest, sinister grin forming on her lips. "I had to get myself off this morning at the thought of tonight." Her confession grounds me. "I tried to wait, but..." She trails off, not able to finish her sentence with anything more than a wobble of her head.

Her admission turns me on even more. Desperate for the sexy portion of the day, I rush for her bedroom.

"That's so hot, Tate," I whisper gravelly in her ear, nibbling her earlobe. "Since you're ahead in the orgasm count, it's only fair to start with a blow job lesson. Then we'll be even."

Her face contorts, my declaration gaping her jaw.

"Um, like right now? First?" Her nervousness is adorable. And even if she sucks at it—no pun intended—it won't matter. I'm hard as a rock, and the second her lips touch my dick, I could blow.

I let her go on the bed gently. As she lies down, I crawl on top of her, caging her body under mine. I shove my hard dick into her thigh for sympathy.

"Right. Now. Can you feel how hard I am for you?"

"Me?" she squeaks.

"All you, babe." I want her to know how she makes me feel. Not the thought of sex or a blow job, but the thought of sex and a blow job with *her*.

Pushing to my feet, I slide my pants and boxers down my legs, kicking them to the side. My hoodie and shirt come next. Tate's eyes widen with every article of clothing I remove. When I'm completely naked for her viewing, her eyes flutter shut. My vision trained on her chest, her breath hitches.

Opening her eyes, she swallows. Twice. "You weren't lying. It's hard."

I try to hide my chuckle, but it releases. "I'll never lie to you. Especially when you could call me out so easily."

Her head tilts to assess me. An air of confusion surrounds her, almost as if she has no experience with a penis. Which isn't true. One, she's not a virgin. And two, she saw it a few weeks ago.

But we're not talking about my botched plan. Nope, we're staying in the present here, focusing on now.

I stroke myself once.

"I might choke," she voices quietly, her gaze locked on my cock, stuck on the size.

"We'll make sure that doesn't happen."

As much as I'm ready for her to take me in her mouth, I have to go slow. Slowish. At her pace so I don't scare her any more than she's already freaking out.

"I don't know about this. I said I wanted lessons, but—"

I interrupt her excuse. Not to minimize her doubts or worries, but to assure her she can do this. "Touch it with your hands." My demand is unobtrusive, tender. Her fingers twitch. As doubtful as she is about herself and her abilities, her eyes betray her. A hunger swims in the darkened browns.

A bit of precum leaks out the tip. She must notice because suddenly, she's moving closer. Kneeling in front of me, her hand quivers as she reaches out. Her finger meets the tip, and she swipes away the liquid. Without further prodding, she wraps her fingers around my shaft, tugging gently.

With hooded eyes, she looks up at me. "Like this?"

"Perfect," I whisper. "Maybe a little more pressure." She grips harder. "Yep." I will myself to stay in control, to teach this lesson without shooting my load until she's ready and prepared. I cover her hand with mine, squeezing before sliding it up and down the shaft in a steady rhythm. "Now your turn."

She sucks in a breath, then moves her hand.

Her soft hand works me a few times. The amount of pressure she uses remains constant, except for one hard jerk.

"Oops," she says with a giggle when I grunt. "Sorry."

"Feels so good. Don't stop." My eyes slam shut, her gentle touch too overbearing. *I won't blow early. I won't blow early. I won't blow early,* I coax, hoping I have the stamina to uphold the directive.

I allow her one more minute to get used to this before we move on to the next part of the lesson.

Stilling her hand with mine, I tip her chin up with my other hand. "As good as this feels, want to try with your mouth?"

"Um, yeah." Her shaky voice isn't quite convincing. Neither is the shocked countenance, but when she widens her legs and sinks down, her face is level with my cock. She stares long and hard at it, examining and scrutinizing, studying it from all different angles. I don't stop her.

Again, precum leaks out. "Just put it in your mouth, Tate."

She mumbles something incoherent under her breath. The only

words I interpret are "you can do this." If she needs a vote of confidence, I can give it.

"Hey, look at me for a sec." I wait for her attention before continuing. She draws her eyes up to me, still hooded, a bit freaked out. "You *can* do this. Go as slowish as you need, but you can do it."

"Right. Just put it in my mouth. Seems simple enough. I do that all day long with food."

"No teeth or biting," I blurt, in case she needs a reminder.

"I could see how that would hurt. No teeth or biting. Licking?"

"Lots. Licking's good. So good." I stop myself before I moan, my dick getting harder and more painful by the second, needing a release.

"Okay. Here goes. Let's hope I don't suck."

My eyes roll. "You're such a tease."

"I'll show you a tease."

Without further warning, she licks the tip of my cock, lapping up any trace of precum. It's sloppy at first, like a kid with her first popsicle, but she needs only a few trails of her tongue down the shaft to correct her mistakes. And by then, I'm gone.

She brushes her tongue back and forth on the top, then the bottom, back to the top. She makes a rhythm all her own. She owns this blow job. Well, this part of it anyway.

Jutting my hips toward her, I enthuse, "Put it into your mouth. As far as it will go without gagging." She follows my direction, opening her mouth wide to fit my dick in. As much as I want to plunge inside, I resist, trying to be the gentleman but unraveling quickly.

She somehow manages more than half in her mouth. Just as I'm about to give her more guidance, she gags. I withdraw a step back from the bed, my cock falling from her mouth, jutting straight out.

"I'm sorry," Tate apologizes, a tear falling out of one eye.

"Hey, it's fine." I can't quite read her expression, how she's feeling about it. "Are you okay?"

She nods. "Yeah. Just embarrassed."

I sit down on the bed, cognizant I'm still naked, and face her. Rubbing my fingers against her thighs, I comfort her with my actions and my words. "Don't be. Please. It was good. See? Still hard." In case she needs a reminder, I point to the evidence between us.

"It seems…painful." The red color of her cheeks faints.

"Not going to lie. It kinda is."

"I can try again," she starts, leaning over. I stop her before she can get her mouth close. As much as release is imminent, I don't want to push her too far.

"No, Tate. Another time. I can think of plenty of other ways to relieve this and get you another orgasm as well."

Intrigued, exhilaration splays over her face.

"You got the condoms?"

"Yep. In my bag. Get undressed and comfortable. I'll be right back."

I don't bother with clothes, and I make quick work of grabbing the box of condoms from my bag. Upon return, she's nestled under the covers, her clothes piled on the chair in the corner.

As much as I tried not to let it, there's a lot of expectation riding on this. For me. For her. For us. I plan to make it as good for her as possible. As long as I get to bury myself in her, I have no doubts I won't enjoy it. I can't wait to take this to the next level, to extend the physical connection we share to a more intimate one.

The box of condoms on the nightstand, I climb onto the bed, slipping under the covers next to her. I hold them up, drinking her in, soaking up every ounce of naked Tate Winchester. Her breasts, her curves, her body mine for the taking.

"You good?" I ask. I'll only stop if she says no, but man, do I hope we don't have to stop. Not when we're this close.

"I'm not sure." Her tiny voice sounds so insecure. I hate how she's having doubts, but I understand.

"What will make you more sure?"

"I keep thinking about last time. The time I got pregnant. You're not my ex, but this is a huge step. And there are consequences to our actions. It hasn't been too much of a hardship to go without sex for the past six years. It's not like it was any good."

She gives me the opening I need.

Leaning on my elbow, I wait until she concentrates on me. "The one thing I can promise you is it will be good. Whatever it takes to make it the most pleasurable for you, I'll do."

"And the other?"

How do I convince her she won't get pregnant? The risk is always there, no matter how many precautions put into place. She and I know better than anyone.

"Are you on the pill?" A shake of her head. "Really?" *Oops.* The word slips out. Thought it might be a given. The first thing Megan did after birthing Lennon was get on the pill.

"It seems stupid, but every time I went to the doctor, I couldn't make myself bring it up. Since I swore off sex after getting pregnant, I figured it didn't matter much." She hesitates and worries her bottom lip into her mouth. "I wasn't expecting you, Walsh. Certainly not now."

I can't resist a kiss on her forehead.

"I get it. I'm irresistible. You can admit it." A shy smile finds its way onto her lips. I can work with that. "We'll come back to this later. Maybe it's time to finally inquire about it." I don't want to put any pressure on her, but damn it. I want to have sex.

Thank goodness she can't read my mind. Not sure she'll like my thinking.

"Did he use a condom?"

"No." The one-word is barely audible.

"No judgment here. We conceived Lennon with an expired one." Megan's the only person who knows, but there's freedom in sharing it with Tate. "Was it your first time?"

"No. Yours?"

"Nope. I should have known better. But, if I could go back and change it, I never would. Lennon's worth every sacrifice."

"I feel the same way about Aubrey." She's quiet for a few minutes, then her head bobbles. "This is supposed to be adults only. Why are we talking about the kids?"

Needing her closer to me, I tug her into my side, wrapping my arm around her back, my hand landing on her bare ass.

"Can we have sex now? Please? I get you want to take things slowish, but I'm dying here, Tate. Having you naked in your bed, all to myself, makes it hard to think about anything other than burying myself inside you."

She cocks her head to regard me. "When you put it like that, by all means. Let me hand over my vagina on a silver platter."

"So that's a yes?"

Her breath catches.

I can't be mad. It's a big step for her. But fuck. I don't want to feel like it's a slap in the face, but it does. Maybe I shouldn't have made it such a huge deal. But the fact of the matter is it *is* a big deal. Not just for her. It's the first time since Megan I feel something for a woman, something beyond just sex. I've been careful who I've slept with since Megan—because like Tate, I couldn't risk the chance of getting another girl pregnant. I get where she's coming from. So I took every precaution and only had a few one-night stands when a need for sex consumed me.

It's different with Tate. I want more than one night. I want more than just sex. I want a relationship if she'll let us.

"Yes, Walsh. It's a yes."

So lost in my woes, her answer doesn't register right away. Not until she scrambles to reach for the condoms.

With one secured between her fingers, she drops it on my chest and lies down. When I don't move quickly enough for her, she lets out a deep sigh. "Well? Are we doing this or not?"

"Oh hell yes, we're doing this."

CHAPTER 22
TATE

don't let Walsh see how terrified I am. Because I am scared shitless of having sex with him. No, scratch that. I'm scared shitless of having sex. It has nothing to do with him. He's the unlucky guy who gets to deal with my ups and downs, my indecision about this choice.

I could say no. He'd be upset with me for a little while, but he'd get over it. But, it's not fair to him, and frankly, not what I want.

I may dread the consequences of having sex, but one thing I'm certain of—Walsh. He's proven he'll go at my pace. If all he wanted was sex, he would have walked away weeks ago. Or he would have pressured me into doing it before now.

He wants more than sex. He wants *me*.

And I want him. I want him in such a way it hurts. Probably not as painful as the erection he's been sporting for the last hour, but there's an ache in me soothed only by him. Right now, sex with him.

Hell, he even promised he'd make it good for me. When I gagged on his dick and he didn't push me to continue, his personality shone through. I shudder at the memory. I barely had it in my mouth.

"Earth to Tate." His voice pulls me out of my trance, and at the sight of his eagerness, all traces of fear vanish.

Maybe not all, but most.

"Hi."

"What are you thinking about?"

"How much I want you inside me. No matter the consequences, I want this. Give me an orgasm."

Cockiness has replaced my fear. I'm not sure which one is worse.

"I think I will."

He springs up, urging my shoulders to rest on the bed. Fuck, his body's sexy. In all honesty, I want to lick his six-pack abs, not his dick. I want to trail my tongue over each divot, every crevice. I slap my hand over my mouth when I moan. Walsh quickly yanks it away.

"Unless something other than what's happening in this room elicited the moan, don't stop."

"All you. Just thinking about how good my orgasm will be. When you get to it."

He raises the eyebrow with the scar, the faded reminder of an injury enhancing his sexiness. "I'm not the one stalling here."

His unintentional words slice through me. He's right. I'm totally stalling, yet begging him to get on with it. He must be some kind of saint. Any other guy would have bailed by now. Even if they were okay with my mom status, this would have sent them packing. But not Walsh.

"You're incredible." I speak the words aloud as my brain processes them.

"You're pretty special yourself, Tate. Now, can I get on with it already?"

He doesn't wait for my answer. *Smart man.*

Within a minute, he's sheathed himself.

As I lie down in a semi-comfortable position, I drive away any negativity creeping in, tuning in only to what's happening between Walsh and me. Not what happened in the past. Not what comes next. This moment right now. The one in which he moves into position over me, resting on his forearms. I sneak a peek at his muscles, the way his arms flex causing the veins to protrude. My tongue darts out of my mouth at the spectacle.

"Eyes up here," he commands. "Are you wet for me, Tate?"

As if on cue, the moisture pooled in between my thighs trickles out. At least lubrication won't be an issue. "Yes. So wet." I reach a hand down there, but he bats it away.

"Oh no. There won't be any of that. This is all on me, babe. I dole out the orgasms."

I want to laugh at his comment, but I refrain, keeping any comical notes to myself. Besides, my head's stuck on his use of "babe." It doesn't escape my notice he's used it twice since we've been in the bedroom.

He reaches his right hand in between my legs, checking for evidence I'm telling the truth. His fingers inch their way in, my body responding in a way I've never felt before. Wound up tight like a coil is the only analogy my mind can supply. Unlike a coil, the need for release is strong.

My body writhes with need, my fingers fisting the sheets. "Don't make me come on your fingers. I want to feel more," I plead, as his fingers work me into a frenzy. So close, yet I don't want to fall. I want his dick.

"Bossy."

I lift my head off the pillow to observe him but get a view of the top of his head. He shifts himself to fit between my thighs. I widen them for ease.

Letting go of every inhibition I had mere moments ago, I wait with bated breath for him to breach my opening. And when the tip nudges in, I call out. Not in pain, but in genuine pleasure. Six years is a long time to go without sex, especially for someone so young. By the time I got pregnant, I had only had sex a handful of times.

"Fuck. I said not to stop moaning, but damn girl. I'm on thin ice here and can't make it good if I come early."

"It's already better than I could have imagined. Go deeper. I need more of you. So much more."

My walls grip him tightly as he pushes in. Slow at first, but at my insistence, he moves quicker, sensing to propel swiftly past the spot of pain. Although subtle, it still causes me to wince. Guess delivering a baby hasn't lessened the pain.

Once he's seated all the way in, he chooses when to move, thrusting in and out, my body reacting to every push and pull.

Pleasure consumes me. This isn't the experiences I had before.

There's more to this than sex. More of an emotional connection among the physical.

My hands grip his back, tugging him nearer, as close as I can get him. My fingertips dig into his shoulders, paralleling the throbbing where he pistons inside me.

The orgasm barely starts before it full-on floods me. Waves and waves of ecstasy pulsate every crevice, and I feel it everywhere, not just in my abdomen. Warmth spreads throughout me, the sensation unmatched.

I scream out Walsh's name as my name falls from his mouth with a grunt. It brings some awareness back. So blissed out, I forgot there was someone else in the room for a moment. A feeling of such strong elation took over, rendering me oblivious.

When the pulses stop, I bring my head down, my eyes opening to find Walsh's sated expression peering back at me.

My fingers tangle in his hair. "Thank you for not letting my fear win," I whisper.

A smile graces his lips. "The pleasure's all mine."

Motioning down to where he's still inside me, I ask, "Not as painful?"

"Nope. But damn, that was a lot. Hopefully, the condom can handle it all."

His words seep in one by one, the exact meaning not clear immediately. But when it fully sinks in, I freeze. Literally, go still. About the same time, he grasps his mistake.

"Shit, Tate. No. It's fine. I promise you, it's *fine*." He stresses the last fine, but I can't help thinking it's not. Nor can he make such a promise.

"You need to check." He doesn't move fast enough, so I repeat it, a little more harried this time. "Walsh, you need to check. Please."

Yes, I sound desperate. Yes, it's most likely irrational. No, I won't apologize.

The frantic tone gets him moving. He pulls out of me carefully and takes off for the bathroom, presenting a splendid view of his ass I can't even appreciate because I'm so worried.

When he returns, my clothes are back on. His body language conveys he doesn't like it. He holds a washcloth in his hand, his expression giving nothing away. It makes me cagey not being able to read him. How can he be so nonchalant, so blasé? Why he is not freaking out? A pregnancy is the last thing he needs on top of everything in his life.

"Well?" I blurt.

His smile should be comforting, but it's not. Even his "all good" does little to appease my fears.

I cannot get pregnant. Not now. Not when I'm navigating this new life. Oh, why was I so stupid? Why did I have to be so selfish and break my own rules? Why does he have to be so damn sexy and sweet?

Tears pool at the corners of my eyes. Concentrating on the ceiling, I blink rapidly, not wanting them to fall.

The bed dips next to me, Walsh's hand falling on my thigh. His expression mirrors mine when I meet his eyes.

"It'll be okay, Tate. Whatever happens. But I'm sure everything's good. No tears or spills. Promise." Not even his sad smile can elicit one from me.

"And if it's not?" I can't ponder the possibility if not, but it's kind of hard not to.

He pulls me to his side. When did he put his clothes back on? "We'll cross that bridge if we come to it. But please understand, my mouth got away from me. It was a stupid thing to say in the heat of the moment."

"You think?" I retort. "So I shouldn't be freaking out?"

His heavy sigh fills the room. "I can't tell you how to feel. But based on what I cleaned up, I'd say we're safe. I apologize for uttering something to make you freak out. Believe me, I understand what must be going through your head. And I'm sorry for putting it there. However, I won't apologize for wanting to be with you. For wanting to have sex with you. That was fucking awesome, and if I haven't ruined everything, I'd very much like to do it again with you."

His comment makes me laugh. Not in a "ha ha" way, but ironically. I'm sitting here, barely able to think about anything else except for getting pregnant, and he's cracking jokes about having sex again.

"Talk to me in a few weeks." I go to stand up, but he tugs my wrist back. "I wasn't ready."

My words slap him in the face. "That's not fair. I didn't force you."

I hate how he's right and how disappointment infuses his tone and mars his handsome face. I have to own my emotions. He's not to blame.

"I can't get pregnant again, Walsh. I love Aubrey, I do, but I can't do it again. Not on my own. Not with two of them." Every other thought dies on my lips as tears consume me. I don't know how I end up in his arms—did I collapse or did he pull me there—but a certain peace sweeps over me with his hand rubbing my back. As if it would be okay. We could make it work. If. *If* we get pregnant. I wouldn't be alone this time.

"You're not alone, babe. We'll get through any consequences of our behavior together."

I can't be sure he intends to, but there's so much emphasis on the *we, our,* and *together.*

I pull my head back so I can see his face. His expression displays concern. "Why are you so sweet?"

"Ha. Hardly."

"You are. You're a wonderful dad, a great friend, a remarkable man." I stop myself before I spill every single exceptional quality about him. "Did I thank you for today's flowers? I'm always forgetting to show my appreciation. They're my favorite."

My accolade earns more of his devotion. "Which ones?"

I smile. "All of them. Any of them."

"But which ones do you like the most?" His curiosity is adorable and coupled with how he's made sure I'm okay with what's currently happening, I can't help but grin wider and give him more of my truths.

"The ones that come from you." I wiggle myself out of his arms and onto his lap, my thighs straddling his as I face him. "The thought, the simple gesture, the pretty colors. I love them all."

His scrutiny of my face makes me blush slightly. Apprehension fills his features, but it's more for me than him. Especially when he asks, "You're okay?"

My go-to answer—yep—seems too flippant. And besides, I'm not fully okay. I won't be until knowing, without a doubt, he's right, and we didn't make a colossal mistake.

I shrug. "Meh. I want to be, but until I know for sure, the thought will linger in the back of my mind, the 'what if' and 'we should have been more careful' opinions screaming at me."

"It kills me I was so stupid to say something so dumb, but no matter what, I don't regret what we did. Do you?"

"You kept your promise."

Do I explain I have regrets? I regret being so selfish and needing to know what it was like to feel him inside me.

His fingers run through my hair, brushing wayward strands out of my face. "It was amazing for me too. One day, I hope we get to experience it again. Just think of how much better it will be."

The potential for what he suggests thrills me. The parts of me not currently freaking out about the consequences of our actions. Because he's right. It was damn amazing. I always heard sex should be pleasurable and fun, but that was never my experience. Until Walsh.

I divert his thinking away from this subject. "Want some pie now?"

"Damn straight." He makes no move to get up. A subtle crease on his forehead, below his healing battle wound scar, forms. "Are we okay?"

The words get stuck in my throat, so I nod my answer. From the way he doesn't immediately relax, it's not what he was hoping for, so I whisper, "I think so."

My cheeks cupped in his palms, he brings my head closer to his. He leans in for a kiss but instead of the passionate ones we've partaken, his lips leave the sweetest, most chaste kiss on the corner of my lips. At the moment, it's exactly what I need. And damn if my heart doesn't shout, *Hey, Tate's head, get on board with this!*

"Think we can still shower together?" He sets my feet on the ground as he stands from the bed.

I don't let his question get to me. Just because I haven't had a chance to fully ponder it yet doesn't mean I want to say no.

"There's a high probability of a positive outcome."

I turn for the door, heading for the kitchen, his body heat surrounding me as he drapes his arms over my shoulders from behind.

"I'll take those odds."

"I thought you might."

Over pie and leftovers, Walsh fills me in on the details of the fundraiser, gives me a crash course about members of the hockey team, and compliments the pie no less than a dozen times.

"Can we make this together one day?"

I raise my brow at his use of "we." "Like *we* made all the other things? I cook, you clean?"

Before speaking, he swallows the last bite, savoring it. His eyes fall closed on a moan. "I want to help. Will you teach me?"

I confirm what he's asking. "To make pecan pie?"

"Yep."

"In exchange for blow job lessons?" I utter. Although, I'm not sure he could be any worse a student in the kitchen than I was in the bedroom. Then the image of him peeling potatoes emerges and confirms he could be. "Yes. I'd like to teach you how to make pecan pie, as inept as you are in the kitchen. I'm up for the task."

"Gag-cough-gag," he mumbles.

I can't even argue because he's correct again. I've lost count of how many times he's been accurate.

"I feel like there's a dare in there somewhere."

I study his face, seeking clues about how serious he is. The only hint I get is the tic of his left eye, but hell if I know what it means.

"I'm at a disadvantage to practice, considering we hardly get any alone time together, but you could show up at any time and help in the kitchen."

He thrusts his hips out to me. "We have all night after the fundraiser." I can't be certain through his pants, but I swear he's sporting a semi.

"Taken under advisement." The clock behind him alerts me to how little time we have left to get ready for said fundraiser. "We should get ready soon."

"Right. Although we're saving time by showering together."

Even if I wanted to turn him down, I can't with the way he tells me what we're doing. I glance at his crotch. "No funny business in the shower. One, we don't have time. And two, you know." A shiver runs through me at the thought of our earlier discussion.

Walsh grabs my hand and squeezes once, communicating everything with his action.

At the moment, it's precisely what I need.

Walsh senses the purpose of the shower—to get clean. Sure, maybe his hand lingers a little longer on my breasts and ass, but other than that, he's a true gentleman.

We arrive at the restaurant around seven. I've yet to try it mostly because I don't eat out much and because it's off the beaten path, located just within the town limits. I stick to areas I'm familiar with.

I wasn't sure what to expect with a name like Orchard View Tavern, and I didn't have a chance to check out the menu. From the outside, it's big like a warehouse, almost too large to be a restaurant. Lights along the top of the flat roof illuminate the brick façade. The name of the restaurant stands out in big, bold black letters above double glass doors.

Inside, the space is a large open area, with tables spread throughout. The brick extends to the interior, one wall painted white, the others original. Wide, exposed beams run from ceiling to floor in a few places. Rows of track lighting brighten the space well. From what I can tell, there's a section in the back for games of some sort.

Most of the tables are full, which hopefully bodes well for the fundraising efforts.

We sit with his teammates at a long table seating at least twelve. Walsh introduces me to them, and all but one size me up. I'm pretty sure his allegiance to the other team accounts for his lack of analysis.

It's strange for me to be part of a duo—holding hands, being introduced as his girlfriend—but it feels right. Well, maybe not the *girlfriend* moniker. I almost choked on a sip of water when he said it. We've yet to discuss a label for what our relationship is. Now is not the time to discuss it. I'm too enthralled by the banter between teammates.

"First time here. What should I get?" one of them asks. Gabe, maybe.

"If you're in the mood for meat, their burgers are good. I'm partial to the Hangover Cure," another one answers. A backward Aspenridge hat hides his curly locks.

"Why am I not surprised?" the one with a shaved head responds. Backward hat guy salutes him with the finger.

"And if I'm not in the mood for meat?" The way his voice intones on *meat* confirms my suspicions about his being gay.

"Veggie Delight burger, duh."

"Or a salad," another player adds his two cents.

I don't hang around many—if any—college students. I lost touch with most of my high school friends except Carley. Any other friends I left behind in Kansas were other moms. Most were older, and the only thing we had in common was our kids, so the relationships were superficial. Haven't given them much thought since I arrived in Vermont.

College athletes seem to be a different breed, at least these hockey ones. In the ten minutes we've been here, they've shown a sense of camaraderie but also ragged on each other the way only people who are comfortable with each other do. It's fascinating and entertaining for this girl with no college experience. The fact they're easy on the eyes doesn't hurt. When the conversation turns to hockey, I zone out.

"What are you thinking about ordering?" Walsh's husky voice tickles my ear.

"Um, haven't decided yet."

I haven't even looked. I've been too busy enthralled with these attractive college hockey players.

"I'm gonna grab a beer? Want something from the bar?"

"Sprite or ginger ale, please."

He disappears from the table, and my eyes note his ass in his khaki pants as he saunters to the bar with a few of the other teammates.

His seat vacated, another player slides down, the one in the backward hat. "Cody McGuire."

"Tate."

"Right. I can remember one name but figured you're the one who's meeting all of us and probably won't remember all the names."

"Or any," I mumble, hoping he can't hear me. He doesn't sit too close to be uncomfortable, but what exactly am I supposed to talk to him about? Hockey? No. College? Negative. Vermont? "Where are you from and what brought you to Vermont?"

"Lyndon, a small town in Oregon. My former coach talked me into applying to Aspenridge. My folks were convinced I wouldn't get in, but I proved them wrong, didn't I?" He smiles, but it doesn't reach his eyes. A hint of embarrassment hides in his tone. Shouldn't he be happy about his acceptance?

"You did." I flash him a wider smile, showing him a little kindness. "What's your major?"

"Biology. Not for the fainthearted."

I laugh. "Indeed not. But either is hockey."

His entire demeanor changes with my simple statement. "Have you been to a game yet?"

"Can't say I have."

"Too busy with classes?" he guesses.

A kid and a job. "Something like that."

Thankfully, Walsh is back, along with a server to take our order.

"Stop macking on my girlfriend, McGuire."

"Keeping her company until your ass came back. Pipe down." Cody makes no move to shift back to where he was sitting until Walsh puffs his chest. Not quite a pissing match, but my heart celebrates Walsh's protectiveness.

I think I quite like being Walsh Keeley's girlfriend.

"I didn't realize we were at the girlfriend stage of our relationship." The words leave my mouth while we stand in line for a game of cornhole after we've eaten. Best yard game ever. Never thought to play it indoors, but the games area provides plenty of space for it. Including a "grassy" area.

"Right. Sorry. 'Lennon's friend's mom' sounded too cultured for this crowd. 'Friend' seemed like a dig to you. You can't be a 'fuckbuddy' after only one time. All I was left with was girlfriend. Unless you have a better term you'd prefer." He sips his beer bottle, the one he's allowed for tonight, nursing it slowly. As much as he didn't ask anything, he's waiting for an answer.

"Think they would have believed escort?"

Beer sprays out of his mouth like a geyser, coating the table next to him in liquid. He coughs and spurts before getting control of himself. With a narrowed glare and pointed finger, he mutters, "I wasn't expecting that."

"We're even then." Although the more I think about it, the more the title of girlfriend has a nice ring to it. But what's better is I get to call Walsh my boyfriend. Which doesn't suck in the slightest. I kiss his temple. "Going to the bathroom. Be right back." For shits and giggles—because I need to try it out—I add, "Boyfriend."

I'm too nervous for his reaction, even though he said it first and I'm agreeing.

The bathroom has three stalls, but all three are empty, which means there's no one to witness my ecstatic reaction to my period starting. The laugh starts low in my abdomen, and by the time it's liberated, it's a full-on cackle. Guess I freaked out for literally nothing earlier.

I finish my business—learned the hard way to always carry pads and tampons in my bag—and exit the stall. As I'm washing my hands, another girl enters. She's dressed in a little black dress, her shoulders covered with a short sweater. Her hair's pulled up in some sort of fancy updo I wish I could replicate and pull off. Her eyes rake over me, scanning from head to toe.

"Oh, Walsh's new girl, right?" I can't quite decipher what emotion fills her tone. Envy? Resentment? Bitterness? However, I don't like the way she emphasizes *new*.

"Yes." Another lesson I've confirmed: answer only the question asked and keep it simple.

"Where'd he find you? Haven't seen you around campus."

The hot water scalding my fingers matches the temperature inside at her insinuation.

"I'm not a student." Soap rinses off my hands, falling into the drain. I kinda wish I could swirl after it to avoid this confrontation.

Her hip leans up against the sink farthest from where I stand, arms crossed over her chest. "Yeah, didn't think so. Did you ride the Keeley cockcycle yet?"

There's no way I heard her correctly. She asked...if I...rode...the *Keeley cockcycle?*

"Um, not sure how that's your business."

As much as I don't relate to the other moms in Aubrey's class, catty college girls aren't my style either. Too much drama.

"Mark my words. Don't get too invested. He'll be bored with you within a week. Especially if you aren't into kids. You know he's a dad, right? Or did he leave that part out?"

I stare in abject horror, not comprehending her words. She stands there, clearly not in any rush to take care of whatever led her into the bathroom, waiting for an answer. A real answer, as if I'm going to spill my secrets about my relationship with Walsh to a stranger.

After a brief silence, when she doesn't get what she wants, she uncrosses her arms and throws them in the air. "Suit yourself. Don't say I didn't warn you." Her "advice" issued, she finally makes her way to a stall.

I exit the bathroom as quickly as possible, trying to make sense of what she insinuated. It contradicts everything I know about Walsh, everything he's told me, everything he's shown me. But could her words possibly have any truth to them?

Not watching where I'm going, I slam into a hard body. Strong arms grip my biceps to keep me upright, and Walsh's voice filters in through the rampant thoughts swirling around my brain of the man himself. My body reacts to the zap of electricity flowing through at our connection.

"Hey, all good?" His expression is equal parts concern and content.

"Honestly, I'm not sure." Do I attempt to bring up the weird conversation with the girl? Who even was she? A fundraiser for his hockey team is probably not the best place to have this discussion if I decide to bring it up. "How much longer are you obligated to stay?"

Not wearing his watch, he pulls his phone out of his pocket. "An hour tops. Okay?"

No, not really, I want to confess, but my head nods. "Oh. About earlier. I think maybe I overreacted a little." His brows furrow, but he lets me continue. "I got my period. Pretty sure we're safe. Just in case."

"Are you freaking kidding me?" He winks, but his tone and ensuing laugh oppose his sarcastic comment.

"But don't get any ideas we'll be doing anything else tonight or tomorrow. Just, gross. Ew. No."

"Tell me how you really feel about it."

Rather than do that, I ask, "How do you feel about cuddling?"

His actions scream louder than any words as he pulls me into his side and kisses the top of my head. "It's one of my favorite things in the world."

While I highly doubt that, right now, I'll accept it.

As he steps up to play the game, I can't help but wonder how much truth there is to everything I know about Walsh Keeley.

CHAPTER 23
WALSH

Tate seems off or distracted when returning from the bathroom. Once she told me about getting her period, I thought she'd relax a little, knowing my stupid mistake was just that—stupid and a mistake. I didn't mean to set her off, spiral her into a freak-out, but I get where she's coming from. Obviously, I need to be safe as much as she does. I can't "afford" an unwanted pregnancy in my life now. Actually, never. Not when graduation looms and I'll soon be starting my career.

I was fortunate when Megan got pregnant with Lennon—my life didn't change a whole lot. I still got to attend college, play hockey, and work toward my dream of becoming an athletic trainer, all with a baby and toddler in tow. Megan wasn't initially wrong—her life changed the most—but we've both altered our plans for Lennon's sake and make sure she gets what she needs before her parents. It hasn't always been easy, but we've made it work. A similar situation would upset the balance in our lives…and not in a good way.

"She's a pretty one. Where'd you find her?" Cody asks, bringing me out of my head with a nod to Tate. He's drunk more than his allotment of one beer but still on the right side of tipsy. He seems to think some rules don't apply to him.

"Her daughter and Lennon are in the same preschool class."

He almost chokes on his beer. "She's a mom?" His subtle once-over of Tate doesn't go unnoticed. "Damn. Can you hook me up with any other moms?"

"Um, no. Not happening. Pretty sure they're all married or way older than us."

"Dude, I'm totally into cougars," he drawls, his non-Vermont accent stronger with each sip.

I pat him on the back. "I think you should stick to bunnies for now. Less baggage. More action." He doesn't miss the exhaled sigh complementing my words. It's the complete opposite of how I feel about Tate. Since she and I have similar baggage, I'm in no position to judge her. And as far as action goes, it's not like I want or need to go out every weekend and pick up some random bunny. Not my style.

Walking away from Cody, I sidle up to Tate, who's studying the items up for auction. "See anything you like?" Goose bumps erupt on her neck.

Her hand flies to her chest as she swivels around, her relief palpable at recognizing me. "Walsh, you scared me."

"Sorry, babe." I pull her into me, my hand splaying her abdomen. Instead of melting into me, her body stiffens, and she tries to jerk away. "Hey, what's wrong?"

"Can you just not?" Her tone is unfamiliar—high, pitchy, full of uncertainty yet underlined with indignation. I want to push her, ask for clarification, but two puck chasers arrive at the table.

"Hey, Keeley. Having a good night?" The taller of the two speaks. And by taller, I'm talking an inch or two. I've seen them around campus before but uncertain of either of their names. Bianca? Erica?

I'll never understand the fascination of the revolving door of sexual partners from these types of girls. I don't see the full effect of their behavior because I don't live in the hockey house or on campus.

"Sure," I mumble, trying to avoid too much conversation with them and also attempting to gain Tate's attention. Tate's entire body stiffens in the proximity of the two girls. Ignoring them, I turn her toward me, my hands on her shoulders to help relax her. She keeps her head down, her gaze cast toward something on the table. Even when I tip her chin up, her eyes dart around, never once landing on me. A sinking feeling weighs my stomach down. "Tate, talk to me. What's going on?"

Suddenly more aware of the extra sets of eyes I don't want privy to this conversation, I guide her away from the table. Thoughts swirl through my mind of what could have set her off and made her so uncomfortable.

I don't stop until we're in a corner of the room, away from most of the people enjoying their food. Trepidation hides in all areas of her face and posture, sending me into overprotective and "fix it" mode.

"Babe, I'm thinking the worst. Care to clue me in?"

"How many girlfriends have you had?"

Her out of left field question throws me off-kilter, but I rebound quickly. "One."

"And girls you've slept with? I assume it's been more?"

My brain circulates through the handful of girls there have been after Megan. "Six?" I should be more certain of the number, but they all seemed so insignificant after Megan. Until her. Tate.

"So there could be more than six?" she challenges, her laser gaze holding steady with mine.

"One, maybe two at the most. One-timers mostly." I should probably shut up now. This conversation is better suited for her house later. Maybe not the bedroom, even though we're not having sex tonight.

Her brow quirks at my use of "one-timers." "Just a quick ride on the Keeley cockcycle?"

The what?

Was that even English?

Did she use my last name and some sort of bicycle reference?

"WHAT? What in the hell does that mean?" My voice pitches high, but I tamp down the emotion behind it.

Or, I attempt to tamp it down. Not sure my emotions will stabilize until I understand what she's said.

"You tell me." Her arms cross over her chest, the action drawing my focus there. I sense the way her heart pounds. She's uncomfortable. I can't tell if it's because of the confrontation or the subject or me.

"Tate, I have no clue what the fuck you're talking about. The Keeley…what did you call it?"

"Cockcycle." Such disdain in her voice. Such disgust in her expression.

"Right. Cockcycle." I run my hands through my hair, blowing out an exasperated breath. "And I'm supposed to know what it means?"

The first slip in her demeanor breaks through. The fact I'm shocked at this news surprises her.

"Something to do with hockey maybe? Sorry if I was too stunned to ask for clarification."

Her snarky attitude does little to assuage the way I'm feeling, the way my pulse continues to throb stronger. "Where did you hear such a crude thing?" Perhaps that should have been the first thing I asked, but like her, the shock of hearing something so revolting rocked me.

"In the bathroom. From the girl who was just at the table."

"Which one?" As if that's the most important piece to this mystery.

"The platinum blonde."

Yep, see. No real difference since I don't remember either of their names. But I know for certain, without a doubt, neither one of them is one of my handful of one-timers.

Without a better option or way to control my emotions, my feet pace around the corner we're standing. How does a rumor like this even start? Better yet, who the hell came up with the name?

Cockcycle.

Even thinking it has my blood boiling.

A thought occurs to me. A worse thought than all others taking precedence in my mind since Tate brought it up.

I stop right in front of Tate. "Oh my god. You think it's *true*? That's why you're acting all cagey, asking these questions. You think I'm what? Like a manwhore?"

Her gaze flicks down for a brief second before her shoulders slump. "I don't. Not the Walsh I know. But the doubt started creeping in, especially because we haven't known each other long. I don't know what it's like to be in college, and when you add hockey…" She's unable to complete the thought. I don't like how she's bothered by this, and how I'm the source.

"It's not true, Tate. Not any of it. Not even a single bit. I wouldn't ever get involved, even for one night, with a bunny. I hate knowing girls may be with my friends before or after me. That's not the type of guy I am. Have I not shown you that?" The defensiveness in my tone bleeds through.

Never did I think I'd be having this conversation with her. Not ever. And not because she's not at school with me or into hockey. Because I thought she knew me. Knew what I was capable of. Or in this case, not capable of.

Her eyes dampen with tears. "I'm sorry. I was caught so off guard when she was spewing it, I didn't know what to think. But I want to believe you."

"But you don't?"

She grabs for my wrists, but I keep them out of reach. I'm not ready to be touched by her. Not when she's not completely convinced the rumor has no basis in reality.

"How do I prove it's a total fabrication? A horrible one."

"I-I don't know," she murmurs softly and unconfidently.

"And my word's not good enough?"

I'm at a loss for how to get her to trust me, or even where we go from here. Do I drop her home and leave? Is my invite to stay still valid? Is this the end of the possibility of something more between Tate and me? That thought has my skin crawling.

I like her, everything I know about her, as little as she thinks it is. There's not a doubt in my mind she isn't who she's portrayed or has any skeletons in her closet causing me to distrust her. Obviously, she doesn't share those same sentiments about me.

I've never been in a situation like this before. I've never been involved with bunnies. Because with me, what you see is what you get. I just need to figure out how to make her understand.

"How do I get rid of the doubts?" Her voice is so small, so soft-spoken, I barely hear her. I also don't have an answer for her. I can't tell her what to believe, what to do, how to handle this situation. She has to make the choice—whether to put her trust in me or in what some sex-hungry cunt told her.

"What's making you believe a stranger over me? Like, why do

her words hold more clout than things I've said and done to the contrary?"

"A manwhore can still be a gentleman, Walsh."

Damn, she has a point. Cody's proof.

"I'll give you that. Plenty of guys on the team fit that mold. None of them are me, though." I pause, unsure what else to say or do. "What the hell even is a cockcycle? And no, it has nothing to do with hockey."

"I've asked myself the same repeatedly. A cock taken for a ride, like a bicycle. That's the best I can come up with."

"Hmm. The more I think about it, the more it has a nice ring to it. Keeley cockcycle." Using a short i versus the long i changes the effect. It's also exactly what we need to break through the tension. "Too bad you didn't have time to ride it, try it out for size. You're missing out on something special."

"Why can't I sometime soon?" She slaps a hand over her mouth, my bad habits rubbing off on her.

She didn't mean to say it, but it's the in I need.

I step an inch closer, wanting to touch her but not pushing my limit. Parroting her words from a few days ago, I plead, "It's yours for the taking any time you want." Then I include a caveat of my own. "*Only* yours, Tate."

A flash of concern swipes over her face. The need to protect her, show her she's mine, is fierce.

"Why would she say it if it's not true?" The uncertainty is back, but this time, it's not so much directed toward me but the girl.

Despite the absurdity of the situation, I don't have to think too hard for a reason. "Because she's jealous. Because she's a bitch. But mostly because she wants a piece of the action, to ride the Keeley cockcycle, but will never get the opportunity." Taking a bigger chance, I grab her wrists, bringing her nearer to me. It's a good sign when she doesn't hesitate. "I don't want any of them, Tate. Even if I did—which I don't—it would be a means to an end, a onetime thing." I repeat those words slowly, allowing them to sink in. "One. Time. Understand I want more with you. Today was not enough." I allow her the time to process, hoping she undoubtedly accepts my point. "Please believe me. I'll do whatever's necessary to prove to you how serious this is, how much I want this between us. How much *you* mean to me."

"Walsh, I..."

My finger to her lips cuts her off. Figuring I have nothing to lose, I go for broke. "Not here. Give me tonight at the very least. I'm not ready to say goodbye to you when I drop you off."

Her head nods the slightest bit. "Okay."

"Fuck." I wrap her in my arms, waves of tension rolling off me with the action. As crappy as it feels dealing with this, holding her feels right. Like it's something I'm meant to do.

And not just in this moment.

Tate moves her head away and peers up at me with sad eyes. "Is it time for us to leave yet?"

I don't even pull out my phone. Not caring the auction hasn't ended yet—not like I bid on anything—I lead her over to my coach. He's finishing up with a man, most likely some influential bigwig in the community. I wait until he's finished before speaking.

"Hey, Coach. I have to head out." I give no reason because I'm not about to lie in front of Tate when I'm proving she can trust me. He shakes my offered hand.

"Walsh, see you at practice on Sunday." He then reaches out to Tate, who doesn't hesitate to shake his hand. "Tate, nice meeting you. Hope to see you at a game soon."

She's no doubt startled by the fact he remembered her name. But that's Coach. As great of a coach as he is, he's a people person at heart.

"Nice to meet you. I'll try to make it to the rink."

My ears perk up at her comment. I've only been trying to get her to come to a game for a month. The woman is full of excuses.

We bid farewell to a few more teammates before grabbing our jackets from the coat check. I help her into hers without conscious thought, not to demonstrate a point, but because it's something I'd do anyway.

Once the sun went down, the bitter cold characteristic of Vermont winters rolled in. I tuck Tate into my side as we walk to the car. She seems to be over what happened earlier, or at least feeling better about it. Or me. Or she's just cold and wants my warmth. The walk to the car is just long enough for the wind to whip through.

"Sorry I don't have a car starter," I apologize as I hit the button to unlock the doors.

"I drive a ten-year-old Honda Civic. I barely have heat."

Her comment evokes something deep within me. As much as I hope she's not serious, it still rattles me. "I hope you're kidding."

Her hand on my arm, she smiles tenderly. "Relax. I am. The heat works fine, but I'm worried a little about the snow. We got some in Kansas, but nothing like Vermont. A new car isn't really in my budget this winter."

"At the very least, you'll need snow tires." I add "put snow tires on Tate's car" to my mental running list of things to do in the next week.

"Okay."

The drive to her place is quiet. While it's not entirely unpleasant, it's not entirely comfortable either. If that doesn't change by the time we arrive at her place, it's going to be a long night.

The silence continues while I park and we head inside. After making sure the door is locked, she slips down the hall to her bedroom. My first instinct is to follow her but quickly think better of it. If she needs space from me, I can give her that.

I flop down on the couch and dig my phone out of my pocket. There's a text from Meg with a picture of Lennon sleeping the wrong way in her bed.

> Adorable. You're dropping her off at 3 tomorrow?

> She conked out early like this. Didn't even stir when I changed her into PJs.

> Yes, we'll be there around 3

> Must have had a busy day of play

She'll only message back if she needs the last word, which is the case with her when she's mad at something I've done or just pissed off. Hopefully not tonight. I can't deal with her bullshit.

One moody woman is enough.

Speaking of, Tate saunters back into the room a few minutes later wearing flannel pants and an oversized hoodie. Another thing jotted on the mental to-do list: Get Tate an Aspenridge hoodie with my name and number on it. She wiped her face free of the minimal makeup she wore to the event and pulled her hair into a messy bun. Her beauty astounds me. And the compliment tumbles out of my mouth.

"Stunning, babe." I attempt to pull her onto the couch with me, but she's slightly out of reach.

"Don't feed me lies. That's the exact opposite of what you're trying to prove."

Momentarily stunned by what she thinks of me, I recover quickly.

"Sorry. Let me try again." I drag my eyes up and down her, my perusal slow and lingering. "Tate, how dare you walk into the living room wearing such a heinous outfit? And no makeup? Whatever are you thinking?" I wait to capture her attention with mine before adding, "Better?"

"Totally believable. I'll never doubt you again." Too bad her words are laced with a sarcastic tone. "Coffee?"

"Sure. And some cookies?"

She turns for the kitchen, and I quickly follow behind. "Let me see if I have any left. *Someone* might have eaten all the leftovers."

It shouldn't affect me the way it does, but I can't help the emotion of frenzy washing over me at her emphasized use of someone. Because obviously, *someone* is me.

In the kitchen, she busies herself making a pot of coffee. Next to my mom, she makes the best-tasting coffee, and I'm yearning for another taste of the way she prepares it with coconut milk. If she'll let me steal a sip.

Tate opens up the container for the cookies with a smile. "Three left. All yours."

Yesterday I would have taken them all. Hell, six hours ago, I would have acted the same way. Yet right now, I choose two, leaving the last for her. The gratitude for my act displays on her face, a beaming smile gracing her lips.

Point one to Walsh. Don't screw this up.

"What's on your agenda for tomorrow?"

"Lennon comes back around three, then I'm volunteering at a hockey clinic."

Astonishment parades across her facial features. She hadn't foreseen my comment.

"Um, wow. That's cool. I wouldn't fathom you have time for something like that given school, hockey, Lennon…" She trails off, but the implication of more lingers in the air.

"It's not a huge time commitment. And Lennon will sit in the stands and watch, or she'll jump on the ice and stay out of our way. She'll be in her glory."

A small smile graces her lips. "Fun for her and generous of you."

"I owe a lot to hockey, to the people who work the rinks. I like to give back when I can."

It's more than "a lot." Since I was three years old and learned to skate, all I wanted to do was play hockey. Mom and Dad had no qualms about supporting my love of the sport, except equipment and travel leagues aren't cheap. And when Dad lost his job when I was in middle school, it put a damper on the prospect of continuing to play.

It was Millie who approached me after practice at Nordic, and without her uttering a word, I understood by the way her shoulders slumped and the defeat in her eyes. Hockey wasn't on the essentials list.

Except I was determined to play. I mowed lawns, shoveled driveways, walked dogs, returned cans and bottles. Any chore someone would pay me for, I did. And when I was about one hundred dollars short by the time the next season rolled around, Wayne, the owner of the Nordic Rink, paid the rest with a mention of "working it off." In the years since, I more than have, while also gaining an appreciation for giving back and helping whenever I could. Especially when it involves hockey.

Tate's voice brings me out of my memories. "An admirable quality." She casts her head down, her fingers gripping the handle of her mug a little tighter. A beat of silence commences, but the tension in the air isn't stifling. When she looks back up at me, a sadness hangs over her. "I owe you an apology, Walsh."

"For what?"

"For letting that girl get in my head. For not trusting you at your word. You've done nothing, and I mean *nothing*, to make me think less of you. And honestly, if the Keeley cockcycle was a thing, if you could have any girl at any time, you wouldn't be here right now with me. You wouldn't have worked so hard to wait until I was ready. The chase wouldn't have been worth it."

"It's not a thing," I stress, unable to repeat the actual words.

"I believe you. But the rest is still true. My emotions are all over the map between thinking there was a possibility of getting pregnant and my period arriving. It doesn't excuse my behavior."

"I'd very much still like you to be my girlfriend. If you can stand it," I tack on.

She retorts sassily, "Only if I can ride the Keeley cockcycle."

To say I'm shocked is an understatement, but damn if it doesn't turn me the fuck on. Which isn't the best place to be right now considering she's off-limits for a while. It's so unfortunate since we have the place to ourselves, no kids needing us, all the time...

No. I can't let my thoughts drift there.

"As long as it's ultimately protected. I don't need the added stress of a possible malfunctioning condom."

"You need to get on birth control." Not my best comeback for a variety of reasons, especially when she raises her brow. I continue, without screwing things up more. "As a backup protection. Between the two, we should be good. Birth control and condoms. Used in conjunction."

Great. Now I'm babbling.

"Fair enough. If you're willing to wrap it up, the least I can do is remember to take a pill every day."

"That was easier than I thought."

"Don't push it and make me change my mind."

I heed her advice and shut up, her narrowed stare even more of a deterrent.

"How about dinner at my house on Sunday with the girls? Maybe if we're really lucky, Mom will let us escape for an hour to Target. Hell, the grocery store."

"Shouldn't you check with your mom first before inviting us?"

"Nope. 'The more the merrier' she'll say."

She laughs at my lousy impression of Millie Keeley.

"Let me just check with Aunt Marsha since we usually go there for dinner on Sundays. But we've been there a lot this week, so she may be sick of us."

I shrug. "Lunch works too. Hell, how about breakfast? Come for some meal on Sunday."

"Sheesh. Okay. You don't have to beg. It doesn't suit you."

"Yeah, but it worked, didn't it?" She rolls her eyes at my wink.

We sit in the kitchen a little longer, sharing our favorite Thanksgiving weekend traditions before we turn in for the night.

I change into flannel PJs and a hockey T-shirt before climbing into bed. Dressed in the T-shirt I wore earlier and PJ pants, she makes it very clear which side I'm to sleep on. It does little to discourage my cock from thinking it's time to play.

Damn period.

CHAPTER 24
WALSH

Cuddling Tate all night long changes something between us. I can't put my finger on what exactly, but there's a distinct glow about her this morning, a renewed energy radiating off her. I'm not stupid enough to ask. She'll tell me when she's ready.

She cooks pancakes for breakfast—a triple batch with some "to freeze for the week." I wish I had an ounce of her organization and productive nature. After I clean up breakfast—loading the dishwasher how she likes—we curl up on the couch to finish the movie we started weeks ago before I have to leave.

As much as I'll see her around, a part of me doesn't want to leave. The last twenty-four hours have been overcharged with emotions, for both of us. I'm glad we worked through it all to end up here: Tate as my girlfriend. Even thinking those words has my heart beating faster. I should pinch myself to confirm I'm not dreaming.

The movie ends, and it's time to say goodbye. Tate's wrapped in my arms. It's coming to be my favorite place for her. Too bad it's only when we're alone.

"I'll text you later to let you know what time to come for breakfast."

She pulls back to peer at me. "And to let me know what to bring."

"Sure, that too," I appease her. My mother won't ask anything of her. "I'm going to miss you. Miss this. Miss the way…"

"Stop talking and kiss me, Walsh," she demands.

On her tiptoes, she meets me halfway, our lips crashing together as if this is our last kiss. And it will be for a while considering I don't know when we'll have another chance to be alone.

Each kiss from Tate stirs up emotions inside me, begging for more.

More kisses.

More emotion.

More everything.

Our tongues duel for control. Usually she gives it up easily, but she seems to want it now. I back off slightly, encouraging her to take the lead. Our mouths still connected, she leaps into my arms, immediately wrapping her legs around my waist. Her tongue delves deeper into my mouth, rubbing against the inside before assaulting my tongue. Will I ever get enough of this?

In my pants, my cock grows hard, the hint I need to break away.

Tate pouts, her eyes flying open at the loss. "Why did you stop?" I thrust my hips up, allowing her to feel the reason. "Oh. Yeah, I could see how that's a problem."

"You think?"

She giggles. "It still amazes me the effect I have on you."

"Get used to it. I don't see it changing soon."

"Promise?"

"Yep." I pop a last chaste kiss to her lips and slowly lower her down. "Hope Aubrey had fun at her sleepover."

She perks up. "I can't wait to hear how it went. Her call last night was too quick. Have fun at practice."

"Thanks, babe. I will."

I grab my bag from the floor by the door and wiggle my feet into my sneakers. As much as I don't want to go, I can't stay any longer. One last wave and I'm out the door, on my way to see my other favorite girl.

I let that sink in for a minute as I warm up my car.

Damn, I've got it bad for Tate.

Hope Lennon won't mind sharing her top spot with a new person sometime soon. Or two.

That thought causes a stupid grin.

✕

Lennon observes my skate bag the moment she walks through the door and disappears up the stairs. Out of curiosity, I follow her. She runs to my room and swaps the blankets, bringing hers to her nose, the scent appealing enough to warrant a smile. Back to her room to leave her blanket on her bed and grab her skating bag. It doesn't even faze her as I watch from the hallway.

"I'm ready, Keeley. I skate too?"

"Most likely. But there's going to be a team of other kids there who I'll be helping. Mr. Kenny's daughter will be there to keep an eye on you."

"What's her name?"

"Liliana. I think." I scratch my head. "You know I'm not good with names."

"Is she pretty like Tate?"

"I've never met her."

"Can we see Tate soon?"

"She and Aubrey are coming for breakfast tomorrow."

"Is she your lady friend?"

I'm unprepared for her query. "Where did you hear that?"

"I heard Momma talking on the phone about 'his new lady friend.'"

Damn, Megan. And she's always on my ass about how I say inappropriate things in front of our daughter.

"Can we talk about this later? We don't want to be late to the rink."

"Gosh, no. Let's do this." She hands me her bag and scurries down the hall, leaving me reeling after our conversation.

By the time Lennon and I arrive at the rink, our conversation seems forgotten. From Lennon's point of view. Her question spirals through my mind on a loop, something I'll bring up to Megan later.

Kenny greets us by the entrance, a girl around my age standing next to him. His hand out in greeting, his eyes land on Lennon first.

"Lennon, so great to see you. Are you ready to skate?"

"Yep. All set." She bobs her head, her enthusiasm infectious.

"Great." He motions to his daughter. She's pretty in an understated way, although the way her makeup cakes on her face is quite off-putting. Her light brown hair is pulled into a braid, and she's dressed in leggings and a heavy fleece zip up. "This is Liliana. She's going to sit with you in the stands or take you on the ice when you're ready."

At least I got something right today.

Liliana bends down to Lennon's level. "Lennon, so great to meet you. My dad told me all the great things about you. I can't wait to see you skate."

"Nice to meet you."

Still crouched by Lennon, Liliana looks my way. "Hey, I'm Liliana."

"Walsh. Thanks for agreeing to monitor her. If she wants to skate, just tell her where she's allowed to stay. She'll behave, right, Squirt?"

"Absolutely." There's a little devil in her smile, but I think I can trust her.

I drop Lennon's bag to the floor. "There are some pancakes for a snack in there. Sorry they're cold, but Tate made them, so they're yummy."

The moment I mention Tate, I regret it.

Lennon spins to me, hands on her hips, nostrils flaring in annoyance. "Tate made *you* pancakes?"

"And for you." I point to her bag.

"When did you see her?"

"Later, Len. We'll talk about this later." Over her head, I mouth *Sorry* to Liliana, who waves it off with a flick of her wrist.

Lennon stomps her foot once, and when I'm about to reprimand her, she turns and stalks away from me.

"I'm sorry," I start to poor Liliana, caught in the middle of our showdown.

She smiles warmly at me. "We'll be fine."

"If you need anything, grab me off the ice. She needs help lacing her skates. There's also a thermos of water in her bag. Make her drink it even if she refuses, please?"

"Sure thing. Don't worry. I've got this. Kids are my specialty, and this age is right up my alley."

"Okay. Thanks again."

She turns away and jogs to catch up to Lennon. A small wave of guilt niggles me, but I remind myself Lennon enjoys ice time no matter who she's with.

Kenny clears his throat from behind me. "She'll be fine. And if she's not, we know where to find you. Shall we?" He motions to the other side of the entryway toward the office.

Exhaling and hoping for the best, I agree to follow him.

The clinic is fun. The kids range in age from eight to about twelve. Some of them have never skated before, let alone played hockey, so that's a bit of a hindrance. But there are about five other coaches, which is super helpful.

I sneak peeks at Lennon, who's skating on the opposite side of the rink while we run drills, although "drills" is a very loose term. It's more about getting the kids used to feeling comfortable on skates and making contact with the stick and puck. Lennon seems to behave for Liliana. It doesn't escape my notice Liliana's quite the skater. Guess it's not too surprising given her dad's career choice.

The clinic runs for two hours. I'm groomed for longer practices, but this one seems more exhausting. Mostly because I'm bent over more, holding the kids up, rather than skating hard. Different muscles than I'm used to using.

Once it's over, the coach in charge gives a speech. A round of applause follows, started by one of the younger kids. It soon ripples through the rest of the group and after a few seconds, all of us in the rink are hooting, hollering, and cheering. Liliana and Lennon join us on the ice, clapping away.

Once the attendees have left the ice, I skate over to where Lennon is showing Liliana some trick she's been working on—a two-footed jump about an inch off the ice. She must have taught herself because I didn't.

"Hey," Liliana says as I approach.

"Hi. Thanks for keeping an eye out for her."

"Anytime. She's got quite the personality. I sometimes questioned if I was talking to a child." She laughs, a bright smile in my direction.

"She keeps me on my toes, but in a fun way." Lennon skates over, using a T-stop before she barrels into me. "Right, Squirt?"

"Keeley, did you see my jump?"

"Sure did. Where did you learn that?"

"I just did it myself. I thought really hard about lifting my feet off the ice, and I jumped."

Holding my hand out for a high five, I say, "Great perseverance. Did you eat your pancakes?"

"Yeah, but don't think I'm not still mad you got to see Tate without me."

"Of course I didn't." My sarcasm goes over her head this time. "Ready to be done?"

"Just one more jump. Be right back."

She skates away without waiting for a response.

"I'm amazed at the way she skates so well. How long has she been skating?"

"I had her on skates as soon as she could walk, but she's made strides the past year. It helps she loves it and never passes up an opportunity to practice."

Liliana and I slowly skate toward the rink exit, one eye trained on Lennon. An awkward silence ensues.

In the stands, I slip off my skates and put my sneakers on. Lennon comes off the ice slightly out of breath.

"Oh, her stuff's still up on the other side. Let me grab it."

I'm about to tell her I'll get it, but Liliana takes off before I get the chance.

"Did you behave?" Sitting on the bench, I loosen her laces and remove her skates before standing her on the bench to remove her snow pants.

"Yep," she states, popping the p. "Liliana's nice. And she's super good at skating. Even better than Momma." Her nose scrunches at her comment. "But don't tell her. She'll be mad." She's got her mother pegged.

It wasn't hard to convert Megan into a skating and hockey fan. She learned early on in our relationship that if she wanted to see me, she'd find me at the rink. Better yet, she'd strap on her skates and join me on the ice for free skate. Her skills improved each time, but she likes to be the best, and skating is no exception.

"Your secret's safe with me."

Liliana reemerges with her bag, her street shoes replacing her skates.

"Will you be here again? I want to learn how to do a real spiral. Can you teach me?"

Liliana volleys between the two of us, her gaze remaining longer on me. "I'm heading back to school tomorrow, but I'll be home for winter break. I'm sure we can find a time to skate together again, even if Daddy's not busy."

Lennon agrees with a head bob before Liliana finishes speaking. "Yes." Her scrutiny fixates on me. "Get her number."

"Lennon, manners," I chide. The brat rolls her eyes at my reprimand.

"Keeley, can you please get Liliana's number?" It's not much better, but it's not an argument I'm prepared for now.

Liliana covers up her smirk with her hands.

"Liliana, would you be so kind as to put your number in my phone so we can text when you're in town?" I hand over the phone to her.

"Of course." She hands it back after her fingers fly over the screen. "I texted myself so I have yours too." A tinge of red flushes her cheeks, but she covers it up by quickly shifting her focus to Lennon. "I had a lot of fun and can't wait to skate again."

"Me too. Maybe you can meet Aubrey." She must have discussed her friend with Liliana because she doesn't appear confused. "She probably won't skate. Oh, and she won't eat any of those cookies you were talking about, but you should still bring them 'cause I can't wait to try them." In true Lennon fashion, she rubs her belly and smacks her lips. As much as I try, I can't control my eye roll.

"Sounds good, Lennon." With a pat on my shoulder, she says, "I wish you luck for the future," before walking away, a hearty chuckle following her retreat.

As much as I shouldn't foster this type of behavior, I can't help asking, "What type of cookies?"

Lennon's entire face infuses with excitement, and when she answers, I understand. "S'nores cookies!"

I chuckle at her mispronunciation of the word. "Oh, snap. Think you'll share with your old man?"

"If I have to." With the strength of Midas, she somehow refrains from rolling her eyes.

"You're the best, Len."

It takes a few more minutes to pack up all our stuff, but soon we're on the way out of the rink. A wave over my shoulder to Kenny, Lennon trails behind as we exit.

"You should call Tate," she suggests as we climb into the truck.

Every time she mentions her, I'm conflicted. First, I can't figure out where this sudden interest in Tate is coming from, besides what she heard from her mother. But second, does she know there's something between us? She can't be that intuitive about my feelings for the woman, can she?

I decide to test out the waters, feel her out to see where she's coming from.

"Why should I call her?" I watch the rearview mirror for clues. Her head's down, her effort on buckling her straps.

"'Cause I want to see her."

"Tate or Aubrey?" I stress Tate's name just slightly.

"Tate, duh. I have so many things to tell her."

As kooky as she is with the things she says, there's always a reason behind her words. It sometimes takes a while for the reason to be revealed, but there is *always* a reason.

"Can you wait until tomorrow when she and Aubrey come for breakfast?"

"Are you going to let me have alone time with her?" she retorts, her eyes meeting mine in the mirror.

My loud gasp fills the truck. "Lennon, where is all this coming from?"

"She's your girlfriend." No hesitation or doubt in her tone.

"How do you know?" Let's hope she's not smart enough to pick up on the fact I confirmed what she's telling me. But seriously. How the hell did she figure this out? She's freaking five.

"You buy her flowers."

Oh.

I can work with this.

"Flowers make her happy."

"You do her dishes. Like Poppa does for Mimi."

Not entirely the case, but in her mind, she won't see the difference.

"Like Mimi, she cooks, so I clean up. Like I do for Mimi too."

She has no comeback. A part of me wonders why I'm justifying myself to my preschooler, and why I'm entertaining this line of discussion. But it's what I do. I'm not always the adult in our dynamic. At least not the way I should be. Hopefully, by the time she's a little older and wiser, my life experience will kick in and she won't be able to rattle me so easily.

I won't hold my breath.

Lennon's quiet the rest of the short ride home, staring out the window, lost in her little world. She seems to have forgotten—or let it go—her request to call Tate. Don't tell her, but once she's in bed for the night, I plan to do that.

I should have known she wouldn't let it go so easily.

At home, she empties her bag, and my mom gets a hold of her for her bath. Bless you, Millie Keeley. I throw in a load of our laundry, suddenly tired. Maybe if I let Lennon sleep in my bed, it will be an easier bedtime tonight.

No. I'm supposed to work on curbing her bedtime bad habits, not encouraging them.

Lennon joins me in my room, freshly bathed in PJs, her hair pulled back in two braids. Scrambling up on my bed, she settles in my lap. I think back to Tate's comment about the bond between the two of us and can't help but smile. I would like to believe I'd love any kid of mine, but there's something uniquely special about Lennon.

"I love you, Squirt. Did you enjoy Thanksgiving with Momma?"

"It was so boring. And Grandma made me eat all the stuff on my plate. Even those yucky sweet potatoes." I can't see her face, but I'm sure it's one of disgust.

"Did they at least have marshmallows on them?"

"Nope." She leans back, rubbing her head against my chest, trying to get comfortable, one of her telltale signs she's tired.

"Want me to read you a book and then tuck you in?"

"We didn't call Tate," she says with a yawn, completely ignoring my question.

Jeez, kiddo. Why are you suddenly trying to steal my girl?

"She's busy putting Aubrey to bed. And she'll be here in the morning."

"Okay. How about two books?"

Her ability to move on from one topic to another astounds me. Sometimes I have a hard time keeping up with the five-year-old.

"Deal."

By some miracle, Lennon only gets out of bed once tonight. I text Tate but don't hear from her.

I'm glad she's coming for breakfast tomorrow for both Lennon's and my sakes.

CHAPTER 25
TATE

The three weeks after Thanksgiving seem to fly by, and soon enough, the holiday season is upon us. The days have been a good balance of work and fun, busy times with some downtime for me, and for me and Aubrey together.

We hung out at Walsh's house for Sunday breakfast Thanksgiving weekend, but that's the last time he and I got to be together. We spent an hour to ourselves walking around Target. He held my hand down every aisle, which made my inner self scream with delight. It was freeing, being so comfortable with him, doing such a mundane task as shopping.

It felt *right*. I can't remember the last time I ever felt so comfortable with someone other than a member of my immediate family. While that's scary as shit, it's because it's Walsh. *He* makes it much less scary.

I've seen him in passing at drop-off and pickup, but since the cold weather of December has hit Vermont, we don't stand around the door waiting for the kids. The winter weather ushered in a pickup line, saving all of us from having to brace the cold and/or snow. As the cars line up, an adult brings two children out. The most we manage is a wave and a smile if our cars are near each other.

Lennon texts me every night she's with him. Walsh mentioned something about her being relentless and not letting up on sending me a goodnight text. I think it's sweet, and after Aubrey, she's quickly becoming my favorite five-year-old. I miss the texts the nights she's with Megan, but texts from Walsh certainly help ease the ache.

It's amazing how all out the town goes for the holiday season. There's a huge decorated tree on the town green, and with the fresh snow last night, even in the daytime, it's alluring. I make a mental note to load Aubrey up in the car one night soon and drive around to see the lights, something we've never done before.

Main Street is all decked out with decorations. The lights are dim in the daytime and it would be way more impressive in the dark, but a magical aura permeates the air, the allure of the holiday spirit evading my senses.

I've finished my shopping for Aubrey but have Aunt Marsha and my family left to buy for. For our present this year, Mom and Dad bought us plane tickets to Kansas. I'm a little ambivalent about going home. There's going to be subtle guilt about how much they miss us, especially Mom. I can't let it deter me from building this life in Vermont. I have no desire to deal with Damon's family if they find out we're home. The threatening emails have dwindled to one every few days. I delete those suckers as fast as my fingers can.

I shake off the past, their efforts of trying to take Aubrey from me a mere memory. Their custody battle has no root in reality, and I pray they've given up. We're both better off without them and their support.

Besides, tonight is Walsh's birthday and we're celebrating with a date at Dolce Vita. To say I'm excited is an understatement. Aubrey is sleeping over at Aunt Marsha's, the idea hers. When she asked when she could "be a big girl and sleep over by herself at Aunt Marsha's," I couldn't ask my aunt fast enough. Not sure the words I used were coherent, but Aunt Marsha understood my gibberish and agreed lickety-split. I'll drop her off and then get ready for my date.

"Hey, you," Walsh drawls when I slide into the passenger seat of his truck. He kisses my cheek and fingers the ends of my curled hair. I went for loose curls, and by the way his lust-filled eyes widen, he approves.

"Is my outfit too casual?" I blurt, nerves fluttering in my abdomen. The restaurant isn't super fancy, but I want to look good for Walsh's birthday. Though the actual day was earlier this week, tonight's the first—and only—chance we have to celebrate alone.

He scans me over from head to toe, taking in the purple blouse and jeans I purchased earlier today. It's his birthday, but I splurged on myself. On new undergarments as well. As much as I want to cower from the heated scrutiny, I don't.

"Gorgeous, Tate."

"Wait until you see what's underneath."

His head leans against the headrest, his eyes closing, a deep groan exiting his mouth. "Why must you torture me?"

"Because it's fun." I hesitate to mention the rest of what's on my mind, but drop the pretenses and do it. "The shorter our meal, the longer the dessert." I waggle my brows, falling into the role of a seductress.

He rolls his head toward me, his heated blues staring my way. "About dinner."

In the brief silence, the hairs on the back of my neck stand on end, but I don't let my mind wander to what he could say. Thankfully, he doesn't make me wait long.

"Would you mind if, after the restaurant, we make a stop at the hockey house?"

I intend to tell him that's exactly the opposite of what I want, but my mouth utters, "It's your birthday."

Walsh fits his palm over mine sitting on my thigh, enveloping my fingers in his. It immediately comforts me. "An hour tops. Cody's been riding my ass because 'I'm too busy for my friends.' As if he doesn't see me every day at practice and games."

A tinge of guilt worms in. He's a busy guy, but he's also the one who makes most of our plans, tells me he's dropping by after Aubrey goes to sleep. If he wanted to hang with his friends, he would, right?

"But you're bringing me. Will they be upset to not have you alone?" I bite the inside of my cheek, holding my breath.

A lazy smile forms on his lips. Ones I haven't kissed in too long. "They want to see you."

My brows rise. "Really?"

He nods. "After the fundraiser, they're more curious about who I'm spending my time with, and they need a breath of fresh air from all the puck bunnies and college girls."

"And I'm someone who fits the bill?"

"Indeed. Very much so. We'll chat more at dinner."

And with a chaste kiss on my cheek, the discussion ends as he pulls out and drives us to the restaurant.

The drive takes us down Main Street. As I predicted, it's stunning, the allure magical.

"Want to take the kids for a drive one night to see the Christmas lights? Lennon could use the boost in her spirit, and we haven't done it yet. Mom will make hot cocoa. Lennon lasts about an hour, but if that's too long or late for Aubrey, we can shorten it."

It's like he read my mind. I shake my head. "It's perfect. I was thinking as I drove through town this morning, it's something we should do. Although she won't drink the hot chocolate."

"I'll get her some carrot sticks." His comeback is immediate, as if no thought went into it, even though it's extremely thoughtful. When I don't respond—because I'm too busy trying not to cry—his face flushes red. "That's like so dumb. Never mind. Tell me what she would want, and I'll get it for her."

"It's the sweetest ever, Walsh," I express, my voice watery with unshed tears. "I love how you know her so well and what would make her happy. And if you do actual sticks rather than the rounded ones, she'll love you forever."

Oops. Not quite the words I should have spoken. I mean, she will love him forever, but I shouldn't be putting parameters on our relationship. Especially for the kids.

The conversation is cut short as he pulls into a spot in the lot. "Great. Carrot sticks it is. We'll plan a night soon." His body angles toward me. "For the rest of the evening, no more kid talk. Two college-aged kids out for a night on the town."

Being with Walsh has allowed me to feel like Tate Winchester again. I don't forget I'm Aubrey's mom, but I enjoy being Tate, a woman who goes on dates and has sex with this hockey-playing hunk of a man. I've stopped questioning why he's chosen me and permitted the relationship to unfold to suit our needs.

"Best plan ever."

Over a communal dinner of chicken parmesan and fettuccine Alfredo, there's no chatter of anything children-related. Walsh entertains me with tales of college hockey antics, the ins and outs of the sport, growing up in Havenwood, and more hockey. He can't help himself. It's sewn into the fibers of his being. His passion is contagious, and a part of me gets tingly with the prospect of watching him in action. I can't apprise him of my desires and get his hopes up even slightly. He won't let it go until I've attended a game. When I'm ready, I'll divulge the yearning secret.

We order one piece of apple pie—pecan wasn't an option—to split. I'm giddy whenever our forks clank together. It's childish and immature, but Walsh brings out my inner child, the reckless one I was before I became a mom. I have six years' to make up for, and the more I get acquainted with Walsh, the more layers I shed.

Once I've paid the check, we walk to the lot, his hand on the small of my back. Cue a girly swoon. "Who's going to be at the house?"

The question has been sitting on the tip of my tongue all night, but he was so in his element, I didn't want to interrupt. I'm nervous about spending time with his teammates. I'm not the most outgoing person and prefer to hang out with adults in small groups or one-on-one. And I have nothing in common with these guys except our age, which makes it harder to relate. I'm doing this for Walsh. If roles were reversed, he'd do it for me.

He rattles off about half a dozen names, the only one I remember is Cody. I met them all at the fundraiser, but their names went in one ear and out the other.

Too soon, he maneuvers the truck down a side street near Aspenridge. "When the weather's a little nicer, I'll show you around campus."

"I'd like that." I want to see the campus and can handle a short visit to the ice rink. Especially to see where he spends most of his hours away from home.

I'm out of the truck before he can come around to open my door. He fits our hands together. An instant wave of comfort sweeps over me at the gentle touch. "I can do this," I whisper. "College hockey players don't scare me."

Beside me, Walsh chuckles, overhearing my words. "Probably no different from the guys you're used to."

"More muscular. More brawny. More flirty," I deadpan.

"Fair points," he agrees.

The house is an old Victorian, complete with a front porch held up by columns. Strands of white-colored lights hang from the top, illuminating the oversized porch. It seems out of place for a bunch of hockey guys. I don't ask about it before we're inside.

The faint bleach smell teases my nostrils. It's not overwhelming, though I wonder about the need for bleach at all. Is this their way of cleaning?

"Keeley!" a deep male voice shouts, my vision drawn to the top of the staircase. "You made it." A college male hangs over the railing, smiling in greeting. With one hand, he shifts the locks of his thick, wavy brown hair out of his eyes.

Walsh points up the stairs. "Tristan Ford. Center."

Another guy with shorter hair joins him. Standing next to him, he's taller than Tristan. "Gabe Kolligan. Goalie."

"Best in the league."

Walsh rolls his eyes and leans in so only I can hear. "Inflated ego, but sometimes warranted. He has the most saves in our league all three years he's played."

Walsh leads me into the kitchen, grabs each of us a bottle of water and a can of seltzer for himself, then ushers me into the back of the house where more people congregate. Three more players and a girl about my age. She wears black glasses and has her nose stuck in a textbook. Walsh reminds me who the other guys are, Cody being one of them, and introduces the girl as Arielle.

"Nice to see you again, Tate. Glad you could join us for the fun tonight."

"Game night," one guy jabbers. Maybe Clayton?

Arielle assesses us. "I call Tate on my team. Us girls have to stick together, am I right?"

"Uh, sure," I mutter, totally intimidated by the environment.

"If you're completely uncomfortable, we'll leave." A hopeful lilt infuses Walsh's tone. He wants me to be comfortable.

For him, I'll do my best.

Turns out, his teammates are hysterical, kind, and unexpectedly more like Walsh than I would have predicted. Cody's the biggest "manwhore" of this bunch, followed by Clayton. Arielle and Tristan have been dating since freshman year. She's the epitome of an intelligent nerd, but she's got a sense of humor I enjoy. Someone I could see being friends with.

If I were in the market for female friends my age.

Game night consists of video games. Some sort of hockey game. Seems none of them can ever get enough hockey. I observe it all next to Arielle on a black leather couch while she studies for a chemistry final.

The conversation revolves around hockey, finals, and hockey. Walsh fits right in, having been teammates with them all four years. Two of them will graduate in the spring with Walsh, but two others are juniors and one is a sophomore. Of the six guys, only four live here, but I'm gathering the house is used as a "home base" for parties in the offseason and gaming nights during the season. I learn the freshmen and the sophomores on the team live in the dorms and there's another hockey house for more upperclassmen on the next road over.

The night is an education of the ins and outs of the life of college athletes. Most of which goes over my head, but I nod, laugh, and mm-hmm at appropriate times.

At one point, Ford occupies the vacant cushion next to me. "Tell me about yourself, Tate."

"Not much to tell. Moved to Vermont a few months ago, settling into New England life one day at a time while I try to get my bearings."

"Where did you live before?"

"Kansas."

A flash of light brightens his eyes. "No shit. I'm from Iowa."

We engage in a conversation about the Midwest, what we miss from home, how it's different from Vermont. It's freeing and refreshing, the most I've talked about home since I moved here.

"Ford, stop hitting on my girl," Walsh growls, a deep rift of envy lacing every syllable.

Tingles erupt in my lady parts at his protectiveness. Damn, it's sexy. And makes me hot and bothered. I shift discreetly in my seat to hide the effect his words have on me.

"Can't help it if she wants to talk to me," Ford tosses back.

"On that note, we should get going. Our plans won't do themselves."

A chorus of laughter overpowers the sounds of the video game. The guys are nothing more than prepubescent boys in college bodies.

Gabe composes himself first. "Going back to Mommy and Daddy's house 'cause it's past your curfew?" he goads.

Walsh ignores the bait. "My parents are out of town for the night." He thrusts his hips in the air. "Anytime we want."

"Puh-lease. Like that stops Cody from bringing the girls to his room," Clayton chides, glancing at Cody. "Who's coming tonight?"

"Andddd, we're leaving. Say goodbye, Tate."

Chants of "Goodbye, Tate" echo around the room.

"Until next time, boys. Arielle, it was nice to meet you. Let's definitely meet for coffee after the new year."

"Yes," she confirms. "I'll text you once I'm back on campus in January."

Without another word, Walsh lugs me behind him outside into the cold nighttime air. Even with a warm winter coat, the breeze chills me to the bone.

"'Anytime we want,' huh?" I joke.

The streetlight highlights the red in his face. "Anytime we want tonight. Better?"

"I do like the sound of that. Take me home and ravage me in all the ways."

CHAPTER 26
WALSH

"'m on the pill," Tate discloses nonchalantly the minute we're in my bedroom.

Not something I expected, I gasp at the shock value of her statement. "When'd that happen?" I strip off my sweater, watching her intently.

"At my last appointment. Maybe it was because the doctor was unfamiliar, but the words barreled out of my mouth the minute she walked into the room." I advise Tate to remove her clothes. As hot as she looks in the purple top and black jeans, I'm itching to get inside her, this new tidbit adding to my impatience. "It's not one hundred percent effective, but between the two forms, it's a safer option. The safest one is off the table."

I dare a tiny smirk. "What's the safest option?"

"Abstinence," she murmurs, the word distasteful on her tongue.

I nod, contemplating how best to respond. "Are you prepared to deal with any consequences of our actions?"

"If you're in it with me, yes." Her words come quick with no hesitation in them. No matter what happens, we'd deal with it. Together.

"I'm totally in." My fingers trace her jaw with tender pressure, as if we have all the time in the world.

In tonight's case, until tomorrow morning.

Tate swallows, gearing up for something I probably won't like. "I'm not ready for another baby. Even with you, Walsh."

I try to hide the amazement at the complete contradiction to what she's just told me.

"I'm confused. You want to have sex?" She nods vigorously. "You're okay with the consequences of having sex?" Another nod. "But you're not ready for another baby? How the hell am I supposed to decipher that?"

"Guess we just hope and pray the birth control doesn't fail."

My brow furrows. "And if it does?"

She shrugs. "Then I guess I'll have nine or so months to prepare." She grips my hands and steers me to the bed.

"I probably should stop whatever's going to happen now based on the way you've just fucked my mind over. But it's been way too long since I've kissed you and even longer since I've been inside you. So if this is a green light"—I wave between us where we stand in front of the bed—"selfishly, I'm taking it. Unless you tell me to stop."

She gives me one word. "Go."

With her permission, I push her to my bed. She scurries up to the pillow, leaving her legs spread wide, her pink pussy on display, mine for the taking.

"Wet for me?"

"Since you picked me up," she admits sheepishly, the pink in her cheeks showcased by the soft light from the nightstand.

"What a bummer I've made you wait so long to do something about it."

"So rude," she deadpans with a giggle. "Didn't think it was appropriate to relieve myself in the bathroom of the hockey house."

"Those sounds are mine." My voice is raw and throaty at the image of her threat.

"Only yours, Walsh." A hint of affection shimmers in her confirmation.

My cock hardens, though he'll have to wait until I've lapped up the mess and fucked her with my tongue and fingers.

Raking my eyes over her naked body, admiration sinks in. Her naked body is a glorious sight, one I could stare at all day. If we had that option.

I drag my tongue along her right leg, one long trail up the entire leg. When I get to the apex of her thighs, I seek her out. Lust swims in her eyes, the hunger for sex clear in her deep browns. It's a heady feeling, giving this woman the sensation of such a hankering of desire. My left eye winks, eliciting a dirty giggle from Tate, propelling me into action.

My sight zeroes in on the glistening wetness. Wasting no time, my tongue finds home in her slit, licking and tasting her pussy. Her unique flavor bursts on my tongue, encouraging me to continue. To lap up every bit of sweetness, every drop spilling out.

I set a leisurely pace, thoroughly fucking her with my tongue before inserting my fingers. Tate mewls, moans, and groans at my assault. My cock hardens with each new sound, precum leaking out of the tip. When her thighs try to close against my head, my hands hold them open while I work, one hand splayed on each thigh. She can make all the noises she wants, but I require space to ensure her orgasm hits her.

"I'm super close. Like so close, I can taste it. Whatever you do, don't stop. Make me come, Walsh. Make me see stars."

Invigorated by her requests, I go to town.

Swirling my tongue around her slit.

Sucking her clit into my mouth, then flattening my tongue against the tight bud.

Adding a finger inside her.

I'm rewarded with incoherent sounds as she detonates. Her hips rise off the bed, falling with a thump. Her lower body writhes in need as my tongue never lets up. A splash of wetness coats it as her moans louden. My lips curl into a smile against her at the volume level.

Uninhabited and free to be as loud as she wants, she's delivering. Thankful for the time alone, I'd hate to shush her.

Her noises egg me on, lasting until she's spent. My cock painfully hard, he impatiently waits his turn. To be inside her again. To give her another orgasm on the heels of this one. To score in overtime.

I lick until there's nothing left, until every trace of her wetness disappears. Her chest heaves with deep breaths as her body comes down from the high.

"Stars?" I inquire.

"A night sky," she breathes, her tone panty. "On a clear night in Vermont but even more twinkling in Kansas."

I inwardly pat myself on the back for pleasuring her.

"Ready for more?"

"Gonna need a few minutes."

Her words crush my cock's ego, but the brain in my head urges me to lie down next to her. Slipping my arm underneath her, I ply her rag doll body to me. She comes easily—whether because she wants to or doesn't have a choice against the way I draw her in. Her sluggish smile informs it's probably the former. My fingers draw lazy circles over her breasts.

"Walsh, you're too good to me. Too good for me." Her head tilts back and hooded eyes peer at me. Sated after her orgasm, they shine with an unfamiliar emotion.

I brush a stray hair off her forehead. "I aim to please." I can't help the corny cliché, but I can't confess what's on my mind. She's the one who's too good for me. Not the other way around.

"Kiss me." Her demand is too hard to ignore, the allure of kissing Tate too difficult to reject.

"Thought you needed some time."

Her left shoulder shrugs. "I'm not sure what I need. Being here with you, wrapped in your arms, only having tonight—"

"But we have all night," I interrupt and remind her. "We could go at it until the wee hours of morning."

"Hence my dilemma. I want it all. The sex, the kissing, the cuddling, the recovery time. I'm selfish that way."

"And I'm unselfish enough to give it to you."

I fuse my lips over hers, swallowing the surprised moan escaping her lips. Her tongue snakes its way into my mouth, tangling with mine, battling for control. I yield to her, not able to deny the woman what she craves. I don't need control of the kiss but am a happy participant.

For what feels like hours, our mouths meld together, kissing, nipping, nibbling. Each kiss with Tate is better than the last. As much as a forbidden kiss—hidden from the kids—brings its own magnetism, there's something unique about this kiss. A freedom of sorts, knowing we don't have to rush, we don't have to deny ourselves the pleasure. Though it leads to more, the kiss is unhurried, relaxed, and lazy. Almost as if I was put on this earth to kiss Tate and have her kiss me back.

Tate pulls away first, breathless when she speaks. "I want you. Fuck me, Walsh." She nibbles her bottom lip into her mouth, spurring me into action.

Faster than a winger can take the puck down the ice, I sheathe myself and line up at her entrance, my body caging hers. At her nod, I thrust in. A sense of overwhelming relief sweeps through, a coming home, a shooting for the goal and it hitting the net.

As much as I want to savor this feeling, this intimacy with Tate, I'm on edge and ready to blow. But she deserves another orgasm, and I want to give it to her before my own.

"Much as I enjoy being filled by you, if you don't move—"

My actions cut her off.

Seated all the way inside, I pull out, only to piston my hips forward and shove back in.

"Yesssss," she drawls, her head falling back and exposing her neck. Like a beacon, it draws me in. But I don't shower it with the affection it deserves. I'm afraid I won't be gentle and whatever I do will leave a mark.

Instead, I focus on not blowing before she finishes, though it's all I want to do. I'm so close to exploding. And it wouldn't be such a bad thing. It's not like she hasn't had an orgasm yet tonight. But no. Still wrong. Tate comes first. Always.

Her fingers grip my shoulders, the tips leaving marks. I wish this pain would lessen the one below, but it's the opposite. She's got me so hard up, the explosion's going to be earth-shattering, a reaction I only feel with Tate.

"Babe, I'm on edge here. You close?" My words are clipped, an unintentional sharpness to them. But I can't hold back much longer. Not when her vagina clamps around me like a vise, holding me hostage and squeezing with its movements. It's heaven and hell.

She snakes her hand between us, giving her clit a rub. "I'm com—"

The sign I need, the word isn't out of her mouth as my orgasm pummels me. I don't let up the pounding into her. I can't control the speed and power as I pump myself inside her, chasing the high of letting go.

And damn, is it euphoria. An intoxication unmatched anywhere except maybe scoring the winning goal in a championship game. It's something I don't want to come down from, a feeling I don't want to let go of. A feeling passing way too quickly as I pull out and topple onto Tate's limp body. My breaths are heavy and fast, my stamina needing time to recover. As much as I want to move, I'm sated and comfortable. I hope she's not crushed under my weight.

"Give me a minute to recoup, and I'll clean you up."

"I thought last time might have been a fluke." Her timid words dribble in slowly.

"A fluke?"

"Yeah, like how could it be that good, you know?"

She's mentioned having sex with Aubrey's father. Back when we were teens, I thought sex with Megan was good. And for most of my years, it was better than most.

Until Tate.

So, I get where her head's at.

I peel myself off her, peering into her satisfied gaze. "Not a fluke. Simply that great." I leave a chaste kiss on her forehead before getting up.

When I return with a washcloth in hand, Tate's glassy eyes land on Lennon's blanket, and she queries me with a raise of her brows. "Kinda old for a blankie, aren't you, Walsh? And a pink one."

"Lennon brings mine to Megan's house, so I'm stuck with hers while she's gone."

My comment takes a while to sink in fully. "I have so many questions."

"I'm an open book, if you haven't figured that out already."

I wipe her legs, gently washing away the evidence of our fun. She sits up, her legs crossed in a pretzel position. "This is Lennon's blanket?" She points to it.

"Yep."

"But doesn't she need it to sleep?"

"She has mine."

Her eyes slide sideways to me. "Your blanket?"

"Yeah. Because it smells like me."

"So you get hers?"

"Yes. It's a trade-off. When she comes home, we exchange back, each sleeping with our own."

She's still confused but intrigued. "Whose idea was this?"

"I started it when she was super young. I'm not sure if it was for her or me initially, but now it's kinda for both of us. It's the only thing she packs when she goes to her mom's, and it's always the first thing she does when she gets back here. Takes hers and leaves mine on my bed."

"That's the sweetest thing ever."

"Ha. I'm glad someone thinks so. Megan thinks it's the most ridiculous thing and can't understand why Lennon wouldn't want the same blanket every night."

I stopped justifying it a long time ago. I'm fortunate Megan doesn't express her opinions to Lennon because then we'd have a real problem.

"She's jealous," Tate states simply. She rests back against the pillow, pulling the comforter around to ward off the cool air. Or to be more comfortable without clothes.

"Why would she be jealous of me?"

"Seriously, Walsh? You comprehend what a unique bond you possess with Lennon, right? How fortunate Lennon is to have you for a dad?"

"But she's her mom. She wins by default. Who doesn't love their mom the most?" I speak from experience. I love Dad, but Ma? My love for her is on another level. And it's more than because I share similar personality traits with her.

"I'm sure she loves Megan, but she idolizes you. I see it every time we're together. Hands down, you would do anything for her, and in her little five-year-old way, she knows it."

There's a wistfulness in her tone. I have to wonder if it's coming from her experience with her father or with the lack of a relationship between Aubrey and hers. I curl around her, fitting her into my arms, a favorite position of mine.

"You do the work of two parents. Aubrey's incredibly lucky with you as her mom." I kiss the top of her head. The weight she was holding drops off as she sags more into me.

"I'm just doing my best. I got lucky she's so easy."

"You say that as if you have nothing to do with it."

"I've never been one to toot my own horn."

Her comment loiters around us, the truth of it hanging heavy in the air.

"You should. You have much to brag about."

I rest my head against the pillow, my eyes fluttering closed. Tate in my arms, I'm pretty damn comfortable. It's a feeling I could get used to.

I never appreciated the way the town decorates for the holidays until I experienced it through Lennon's eyes. Watching her discover the world can change my mood drastically, but there's something so magical about this time of year. Lennon's always been about the lights. The more color, the better.

Last year, Mom decided we needed white lights on our tree. My girl was pissed, and she let her grandmother have it. And as much as we tried not to pamper the then four-year-old, two days later, the tree was undecorated and redecorated with colored lights. Lennon profusely thanked Mom, her joy evident in the way she stared at the tree for hours at a time, lying underneath it for a better angle of just the lights. And to think I almost gave my mom a hard time for making the change. It seriously made Christmas.

Every night during the season—unless the weather's terrible—Mom sends us off with mugs of hot chocolate for our nightly "lights viewing." On the days we have nothing going on, I've driven a good thirty minutes to neighboring towns for their displays. The elation on her face makes the amount spent on wasted gas worth every penny. Plus, I've learned to budget for it in the past few years.

Tonight, it's extra special because we've got Tate and Aubrey along for the drive. I can't contain my enthusiasm for showing Aubrey how much fun lights can be.

When they arrive, I usher them into the house. "Dinner's ready. We have to eat quickly so we can get on the road."

Probing me with a lift of her brow, Tate asks, "I didn't realize driving around to view Christmas lights was such a production."

"You haven't seen Lennon Keeley in action."

"Oh, she enjoys light displays?"

"Like a cat on catnip. You'll see." With a wink of my eye, I disappear, hoping she and Aubrey follow me to the kitchen.

After a quick, delicious meal of chicken soup, we pile into my truck. I had the foresight to move the car seat from Mom's van into my truck earlier. Three travel mugs of hot cocoa, cookies, and a glass of milk and carrot sticks for Aubrey, we set off. I wind through back roads, past farms I can barely make out in the dark until we come to a street about fifteen minutes away.

"Look, Keeley. It's the Grinch," Lennon's enthralled voice drifts to the front. "And Santa. And Rudolph. Oh, yes! Olaf!"

My attention drifts to the rearview mirror, watching them as we stop in front of each house on the street.

A mini-squeal makes Aubrey gasp but not because she's scared. Oh no. Because she's spotted Anna and Elsa blow-ups. Her exhilaration displays differently. While Lennon's all about pointing, screeching, and bouncing in her seat, Aubrey's more reserved, her eyes glued to the window, her smile growing wider as we pass each new house, completely enchanted by the scene in front of her. Her eyes barely blink.

"I think she likes it," I mutter from the driver's seat, discreetly folding Tate's hand in mine.

"Just a little."

As inspiring as the light displays are, I focus solely on Aubrey. Watching her experience this for the first time is as mesmerizing as I predicted. Her joy is infectious, her eyes glowing as the multicolored lights reflect off the windows, her lips spread into a huge grin, elation exuding off.

We spend another twenty minutes driving around to different houses. My favorite is the one with the light show set to music. Despite the yawns from the back seat, I convince Tate to stay an extra few minutes so I can enjoy the display.

"Thanks for tonight."

"You're welcome, Tate. We'll hit up another town this weekend if the weather's good."

"Another one?" she prods, confused by my suggestion.

"It's what we do. Every night during the holiday season. A

different part of our town each night or a different town altogether, like tonight."

"Wow. I'm honored to be included."

Stopped at a red light, I study her, fighting any urges of wanting more. "I'm pretty sure she'll let you share it with us, even beyond this year. What do you think?"

It's a bit of a rhetorical question, but I wait expectantly for an answer.

"Yes. I think I'd like that."

"Great. This time next year, pencil us in for the holiday lights tour."

It should feel weird to be making plans for a year in advance with our relationship being so new, but it only feels *right*.

CHAPTER 27
TATE

f I thought the time between Thanksgiving and Christmas flew by, it's nothing compared to Christmas and the start of the new year.

Aubrey and I hopped a plane to Kansas for two weeks, and Aunt Marsha joined us the first week so I didn't have to fly alone. My mom couldn't contain her elation at having us home and Marsha visit. She cried no less than a dozen times. Each occurrence, I guarded my heart against the guilt trying to worm in.

It was nice to be back in Kansas, spend time with my family, and even sneak out for a coffee date with Carley. Except being cornered by Damon's mom. She looked paler and more frail than I remember, certainly not the regal woman who spat horrible things in my face when she learned I was pregnant. My defenses up, they weakened slightly when she told me they were dropping the custody suit and would leave me and Aubrey alone for a peaceful life. Through tears, she asked for an updated photo once a year, and putting myself in her shoes—losing my child and the only piece to her—I agreed. She thanked me profusely and walked away.

With the final burden completely lifted, I enjoyed the rest of my trip. But it didn't feel like "home" anymore. By the end, even Aubrey was itching to get back to our new normal, the chaos of the holidays and being constantly crowded by her grandmother setting the introvert in her on edge.

It took us about a week after traveling to get back into a routine, but three weeks into January, it's almost as if we'd never left.

This afternoon we're making apple cider donuts at Walsh's house. Aubrey mentioned something about donuts earlier in the week and when Walsh heard it, he took it upon himself to get everything we needed. My heart nearly burst into pieces at his generosity and accommodations for my girl. I got the sense Lennon wasn't happy about it, but I assured him I'd make it up to her with cookies. That's on tomorrow's agenda.

As short as the drive to the Keeley's usually is, the snow makes it a little more treacherous. I'm still overly cautious, even though it's been about two months with it here. Thank goodness it's not still snowing.

White knuckles grip the steering wheel the entire drive, but soon I'm pulling into their driveway. I spot Lennon in the front window watching for us.

The front door flies open, and she and Walsh stand there, huge matching grins on their faces. Emotion explodes in my chest at the sight. It's not just Walsh who invokes these newfound feelings of love. His little girl has captured my heart too.

As I unbuckle Bree from her seat, her hands find my cheeks. "This is going to be so fun. I love you, Mommy."

"I love you, Bean. No matter what happens, my love for you won't ever change."

I don't know why I feel the urge to make the statement, but she accepts it easily. If she even comprehends it. If she doesn't, it's a reassurance to me.

Upon entering the house, Lennon throws her arms around my legs, her new favorite way to greet me. It took me a few times to get used to it, but now I expect it. She lets go and looks up at me.

"I missed you, Tate."

"And I missed you too."

She gives one last squeeze before pulling away completely. On my right, I find Aubrey in the air, embraced by Walsh. He's holding her exactly the way he does his daughter, and for a brief period, I can't breathe. The way she's snuggled against him leaves me overcome with feelings. Because for all this time in her life, she's never once had that—the devotion of someone akin to a father. And damn if I don't want to give her one. Specifically, the one currently holding her.

"I want a dad like Walsh."

Her words from months ago ring in my ears, matched in intensity with the pounding of my heart. It's so loud I wonder if anyone else can hear it.

She moves her head to the side before leaning in and leaving a kiss on his cheek. "Thank you for letting us make donuts, Walsh. I hope they taste so yummy."

I've seen Walsh dole out love and affection for Lennon many times, and it hits me right in the feels. But the way he responds to Aubrey's comment—with the same twinkle and care in his eyes—about does me in.

Finding a man who'd love me hasn't been high on my radar. I'd nearly come to terms with Aubrey and me always being a family of two. I never expected Walsh, with his generous personality, his quirks I can't help but love, a daughter of his own. But damn. Now that I found him, I don't think I can give him up. Not either of them. And by the looks of it, neither can my daughter.

I'm brought back to the present by Walsh's deep voice. "You're welcome, Aubrey. Think you can talk Lennon into helping us in the kitchen?"

Aubrey ponders for a minute, her finger tapping her chin. "I'll see what I can do." I can't keep the giggle inside, and Walsh complements it with a chuckle. She wiggles out of his arms, eager to play. Before she disappears in search of her friend, she turns and locks eyes with me. "Call me when you're ready to make the batter, Mommy."

I can only nod. Not because of the comment, but because of everything transpiring in the last ten minutes. Or longer. When I stepped outside and found my car cleared of snow.

I may regret my action later, but I immediately fall into Walsh's arms, hoping beyond hope neither of the girls sees our embrace. The surprise on his end is evident, but he accommodates appropriately, wrapping his arms around me.

Unsure of how long I stay tucked into him, I don't move until my heart rate is back to normal.

"Hey, you're good?" He holds me at arm's length to assess my mental state. Ever since we had sex, he's been more attuned to my moods and emotions.

"Yeah. Happy to be here with you, to spend the afternoon in the kitchen watching you try to 'help.'" There's so much more I want to say, so many secrets to spill, but I rein it in. The entryway of his parents' home is not the place to clue him in. He deserves privacy.

"I'll have you know I've been working on my skills. Even boiled water yesterday for pasta all on my own."

I pull out of his embrace so I can slow clap and observe his cheesy grin. "Boiled water. Wow. Super impressed. I should hand over my apron to you for every meal."

The shock on his face is priceless, as if I'd do that.

"No. Please don't. I won't survive on my own. Who will feed me? And my child? We'll starve."

"Pretty sure Millie wouldn't ever let that happen."

She never would. Even when he moves out and gets a place of his own, unless he moves super far away—something I don't foresee—she'd never let them starve. At least not Lennon.

But most likely not her son either. Heck, she feeds his teammates. I haven't been privileged enough to attend a hockey dinner at Millie's, but I learned all about them the night at the hockey house. Seems she's a bit of a celebrity with the team. For good reason.

He swipes a hand across his brow. "Phew. Thank goodness one woman in my life has my back."

A smile brews on my lips, and the emotion in my chest expands. Not sure how much space remains.

"Come on. I need your help reducing the apple cider before the girls assist."

His head shakes. "May just be your girl. My girl might bail." A deep sigh rumbles out. He starts for the kitchen, and I trail behind.

"That's okay. I've got lots of time to work with her to love cooking and baking."

My feet stop moving. What the hell am I saying? She's not "mine" to work on. Sure, I *hope* this relationship lasts for "lots of time," but is there a guarantee it will?

That would be a big fat *no*.

All the emotion filling up my chest deflates rapidly at the thought.

Forcing my feet into action, I join Walsh in the kitchen. He hands me a brown paper package with a bow tied with a string.

"What's this?"

"A gift. Open it."

I scan his face for hints of what it could be, but his expression remains stoic. So unlike him. Ideas of what could be inside dance across my mind as I rip into it.

"Nice wrapping job."

"Millie's good for more than just food and baths."

I love how he's got no shame about the fact his mom does so much for him. Having met Millie, if she felt he was taking advantage of the situation, she'd nip it in the bud. He may be her "baby," but she's not afraid to speak her mind when being taken advantage of. And if I had to guess, she loves being able to dote on her granddaughter.

Inside the package I find a plastic bag, giving nothing away what the gift is. I discard the wrapping and dig into the plastic, pulling out two aprons, the words "Head Chef" on the front of mine and "Junior Chef" on the second, smaller one. Matching aprons for Aubrey and me.

"Walsh," I breathe out, words escaping me at this truly touching gift. "These are adorable. Aubrey's going to love it."

"I'm more interested in your opinion," he retorts quickly.

Again, not heeding where we are, I throw my arms around his neck, my lips planting a kiss on his cheek.

"I love it. This is so sweet of you."

Our moment's cut short by Millie entering the kitchen, but Walsh doesn't drop my hands. He holds them tighter.

"My boy did good." She motions to the aprons where I discarded them on the table when I went in for my hug.

"Amazing. You're doing something right with him."

"Hey," Walsh protests, his gaze flittering between his mom and me. "I have a lot of noble qualities. I don't always show them in the right ways."

"That's why we're here, right, Tate? To show him the error of his ways?"

My sight lobs from Millie to my boyfriend, who's expectantly waiting for an answer. "That, and for a few other reasons." If his mother wasn't standing right here, our lips would be meeting. If the girls weren't down the hall, a few other parts might do the same. Clapping my hands, I say, "Okay, enough sappy stuff. Let's get to work. You got the goods, Keeley?"

Walsh groans at my use of his nickname. It gets him. Every. Single. Time. I couldn't love it more.

He sets out all the ingredients we need to make the donuts while I reduce the apple cider. Thank goodness he bought double the amount the recipe calls for because the smell was too inviting not to pour myself a cup. There's nothing like pressed fresh apple cider from the farm. It doesn't compare to the stuff they pass off as cider back home.

I invite the girls down to the kitchen once we're ready to make the batter. Lennon lags behind Aubrey, who bounds in, ready and willing to get to work. She notices the apron immediately.

"Mommy, where did you get that apron? I love it." Her fingers reach out to touch the image.

"It's a present from Walsh. It's great, right?" She nods. The only telltale sign she's the least bit jealous is one corner of her mouth remains turned down.

Walsh hands hers over, and the brightest grin illuminates her face. She barely glances at it before she throws herself at him, her cries of, "Thank you, Walsh," stirring up those emotions again. I'm near tears, devotion filling me like helium in a balloon.

He scoops her into his arm, soaking it up with only a glance over at Lennon, who's preoccupied with something on her shirt. A part of me wonders how she'll handle this—her father giving gifts to her friend but not her, her friend currently in her dad's arms, receiving a great deal of comfort from him.

Walsh makes it a point to help Aubrey with her apron. When Lennon finally notices what's going on, she asks, "Keeley, where's mine?"

I suck in a breath, prepared for some sort of meltdown.

A stare-down ensues between father and daughter. "Are you planning on helping in the kitchen anytime?"

"Wasn't planning on it."

I stifle my giggle, but Walsh takes it in stride. "Yours is coming when you *plan* on helping."

Lennon shrugs, as if it's no big deal. Which I'm grateful for. I never want her to feel like Aubrey or I are trying to steal her dad away from her or that he's giving us too much attention and she feels left out.

Kneeling in front of the chair where she sits, I speculate, "Do you maybe want to help us make donuts today? They aren't your favorite, but maybe if you help us make them, you'll want to at least try them." I don't have any expectations she'll agree.

"Is it going to take a long time?"

"No longer than one episode of *Little Einsteins*."

Her eyes travel to each of us, the three of us eagerly awaiting her answer. "Fine. It's not like I have anything better to do."

Walsh immediately grumbles, "Jeez, Squirt. Don't let us twist your arm."

"Yay," Aubrey cheers. Her good mood instantly sours. "But she needs an apron too." She examines the one she's wearing, the wheels turning in her head, the conundrum more than she can handle.

"I'm good. Mimi can wash my clothes if they get messy. She's better at it than Keeley."

"I would argue, but the girl's got a point."

The laugh I held in earlier reappears, and this time, I set it free.

Once I've calmed down a bit, I say, "Okay, troops. Time to make the donuts." It goes over their heads. Even Walsh's based on his perplexed countenance. "Really? You don't know the saying?" I'm not even sure where I picked it up since it's from a Dunkin' Donuts TV commercial from the eighties.

"Um, no. I don't make donuts. Just eat them after buying them."

Shaking my head, I usher them to work, assigning each one an appropriate task. My girl gets the most difficult, the only one who can handle anything without having to be asked more than once.

About ten minutes in, we lose Lennon, who ventures somewhere else in the house. I don't take it too harshly. The kitchen isn't everyone's domain, but her effort while she was here was decent.

Amidst preparing the batter, the kitchen looks like a tornado hit. Millie appeared in the doorway once, raked her eyes over the mess, but left us to it. I assured her we would clean it when we were done. She mumbled something like "Keep teaching him skills, I'll do the cleaning." Millie Keeley is a good egg. What's one more Keeley family member to love?

The last of the donuts in the pan, I put them in the oven and set the timer. Aubrey's chowing down on her second donut hole, enjoying it immensely. Walsh sits next to her, relishing his. They engage in some sort of conversation about donuts, whispering as if they've known each other forever. I can't help but whip out my camera and snap a picture of the image of their heads together. There's no doubt my girl has fallen for him, just like her mother.

The doorbell rings as the last batch comes out of the oven. Thinking nothing of it, I set the pan to cool and turn off the oven. The recipe I found online is a keeper, and my new donut pan came in darn handy. Donuts are at the bottom of my list of sweet treats, but apple cider donuts are palatable.

An unknown pregnant woman materializes in the kitchen's doorway. Her mousy brown hair is matted down and in need of a good washing. Her makeup is subtle but doesn't hide the bags under her eyes.

"Walsh, this young woman is here to speak with you," Millie voices, an edge to her tone, one contrasting her easygoing demeanor and causing goose bumps on my arms.

Walsh pulls his attention from Aubrey and scrutinizes the woman.

"Hey." The girl's voice is shaky, as if she's nervous to be here.

"Hi. Can I help you?"

"I hope so." She steps nearer to the table, her eyes bouncing between Aubrey and Walsh. "Is this your daughter? She's adorable."

"He's Lennon's dad," my girl clarifies. "I don't have a dad."

If she's fazed by Aubrey's comments, she doesn't let it show. "But your daughter, she's about her age, right? I think that's what I remember you telling me six months ago."

A light bulb goes off for Walsh. "Oh. Raquel. From the bar."

"And the hotel." She giggles. Fucking *giggles* at the mention of the hotel. Walsh's face pales instantly.

"Ma, can you bring Aubrey to see what Lennon's up to?" Walsh grits out, his laser focus aimed at me.

"I'll do it," I suggest, not wanting to be privy to anything this girl has to say to him. But he shakes his head. As much as I want to flee the room, I give him the courtesy of staying. Tension coils tightly in my abdomen, but I put on a brave façade.

Millie quickly ushers Aubrey—who thankfully has no inkling what's going on—out of the kitchen. Before Millie goes, there's a definite glare shot in the girl's direction.

Raquel. Fitting.

She sits at the table, eyeing the donuts. I can't help but plate a donut and slide it over to her.

I was pregnant once, and donuts were my kryptonite.

"Thank you." She smiles warmly at me, but her concentration returns to Walsh.

The air in the kitchen thickens, the only sounds are of her munching on the donut and my pounding heart. I can't tell for sure why it's beating so fast, but my flight instinct's activated.

Trouble's on the horizon.

CHAPTER 28
WALSH

Oblivious to the thrumming of my heart, Raquel sits and eats the donut Tate offered her.

Why is she here? What does she want from me? How did she find me?

I barely remember our night several months ago. And not because I was drunk or high or in any other way impairing my ability to remember. It's because she was not memorable. We had sex, and I regretted it immediately.

It was the last time before I met Tate. I'd gone almost a year without it, and I caved that night. With this girl. Damn. Something must have diminished my judgment.

Your cock, dude. It was your cock.

Still. What the hell is she doing here now, eating donuts given to her by my girlfriend? Tate's affected by her presence. She's trying to hide how much.

"That was delicious. Thanks." Raquel wipes the leftover crumbs off her mouth with the back of her hand. *So classy.* "It's yours."

I'm too busy lost in my head to discern what she means. But Tate's gasp clues me in I should heed the words.

My eyes fly to Tate, her hand covering her mouth, her eyes wide in shock. Literal shock. White pales her face, and a heavy weight rests on her shoulders.

I rewind Raquel's comment.

"*It's yours.*"

"What is whose?" I stammer out, my gaze not once leaving Tate's. My pulse beats faster. What am I missing?

"The baby. It's yours, Walsh."

Oh.

OH!

Oh shit.

My body pushes out of the chair.

"It's not, Tate. It's not mine."

I stand in front of my girlfriend, begging her to listen to me, not some puck bunny who showed up here. If memory serves, she had no reason to believe I was a hockey player. Just some lonely girl wanting a good time. Does that make it better?

No.

Tate's eyes glisten with tears, the crushed guise of betrayal seeping into every pore. Shit. I have to make this better. I have to make her see the girl's lying.

"How do you know?" Her words are barely audible, and I'm standing six inches away.

"We used a condom."

"Newsflash. They don't always work. Clearly." Her shaky finger points toward the smug girl sitting at the table.

The thing is, she's not wrong. No birth control is one hundred percent effective. Lennon's proof.

Oh shit. Oh shit. Oh shit.

Lennon.

This will rock her world. Because I was stupid enough to have a one-night stand?

Oh my god.

My thoughts spiral out of control—to that night, to the future, to what this means.

I can't do this again. With a stranger, no less. At least I loved Megan. But we were too young. Hell, I'm still too young. And stupid. Why? Why was I so stupid?

Tate.

What must she think right now? I assured her I wasn't this guy, the one who sleeps around, letting girls ride my…what the hell was it? Now, here's this girl, claiming I did exactly that. And Tate's witnessing it all.

Before I can deal with Tate, I turn to Raquel. "I want proof. Not just your word. Actual medical proof it's my baby. As soon as possible. Is there a chance it might not be mine? When are you due?"

Disbelief coats her face, but she subtly schools her features. "It's yours, Walsh," she states again. It's subtle, but there's a hint of doubt.

"Medical. Proof." My tone leaves no room for misinterpretation. I'm certainly not going to take her word for it.

"We can't do a DNA test until the baby's born."

"Bullshit we can't." Fury races through me, fueled by adrenaline.

"I think I should go."

"That would be best." Except I don't understand it's Tate who voices the words until she disappears down the hall.

"Wait. No. Not you, Tate." Emotions threatening to pervade my body, I chase her up the stairs. "Please don't," I beg in the hallway outside Lennon's room.

"You have to deal with this, Walsh. And I can't be here while you do." Silent sobs accompany her words. Without waiting for my response, she wipes away her tears, putting on a fake cheerful face before she opens the door. "Hey, Bean. It's time to leave. Can you say goodbye to Lennon and Mimi?"

It's Lennon who reacts first. I don't know how, but she comprehends something is amiss. "Daddy?" she questions, looking between Tate and me. It about does me in.

The heavy tension weighing down on me unleashes, and I stumble, steadying myself on the dresser by the doorway. I compose myself as best I can and push out words I never thought I'd have to admit like this.

"It's time for them to leave, Squirt. Say goodbye to Tate and Aubrey." My voice shakes on the *goodbye*. An omen of sorts.

A stronger man would stay and watch the exchange, but my weakness shines through as I step into the hall.

As much as I want—no *need*—Tate to stay, I understand why she can't. And this goodbye isn't just for tonight. My brain makes me highly aware there's a real possibility I could lose her. Over a choice

I made months ago before I knew she existed. Before I knew my heart only beat for her. And our children.

Children.

There's a fifty percent chance I'll have another child in a couple of months. With someone I don't know, and what I remember about her, I didn't like. How's that even going to work?

Children.

How will this affect Lennon and Aubrey? My girl's going to be devastated to lose her friend. All because her dad couldn't keep his dick in his pants. She'll end up hating me, something for which Megan will lord over me until the end of eternity.

I never once thought my life was over with the positive pregnancy test years ago. Call me naïve, but in no way did having a baby in high school "ruin" my life.

But this? This one stupid, asinine mistake?

This one could surely do me in.

Slumping against the wall, I slide down to the floor, my legs flopping out in front of me. I hide my face in my hands and try to ignore Tate and Aubrey passing me by, Aubrey's appeal of "But why do we have to leave?" ringing out loudly in the hall. I'm sure she's not screaming, but to my guilty ears, it's deafening. I strain to hear Tate's answer, but she either doesn't or whispers it so quietly, I can't hear.

My mother joins me in the hall.

"Did the other girl leave?"

Oh shit.

"No." Should I make more of an attempt to get back to the kitchen? Absolutely.

Do I do it? No fucking way.

I pick my head up and peer up at my mother, the one person in my life who's had my back no matter what I did wrong. "What do I do, Ma?"

"The right thing."

"Gee, thanks. I was kinda eager for more than an ambivalent answer," I sass. Luckily, she's used to my sarcastic nature, having inherited it from her.

She glares at me, the one that made me cower when I was little. "First, pick yourself up off the floor so Lennon doesn't get any inkling something's wrong. Second, go into the kitchen, offer the girl a drink of water, get her number, tell her you'll be in touch, and send her on her way. Then, pray like hell it's not your baby."

"And Tate?"

"She's scared, Walsh. It's easy to see how much you mean to her. She wasn't expecting something like this to happen—"

I cut her off. "Neither was I." It comes out way harsher than I intend. I blame the emotional turmoil.

Again I'm on the end of a Millie Keeley glare. "Let me finish." She pauses, waiting for my "I'm sorry" before she continues. "Give her time. She has a choice to make, but so do you. Nothing can be decided until you know for sure." She pauses again. "Is there reason to believe it could be your baby?" she finally asks in a quieter voice, her tone somewhere between soothing and angry.

"If you're asking if we had sex, yes. But we used protection." She raises an eyebrow in challenge. "I know, but seriously. What's the alternative? To be celibate until I get married?"

"When you put it like that, no. That's not a viable solution either."

"Pretty sure you said those exact words the last time we had this conversation. Although last time, I was confident the baby was mine."

She cracks a smile at my paltry attempt at comic relief. As if anything is a laughing matter in this situation.

"You're a good man, Walsh. No matter what happens, your father and I will support you."

"Like another grandkid living here?"

"At least I'm over fifty now. The stigma isn't as bad."

Now it's my turn to chuckle. "I'm never going to live that down, am I?"

"Never, boy. Just wait until Lennon tells you she's having a baby at sixteen. See how you react."

The horror! I've considered it before, but the image of Lennon as a teenage mother doesn't sit right with me.

"Please no. Since we'll still be living here, we'll have your help. Then you can blame her for making you a great-grandmother before you're ready."

Her hands cover her ears, her face a mask of revulsion. "Don't say such wretched things."

"I believe you started it, Millie Keeley."

Removing one hand, she points her finger at me. "That's Mom to you. I raised you to have better manners."

My mouth opens, but no words come out. She always gets the best last word. I confess, "I love you, Ma. I'm so glad I chose you." Standing, I pull her into me, towering over her short statue.

"I've always thanked the higher beings for bringing you into our lives. You make life so much less boring than your sisters, Walsh, but I'm utterly grateful for receiving only *one* of you."

"The best compliment a mother could give." I let her out of my embrace, leaving my hands on her shoulders. "Can you do me one more favor and keep my kid entertained for ten more minutes while I get rid of the hopefully not-mother of my child?"

Mom shakes her head. "So eloquently put. I'll do my best."

"Thanks. Oh, and then totally taste the donuts. We did a smashing job. And by 'we,' I mean Aubrey and Tate." Her name tastes bitter on my tongue, of my doing no less.

"Feel free to knock her up. Your kid would be the cutest." She smirks, thinking she's so funny.

"Millie! No. You should not be fostering this."

She throws her hands up in the air. "I meant in the future, jeez. A few years in the future. When I'm more of a grandma-appropriate age."

"I'll take it under advisement."

She disappears into Lennon's room, shutting the door behind her. I take a few minutes to compose myself and decide on the action needed to get Raquel to leave.

Hefty weights tied to my ankles leaden down my legs on the walk to the kitchen. Raquel's sitting at the table, scrolling through her phone. One hand lazily rubs her stomach.

For one minute, I allow my mind to wander to a place of it being my kid. The scene darkens when Tate's face fills it, disgust so strong claiming her beautiful features. And while she's no less beautiful, I can't help but feel like I've let her down.

She and Aubrey both.

Clearing my throat to speak, I offer, "Can I get you a glass of water?"

Raquel's concentration leaps to me. "Oh, Walsh. You scared me. Do you have milk?"

I answer with a nod of my head and grab a cup from the cabinet. I fill it halfway with milk—I need to get rid of her as fast as possible—and set it in front of her.

"I think it's best if we don't communicate until we have the results."

"It's your baby, Walsh," she maintains, although the shakiness in her voice is back.

"If it is, we'll cross that bridge then. Before, I'm going to assume it's not." She hardly reacts to my harsh words. "Give me your number." I dig my phone out of my pocket, poised and ready to type in the number she rattles off. "I'll research paternity tests and be in touch. It's best if you go."

Standing, I give her no room to argue. *If the kid is indeed mine, I'll do what I have to do. I won't abandon him or her, but I'm also not taking some woman's word it's my kid. Where has she been for the past six months? Why didn't she speak up as soon as she found out she was pregnant?*

Before Tate came into my life.

An unintentional sigh tumbles out of me.

"When did you say you were due again?" I ask, helping her into her coat, her belly making it a little difficult.

"Um, April?" The way she's doubtful raises suspicions.

"You don't know?"

She realizes her mistake. "March." This time it's a statement, but uncertainty lingers around the one word.

I'm too frustrated to do baby math, but this is exactly why I'm *not* taking her word for it.

"Right." I punctuate my answer with a nod of my head. "I'll be in touch this week once I determine the protocol. Are you local to Havenwood?" For the life of me, I can't remember if we exchanged any type of information the night we met.

"I live in Riverbend." Two towns over.

"K." Somewhat local, she must have a place to stay. There'd be some guilt on my end if she wasn't from around here. I surely wouldn't invite her to stay here, but I'd have the decency to help her find a place to crash.

With each step toward the door, the tension in the room increases, a weight crushing on my chest. Even though she's leaving, this is far from over. Until we have an answer. And depending on what the answer is will determine if this is the end or the beginning.

Please let it be the end, I beg.

Raquel turns at the closed door. "I'm sorry I came crashing in like this. I've been meaning to get in touch with you sooner."

"Why didn't you?"

My question catches her off guard, even though she's the one who gave me the opening.

"Oh. Well…I…um, I couldn't remember what you said your name was. Where you were from. But then a friend remembered you played hockey for Aspenridge, and we tracked you down."

"How convenient."

She smiles, like I've said something amazing. "It was."

I open the door, ready to shove her through it, but she doesn't move. "This baby will be lucky to have you as a father."

"How could you possibly know?"

She flusters, a dark red staining her cheeks. It makes her exposed rather than how Tate looks sweet.

Tate.

My irritation at the situation at the highest, I shake my head. "Don't bother answering. I'll text you." Hopefully, she forgets she doesn't have my number, exactly how I want this. Sure, she could show up here at any time, but at least she can't bother me with unnecessary phone calls and texts all hours of the day, which is far easier than making the drive from Riverbend.

I coax her out the door, slamming it behind her. She may keep talking, but I've heard enough from her for tonight. For a lifetime, in fact.

With one goal in mind, I head to the kitchen for my phone. It buzzes in my hand as I pick it up. To my dismay, it's not Tate's name displayed on the screen.

MA

Can we come out now?

Despite my sour mood, a smile spreads on my lips.

She's gone. All safe. I owe you one

She doesn't respond, but the sound of footsteps reaches my ears, right before the assertive voice of Millie.

"Boy, you owe me way more than 'one.' I'll decide later how you'll pay up." She's only teasing, but it does little to sway my mood.

What does it is my daughter. With her blanket in her hands, she stands in front of me, her identical blue eyes to mine, assessing me.

"Tate seemed sad, Dad."

She can always bring me to my knees. This time, her use of "Dad."

"Yeah, Squirt. She was. But I'm hoping not for long."

Please don't let it be for long. Please, by some miracle of miracles, don't let it be my kid.

"Remember, she loves flowers. Maybe we should go to the store tomorrow and pick some out for her. You know her favorite kind, right?"

"Flowers," I whisper, both to acknowledge her suggestion and to answer her question. Although I'm thinking she won't accept any tomorrow. And it may be a while before she ever will.

If ever again.

That thought makes me cringe, the lead ball in my stomach cracking, its contents leaking into every crevice.

A shroud of foreboding envelops my being, casting doubt upon what lies ahead.

CHAPTER 29
TATE

've read and reread Walsh's texts about one hundred times. And those are from the first day. Every day since I left his house in a haste—three long, agonizing days—he sends at least four.

The day after, he sent a gorgeous bouquet of winter flowers. I forced myself to send a text to thank him, then immediately ignored the rest of his messages. But I couldn't not acknowledge the receipt of them. I'm not inconsiderate.

I wish I were mad at him. I wish he had hurt me purposefully so these damn stupid emotions of loving him would quit. But I can't. He did nothing wrong. He did what any other college student his age is doing—or probably worse. He had shit luck. I have no right to fault him for something he did before we met. Hell, before I even moved to Vermont. It's not fair of me. But I also can't bring myself to see him, to reach out, to let him know how I feel. In no way do I want what we have to be over, not by a long shot. However, we both need time to process this on our own, him more so than me. His life could change drastically. The changes to mine will just be a by-product of those in his life.

I can't let myself picture the result—Walsh with a newborn. The mere image makes me flinch.

Needing something to keep my mind off him, Aubrey and I went through the last few boxes. It was mostly summer clothes, so it took approximately two hours to get the boxes into storage. So much for it killing a lot of time, but all the boxes are finally unpacked.

Another tactic was to cook meals for an entire week. Until I ran out of room in my freezer and had to stop. I found a new cookie recipe, so we made those. Aubrey refused to try them, so I ended up eating at least half the batch and tossing the rest after she went to bed. They weren't bad, but I've consumed a lot of unnecessary calories the past few days and didn't need any more.

Now it's day four and the potential to run into him at preschool is real. I avoided him the past two days since Lennon was with Megan, and I purposely dropped Aubrey off late on Monday to avoid a sighting of him. I can't stall any longer, and it's not fair to my daughter to pick her up early or allow her to be the last one picked up to evade him.

I arrive about five minutes early and end up in the middle of the line of cars. A familiar truck pulls in behind me. In my rearview mirror, Walsh hangs his head against the steering wheel. My heart pinches at how miserable he appears—his chin covered in unshaven scruff, his hair wild and unruly, no doubt from running his hands through it. His handsome face is paler than normal, but from this angle, it could be my imagination. Or hope he's as miserable as me.

His door opens, and my heart pounds wildly in my chest.

Please don't come talk to me. I don't have the strength to turn you away.

He ignores my unspoken plea and knocks on my window. I have little choice but to put it down. The cold January wind whips through the cracked window.

"Tate. How are you?"

"Fine." *Lie.* I'm not *fine* by any stretch of the imagination.

"Do you think we could talk?"

"Still having a baby with someone else?" Damn, that was harsh and uncalled for, so I apologize. "Sorry. The question is valid. The tone is not."

He cups his hands together and blows into them, then rests his elbows on the door. "There's a few days' waiting period for the results of the test. I'll have them by early next week at the latest."

Credit to him for not taking the bimbo's word.

"Okay."

"I miss you." His voice turns my insides to goo. I tear my eyes away, staring straight ahead to not say something I'll regret or can't take back.

I have to stay strong, at least until I know if his life's about to change.

"How's Aubrey?"

"Fine." A little less of a lie. She's asked no less than a dozen times—each day—when she can have a playdate with Lennon. "She wants to know if you ate her donuts."

"Oh." His voice gives little away, but curiosity gets the better of me, and I meet his gaze. His cheeks tinge slightly pink. "I may have devoured them all after you left. Paid for it big time on the bus ride the next day. Had to sit out the first period of the game because my coach didn't believe it was motion sickness with the amount of vomit I left on the bus."

"Man, that must have sucked." I make sure my voice is as genuine as possible. No one deserves that, least of all Walsh.

"Pretty sure I won't live it down soon, if at all. Just another stupid mistake I made regarding a woman."

I don't know if he's trying to goad me, but I don't take the bait. And just in time, the doors to the building open, forcing him back to his truck.

"Please tell me this isn't over. That I still have a chance. Don't give up on us over a choice I made before I met you. Please, Tate. At least consider it."

He walks away without my response, which is good because the mortar on the walls around my heart is loose. It's not just in his pleading tone. It's in the way his eyes are downcast and the spark in them has dimmed. He's not done with me. And I'm not done with him. We have so much more to learn about each other, go on more dates, have more sex. Like, lots more sex.

I hold steady in my decision not to cave until the results come in. Either way, I need to know what I'm facing. Once we know what the future holds for him, we'll carve out the path we need.

If there's a path for us.

One lone tear slips past the barrier of strength I don't possess. Swatting it away, I pull up to the door and plaster on a fake smile as I make my way to the passenger side and await my daughter.

But it's Lennon who perceives me first.

"Tate. Tate," she calls out, breaking free of the teacher's hand to dart over to me. "Tate, did you get our flowers? Did they make you less sad?"

Tears threaten again as this little girl I adore dearly regards me expectantly. It's only been several months, but she's left an imprint on my heart. A part of me believes she and Aubrey could stay friends no matter what happens, but it won't be the same relationship between us.

"Did you help Daddy pick them out?" I manage around the ball of emotion in my throat. Her head bobs up and down excitedly. "They made me so happy. Thank you for knowing what I needed."

She looks over her shoulder at the man standing behind her. "Told you, Keeley. She just needed some flowers."

"You were right, Squirt. Good thing I listened to you."

Aubrey has joined us, her little foot tapping, her hands resting on her hips. "Are there any donuts left?"

"No, Keeley ate them all," Lennon explains. "Should you make more?"

Walsh's silent panic mirrors my own, my breath catching in my chest on how to respond. Without letting them down.

Fortunately, Hannah makes it clear we're holding up the line.

"Bean, we'll talk about it at home. I may have the ingredients we need."

"Fine," she huffs, turns on her heel, and climbs into her car seat.

I let go of the breath I'm holding, and with a wave to the Keeleys, I concentrate on tightening Aubrey's buckle.

"Too tight, Mommy. Too tight," Aubrey fusses, batting my hand away from the clip. I'm so flustered, I don't realize how much strength I put into it.

"Sorry, Bean. Let me fix it." I loosen it so it's secure, then briskly walk around the hood of the car, willing myself to calm down. No use in getting more upset. Thankfully, the director of the preschool waves me along, forcing me to be on my way.

It takes the entire short drive home for my pulse to regulate and the butterflies storming my stomach to finally settle.

"Mommy, I think we should have Lennon and Walsh over after school this week. He can bring lunch for all of us and then Lennon and me play. Good plan?"

God, how much I want to consent to her plan. But deep down, I can't. I can't have him here, no matter how much I want it. No matter how much Aubrey begs. For the first time in a while, I put my foot down on something she wants, something so innocent as a playdate with her friend.

Of course, I'm not quite ready to admit that to her, so I smile and reply, "I'll text him and see if he's free."

I'm a coward, and now I'll have to lie more and say he's busy. Which isn't fair to anyone, most of all Walsh. Yet the alternative pains my heart too much.

"Great. Let me know what he says." She unclips the top but can't manage the bottom. While she usually takes it in stride, like so many other things in her life, today she's super frustrated. "I can't do it still."

"I'll help." I maneuver my fingers to loosen and release the straps. "All set." My smile is weak. While she deserves better than my half-effort lately, at least she's fed, bathed, and dressed. And mostly happy. All things considered, can I ask for more?

The next few days are more of the same: wake up to thoughts of Walsh, drag my ass out of bed, think about Walsh, go through the routines of the day, think about Walsh, wonder what he's doing, how he is, remind myself this will all be over soon but might not end up with the outcome I want, "take care" of Aubrey, convince her Walsh still cares for her even though he can't come over and we can't go there, cry myself to sleep where Walsh invades my dreams.

Wash. Rinse. Repeat.

On Monday, a little over a week after what I've deemed "Baby-gate," I drive around town. With about half an hour to kill before pickup and as if on autopilot, my car drives to the floral shop. In all the time we've lived here, I haven't stopped in and checked it out for myself. And I have loved every single bouquet Walsh has gifted me.

Parking my car a few spots down from the door, the walk isn't too unbearable with today's mild-ish weather. Even with an inch of snow on the ground, I get inside unscathed.

A bell rings upon entering, the floral scent invading my nostrils but somehow not overwhelming. The shop is small, maybe ten feet by ten feet at most. Blossoms of all shapes, sizes, and colors perch against two of the walls, a refrigerated case taking up half of the third wall, with a counter to pay on the back one.

My eyes are immediately drawn to a stunning bouquet full of seasonal blooms, including vibrant deep pink and white carnations, cream roses, pink chrysanthemums, and another pink one I can't name. They smell almost as pretty as they look.

"Hi. Can I help you find something?"

The voice at my back startles me. Hand to my chest, I turn around and am met by a woman in her mid-fifties, her hair full of gray pulled into a messy bun on the top of her head. The eyes on her roundish face are kind, her smile sweet, a perfect combination for a small-town florist.

"Hi. I'm just browsing."

"Of course. Let me know if you need anything or have questions. The name's Jenny."

"Tate," I reply instantly, her entire demeanor setting me at ease.

Her golden-brown eyes widen. "Very nice to meet you, *Tate.*" The emphasis on my name raises my suspicions, but she skedaddles away before I can interrogate her.

I amble around the store, my fingers touching, my nose smelling, all the merchandise. For the first time since Babygate, a sense of peace infiltrates me. As if things will be okay and work out for Walsh and me.

The flowers Walsh sent last week have seen better days, but I don't have the proper time to pick out something I equally like. Except for the pink and white arrangement. Maybe she can do it on a smaller scale.

Making my way to the back counter, I find Jenny feverishly texting on her phone. "I have a question when you're finished," I interrupt.

She fumbles the phone at the sound of my voice but catches it before it falls to the floor. Guilt washes over her face as if I've caught her red-handed. "Sorry. Let me just finish…this…text." A minute passes as she completes whatever she's doing, but she places the phone, screen side down, and gives me her full attention. "What can I answer for you?"

"The pink and white carnations in the front. Can you do something on a smaller scale?"

She nods enthusiastically before I've finished speaking. "Of course. Though I have to order them so it wouldn't be until Friday at the earliest."

"Oh." My eagerness dips, but I fancy them on my table. "Yeah, that would be fine."

Her smile convinces me it will be fine to wait. "Awesome. Let me get some information." She has me fill out a card with my name, address, and payment information. Then she makes a few notes on the card about my order. "Do you want to swing by and pick them up Friday or have them delivered for an extra five dollars?"

"I'll pick them up." They were already a little pricier than I wanted to spend, so I'll save the delivery fee.

"Super. I can text you when it will be ready. Probably Friday after noon."

"Okay. Thanks."

My transaction complete, I turn to leave, but Jenny's voice calls me back.

"Tate, one flower-loving gal to another. What's your absolute favorite?"

I don't hesitate. "Dahlias. In peach or purple."

"Great choice. See you Friday."

"See you then."

The bell chimes as I exit the store. As I stride quickly to my car, I can't help but recognize the change in my mood.

Put there by flowers, enhancing the magic in my life since I was a little girl.

CHAPTER 30
WALSH

Any time spent waiting, no matter what it's for, is torture. Lennon was three days late. I thought my life was going to end in those three days because Megan was miserable. However, I'd relive those days and then some compared to what's going on now. Because it's pure torture. With a capital T-O-R-T-U-R-E.

Once Raquel got ahold of my number, she hasn't let up on the texts. I had to put her on Do Not Disturb and text her every few days. It's selfish and mean, but until I know for sure the baby's mine, I don't owe her anything. That's how I'm choosing to justify it.

But her texts aren't the worst part about any of this. No, that would be missing Tate. And Aubrey too, but mostly Tate. She never responds to my texts, but I can't blame her. I get why she won't talk to me. It makes *rational* sense, but my heart hates it. When I see her at preschool, she's so close, yet so far away. Some days, she barely glances at me. I hate how sad she is, so forlorn, but mostly I hate putting her in this position.

I can't focus in class, which sucks because the semester just started. On the ice, I'm distracted but haven't been too sloppy. Heck, I even scored a goal and had an assist in this weekend's home game. It helped Lennon was there cheering me on in the stands. She's been the only bright spot in all of this. Despite my crappy mood, Megan hasn't asked what's up or given me too much shit. It's like she can tell I'm not prepared for an interrogation or her nonsense. No matter the reason, I'm grateful for it.

The results of the paternity test should be back today. At least that's what the lab promised when we sent the results out. I've been checking my email nonstop, hitting refresh like nobody's business. I only have one class on Monday mornings and practice in the evening.

Right after class, Jenny blows up my phone.

Your girl's here.

In your store? Tate?

My pulse quickens at the thought of her being in the floral shop. Then I remember I can't be too excited about it yet.

Yep. Unless there's another Tate here in Havenwood

If there is, I'm unaware

Take notes of what she wants

Already on it

I smile because of course she is.

She doesn't text back, so I pack up my stuff from the Student Center, wave to a couple of teammates, and make my way to the parking lot. Running late this morning, I had to park across campus, so now I have to hoof it to my car. I lost track of time—thoughts of Tate Winchester will do that—and I hope I'm not too late for pickup. Luckily, Lennon's school isn't far from mine, a fact that makes her almost giddy, though she's never given a reason why it's so funny to her.

My phone pings with a text on my drive, the thin layer of snow coating the ground causing me to drive at a slower speed. Every time it snows, I'm grateful for putting those snow tires on Tate's car, knowing she and Aubrey are safer. If she'd let me, I'd just grab Aubrey every day for her, but her independence is important to her, and I don't want to make her feel incapable. My reasons have nothing to do with capability, which I think she understands on some level. At least I hope.

Pulling behind a Tahoe in line, I shift into park, letting the engine idle. The doors will open soon enough, but given the short drive, the car has had little chance to warm up. Lennon's used to the cold of Vermont on top of the ice rink and hardly ever complains. If we let her, the girl wouldn't ever wear a jacket—she discards it as soon as she enters somewhere: car, home, a store, school. It's been a battle at school because they make her zip it all the way up whenever she has it on. I've tried explaining why she needs to follow their directions—using it as a "rule" rather than keeping it zipped for warmth —but my arguments fall on deaf ears.

I check my phone.

> Dahlias are her favorite. But save that for another time because I'm already working on something.
> Just let me know when you want to grab it. Today or tomorrow

I sigh.

Today. Please let it be today.

And let it be an "it's not my baby" bouquet rather than an "I'm not sure how to navigate this" arrangement.

> I'll let you know as soon as I get the results. Will it apply to either scenario?

Jenny knows the whole sordid tale. I poured my heart out to her last week when I picked out the bouquet Lennon made me buy. Thankfully, I was wise enough to leave her home with Mom.

> She'll love it either way. Fingers crossed for you it's a joyous occasion

> Cross your toes too. I need all the luck I can get

> *prayer hands emoji*

The doors to the school open, shortening my wallowing time. I'm in the middle, so I don't expect Lennon right away. I haven't spied Tate's car yet, but she was at the floral shop not long ago. I hope she's driving safe.

The urge to protect her is something fierce, a feeling I've only ever experienced with Lennon and when Megan was pregnant. I've given up trying to explain it. This last week has only proved how much I love Tate. I don't know what I'll do if the baby's mine. And in some ways, Tate's the least of my concerns.

Lennon.

Her name conjures up my girl at the door, holding onto Hannah's hand. Or more like Hannah assuring Lennon doesn't let go. It's for safety only, but Lennon knows not to run away from the teacher, and to stay on the sidewalk, but I'm not one of those parents who would go against the rules enforced by the teachers. Except maybe with the coat. We can be a little laxer with the coat.

Pulling up in front of the door, Lennon's not her usual self, and it raises my fatherly instincts. "Hey, Squirt," I exclaim, rounding the front of the truck. "Why the long face?"

She shrugs, half-hearted. "I'm sad, Dad."

"I can see. You want to tell me about it in the car?" I grab her hand, give Hannah a nod, and walk her the short distance to the back door of the truck.

"Can we go skating now? I think that would cheer me up. It would cheer me up a lot." She pauses, then adds, "No, a ton." Her door open, she faces me, wanting to be excited at the prospect of skating but whatever's eating at her is too big to combat.

"Maybe tonight. I have practice, but maybe Mimi can swing open skate at Nordic."

"That's a long time from now." Her usual spunk is missing, the sass behind her words barely there.

Instead of getting into everything now, I shut the door as she buckles up. When I'm in the front seat, I make sure it's tight before driving off. And then I ask again.

"Want to tell me why you're so sad?"

"I miss Tate."

Shit.

As much as my girl loves Tate, I didn't account for how much not seeing her this past week affected her. We've gone a few weeks without seeing them before, but ever since Thanksgiving, there's been a change in Lennon, a stronger bond between the two of them, forged completely by my five-year-old. I'm grateful Tate indulged her, sharing the same sentiments.

"It stinks, doesn't it?"

"Can't you just call her and tell her you're sorry? And whatever you did, you won't do again?"

"I wish it were that easy." I aim to keep the words in my head, but the response escapes.

"Dad, we need to stop at the flower store."

"Wow, two 'Dads' in less than ten minutes. Are you sick?" Again, not to indulge her wish, I park a few doors down from Whispering Petals. I could convince myself I had to stop in, but I never let Jenny know when I'd be by. Of course, I won't apprise Lennon her idea was a good one, but the way she claps her hands once lets me know she approves.

By the time I get around to the other side of the truck, she's unbuckled. I don't even bother with her coat, just lift her and tuck her into my arms. She shields her face from the elements.

The bell to the store rings as we step inside, Lennon scrambling to get down.

"Don't touch anything, Lennon. Look only with your eyes." I wait for some smart response, but nothing comes.

"I'll be right with you," Jenny calls from the back where she must be working.

While we wait, I search around the store at the updated displays after the holiday season. A blue, white, and silver bouquet catches my eye. Its simple color tones beckon me.

I don't know the first thing about flowers, but I've learned some since I'm here at least once a week. And the occasional pop-in to see what's new. No clue which type make up this arrangement other than white roses. These others don't grow the color we see, can they? Flower dyeing is a thing, right?

"Oh, Walsh. Hey." Jenny's voice greets my ears, her upbeat tone a salve for my miserable heart. "It's not ready yet. There's one flower I need I couldn't get today, but my supplier assured me she'd have it tomorrow."

A nod to Lennon, I turn to face Jenny. "My daughter requested a visit. Results are still not in." I don't mean to sound so bitter, but the waiting is getting old.

And ridiculously overrated.

"This is madame Lennon?" Jenny walks over to Lennon, who seems the least bit interested in any of the merchandise. "It's so good to finally meet you. What brings you by today?"

Lennon sizes up Jenny, who's crouched by her side, giving her a wide smile when she passes her assessment. "Flowers for Tate. Because Aubrey says she's so sad. And since Keeley still can't fix whatever he did to make her sad, I want to send her some to make her smile."

Her words power me into action. Not sure which part of her comment affects me more, I eliminate the distance between us. "*You* are sending Tate flowers? On whose dime?"

Without missing a beat, my five-year-old sasses, "Hey, Dad, can I borrow like ten bucks to send Tate flowers?"

After a moment of pure shock, Jenny covers her chuckle with a cough.

Before I answer her, I address the other part of her statement. "What did Aubrey say exactly?"

"She's sad," she repeats as if I didn't hear her and wasn't asking for clarification.

Helpful.

"And who says it's on me to fix?"

"Mimi."

Of course.

"You are incredibly sweet, Lennon." Jenny stands up, grabs Lennon's hand, and walks to another part of the store. "Tell you what. If Daddy won't buy them for you, I will."

I go to protest—Jenny owes me no favors. Quite the opposite. She does so much for me, I'll be making payments on my tab for about as long as my student loans.

"If you're okay with this kind," she points to a vase holding a myriad of different colored blooms, "I'll let you pick out the colors."

Lennon doesn't hesitate. "Yellow and orange, my favorites."

"Perfect. Let's see what we can put together."

While the girls busy themselves with a bouquet, I dig my phone out of my pocket and refresh my email. It takes forever to load, but once it does, there's one from the testing lab.

Finally.

My heart kicks up into a rhythm similar to when I take the ice in an important game, the beat strong and unsteady. I take three deep breaths, closing my eyes as I exhale the last one slowly, sending up one last prayer for good news. My finger clicks the email open, my eyes already scanning for the words to determine my fate.

"Come on, come on," I chant under my breath as the words blur with my haste. Eventually, I decode them.

"YES!" My shout of glee ricochets off the walls of the small floral shop. "YES!" I repeat. Then I read the words four more times, to make sure my eyes aren't playing tricks on me.

NOT A MATCH.

Pure adrenaline propels my feet. I grab Lennon in the air and swing her around, cognizant not to knock anything over in my excited state.

"Good news?" Jenny surmises with a smirk.

"Only the best." I swipe one hand across my forehead. "Phew. Dodged a bullet." I can't even let my mind drift to the possibility of being the father.

And all I want to do is tell Tate. Tell her it's over. Tell her we can move forward in whatever way she wants. Tell her I love her, and no matter what life throws in our path, I always will.

Setting Lennon back to her feet, I focus on my phone.

"No. Don't let her know yet," Jenny stresses.

My good mood instantly deflates. "Why not? She deserves to know. The waiting has tormented her enough. You heard the girl— she's sad."

Jenny and I enter a sort of stare-down until she relents first. "You could tell her the good news, or you could *show* her." Confusion sets in. Show her how? The email on my phone? Jenny senses my bewilderment. "Flowers, dude. Show her with flowers."

Oh right. But hadn't I already planned for that?

"Sure. The ones you're already putting together." Then I remember they wouldn't be ready until tomorrow. "I have to wait until tomorrow to tell her? No way. I need to tell her today." I can't help the whine in my voice, but I also can't let her go another second without knowing the truth. And I've already wasted precious minutes debating with Jenny.

"I'll have them in the morning by like seven a.m. What time can you stop by and grab them?"

"Noon," I state, thinking about tomorrow's agenda. "And the girls have their long day at school." A plan forms in my mind. I could show up with lunch. She might be working, but surely she needs a lunch break, right? "Noon," I repeat, more certainly.

"And now he gets it."

All the while we've talked, her fingers have been creating the small bouquet Lennon requested. "Wait. What do I do about this?" I point at her hands.

Jenny studies Lennon with a smug smile. "Lennon, when do you want to give Tate the flowers?"

"Today."

"Great. You can bring them to her when Daddy can drive you there."

I'm thoroughly confused. Running my fingers through my hair, I declare, "But you just said…"

"Lennon has nothing to fix with Tate. Hers can go today."

I roll my eyes at her use of having to "fix" things with Tate. It makes it seem like I did something intentionally to hurt her. I didn't. All I did was fall for her. And honestly, I hope I never have to *fix* that.

"Fine." I huff out a breath. "I can wait until tomorrow at noon."

Jenny pats my shoulder, mocking my good choice to accept my fate. "Great, we'll just finish this up, and you guys can be on your way to Tate's." Her attention on my daughter, she continues, "She's going to love these even more because you picked them out."

"I love Tate."

Lennon's words momentarily paralyze me. It's the simple way she declares it affecting me most. While I was busy falling in love with her, I missed how Lennon was as well. All the more reason to be fucking grateful the test wasn't a match.

"I bet she loves you too." The wistfulness in Jenny's tone adds to my relief. "Okay, all set." She hands Lennon a card. "Why don't you write her a message so she knows who they're from?"

Lennon eagerly accepts the pen and sets to work. Heaven knows what she'll write. She's good with her name, but the rest of the letters are quite a hindrance. Though with Aubrey, Tate can hopefully decipher whatever message the lines and marks conveys.

"She's a sweetie," Jenny muses, a motion of her head to Lennon.

I guffaw. "Not the first word I'd use, but she has her moments. She saves her love for special people."

"Tate's a lucky woman." She goes back behind the counter while Lennon finishes her card. "And she's quite smitten with you."

"How could you possibly know? You met her once and discussed flowers." Or did my name come up? The possibility both thrills me and makes me nervous. Maybe not so much *nervous* as apprehensive.

"When you've been in this business as long as I have, you learn a thing or two. Have I ever steered you wrong?" She winks at me.

"Never," I confirm. Tate has loved every single arrangement Jenny suggested. It helps she loves flowers and maybe she wouldn't turn any down, but she's gushed prolifically about the specific ones I've had delivered. Deciding to give Jenny the benefit of the doubt, I smile. "Thanks, Jenny. You've been such a godsend the past few weeks."

"That sounds an awful lot like you won't be needing my services in the future." A small frown graces her lips.

I quickly remedy my mistake. "I might as well surrender my credit card now for all future purchases. And not just for Tate." There's Aubrey to consider. And Lennon's feelings are changing. Laughing, I amend, "Pretty sure I'll be keeping you in business for *years* to come."

Without another word, Jenny wraps up the small bouquet and hands it over to Lennon with a smile. She refuses any payment, proving yet again how valuable she is in my life.

We say goodbye, my girl preciously cradling the bouquet one would a newborn baby. In the truck, she insists we go right to Tate's house to drop them off.

Who am I to argue?

CHAPTER 31
TATE

Despite clearing my head and purchasing flowers for myself, once we get home from school, my bitter mood returns. I didn't see Walsh at pickup, which is a blessing and a curse. If possible, I miss him more. Probably because now I associate blossoms with Walsh. The torture is real.

Aubrey begs for mac and cheese for lunch—the kind from the box. I busy myself with tidying up my already neat kitchen while the water boils. As the timer goes off for the pasta, the doorbell rings.

"It's Walsh," Aubrey singsongs from her perch at the table.

I wish.

"I don't think so, Bree. We talked about this, remember?"

I don't blame her for being optimistic. Images of him run rampant through my mind all hours of the day, even though I "remember" he's not around.

Aubrey shrugs and resumes coloring.

How long do these results freaking take?

Before going to answer the door, I dump the pasta and let it cool in the sink. Trudging slowly to the door, I throw it open casually, not at all prepared for what's on the other side.

Lennon stands there, a huge grin on her face reaching her eyes so similar to her father's. In her hands, she holds a bunch of flowers. And not just any kind, but my absolute favorite.

"Dahlias," I breathe out. My eyes drift to the stairs, Walsh leaning against the railing, a little unsure, a lot sexy. Forcing my gaze away, I open the storm door and step outside onto the landing, addressing his daughter. "Hey, Lennon. How are you?"

She heaves the blooms at me. "These are for you. Please don't be sad." Her head tilts to the side, waiting for my reaction.

Unfortunately, I have no words. The fact she's here, the flowers, her comment about not being sad anymore—it's all-encompassing. Too much. Emotion overload.

I can't let her know that.

Tears prick my eyes, but I hold them in. I speak around the knot in my throat. "Lennon, this is super sweet of you. These are my absolute favorites, and I love the yellow and orange. Did you pick these out yourself?" My nose sniffs the floral scent.

If possible, her excitement doubles with my compliment. "Yup. Keeley didn't even have to pay. Are you less sad now?"

I nod, my eyes finding Walsh's. A softness inhibits his gaze as he watches our interaction. My heart beats wildly, growing in size at how much love I have for this man. He's not completely mine—I may have to share more of him soon—but I can't possibly give him up. If the last ten or so days have proven anything, it's that. I've missed him so much. Almost enough for me to say fuck waiting for the results.

No, my brain prods. You need to know. For peace of mind and how to move forward.

"Any results?" I voice in a whisper.

Walsh shakes his head sadly. A nod is all I can give him. He clears his throat. "Come on, Squirt. I've got to get you home because I have practice tonight."

She snarks, "If I must."

I can't contain the heart-melting smile encroaching on my lips. "Thank you for the flowers, Lennon. I'm going to put them in water as soon as I go inside. They'll be so pretty in my bedroom."

She gives me no warning before throwing herself at my legs. "I love you, Tate," she muffles out.

My heart about bursts at her declaration, at how she delivers it with so much affection, even subdued against my leg. As if she's been holding it in for so long and couldn't wait to unleash the sentiment into the universe.

"I love you, Lennon. So much," I mutter in a whisper, bending down to give her a proper hug, cognizant of the flowers still in my hands. Tears threaten stronger this time, emotion swirling through, transferring from me to this little girl who makes my pretty great days even brighter.

Lennon pulls away first, a quick peck of her lips to my cheek. "See you soon. Keeley's going to fix it. I just know it." Without waiting for a response, she bounds down the stairs to her father. My eyes are misty when she fits her hand into his, the bond they share unbreakable. "I'm ready now. Thanks for driving me to bring Tate flowers. I love you, Keeley."

"Back at ya, Squirt." Walsh's voice shakes. Maybe he's not as worked up as I am, but he's affected. His eyes find mine and at that moment, I'm certain everything will be fine. Things will work out the way they're supposed to. "I'm crazy about you," he mouths.

"Back at ya, Keeley," I parrot his words, my audible voice scratchy. I can't tear my eyes away as they walk hand in hand to his truck, Lennon jabbering away.

With one last wave and a kiss blown, Walsh climbs into his truck. Only then do I go back inside, clutching the flowers to my chest. A thoughtful gift from a compassionate child, one who holds a piece of my heart behind Aubrey and her father. No doubt in my mind, it was her idea to get these and drop them off. I can't fault her for any of it. She's just an innocent bystander caught in the crosshairs of a tricky adult situation.

On the way to the kitchen, I do my best to compose myself for Aubrey. I don't want her to think something's wrong. She's seen enough of my emotions lately and taken her share of my anger and sadness. She doesn't need any more.

She's still coloring at the table. "Pretty flowers. It was Walsh." She giggles like it's the best-kept secret.

"Actually, they're from Lennon."

"So you're not sad anymore."

"How did you know?"

"Flowers always make you smile. Me too. Because they're so pretty. Like you and me."

Laying the blossoms on the table, I crouch next to her. "So pretty. You and me. And flowers too." Hugging her into my side, I declare, "I love you, Aubrey Belle."

"Mommy, I know that, silly." She wraps her arms around me. "Can we eat lunch now? My tummy is so hungry."

"Sure thing, Bean. Sure thing."

For the first time since all this started, I sleep like a rock, Lennon's flowers on my nightstand putting me under some sort of spell. They're the first thing I see after opening my eyes, and an immediate smile jumps on my face.

I spend most of the morning listening and re-listening to medical notes, doing my best not to screw them up. I ache to text Walsh, to ask if the results came back yet, even though I'm highly certain he'd let me know when they do.

My phone rings about 11:45.

"Please don't be the school. Please don't be the school." I need the whole day to myself.

The number is unfamiliar, but at least it's not the school.

"Hello?" I answer tentatively.

"Is this Tate?"

"Yep."

"Hi, it's Jenny from Whispering Petals. I have some bad news."

My stomach plummets. "Oh?"

"I won't be able to get the calla lilies in for Friday. Can you wait until next week?"

No rests on the tip of my tongue.

Ever since I walked out of the shop yesterday, the image of flowers brightening up my place on Friday has given me something to anticipate, something to believe in until this mess with Walsh is resolved. Now I'll have to wait some more. Ahh! All I freaking do is wait.

Instead of unloading my woes onto the sweet florist, I reply, "Of course. Let me know when I can stop in and pick them up."

"Thanks, Tate. I'm sorry. I didn't think it would be a problem, but there was a big storm out in the Midwest and my supplier—"

She cuts herself off. "Never mind. You don't need to hear the struggles of keeping beautiful flowers in stock in the winter. I'll call you next week when I know for sure it will be ready."

"Thanks. I appreciate it." I'm about to say goodbye when the small vase on my nightstand catches my eye. "Thanks for the dahlias. They're so pretty and make my room smell divine."

"Oh. You're welcome. That little girl had no intentions of leaving my store without flowers for you."

"She's something else, isn't she?"

"Yes. She's her father's daughter for sure."

"One hundred percent," I confirm with a sigh.

"I don't want to keep you. I'll be in touch soon. Take care. Bye." The line goes dead, Jenny breaking off our conversation.

"Well, that was weird."

Not thinking too much into it—I don't know her, she doesn't know me—I attempt to get back to work. It lasts all of ten minutes when my doorbell rings. I need some serious excuses for my bosses for all the distractions lately.

I reach the front door at a snail's pace, issuing a, "Jeez, I'm coming," when the doorbell rings again.

Throwing open the door, I'm greeted with flowers. An enormous bouquet. Pink and white, almost a replica of the one I noticed yesterday. The one I ordered in a smaller version for pickup on Friday. The one postponed to next week.

"How?" That's the word I manage over my shock.

Walsh's face peeks through the spaces in between the stems. "Let me inside and I'll explain." He holds up a paper bag. "Hungry? I brought lunch."

How the hell do I say no? He's got a floral arrangement he undoubtedly had help picking out and lunch. My stomach rumbles at the mere thought of whatever's in the bag. Walsh only brings things I like, so whatever's in there has to be good.

My good-natured conscious alerts me to the fact I don't know where we stand. Too many balls—or for Walsh, pucks—in the air.

"Walsh, I," I start, only to be stopped by his megawatt smile.

"It's not mine."

Three tiny words. The way my brain processes them, you'd think he just asked how I would cure cancer.

It's.

Not.

Mine.

"Not. Mine." He repeats the last two words. For my benefit. He's had time to process this.

"For real? No chance? Like you're absolutely sure?"

He doesn't answer. Rather, without an invitation, he barges into my condo, depositing the flowers and the lunch on the table before he lifts me in his arms. One hand on the back of my head, the other around my waist, his gaze finds mine. In his pools of blue, fondness reflects, relief swimming in the light color.

"No chance. It's over. Done. Finito."

His use of "finito" breaks me, and tears begin immediately. Tears of joy and contentment. Tears of having answers. Tears of *not his*.

Walsh cradles me to his chest, holding me while my emotions surge freely. All the pent-up ones I've held onto these last, long ten days liberated with just three words. Three words signifying the end of the torture. The end of missing his touch. The beginning of us.

I'm not sure how long I cry, how long it takes to get a handle over my emotions, but when I finally tug free, his coat's stained with the evidence. He shrugs out of it.

All I can do is stare. The way he shakes his arms out of the coat before it falls to the floor. Short stubble covers his chin, and since I can, my fingers reach out and touch it, tracing lines along his jaw. It's coarse to my fingers, and suddenly I can't wait to feel it on other parts of my body.

"Are you hungry?" he asks.

I've been starved the last few weeks, and now I'm going to indulge and engorge myself until satiation.

"Not for food."

His eyes widen. "Should I put the flowers on the kitchen table?"

"After."

"After what?"

I don't answer. Grabbing his hand—I don't care he still wears his boots—I lead him to my bedroom.

Four orgasms later—two for each of us, including the one from my first ever completed blow job—we sit around the kitchen table eating lunch. He had the good sense to bring sandwiches, so they didn't get cold while we had sex. Damn good sex, I might add. Kinda mind-blowing. The sex I've only read about in romance novels but never experienced for myself. Now, there's no going back to crappy sex. Walsh has both ruined and made sex great, the most interesting conundrum if there ever was one.

"Thanks for lunch. And the sex. Oh, and the flowers. I got a call earlier from Jenny saying the ones I wanted were delayed until next week."

A devilish smile graces his lips. "Yeah, those won't be coming next week. I'm hoping the ones I brought today make up for it."

Elation lights me up. "Those are the ones I wanted. Something very similar in size, but after the holidays, I couldn't justify the price for something bringing me such joy but eventually dies." Once the words are out of my mouth, I realize how awful they sound. Unappreciative, almost, of the gift he brought today, but also the many arrangements he's brought the last few months. Placing my hand over his, I exclaim, "That sounds horrible. I *love* the flowers, Walsh. Please don't think otherwise."

"If I thought you didn't appreciate them, I wouldn't bring them. But I understand your logic. I may not be rolling in dough—now or ever—but there will always be money for the things you love, Tate. Always. And that goes for Lennon and Aubrey too." He pauses a moment. "Within reason. Especially for my kid. She's quite the expense with skating gear, lessons, ice time—" He ticks each item off on his fingers, and I chuckle.

I don't allow my brain to travel to a future too far beyond a few months. No matter he implied otherwise, we don't know what the future has in store for us. For the present, I'm living in the here and now, enjoying my time with this hunk of a man while I can call him mine.

"Thank you. Flowers have always had a way of making things better, turning a bad day around. Their beauty is never a waste, no matter how long they last before they shrivel up and die."

"Most eloquently put," he drawls.

"I try." My smile's wide, matching his.

I try to hold the rest in, but my mouth gets ahead of my brain. "I love you."

If I had any reason to worry about how my words would affect Walsh, I shouldn't have. Because he squashes every doubt, every insecurity swirling through me the past few weeks with three words and my name.

"I love *you*, Tate." Total emphasis on you. "Damn, that feels good to get off my chest. Do you know how long I've been wanting to give you those words?"

I shake my head, unable to speak around the lump lodged there. I want him to repeat the words, to make sure I didn't misunderstand him.

"A long fucking time."

"How long?" I whisper. A part of me needs to know.

"The Sunday after Thanksgiving. When it didn't faze you how Lennon practically dragged you to her bedroom because she 'had to talk to you.' And you went willingly. No qualms. Just went with her and listened to her talk about whatever she was going on about. And as much as there was something so special about the act itself, I was so freaking jealous she got to you first. That she could capture your attention when I wanted all your focus on me." As he speaks, his hand reaches out to mine. "I figured the only real reason I was jealous of my daughter was because I had fallen for you."

"Wow." I have no other words. Emotions, yes, but no way to express them.

"And Aubrey too." Not an ounce of sarcasm or fabrication accompanies his declaration.

Which scares the shit out of me, but I hold in my gasp. Because yeah, I could see this ending that way—Walsh, Lennon, Aubrey, and me. But we still have so many hurdles to overcome, things to learn about the other person, growing up to do. It's been five months, and we're twenty-two years old. That seems damned fast to be here.

Except for both of us, we were thrown into the fire as teens, parents to a newborn baby. We've made it this far independently. Imagine where we could go together.

"I don't know what you're thinking, but stop *over*-thinking it."

"Don't take it back," I plead, afraid he'll retract it because he thinks it's upset me.

"I wouldn't dare take it back."

Another question has been on my mind for some time, and it seems as good a time as any to ask now. "Are we at the stage of telling them about us?" I don't have to quantify who "them" are.

"No. At least I don't think so. Do you?"

"I don't know. This is all unfamiliar territory for me. And they're at an age where they could kind of understand it. Maybe. Or maybe not. But I don't want them to get any ideas in their heads about what it means or anything."

"New territory for me too. Lennon knows something's up, 'cause she overheard Meg mention something a few weeks ago."

I nod, the idea not sitting comfortably with me, which solidifies we aren't ready to tell them. Although maybe it's because someone else told her and not us. That's the part making me uncomfortable. And it doesn't help it's Walsh's ex.

"So you told Megan then? About us?"

"I swear I didn't. She assumed but hasn't directly addressed it with me. I was going to talk to her about the fact Lennon overheard her, but with the holidays and then the…"

"Babygate," I supply for him.

"Babygate?"

"That's what I called it in my head." My shoulders lift. "Seemed fitting."

He tries it out. "Babygate. Yeah, okay. Catchy and sensible. And not nearly as offensive as the Keeley cockcycle." Walsh spits the words out, embarrassed.

I lean in closer. "I very much enjoyed my ride on the Keeley cockcycle today. And as long as I'm the only one riding, it's kind of growing on me." Which is a total lie, the part about it growing on me. Walsh promptly calls me out on my bullshit.

He points a disapproving finger in my direction. "Growing on you, my ass."

"It's awful. It makes you out to be a total whore."

"We call them 'players' when they're of the male variety."

"My bad." I glance at the clock. "Shit. It's almost time to get the girls."

"I'll grab them." He stands up. "Wait. Will Aubrey be okay with that?"

I smile, his kind gesture touching my heart. "Yeah, I think she just might," I say with a snicker.

"Cool." He leans down for a kiss. A spine-tingling, over-the-top kiss to keep me satisfied while he's gone. However, I'm not complaining. All things considered, I'll take all the kisses he wants when we're alone. These moments happen few and far between. "You want me to see what Millie's making for dinner?"

"No," I protest. "I'll make us dinner." Damn, I jumped too fast on that one, not wanting to put Millie out. The more I consider it, the more I should have agreed. One less meal to make.

Again, Walsh reads me like the open book I am. "You can cook another day for us. I'll clean up."

Once he leaves to pick up the girls, as I tidy up the kitchen, I can't wipe the smile off my face.

Thank goodness Babygate was short-lived.

He's all mine. I don't have to share him with anyone new, exactly the way it should be.

EPILOGUE
WALSH

SIX MONTHS LATER

My girl snoozes on the couch. Because she refused to sleep last
night, she crashed hard after a morning of swimming at the town
pool with Aubrey and Tate. If I wake her, she'll be a bear. As much
as I shouldn't reward her with skating, if I wake her with the
promise of skating with Liliana, she'll be excited, tire herself out
more, and sleep will claim her. Hopefully, all night.

Gathering our skate bags, I message Tate.

> Can I interest you in free skate at Aspenridge in thirty minutes? No sticks involved

> *shudder*

A cackle jumps free. With a little—a lot—of bribery, I convinced her to watch one of my games. Who could have predicted there'd be an all-out brawl? Not your average hockey fight, but a wrestling match on the ice? I wasn't involved, but she was so spooked, she didn't talk to me for twenty-four hours, pissed at me though I had not an iota of blame. Totes unfair to have suffered the hellish twenty-four hours.

> Just a small group skating for fun. No fights. Come for Lennon

A tad bit mean to use my child as a pawn in my enticement game, but desperate times. Lennon would love for Tate to see her skate, but my motives are purely selfish. Doesn't matter I saw her hours earlier in a two-piece bikini, I can't get enough of her.

We told the girls we're dating, though we're not overtly intimate in front of them. A peck on the cheek or lips here and there, but nothing outlandish. We save that for after-hours. We've had to be creative about sex, but there are certain cases where she's way more agreeable to my demands of having my way with her once Aubrey's sleeping. Fireworks those nights.

> Aubrey and I will sit in the stands. Is it cold in the summer?

> The ice is still as frozen no matter the weather outside

> Bummer

> Want me to pick you up?

> When?

> Uh, like twenty minutes?

Lennon stirs on the couch. I suck in a breath to see if she's going to wake up on her own. I planned to scoop her off the couch and stick her in the car, hoping she'd keep sleeping. Her head lifts, her eyes open, she smiles at me, flips over, and conks back out. My attention returns to the phone.

> I'll drive us. Aubrey's in a mood. Not sure what's up with her

> Aubrey has bad moods?

I've never seen the kid throw a tantrum, be unkind, or put up a fight about anything. Well, except for when I ate all her donuts. She wasn't too happy with me then.

> On the rare occasion. We'll meet you at the rink

> See you later

I fill our water bottles. Mom joins me in the kitchen. "How was the pool?"

"The monster had fun." My mother doesn't conceal her chuckle. "Aubrey made it in the water, with a smile even. Progress."

"She'll get there. No use forcing it."

"Agreed." I top the bottles with ice, tightening the caps, and toss some squeezies and granola bars into the bag.

"Where you off to?"

"Aspenridge to skate." She gives me the "mom glare," the one she perfected by the time I was three. Or so she's led me to believe. She also enjoys pointing out how she didn't need it until I came along. "What?"

"I didn't say a thing."

"Actions speak louder than words, Millie Keeley." She smacks the back of my head.

"Ow."

"Respect, boy." Her grin defies her words. "What time will you be home? Dad and I are going out for dinner, but I've already made a meatloaf. Think you can heat it for you and the underling?"

"Sure." A one-brow raise calls me out on my bullshit. I amend, "I have faith Tate can."

Ma harrumphs and points a finger my way. "Do not take advantage of her kindness."

"I assure you, Tate will be more than willing to heat a dinner you've prepped, will enjoy every bite, and not think I'm taking advantage."

A wistful smile graces her lips. "She's a good egg."

"The best."

I sure hope I don't screw up what we have. I'd be lost without her in my life. We haven't talked about future plans, but she's stuck with me and Lennon for the rest of our lives. Once I can save up enough money for a ring and a house and everything else Tate deserves in life, I'll make it official.

We're young, with plenty of life ahead of us. No need to rush into anything at twenty-two.

X

As I predicted, Lennon's a beast to wake until a whispered, "Liliana wants to skate with you today," perks her right up.

When we arrive at the rink, she jabbers away, her exhaustion almost forgotten. A few small yawns escape, but her overall enthusiasm for skating and seeing Liliana trump them. In the slight chance they don't show up, she doesn't know Tate and Aubrey are coming.

When I open up the back door, she's got her buckle undone and smacks her forehead. "We didn't bring cookies for Liliana. 'Member I told her last time we'd bring cookies? Why didn't we bake cookies?"

True to her word, over winter break, Liliana texted, and we got together. Lennon intended to bring cookies when we saw her next, but she must have forgotten until now. As if the girl would stay in the kitchen long enough to bake cookies.

"Don't know what to tell you, Squirt. Maybe don't mention the cookies."

She gasps, the thought ludicrous. "I don't want to be rude."

"Then you shouldn't have told her *you'd* bake cookies." Rendered speechless, her jaw drops, but no words emerge. "She won't be mad, even if it slips out by accident. She wants to skate with you. Then maybe we can go to the bakery and get cookies as a treat."

I mentally slap myself. Of all the things in the world, Lennon doesn't need sugar after skating. What she needs is rest. If she eats cookies, she'll be up all night. Again. Guess I should heed my own advice.

"Grand plan, Keeley."

"Not in the slightest," I mumble. She jumps into my outstretched arms. With her in one arm and the bags in the other, we head inside.

Lennon inhales the moment we breach the entrance, letting out a long "Ahhhh" on the exhale. I won't ever tire of her love of the ice.

Liliana meets us in the bleachers. Her high ponytail swishes as she walks over. "Hey, Lennon. Glad you could make it." She's dressed for skating: thin zip-up jacket and black leggings pulled over her skates. I shake off memories of Megan in a parallel outfit. As good as Tate would look in something similar, highly doubtful she'll get on the ice. It's enough for her to watch us.

"I didn't bake cookies," Lennon blurts, a wave of apology crashing her words. From where she sits on the bench, she waits for Liliana's response.

A smile glosses Liliana's mouth. "You're in luck. I did."

My kid's eyes nearly bulge out of her head, her astonishment palpable. "The s'nores ones?" At Liliana's nod, Lennon bounces on her toes. "That's the most 'mazing thing ever."

"I'll share some after we skate. Ready to show me your new tricks?"

"Yep." I help her into her skate gear and send the two of them on the ice. I survey the door for Tate and Aubrey, but after fifteen minutes, I lace up my skates and join the girls on the ice.

Even in the offseason, I can't get enough ice time. Until I hear from a few athletic trainer jobs I applied to, I'm working more hours at the Nordic rink and helping with the summer camp for a few weeks in August at Aspenridge. When Lennon starts kindergarten in the fall, if I still don't have the job I want, I'm going to inquire about more hours at Aspenridge. I'm sure Kenny can find work for me.

As I make a lap around the outside, my eyes catch on the

gorgeous woman entering the rink. She holds Aubrey's hand, her eyes flittering around. When she spies me, a smile with enough wattage to power all of Vermont parts her lips.

She's all mine. How did I ever get so lucky?

"Tate! Aubrey!" Lennon sees them too and skates over to the opening. She's a little out of breath, but nothing will dim her enthusiasm. "Are you here to skate?"

"Gosh, no. We heard you were skating and wanted to see you."

Lennon's smile stretches from ear to ear. "This is the best day ever." She points to the stands. "Sit up there. I'll show you my skills."

Liliana and I stifle our laughter.

I motion to Liliana I'm going to watch from the stands. Greeting Aubrey with a pat on the head, I can't resist the pull to Tate. My lips brush a chaste kiss on hers. "Missed you."

"It's been three hours."

"Doesn't change the fact." I loop our hands together, leading her up the stairs. I help Aubrey up and am rewarded with a hug. My heart shatters into more pieces at her sweet gesture.

She shivers. "It's chilly in here." She's wearing one of Lennon's Aspenridge hoodies and thick pants. Tate carries a winter jacket in one hand and helps her into it.

"Thanks for coming. Lennon's a bit excited."

"I'm ready. Watch this," Lennon directs from the ice, shouting to make sure we can hear her. She takes off, her little legs gaining speed and momentum with each glide of the skate. For her age, she's pretty graceful. Her feet coast over the ice, her arms in a T. Skating as often as she does has its merits.

She rounds the corner, one foot crossing over the other, a move she's worked on a lot lately. Her left leg lifts in the air behind her. Damn, she does have new tricks. Her right leg wobbles a bit, but she brings the other down to steady herself. She continues around the ice, Liliana near her. She ends her show with a hop and a twirl, landing it with a toe pick in the ice. It's not a perfect landing, but I'm impressed.

Her fan club claps and cheers, and the ice princess bows before skating our way, Liliana on her heels.

She pants when she reaches us, standing on the bottom of the bleachers. "Tate! Did you see my arabest? Wasn't my leg so high?"

"You were wonderful, Lennon. Amazing skating. You sure can do a lot of tricks."

"Liliana's been teaching me. She's a good teacher. I bet she could teach Aubrey too."

"No." There's no hesitation in Aubrey's voice, and she punctuates her decision with a head nod. A shiver passes through her again.

My girl shrugs, not upset by her friend's decision. She reads her well, partly why their friendship works despite their differences. "How about a s'nores cookie?"

Aubrey's expression sours. "Yuck. Mommy brought carrots."

Lennon turns her nose up at the mention of carrots. "More for me."

"One, Lennon Victoria. Mimi has meatloaf for dinner."

"I like meatloaf," Aubrey pipes up.

"Great. Mimi saved you some. All we have to do is heat it…" I start an internal countdown in my head. Three, two, one…

"Did she leave you strict instructions for what temperature and how long?" Tate inquires.

"Great, than—" The words die on my lips rewinding through what she said. It wasn't an agreement to cook the meatloaf, but a question if I had the directions. Not what I expected from her.

My eyes swing to my right. Tate curls her lips into her mouth, trying not to laugh. Everything I was going to say dies on my lips when Kenny enters the rink from the back hallway. He raises his hand in a wave, strutting toward us. Reaching the stands, he stops next to Liliana and kisses her on the cheek.

"Hey, Dad. What's up?"

"Heard Walsh was here. Wanted to talk to him."

"Me?" My voice is a high-pitched squeak. "What do you need from me, sir?"

He dismisses my use of formalities. "Secure a job for the fall yet?"

"Not yet. I've got feelers out in a few places. Why, do you have one for me?" A nervous chuckle releases.

"Indeed I do."

His words are serious, but it takes a moment for them to sink in. He does?

"You're leaving Aspenridge?" I spurt. Even though I'm no longer a student, I had hoped he'd be my connection here when and if I needed a job.

But wait. He said he has a job for me.

Liliana's gaze flies to her father. "Dad, what's going on?" She rips the question from my brain.

"Coach Pagano was offered a position in Florida. Already packing his bags as we speak."

Coach is leaving? My last season didn't end on the best note. We didn't make it to the tournament, but it's not like we had a losing record. And I thought he liked it here at Aspenridge. The news is mind-blowing.

Again, his words about a job thump into me. He can't mean for me to…

Thankfully, he continues. "I signed the papers. You're looking at the new head coach of the Aspenridge Maple Moose men's hockey team." Under the dim lights of the arena, Kenny's face radiates joy.

Liliana throws her arms around him. "Dad, that's amazing. I'm thrilled for you." Pride exudes off her in waves.

"Wow. Congrats. The team is in excellent hands." I reach my hand for him to shake when their hug is done.

"Thanks, Walsh. They asked if I had anyone to replace me as rink manager. Expect a call tomorrow." His fervor deepens, fine lines creasing his eyes and mouth.

What does he mean by "expect a call tomorrow?" A call from who?

My brain tries to process the significance of the words, but it's not firing on all cylinders. "Huh?" is the best I can do.

"Walsh." Tate tugs on my sleeve. "Say something else. Thank you at the least. Isn't this like a dream job?"

"My dream job?" I parrot back. Manager of the Aspenridge College ice rink. Me, Walsh Keeley. Am I dreaming? "Pinch me."

Tiny fingers squeeze my knee. "Only because you said to, Dad," Lennon squeaks when my eyes nag her sight.

I'm not dreaming. Holy hell. This could really happen.

"Oh, it's happening," Kenny agrees, reading my mind. Or did I speak aloud? "You're more than qualified, and I don't think we could find another candidate as dedicated to the rink as you."

"Hey, can I get a cookie now?"

Leave it to the five-year-old to ruin my moment. Oblivious to how my world's going to change, Lennon sits on the bench, legs swinging back and forth, feet still in skates, a hopeful countenance only an innocent child has settled on her face.

"Sure, kid. Life's all about your cookies."

A chorus of laughter slices the hollowness of the empty arena.

Liliana retrieves the cookies from her bag while Kenny and I chat logistics. As if the job is already mine.

Fifteen minutes later, he's leaving with one last shake of my hand. "I'd say welcome to the team, but you've been a member the last four years. I'll be in touch."

"Thank you, Kenny." I push the words I should have said from the beginning out of my mouth.

"My pleasure." With his arm looped around his daughter, they head back for his office. I can't help but think that will be me some-day. The entire picture, daughter and all.

Tate's voice breaks into the image. "Walsh. This is amazing," she singsongs, admiration evident in her tone.

"I'm a bit stunned, to be honest. *If* I even get the job."

There must be a protocol to follow, procedures, and rules in place. Kenny can't recommend me and voilà. The job is mine. It can't be that easy.

"He seemed pretty confident."

"Guess we'll wait and see what happens."

I don't want to get my hopes up.

Would it be an ideal job? Yep.

Would I accept if offered? Yep.

Would it solve my job woes? Absolutely.

But it's been a hot minute since Kenny mentioned it. Let's not get ahead of ourselves.

"Walsh, I'm really cold. Is it time for Mommy to cook the meat-loaf now?"

"Aubrey," Tate chides, as if the question is rude. Has she met Lennon?

"Nonsense, Tate." I sit down next to Aubrey, loosening the laces on my skates. "Aubrey, would you like it to be time for your mom to cook Mimi's meatloaf now?"

She rubs her belly. "I like Mimi's meatloaf. And Mommy won't mess it up."

I tip her chin up. "She certainly won't." Over Aubrey's head, I wink at Tate, easing the worry creeping in. "The better question is, what should we bake for dessert?"

Aubrey's finger taps her chin, concentrating profoundly. I will my kid to stay quiet and let her friend have this one. "Donuts. Definitely donuts. Do we need to stop at the store for 'gredients?"

"We can grab them from home, kiddo," Tate entices.

"I'll go with Lennon and Walsh to Mimi's house." Like before, her voice never wavers, assertive in her decision.

"You can sit in the new seat Keeley put in his truck for you," Lennon enthuses.

"When did you—"

I cut Tate off with a kiss on the corner of her lips. "We'll talk about it later. You go to your house and grab the ingredients. I'll take the girls to my place."

The girls.

Has a nice ring to it.

So far, I've got three. And counting…

Once we're packed up and ready to leave, with a girl's hand tucked into each of mine, we leave one of my favorite places.

This may not have been the life I'd planned for myself, but this one's turning out even better.

What's life like for Walsh with three girls? Check out what's in store for the Keeleys in this bonus scene.

She's the coach's daughter. He thinks rules don't apply to him. To say *It's Pucking Complicated* would be an understatement. Read how complicated in book two of the Aspenridge College Hockey series.

IT'S PUCKING COMPLICATED

Dad never told me I couldn't fall for one of his hockey players.
But he never said I could, either...

I've followed the Aspenridge College hockey team for years, even when I wasn't a student. Now that I've transferred here, I have up close and personal access to the team, including their parties.

Intending to shed my wallflower status, it's only natural to attend the first party of the season. Reputed playboy Cody McGuire takes me under his wing, and when he finds out I genuinely love his favorite sport, his interest is piqued.

I don't mean to keep running into him on campus, but it happens. And when he tells me to prove I'm not like the usual women he has in his bed, what comes out of my mouth is asking him to teach me things. *Sexual* things. He thinks I'm kidding at first, but I'm not. What better way to learn more skills in the bedroom than from the king of the player's club?

So long as he doesn't find out my dad is his new coach....

AUTHOR'S NOTE

Thank you so much for reading *Pucked Up Plans*! Of the millions of books in the world, I'm grateful you've chosen mine to make your list.

This book has been years in the making, and when I say years, I mean I wrote it in 2020! Back when I was a different writer, way less knowledgeable about marketing and business but still knew how to bring the emotions. The original draft looks way different than the version you read. The bones and plot were there, but the multiple rounds of edits enhanced the storyline and character development. I tried a different method of editing and dare I say, I actually enjoyed the process. It's definitely a strategy I'm going to continue for the foreseeable future.

The seed for this story was a hockey player at a Vermont college. That's all. Of course, that's so little to go on, so I had to expand it. What if…he was a college hockey player but also a single dad? Because in high school, he got his girlfriend pregnant. And what if, somewhere across the country, there was a high school girl who found herself pregnant around the same time? What would it look like when their worlds collided? BAM! The rest of the story took root from there.

The original draft starts with Walsh and Tate both finding out they're going to be parents before it jumps into the present. I loved the prologue, especially my favorite line, *"Yeah, Meg. If it's a girl, she most certainly can play hockey."* If that doesn't set the stage for things to come, I don't know what else will. As I reworked the drafts, the prologue didn't fit. I held on to it for a while, being stubborn, not wanting to give it up, but eventually I cut it out and started with the present.

Fast forward to when I decided I needed a bit of an introduction to this series. I'm not not sure why my brain forgot I had the perfect beginning, but it wasn't until I was in the shower one day (I get the *best* ideas there, and now I even have "shower" notes to write these ideas down, but that's a story for another day), and realized I HAD the perfect way to start the series...and it was mostly written. I spruced up Tate's part, created a cover, and *Pucks and Pink Lines* went up as a free download and introduction to this new series. (If you haven't read it, grab it <u>here</u>). When readers got a hold of it, they couldn't wait for book one, which made my heart so happy.

I can't adequately tell you all my favorite things about this book without making you read an entire novel, but suffice it to say, I love a lot about this book.

First up, Walsh Keeley.

The man has his faults, but how do you not love him? Forget about his relationship with his daughter for a moment, but the flowers, the snow tires, the loading of the dishwasher? Swoon. *fans self* I adore his relationship with Millie (how she calls him "boy" and he calls her "Ma"). Two peas in a pod, these two. I love the scenes with the two of them, how she's so wise and how he's never moving out of her house. Which, in his mind, he's adamant about. At least when he says it. Until Tate comes along. And he's not expecting her. He's not prepared for this woman to captivate him in such a way, it almost knocks him to his knees. But that's love for ya, and this boy is smitten with Tate.

From her very first appearance on the page, Lennon gripped my heart and never let go. Even at five, she's quite a force, a presence, as Tate mentions, and man is she fun. So much sass, sarcasm, and spunk wrapped into a petite package, all passed down to her from her grandmother and father. I've written father-daughter relationships before (hello Brayden and Emmy, to name one), but nothing like the bond between these two. Even in my final read through, my emotions ran strong for their bond, and I laughed out loud at some of the things Lennon says and does. And I was the one who wrote them in the first place, lol.

I could go on and on and *on* about Lennon (how about how she calls him KEELEY?), but I promised myself this note is supposed to be short. So, my final thought about Walsh and Lennon revolves around the blankets. Once the idea formed, I couldn't type the words fast enough. In the original draft, there's more of Walsh's emotions about it, especially when she "steals" them both (which is mentioned in passing in the bonus epilogue). Man, he was NOT happy.

Next up, Tate Winchester.

Here's a girl who's mostly got her shit together, forging a life with a preschooler in this brand-new place, on her own, and making it work. She's sacrificed so much for Aubrey, but wouldn't have it any other way. And while Aubrey's easygoing and mild-mannered, she's got her quirks. She may not stand out as much as Lennon, but when she decides she's all about Walsh, my heart melted. Maybe that's because *he* melted for her too. But back to Tate. She's got her flaws, overreacts at times, but she's quick to realize her mistakes and apologize. I love that about her. Sure, maybe she's a bit dramatic at times (but I'd be hard pressed to find a woman in her position who wouldn't be), but she recognizes it about herself. And hey, aren't we all allowed to freak-out from time to time, especially about the BIG things? I admire how she's not afraid to admit when she's wrong and own her mistakes. That's what life is about.

When I wrote this book, it was supposed to be a standalone. One and done. However, with interconnected series and hockey romances being huge now, it became book one of a series. I've yet to determine how many books there will be. Guess it depends which of the hockey team members speak the loudest in the next few months. I hope you'll stick around for the rest. And don't think we've seen the last of the Keeley family. Nope, not even a little.

As always, a book doesn't get written, published, and marketed in a vacuum, and without the following people on my team, Walsh, Lennon, Tate, Aubrey and the rest of the cast would be collecting dust on my old laptop.

With deepest gratitude and appreciation, thank you:

Denise: for encouraging me to pivot to college hockey rather than stick with my original plan of releasing a different series first. For fried cookie dough bites and movies that make us laugh. For your detailed notes and ideas to improve the story. For being the OG!

Missy: for getting this book done minutes (ha ha) before JTO made his debut. For talking characters quirks out. For blurb help.

Kitty: for your eagle eyes and catching mistakes other pairs of eyes miss. For talking about inappropriate things at Rich Farm with little ears behind us. For loving Walsh and the blanket almost as much as I do.

Arell, Libby, Mary Ellen and Nicole: our daily work time is the highlight of my day. I love knowing that even though I'm alone in my house, I'm connected to the best author friends I could ask for. For title help. I can't remember who it was at this point who came up with it, but it's so much better than anything having to do with lines. Here's to 2024, our year to SOAR to new heights in our businesses. I'll see you at the top! First up, writer's retreat!

Mary Ellen: for taking my cover idea and improving what I gave you. For "critiquing" the blurb. I'd say we're better about keeping distractions to the minimum, but I might be making that up. I am so excited for Denver, among the other times I'll get to see you in 2024.

Vicci: among so many other things you do for me, for plot help on this book.

Kelly and Connor: all things hockey (beyond what Missy added as well). PS "Kenny's" now a good guy. You can let him know.

DJ: for the picture on the front cover.

My enthusiastic **cheerleaders** who've believed in me from the start, even when one is going through a cancer battle (kick ass!) : this is my year. Let's see where I can go.

Members of the ARC team: whether you've been here from the beginning, came along the way, or joined for this release, I'm so thankful for you. Thank you for being amazing and reading my books and helping spread the word. Each one of you is amazing.

Readers/influencers: For choosing my books of the millions available, from the bottom of my heart, thank you! I'm always amazed at how strangers take my words to heart and fall in love with the characters who live in my head. It's definitely a lot surreal.

Members of Taylor Delong's Tribe: I'm coming back, I promise.

Author friends: this is the year I get to meet a lot of you in person, and I couldn't be more excited. Grateful to be on this journey together and to have so many great resources in each of you.

Mom and Dad: I wouldn't be here without you. Literally, lol, but also where I am in life is thanks to you. I love you.

Last, but not least, **E and A**: for not thinking I'm entirely crazy when I talk about plot points and fictional characters and selling books and everything else that goes along with being an indie author. Well, and your mom. It may look like I stay home in my PJs every day, but I promise you, I'm working. Watch how things change this year. Love you to the moon and back!

ALSO BY TAYLOR DELONG

Aspenridge College Hockey Series

Pucked Up Plans

It's Pucking Complicated

Sweet as Puck

Summer Puckin'

Creek Valley Creamery Series

Rocky Road

After Eight

Tin Roof Sunday

Cold Brew

Zero Visibility

Forever in Laketon Series

Waiting on Forever

Forever Squared

Forever and a Day

Laketon 2.0

Love Unscripted

Life Unscripted

Brew Play Love

Rocky Water Series

Defining Us

The Breaking Point

Murrtham's Tree Farm Series

The Magic of Us

The Magic of Her

The Magic of Baseball

Love on the Tree Farm (Box Set)

Standalones

A Not so Merry Rescue (Christmas romance)

The Highway Ride

Up to Fate part of the Steamy Shorts anthology

Opposing Fate part of A Kiss at Midnight

Loving Rebel

Whiskey Tears

Can't Buy My Love (Girl Power Romance)

Where Forever Leads (Falls Village)

The Lawn Boy (All American Boy)

ABOUT THE AUTHOR

Taylor Delong writes small-town, contemporary romances full of heart and heat. Her cinnamon roll heroes protect the ones they love and will leave you swooning. She has been reading and writing for as long as she can remember. It's always been her dream to be a published author. She spends her days chasing after toddlers and her nights scribbling down stories and ideas the characters in her head dictate to her. She lives in CT with her two children.

Check out her website for more.